RULE GOLDEN
AND OTHER STORIES
DAMON KNIGHT

AVON
PUBLISHERS OF BARD, CAMELOT AND DISCUS BOOKS

Cover illustration by Dean Ellis.

AVON BOOKS
A division of
The Hearst Corporation
959 Eighth Avenue
New York, New York 10019

Published by arrangement with the author.
Library of Congress Catalog Card Number: 79-83828
ISBN: 0-380-43646-9

First Avon Printing, April, 1979

Contents

Introduction

In the 1950s, when these stories were written, I began to be preoccupied with what seems to me the great unsolved problem of politics: how to keep the bastards from grinding you down.

All modern systems of government, including the most utopian, are based on the assumption that the system will produce benevolent rulers, but in practice the bastards almost always end up on top, because power is what they want and because the less scrupulous they are, the easier it is for them to get it.

In "Rule Golden" I proposed an utopian solution to this problem, a device which would cause anyone who deliberately hurt another person to feel his victim's pain. (Cyril Kornbluth later pointed out to me that this wouldn't work on masochists.)

I am fond of the design of the alien in this story—trilateral symmetry, which has many advantages. The war in Indochina is called that and not the Vietnam War because Indochina is what we called Vietnam then. The war was going on when I wrote the story, but quasi-formal U.S. involvement came later.

In "Natural State" I tried another solution, the use of genetic engineering to decentralize society and break the pattern of high-consumption, capital-intensive living.

This story was the product of an editorial collaboration with Horace L. Gold, then the editor of *Galaxy*, who was famous for his ability to turn a writer's idea on its head and make it new. My title for the story was "Cannon Fodder"; I wanted it to be about the epic adventures of a squad of soldiers trying to get a living cannon from here to there. Horace probably thought this was a dumb idea, and he was probably right; anyhow, he seized on

1

the notion of an organic "machine" and made me elaborate it. Some of the details, including the knifebushes, were also his. I had to rewrite parts of the story twice for Horace, and that distressed me—I don't know anybody who *likes* rewriting to editorial order—but when I got over that I liked the story, and it is still one of my favorites. I feel a strong sympathy for Alvah Gustad, because although he is both ignorant and innocent at the beginning of the story, there is a core of intelligence and stubbornness in him that eventually makes people stop walking over him.

The character of Wytak is based on that of William O'Dwyer, mayor of New York in the late 40s. I don't know where Beej and Doc Bither came from.

The central idea of the story is foreshadowed in a still earlier effort, "Doorway to Kal-Jmar," which I wrote when I was twenty and have since almost entirely forgotten; but Algis Budrys, who was about twelve when he read it, keeps telling me how great it was. Anyhow, I do dimly remember that the Martians in "Doorway to Kal-Jmar" had split into two races, one dependent on machines and the other relying on their own physical and mental powers. The idea was not new then—John W. Campbell had used it in 1937 in a story called "Forgetfulness," and H. G. Wells before him in *The Time Machine*, published in 1896.

Jawj Pembun, the underdog in "Double Meaning," is one of my favorite characters. I played him off against my version of a typical science fiction hero, Thorne Spangler —an ambitious upstart, tough, clever and unscrupulous. I wanted to show that the bastards don't always win; they are vulnerable because they are self-deluding and humorless.

The aliens in this story again reflect my belief that if we encounter people on other planets they are not necessarily going to look like human beings, or like spiders or lizards or anything familiar. Another point I wanted to make is that the spectacular space battles in science fiction stories are illogical, because it would be so much simpler just to bomb the enemy's planet apart. For this and other reasons I conclude that a galactic empire is a practical impossibility. I like this conclusion, although I don't like the bombs. (My belief is that if the bastards *can* bomb a planet, eventually they will.)

"The Earth Quarter" is in part a reaction to the macho science fiction identified in the 50s with John Campbell, who would not publish any story in which another race turned out to be more advanced, smarter, or in any other way better than us. Considering the size and age of the universe, the likelihood that the human race is the pinnacle of creation seems to me vanishingly small. The villain of this story, Lawrence Rack, is my version of the hero of a story by L. Ron Hubbard, "To the Stars," which Campbell published in 1950.

"The Dying Man," a nonpolitical story, began as an inversion of a familiar science fiction theme, the immortal man or woman in a world of mortals. For several years before I wrote this story I had been reading a lot of speculative psychology, anthropology and mythology. I read eight or nine books by C. G. Jung, always hoping that the next one would explain the fascinating hints of the others, and always disappointed. Nevertheless, I think I got something immensely valuable from Jung, and from his disciple Erich Neumann. I also read Robert Briffault's enormous *The Mothers,* a study of the evidence for a matriarchal society in prehistory; the quotation about the Alfurs of Poso comes either from this or from Frazer's *Golden Bough;* I used to know which, but have forgotten.

One of the early scenes on the beach was inspired by a painting of Pablo Picasso's, *The Race* (1922). The photomicrographs of disease-causing organisms can be found on Plate IV of the article "Bacteriology" in the *Encyclopaedia Britannica,* 1954 edition. The ideas about architecture are a logical development of something that is already happening, the trend toward less and less permanence, more and more temporary buildings. Although this story is a myth, in its general outlines I believe it represents a more likely future than any of the others described in this book.

I think it is worth noting that all these unconventional stories managed to get published in science fiction magazines in the 50s, and I want to express my deep gratitude toward the editors who encouraged me, helped me, and bought the stories: Horace L. Gold, Samuel S. Mines, Harry Harrison, and Larry T. Shaw.

DAMON KNIGHT
Eugene, Oregon
September 26, 1978

Rule Golden

I

A man in Des Moines kicked his wife when her back was turned. She was taken to the hospital, suffering from a broken coccyx.

So was he.

In Kansas City, Kansas, a youth armed with a .22 killed a schoolmate with one shot through the chest, and instantly dropped dead of heart-failure.

In Decatur two middleweights named Packy Morris and Leo Oshinsky simultaneously knocked each other out.

In St. Louis, a policeman shot down a fleeing bank robber and collapsed. The bank robber died; the policeman's condition was described as critical.

I read those items in the afternoon editions of the Washington papers, and although I noted the pattern, I wasn't much impressed. Every newspaperman knows that runs of coincidence are a dime a dozen; *everything* happens that way—plane crashes, hotel fires, suicide pacts, people running amok with rifles, people giving away all their money; name it and I can show you an epidemic of it in the files.

What I was actually looking for were stories originating in two places: my home town and Chillicothe, Missouri. Stories with those datelines had been carefully cut out of the papers before I got them, so, for the lack of anything better, I read everything datelined near either place. And that was how I happened to catch the Des Moines, Kansas City, Decatur and St. Louis items—all of those places will fit into a two-hundred-mile circle drawn with Chillicothe as its center.

I had asked for, but hadn't got, a copy of my own paper. That made it a little tough, because I had to sit there, in a Washington hotel room at night—and if you know a

7

lonelier place and time, tell me—and wonder if they had really shut us down.

I knew it was unlikely. I knew things hadn't got that bad in America yet, by a long way. I knew they *wanted* me to sit there and worry about it, but I couldn't help it.

Ever since *La Prensa*, every newspaper publisher on this continent has felt a cold wind blowing down his back.

That's foolishness, I told myself. Not to wave the flag too much or anything, but the free speech tradition in this country is too strong; we haven't forgotten Peter Zenger.

And then it occurred to me that a lot of editors must have felt the same way, just before their papers were suppressed on the orders of an American president named Abraham Lincoln.

So I took one more turn around the room and got back into bed, and although I had already read all the papers from bannerlines to box scores, I started leafing through them again, just to make a little noise. Nothing to do.

I had asked for a book, and hadn't got it. That made sense, too; there was nothing to do in that room, nothing to distract me, nothing to read except newspapers—and how could I look at a newspaper without thinking of the *Herald-Star?*

My father founded the *Herald-Star*—the *Herald* part, that is, the *Star* came later—ten years before I was born. I inherited it from him, but I want to add that I'm not one of those publishers by right of primogeniture whose only function consists in supplying sophomoric by-lined copy for the front page; I started on the paper as a copy boy and I can still handle any job in a city room.

It was a good newspaper. It wasn't the biggest paper in the Middle West, or the fastest growing, or the loudest; but we'd had two Pulitzer prizes in the last fifteen years, we kept our political bias on the editorial page, and up to now we had never knuckled under to anybody.

But this was the first time we had picked a fight with the U. S. Department of Defense.

Ten miles outside Chillicothe, Missouri, the Department had a little thousand-acre installation with three laboratory buildings, a small airfield, living quarters for a staff of two hundred and a one-story barracks. It was closed

down in 1968 when the Phoenix-bomb program was officially abandoned.

Two years and ten months later, it was opened up
again. A new and much bigger barracks went up in place
of the old one; a two-company garrison moved in. Who
else or what else went into the area, nobody knew for
certain; but rumors came out.

We checked the rumors. We found confirmation. We
published it, and we followed it up. Within a week we had
a full-sized crusade started; we were asking for a con-
gressional investigation, and it looked as if we might get it.

Then the President invited me and the publishers of
twenty-odd other anti-administration dailies to Washington.
Each of us got a personal interview with The Man; the
Secretary of Defense was also present, to evade questions.

They asked me, as a personal favor and in the interests
of national security, to kill the Chillicothe series.

After asking a few questions, to which I got the answers I expected, I politely declined.

And here I was.

The door opened. The guard outside looked in, saw me
on the bed, and stepped back out of sight. Another man
walked in: stocky build, straight black hair turning gray;
about fifty. Confident eyes behind rimless bifocals.

"Mr. Dahl. My name is Carlton Frisbee."

"I've seen your picture," I told him. Frisbee was the
Under Secretary of Defense, a career man, very able; he
was said to be the brains of the Department.

He sat down facing me. He didn't ask permission, and
he didn't offer to shake hands, which was intelligent of
him.

"How do you feel about it now?" he asked.

"Just the same."

He nodded. After a moment he said, "I'm going to try
to explain our position to you, Mr. Dahl."

I grinned at him. "The word you're groping for is 'awkward.' "

"No. It's true that we can't let you go in your present
state of mind, but we can keep you. If necessary, you will
be killed, Mr. Dahl. That's how important Chillicothe is."

"Nothing," I said, "is that important."

He cocked his head at me. "If you and your family lived

9

in a community surrounded by hostile savages, who were kept at bay only because you had rifles—and if someone proposed to give them rifles—well?"

"Look," I said, "let's get down to cases. You claim that a new weapon is being developed at Chillicothe, is that right? It's something revolutionary, and if the Russians got it first we would be sunk, and so on. In other words, the Manhattan Project all over again."

"Right."

"Okay. Then why has Chillicothe got twice the military guard it had when it was an atomic research center, and a third of the civilian staff?"

He started to speak.

"Wait a minute, let me finish. Why, of the fifty-one scientists we have been able to trace to Chillicothe, are there seventeen linguists and philologists, three organic chemists, five physiologists, *twenty-six psychologists, and not one single physicist?*"

"In the first place—were you about to say something?"

"All right, go ahead."

"You know I can't answer those questions factually, Mr. Dahl, but speaking conjecturally, can't you conceive of a psychological weapon?"

"You can't answer them at all. My third question is, why have you got a wall around that place—not just a stockade, a wall, with guard towers on it? Never mind speaking conjecturally. Now I'll answer your question. Yes, I can conceive of psychological experimentation that you might call weapons research, I can think of several possibilities, and there isn't a damn one of them that wouldn't have to be used on American citizens before you could get anywhere near the Russians with it."

His eyes were steady behind the bright lenses. He didn't say, "We seem to have reached a deadlock," or "Evidently it would be useless to discuss this any further"; he simply changed the subject.

"There are two things we can do with you, Mr. Dahl; the choice will be up to you. First, we can indict you for treason and transfer you to a Federal prison to await trial. Under the revised Alien and Sedition Act, we can hold you incommunicado for at least twelve months, and, of course, no bail will be set. I feel bound to point out to you that in this case, it would be impossible to let you come to trial until the danger of breaching security at Chillicothe is past. If necessary, as I told you, you would die in prison.

"Second, we can admit you to Chillicothe itself as a press representative. We would, in this case, allow you full access to all nontechnical information about the Chillicothe project as it develops, with permission to publish as soon as security is lifted. You would be confined to the project until that time, and I can't offer you any estimate of how long it might be. In return, you would be asked to write letters plausibly explaining your absence to your staff and to close friends and relatives, and—providing that you find Chillicothe to be what we say it is and not what you suspect—to work out a series of stories for your newspaper which will divert attention from the project."

He seemed to be finished. I said, "Frisbee, I hate to tell you this, but you're overlooking a point. Let's just suppose for a minute that Chillicothe is what I think it is. How do I know that once I got inside I might not somehow or other find myself writing that kind of copy whether I felt like it or not?"

He nodded. "What guarantees would you consider sufficient?"

I thought about that. It was a nice point. I was angry enough, and scared enough, to feel like pasting Frisbee a good one and then seeing how far I could get; but one thing I couldn't figure out, and that was why, if Frisbee wasn't at least partly on the level, he should be here at all.

If they wanted me in Chillicothe, they could drag me there.

After a while I said, "Let me call my managing editor and tell him where I'm going. Let me tell him that I'll call him again—*on a video circuit*—within three days after I get there, when I've had time to inspect the whole area. And that if I don't call, or if I look funny or sound funny, he can start worrying."

He nodded again. "Fair enough." He stood up. "I won't ask you to shake hands with me now, Mr. Dahl; later on I hope you will." He turned and walked to the door, unhurried, calm, imperturbable, the way he had come in.

11

Six hours later I was on a westbound plane.

That was the first day.

The second day, an inexplicable epidemic broke out in the slaughterhouses of Chicago and surrounding areas. The symptoms were a sudden collapse followed by nausea, incontinence, anemia, shock, and in some cases, severe pain in the occipital and cervical regions. Or: as one victim, an A. F. of L. knacker with twenty-five years' experience in the nation's abattoirs, succinctly put it: "It felt just like I was hit in the head."

Local and Federal health authorities immediately closed down the affected slaughterhouses, impounded or banned the sale of all supplies of fresh meat in the area, and launched a sweeping investigation. Retail food stores sold out their stocks of canned, frozen and processed meats early in the day; seafood markets reported their largest volume of sales in two decades. Eggs and cheese were in short supply.

Fifty-seven guards, assistant wardens and other minor officials of the Federal penitentiary at Leavenworth, Kansas, submitted a group resignation to Warden Hermann R. Longe. Their explanation of the move was that all had experienced a religious conversion, and that assisting in the forcible confinement of other human beings was inconsonant with their beliefs.

Near Louisville, Kentucky, neighbors attracted by cries for help found a forty-year-old woman and her twelve-year-old daughter both severely burned. The woman, whose clothing was not even scorched although her upper body was covered with first and second degree burns, admitted pushing the child into a bonfire, but in her hysterical condition was unable to give a rational account of her own injuries.

There was also a follow-up on the Des Moines story about the man who kicked his wife. Remember that I didn't say he had a broken coccyx; I said he was suffering from one. A few hours after he was admitted to the hospital he stopped doing so, and he was released into police custody when X-rays showed no fracture.

Straws in the wind.

At five-thirty that morning, I was waking up my managing editor, Eli Freeman, with a monitored long-distance call—one of Frisbee's bright young men waiting to cut me off if I said anything I shouldn't. The temptation was strong, just the same, but I didn't.

From six to eight-thirty I was on a plane with three taciturn guards. I spent most of the time going over the last thirty years of my life, and wondering how many people would remember me two days after they wrapped my obituary around their garbage.

We landed at the airfield about a mile from the Project proper, and after one of my hitherto silent friends had finished a twenty-minute phone call, a limousine took us over to a long, temporary-looking frame building just outside the wall. It took me only until noon to get out again; I had been fingerprinted, photographed, stripped, examined, X-rayed, urinanalyzed, blood-tested, showered, disinfected, and given a set of pinks to wear until my own clothes had been cleaned and fumigated. I also got a numbered badge which I was instructed to wear on the left chest at all times, and an identity card to keep in my wallet when I got my wallet back.

Then they let me through the gate, and I saw Chillicothe.

I was in a short cul-de-sac formed by the gate and two walls of masonry, blank except for firing slits. Facing away from the gate I could see one of the three laboratory buildings a good half-mile away. Between me and it was a geometrical forest of poles with down-pointing reflectors on their crossbars. Floodlights.

I didn't like that. What I saw a few minutes later I liked even less. I was bouncing across the flat in a jeep driven by a stocky, moon-faced corporal; we passed the first building, and I saw the second.

There was a ring of low pillboxes around it. And their guns pointed *inward,* toward the building.

Major General Parst was a big, bald man in his fifties, whose figure would have been more military if the Prussian corset had not gone out of fashion. I took him for a Pentagon soldier; he had the Pentagon smoothness of manner, but there seemed to be a good deal more under it than the usual well-oiled vacancy. He was also, I judged, a very worried man.

"There's just one thing I'd like to make clear to you at the beginning, Mr. Dahl. I'm not a grudge-holding man, and I hope you're not either, because there's a good chance that you and I will be seeing a lot of each other during the next three or four years. But I thought it might make it a little easier for you to know that you're not the only one with a grievance. You see this isn't an easy job, it never has been. I'm just stating the fact: it's been considerably harder since your newspaper took an interest in us." He spread his hands and smiled wryly.

"Just what is your job, General?"

"You mean, what is Chillicothe." He snorted. "I'm not going to waste my breath telling you."

My expression must have changed.

"Don't misunderstand me—I mean that if I told you, you wouldn't believe me. I didn't myself. I'm going to have to show you." He stood up, looking at his wristwatch. "I have a little more than an hour. That's more than enough for the demonstration, but you're going to have a lot of questions afterward. We'd better start."

He thumbed his intercom. "I'll be in Section One for the next fifteen minutes."

When we were in the corridor outside he said, "Tell me something, Mr. Dahl: I suppose it occurred to you that if you were right in your suspicions of Chillicothe, you might be running a certain personal risk in coming here, in spite of any precautions you might take?"

"I considered the possibility. I haven't seen anything to rule it out yet."

"And still, I gather that you chose this alternative almost without hesitation. Why was that, if you don't mind telling me?"

It was a fair question. There's nothing very attractive about a Federal prison, but at least they don't saw your skull open there, or turn your mind inside out with drugs. I said, "Call it curiosity."

He nodded. "Yes. A very potent force, Mr. Dahl. More mountains have been moved by it than by faith."

We passed a guard with a T44, then a second, and a third. Finally Parst stopped at the first of three metal doors. There was a small pane of thick glass set into it at eye-level, and what looked like a microphone grill under that. Parst spoke into the grill: "Open up Three, Sergeant."

"Yes, sir."

I followed Parst to the second door. It slid open as we reached it and we walked into a large, empty room. The door closed behind us with a thud and a solid *click*. Both sounds rattled back startlingly; the room was solid metal, I realized—floor, walls and ceiling.

In the opposite wall was another heavy door. To my left was a huge metal hemisphere, painted the same gray as the walls, with a machine-gun's snout projecting through a horizontal slit in a deadly and impressive manner.

Echoes blurred the General's voice: "This is Section One. We're rather proud of it. The only entrance to the central room is here, but each of the three others that adjoin it is covered from a gun-turret like that one. The gun rooms are accessible only from the corridors outside."

He motioned me over to the other door. "This door is double," he said. "It's going to be an airlock eventually, we hope. All right, Sergeant."

The door slid back, exposing another one a yard farther in; like the others, it had a thick inset panel of glass.

Parst stepped in and waited for me. "Get ready for a shock," he said.

I loosened the muscles in my back and shoulders; my wind isn't what it used to be, but I can still hit. *Get ready for one yourself*, I thought, *if this is what I think it is*.

I walked into the tiny room, and heard the door thump behind me. Parst motioned to the glass pane.

I saw a room the size of the one behind me. There was a washbasin in it, and a toilet, and what looked like a hammock slung across one corner, and a wooden table with papers and a couple of pencils or crayons on it.

And against the far wall, propped upright on an ordinary lunch-counter stool, was something I couldn't recognize at all; I saw it and I didn't see it. If I had looked away then, I couldn't possibly have told anyone what it looked like.

Then it stirred slightly, and I realized that it was alive.

15

I saw that it had eyes.
I saw that it had arms.
I saw that it had legs.

Very gradually the rest of it came into focus. The top was about four feet off the floor, a small truncated cone about the size and shape of one of those cones of string that some merchants keep to tie packages. Under that came the eyes, three of them. They were round and oyster-gray, with round black pupils, and they faced in different directions. They were set into a flattened bulb of flesh that just fitted under the base of the cone; there was no nose, no ears, no mouth, and no room for any.

The cone was black; the rest of the thing was a very dark, shiny blue-gray.

The head, if that is the word, was supported by a thin neck from which a sparse growth of fuzzy spines curved down and outward, like a botched attempt at feathers. The neck thickened gradually until it became the torso. The torso was shaped something like a bottle gourd, except that the upper lobe was almost as large as the lower. The upper lobe expanded and contracted evenly, all around, as the thing breathed.

Between each arm and the next, the torso curved inward to form a deep vertical gash.

There were three arms and three legs, spaced evenly around the body so that you couldn't tell front from back. The arms sprouted just below the top of the torso, the legs from its base. The legs were bent only slightly to reach the floor; each hand, with five slender, shapeless fingers, rested on the opposite-number thigh. The feet were a little like a chicken's . . .

I turned away and saw Parst; I had forgotten he was there, and where I was, and who I was. I don't recall planning to say anything, but I heard my own voice, faint and hoarse:

"Did you *make* that?"

II

"Stop it!" he said sharply.

I was trembling. I had fallen into a crouch without realizing it, weight on my toes, fists clenched.

I straightened up slowly and put my hands into my pockets. "Sorry."

The speaker rasped.

"Is everything all right, sir?"

"Yes, Sergeant," said Parst. "We're coming out." He turned as the door opened, and I followed him, feeling all churned up inside.

Halfway down the corridor I stopped. Parst turned and looked at me.

"Ithaca," I said.

Five months back there had been a Monster-from-Mars scare in and around Ithaca, New York; several hundred people had seen, or claimed to have seen, a white wingless aircraft hovering over various out-of-the-way places; and over thirty, including one very respectable Cornell professor, had caught sight of something that wasn't a man in the woods around Cayuga Lake. None of these people had got close enough for a good look, but nearly all of them agreed on one point—the thing walked erect, but had too many arms and legs. . . .

"Yes," said Parst. "That's right. But let's talk about it in my office, Mr. Dahl."

I followed him back there. As soon as the door was shut I said, "Where did it come from? Are there any more of them? What about the ship?"

He offered me a cigarette. I took it and sat down, hitting the chair by luck.

"Those are just three of the questions we can't answer," he said. "He claims that his home world revolves

17

around a sun in our constellation of Aquarius; he says that it isn't visible from Earth. He also—"

I said, "He talks—? You've taught him to speak English?" For some reason that was hard to accept; then I remembered the linguists.

"Yes. Quite well, considering that he doesn't have vocal cords like ours. He uses a tympanum under each of those vertical openings in his body—those are his mouths. His name is Aza-Kra, by the way. I was going to say that he also claims to have come here alone. As for the ship, he says it's hidden, but he won't tell us where. We've been searching that area, particularly the hills near Cayuga and the lake itself, but we haven't turned it up yet. It's been suggested that he may have launched it under remote control and put it into an orbit somewhere outside the atmosphere. The Lunar Observatory is watching for it, and so are the orbital stations, but I'm inclined to think that's a dead end. In any case, that's not my responsibility. He had some gadgets in his possession when he was captured, but even those are being studied elsewhere. Chillicothe is what you saw a few minutes ago, and that's all it is. God knows it's enough."

His intercom buzzed. "Yes."

"Dr. Meshevski would like to talk to you about the technical vocabularies, sir."

"Ask him to hold it until the conference if he possibly can."

"Yes, sir."

"Two more questions we can't answer," Parst said, "are what his civilization is like and what he came here to do. I'll tell you what he says. The planet he comes from belongs to a galactic union of highly advanced, peace-loving races. He came here to help us prepare ourselves for membership in that union."

I was trying hard to keep up, but it wasn't easy. After a moment I said, "Suppose it's true?"

He gave me the cold eye.

"All right, suppose it's true." For the first time, his voice was impatient. "Then suppose the opposite. Think about it for a minute."

I saw where he was leading me, but I tried to circle around to it from another direction; I wanted to reason it

18

out for myself. I couldn't make the grade; I had to fall back on analogies, which are a kind of thinking I distrust.

You were a cannibal islander, and a missionary came along. He meant well, but you thought he wanted to steal your yamfields and your wives, so you chopped him up and ate him for dinner.

Or:

You were a cannibal islander, and a missionary came You treated him as a guest, but he made a slave of you, worked you till you dropped, and finally wiped out your whole nation, to the last woman and child.

I said, "A while ago you mentioned three or four years as the possible term of the Project. Did you—?"

"That wasn't meant to be taken literally," he said. "It may take a lifetime." He was staring at his desk-top.

"In other words, if nothing stops you, you're going to go right on just this way, sitting on this thing. Until What's-his-name dies, or his friends show up with an army, or something else blows it wide open."

"*That's* right."

"Well, damn it, don't you see that's the one thing you can't do? Either way you guess it, that won't work. If he's friendly—"

Parst lifted a pencil in his hand and slapped it palm-down against the desk-top. His mouth was tight. "It's *necessary*," he said.

After a silent moment he straightened in his chair and spread the fingers of his right hand at me. "One," he said, touching the thumb: "weapons. Leaving everything else aside, if we can get one strategically superior weapon out of him, or the theory that will enable us to build one, then we've *got* to do it and we've *got* to do it in secret."

The index finger. "Two: the spaceship." Middle finger. "Three: the civilization he comes from. If they're planning to attack us we've got to find that out, and when, and how, and what we can do about it." Ring finger. "Four: Aza-Kra himself. If we don't hold him in secret we can't hold him at all, and how do we know what he might do if we let him go? There isn't a single possibility we can rule out. Not one."

He put the hand flat on the desk. "Five, six, seven, eight, nine, ten, infinity. Biology, psychology, sociology, ecology, chemistry, physics, right down the line. Every science. In any one of them we might find something that would mean the difference between life and death for this country or this whole planet."

He stared at me for a moment, his face set. "You don't have to remind me of the other possibilities, Dahl. I know what they are; I've been on this project for thirteen weeks. I've also heard of the Golden Rule, and the Ten Commandments, and the Constitution of the United States. But this is *the survival of the human race* we're talking about."

I opened my mouth to say "That's just the point," or something equally stale, but I shut it again; I saw it was no good. I had one argument—that if this alien ambassador was what he claimed to be, then the whole world had to know about it; any nation that tried to suppress that knowledge, or dictate the whole planet's future, was committing a crime against humanity. That, on the other hand, if he was an advance agent for an invasion fleet, the same thing was true only a great deal more so.

Beyond that I had nothing but instinctive moral conviction; and Parst had that on his side too; so did Frisbee and the President and all the rest. Being who and what they were, they had to believe as they did. Maybe they were right.

Half an hour later, the last thought I had before my head hit the pillow was, *Suppose there isn't any Aza-Kra? Suppose that thing was a fake, a mechanical dummy?*

But I knew better, and I slept soundly.

That was the second day. On the third day, the front pages of the more excitable newspapers were top-heavy with forty-eight-point headlines. There were two Chicago stories. The first, in the early afternoon editions, announced that every epidemic victim had made a complete recovery, that health department experts had been unable to isolate any disease-causing agent in the stock awaiting slaughter, and that although several cases not involving stockyard employees had been reported, not one had been traced to consumption of infected meat. A Chicago epidemiologist was quoted as saying, "It could have been just a gigantic coincidence."

The later story was a lulu. Although the slaughter-houses had not been officially reopened or the ban on fresh-meat sales rescinded, health officials allowed seventy of the previous day's victims to return to work as an experiment. Within half an hour every one of them was back in the hospital, suffering from a second, identical attack.

Oddly enough—at first glance—sales of fresh meat in areas outside the ban dropped slightly in the early part of the day ("They *say* it's all right, but you won't catch me taking a chance"), rose sharply in the evening ("I'd better stock up before there's a run on the butcher shops").

Warden Longo, in an unprecedented move, added his resignation to those of the fifty-seven "conscience" employees of Leavenworth. Well-known as an advocate of prison reform, Longo explained that his subordinates' example had convinced him that only so dramatic a gesture could focus the American public's attention upon the injustice and inhumanity of the present system.

He was joined by two hundred and three of the Federal institution's remaining employees, bringing the total to more than eighty per cent of Leavenworth's permanent staff.

The movement was spreading. In Terre Haute, Indiana, eighty employees of the Federal penitentiary were reported to have resigned. Similar reports came from the State prisons of Iowa, Missouri, Illinois and Indiana, and from city and county correctional institutions from Kansas City to Cincinnati.

The war in Indo-China was crowded back among the stock-market reports. Even the official announcement that the first Mars rocket was nearing completion in its sublunar orbit—front-page news at any normal time—got an inconspicuous paragraph in some papers and was dropped entirely by others.

But I found an item in a St. Louis paper about the policeman who had collapsed after shooting a criminal. He was dead.

I woke up a little before dawn that morning, having had a solid fifteen hours' sleep. I found the cafeteria and

21

hung around until it opened. That was where Captain Ritchy-loo tracked me down.

He came in as I was finishing my second order of ham and eggs, a big, blond, swimming-star type, full of confidence and good cheer. "You must be Mr. Dahl. My name is Ritchy-loo."

I let him pump my hand and watched him sit down. "How do you spell it?" I asked him.

He grinned happily. "It is a tough one, isn't it? French. R, i, c, h, e, l, i, e, u."

Richelieu. Ritchy-loo.

I said, "What can I do for you, Captain?"

"Ah, it's what I can do for *you,* Mr. Dahl. You're a VIP around here, you know. You're getting the triple-A guided tour, and I'm your guide."

I *hate* people who are cheerful in the morning.

We went out into the pale glitter of early-morning sunshine on the flat; the floodlight poles and the pillboxes trailed long, mournful shadows. There was a jeep waiting, and Ritchy-loo took the wheel himself.

We made a right turn around the corner of the building and then headed down one of the diagonal avenues between the poles. I glanced into the firing slit of one of the pillboxes as we passed it, and saw the gleam of somebody's spectacles.

"That was B building that we just came out of," said the captain. "Most of the interesting stuff is there, but you want to see everything, naturally, so we'll go over to C first and then back to A."

The huge barracks, far off to the right, looked deserted; I saw a few men in fatigues here and there, spearing stray bits of paper. Beyond the building we were heading for, almost against the wall, tiny figures were leaping rhythmically, opening and closing like so many animated scissors.

It was a well-policed area, at any rate; I watched for a while, out of curiosity, and didn't see a single cigarette paper or gum wrapper.

To the left of the barracks and behind it was a miniature town—neat one-story cottages, all alike, all the same distance apart. The thing that struck me about it was that there were none of the signs of a permanent camp—no borders of whitewashed stones, no trees, no shrubs, no flowers. *No wives,* I thought.

"How's morale here, Captain?" I asked.

"Now, it's funny you should ask that. That happens to be my job, I'm the Company B morale officer. Well, I should say that all things considered, we aren't doing too badly. Of course, we have a few difficulties. These men are here on eighteen-month assignments, and that's a kind of a long time without passes or furloughs. We'd like to make the hitches shorter, naturally, but of course you understand that there aren't too many fresh but seasoned troops available just now."

"No."

"*But,* we do our best. Now here's C building."

Most of C building turned out to be occupied by chemical laboratories: long rows of benches covered by rank growths of glassware, only about a fifth of it working, and nobody watching more than a quarter of that.

"What are they doing here?"

"Over my head," said Ritchy-loo cheerfully. "Here's Dr. Vitale, let's ask him."

Vitale was a little sharp-featured man with a nervous blink. "This is the atmosphere section," he said. "We're trying to analyze the atmosphere which the alien breathes. Eventually we hope to manufacture it."

That was a point that hadn't occurred to me. "He can't breathe our air?"

"No, no. Altogether different."

"Well, where does he get the stuff he does breathe, then?"

The little man's lips worked. "From that cone-shaped mechanism on the top of his head. An atmosphere plant that you could put in your pocket. Completely incredible. We can't get an adequate sample without taking it off him, and we can't take it off him without killing him. We have to deduce what he breathes in from what he breathes *out. Very* difficult." He went away.

All the same, I couldn't see much point in it. Presumably if Aza-Kra couldn't breathe our air, we couldn't breathe his—so anybody who wanted to examine him would have to wear an oxygen tank and a breathing mask.

23

But it was obvious enough, and I got it in another minute. If the prisoner didn't have his own air-supply, it would be that much harder for him to break out past the gun rooms and the guards in the corridors and the pillboxes and the floodlights and the wall. . . .

We went on, stopping at every door. There were storerooms, sleeping quarters, a few offices. The rest of the rooms were empty.

Ritchy-loo wanted to go on to A building, but I was being perversely thorough, and I said we would go through the barracks and the company towns first. We did; it took us three hours, and thinned down Ritchy-loo's stream of cheerful conversation to a trickle. We looked everywhere, and of course we did not find anything that shouldn't have been there.

A building was the recreation hall. Canteen, library, gymnasium, movie theater, PX, swimming pool. It was also the project hospital and dispensary. Both sections were well filled.

So we went back to B. And it was almost noon, so we had lunch in the big air-conditioned cafeteria. I didn't look forward to it; I expected that rest and food would turn on Ritchy-loo's conversational spigot again, and if he didn't get any response to the first three or four general topics he tried, I was perfectly sure he would begin telling me jokes. Nothing of the kind happened. After a few minutes I saw why, or thought I did. Looking around the room, I saw face after face with the same blank look on it; there wasn't a smile or an animated expression in the place. And now that I was paying attention I noticed that the sounds were odd, too. There were more than a hundred people in the room, enough to set up a beehive roar; but there was so little talking going on that you could pick out individual sentences with ease, and they were all trochaic—*Want* some *su*gar? *No,* thanks. Like that.

It was infectious; I was beginning to feel it now myself —an execution-chamber kind of mood, a feeling that we were all shut up in a place that we couldn't get out of, and where something horrible was going to happen. Unless you've ever been in a group made up of people who had that feeling and were reinforcing it in each other, it's indescribable; but it was very real and very hard to take.

24

Ritchy-loo left half a chop on his plate; I finished mine, but it choked me.

In the corridor outside I asked him, "Is it always as bad as that?"

"You noticed it too? That place gives me the creeps, I don't know why. It's the same way in the movies, too, lately—wherever you get a lot of these people together. I just don't understand it." For a second longer he looked worried and thoughtful, and then he grinned suddenly. "I don't want to say anything against civilians, Mr. Dahl, but I think that bunch is pretty far gone."

I could have hugged him. Civilians! If Ritchy-loo was more than six months away from a summer-camp counselor's job, I was a five-star general.

We started at the end of the corridor and worked our way down. We looked into a room with an X-ray machine and a fluoroscope in it, and a darkroom, and a room full of racks and filing cabinets, and a long row of offices.

Then Ritchy-loo opened a door that revealed two men standing on opposite sides of a desk, spouting angry German at each other. The tall one noticed us after a second, said, " 'St, 'st," to the other, and then to us, coldly, "You might, at least, knock."

"Sorry, gentlemen," said Ritchy-loo brightly. He closed the door and went on to the next on the same side. This opened onto a small, bare room with nobody in it but a stocky man with corporal's stripes on his sleeve. He was sitting hunched over, elbows on knees, hands over his face. He didn't move or look up.

I have a good ear, and I had managed to catch one sentence of what the fat man next door had been saying to the tall one. It went like this: *"Nein, nein, das ist bestimmt nicht die Klaustrophobie; Ich sage dir, es ist das dreifüssige Tier, das sie störrt."*

My college German came back to me when I prodded it, but it creaked a little. While I was still working at it, I asked Ritchy-loo, "What was that?"

"Psychiatric section," he said.

"You get many psycho cases here?"

"Oh, no," he said. "Just the normal percentage, Mr. Dahl. Less, in fact."

The captain was a poor liar.

25

"Klaustrophobie" was easy, of course. *"Dreifüssige Tier"* stopped me until I remembered that the German for "zoo" is *"Tiergarten." Dreifüssige Tier:* the three-footed beast. The triped.

The fat one had been saying to the tall one, "No, no, it is absolutely not claustrophobia; I tell you, it's the triped that's disturbing them."

Three-quarters of an hour later we had peered into the last room in B building: a long office full of IBM machines. We had now been over every square yard of Chillicothe, and I had seen for myself that no skulduggery was going forward anywhere in it. That was the idea behind the guided tour, as Ritchy-loo was evidently aware.

He said, "Well, that just about wraps it up, Mr. Dahl. By the way, the General's office asked me to tell you that if it's all right with you, they'll set up that phone call for you for four o'clock this afternoon."

I looked down at the rough map of the building I'd been drawing as we went along. "There's one place we haven't been, Captain," I said. "Section One."

"Oh, well that's right, that's right. You saw that yesterday, though, didn't you, Mr. Dahl?"

"For about two minutes. I wasn't able to take much of it in. I'd like to see it again, if it isn't too much trouble. Or even if it is."

Ritchy-loo laughed heartily. "Good enough. Just wait a second, I'll see if I can get you a clearance on it." He walked down the corridor to the nearest wall phone.

After a few moments he beckoned me over, palming the receiver. "The General says there are two research groups in there now and it would be a little crowded. He says he'd like you to postpone it if you think you can."

"Tell him that's perfectly all right, but in that case I think we'd better put off the phone call, too."

He repeated the message, and waited. Finally, "Yes. Yes, uh-huh. Yes, I've got that. All right."

He turned to me. "The General says it's all right for you to go in for half an hour and watch, but he'd appreciate it if you'll be careful not to distract the people who're working in there."

I had been hoping the General would say no. I wanted to

see the alien again, all right, but what I wanted the most was time.

This was the second day I had been at Chillicothe. By tomorrow at the latest I would have to talk to Eli Freeman; and I still hadn't figured out any sure, safe way to tell him that Chillicothe was a legitimate research project, not to be sniped at by the *Herald-Star*—and make him understand that I didn't mean a word of it.

I could simply refuse to make the call, or I could tell him as much of the truth as I could before I was cut off —two words, probably—but it was a cinch that call would be monitored at the other end, too; that was part of what Ritchy-loo meant by "setting up the call." Somebody from the FBI would be sitting at Freeman's elbow . . . and I wasn't telling myself fairy tales about Peter Zenger any more.

They would shut the paper down, which was not only the thing I wanted least in the world but a thing that would do nobody any good.

I wanted Eli to spread the story by underground channels—spread it so far, and time the release so well, that no amount of censorship could kill it.

Treason is a word every man has to define for himself.

Ritchy-loo did the honors for me at the gun-room door, and then left me, looking a little envious. I don't think he had ever been inside Section One.

There was somebody ahead of me in the tiny antechamber, I found: a short, wide-shouldered man with a sheep-dog tangle of black hair.

He turned as the door closed behind me. "Hi. Oh— you're Dahl, aren't you?" He had a young, pleasant, meaningless face behind dark-rimmed glasses. I said yes.

He put a half-inch of cigarette between his lips and shook hands with me. "Somebody pointed you out. Glad to know you; my name's Donnelly. Physical psych section—very junior." He pointed through the spy-window. "What do you think of him?"

Aza-Kra was sitting directly in front of the window; his lunch-counter stool had been moved into the center of the room. Around him were four men: two on the left, sitting on folding chairs, talking to him and occasionally making notes; two on the right, standing beside a waist-high enclosed mechanism from which wires led to the upper lobe of the alien's body. The ends of the wires were taped against his skin.

"That isn't an easy question," I said.

Donnelly nodded without interest. "That's my boss there," he said, "the skinny, gray-haired guy on the right. We get on each other's nerves. If he gets that setup operating this session, I'm supposed to go in and take notes. He won't, though."

"What is it?"

"Electroencephalograph. See, his brain isn't in his head, it's in his upper thorax there. Too much insulation in the way. We can't get close enough for a good reading without surgery. I say we ought to drop it till we get permission, but Hendricks thinks he can lick it. Those two on the other side are interviewers. Like to hear what they're saying?"

He punched one of two buttons set into the door beside the speaker grill, under the spy-window. "If you're ever in here alone, remember you can't get out while this is on. You turn on the speaker here, it turns off the one in the gun room. They wouldn't be able to hear you ask to get out."

Inside, a monotonous voice was saying, ". . . have that here, but what exactly do you mean by . . ."

"I ought to be in physiology," Donnelly said, lowering his voice. "They have all the fun. You see his eyes?"

I looked. The center one was staring directly toward us; the other two were tilted, almost out of sight around the curve of that bulb of blue-gray flesh.

". . . in other words, just what is the nature of this energy, is it—uh—transmitted by waves, or . . ."

"He can look three ways at once," I said.

"Three, with binocular," Donnelly agreed. "Each eye can function independently or couple with the one on either side. So he can have a series of overlapping monocular images, all the way around, or he can have up to three binocular images. They focus independently, too. He could read a newspaper and watch for his wife to come out of the movie across the street."

"Wait a minute," I said. "He has *six* eyes, not three?"

"Sure. Has to, to keep the symmetry and still get binocular vision."

"Then he hasn't got any front or back," I said slowly.

"No, that's right. He's trilaterally symmetrical. Drive you crazy to watch him walk. His legs work the same way as his eyes—any one can pair up with either of the others. He wants to change direction, he doesn't have to turn around. I'd hate to try to catch him in an open field."

"How did they catch him?" I asked.

"Luckiest thing in the world. Found him in the woods with two broken ankles. Now look at his hands. What do you see?"

The voice inside was still droning; evidently it was a long question. "Five fingers," I said.

"Nope." Donnelly grinned. "One finger, four thumbs. See how they oppose, those two on either side of the middle finger? He's got a better hand than ours. One *hell* of an efficient design. Brain in his thorax where it's safe, six eyes on a stalk—trachea up there too, no connection with the esophagus, so he doesn't need an epiglottis. Three of everything else. He can lose a leg and still walk, lose an arm and still type, lose two eyes and still see better than we do. He can lose—"

I didn't hear him. The interviewer's voice had stopped, and Aza-Kra's had begun. It was frightening, because it was a buzzing and it was a voice.

I couldn't take in a word of it; I had enough to do absorbing the fact that there were words.

Then it stopped, and the interviewer's ordinary, flat Middle Western voice began again.

"—And just try to sneak up behind him," said Donnelly. "I dare you."

Again Aza-Kra spoke briefly, and this time I saw the flesh at the side of his body, where the two lobes flowed together, bulge slightly and then relax.

"He's talking with one of his mouths," I said. "I mean, one of those—" I took a deep breath. "If he breathes through the top of his head, and there's no connection between his lungs and his vocal organs, then where the hell does he get the air?"

"He belches. Not as inconvenient as it sounds. You

could learn to do it if you had to." Donnelly laughed. "Not very fragrant, though. Watch their faces when he talks."

I watched Aza-Kra's instead—what there was of it: one round, expressionless, oyster-colored eye staring back at me. With a human opponent, I was thinking, there were a thousand little things that you relied on to help you: facial expressions, mannerisms. signs of emotion. But Parst had been right when he said, *There isn't a single possibility we can rule out. Not one.* And so had the fat man: *It's the triped that's disturbing them.* And Ritchy-loo: *It's the same way . . . wherever you get a lot of these people together.*

And I still hadn't figured out any way to tell Freeman what he had to know.

I thought I could arouse Eli's suspicion easily enough; we knew each other well enough for a word or a gesture to mean a good deal. I could make him look for hidden meanings. But how could I hide a message so that Eli would be more likely to dig it out than a trained FBI cryptologist?

I stared at Aza-Kra's glassy eye as if the answer were there. It was going to be a video circuit, I told myself. Donnelly was still yattering in my ear, and now the alien was buzzing again, but I ignored them both. Suppose I broke the message up into one-word units, scattered them through my conversation with Eli, and marked them off somehow—by twitching a finger, or blinking my eyelids?

A dark membrane flicked across the alien's oyster-colored eye.

A moment later, it happened again.

Donnelly was saying, ". . . intercostal membranes, apparently. But there's no trace of . . ."

"Shut up a minute, will you?" I said. "I want to hear this."

The inhuman voice, the voice that sounded like the articulate buzzing of a giant insect, was saying, "Comparison not possible, excuse me. If (*blink*) you try to understand in words you know, you (*blink*) tell yourself you wish (*blink*) to understand, but knowledge escape (*blink*) you. Can only show (*blink*) you from beginning, one (*blink*) little, another little. Not possible to carry all knowledge in one hand (*blink*)."

30

If you wish escape, show one hand.

I looked at Donnelly. He had moved back from the spy-window; he was lighting a cigarette, frowning at the match-flame. His mouth was sullen.

I put my left hand flat against the window. I thought, *I'm dreaming.*

The interviewer said querulously, ". . . getting us nowhere. Can't you—"

"Wait," said the buzzing voice. "Let me say, please. Ignorant man hold (*blink*) burning stick, say, this is breath (*blink*) of the wood. Then you show him flashlight—"

I took a deep breath, and held it.

Around the alien, four men went down together, folding over quietly at waist and knee, sprawling on the floor. I heard a thump behind me.

Donnelly was lying stretched out along the wall, his head tilted against the corner. The cigarette had fallen from his hand.

I looked back at Aza-Kra. His head turned slightly, the dark flesh crinkling. Two eyes stared back at me through the window.

"Now you can breathe," said the monster.

III

I let out the breath that was choking me and took another. My knees were shaking.

"What did you do to them?"

"Put them to sleep only. In a few minutes I will put the others to sleep. After you are outside the doors. First we will talk."

I glanced at Donnelly again. His mouth was ajar; I could see his lips fluttering as he breathed.

"All right," I said, "talk."

"When you leave," buzzed the voice, "you must take me with you."

Now it was clear. He could put people to sleep, but he couldn't open locked doors. He had to have help.

"No deal," I said. "You might as well knock me out, too."

"Yes," he answered, "you will do it. When you understand."

"I'm listening."

"You do not have to agree now. I ask only this much. When we are finished talking, you leave. When you are past the second door, hold your breath again. Then go to the office of General Parst. You will find there papers about me. Read them. You will find also keys to open gun room. Also, handcuffs. Special handcuffs, made to fit me. Then you will think, if Aza-Kra is not what he says, would he agree to this? Then you will come back to gun room, use controls there to open middle door. You will lay handcuffs down, where you stand now, then go back to gun room, open inside door. I will put on the handcuffs. You will see that I do it. And then you will take me with you."

... I said, "Let me think."

32

The obvious thing to do was to push the little button that turned on the audio circuit to the gun room, and yell for help; the alien could then put everybody to sleep from here to the wall, maybe, but it wouldn't do any good. Sooner or later he would have to let up, or starve to death along with the rest of us. On the other hand if I did what he asked—*anything* he asked—and it turned out to be the wrong thing, I would be guilty of the worse crime since Pilate's.

But I thought about it, I went over it again and again, and I couldn't see any loophole in it for Aza-Kra. He was leaving it up to me—if I felt like letting him out after I'd seen the papers in Parst's office, I could do so. If I didn't, I could still yell for help. In fact, I could get on the phone and yell to Washington, which would be a hell of a lot more to the point.

So where was the payoff for Aza-Kra? What was in those papers?

I pushed the button. I said, "This is Dahl. Let me out, will you please?"

The outer door began to 'slide back. Just in time, I saw Donnelly's head bobbing against it; I grabbed him by the shirt-front and hoisted his limp body out of the way.

I walked across the echoing outer chamber; the outermost door opened for me. I stepped through it and held my breath. Down the corridor, three guards leaned over their rifles and toppled all in a row, like precision divers. Beyond them a hurrying civilian in the cross-corridor fell heavily and skidded out of sight.

The clacking of typewriters from a nearby office had stopped abruptly. I let out my breath when I couldn't hold it any longer, and listened to the silence.

The General was slumped over his desk, head on his crossed forearms, looking pretty old and tired with his polished bald skull shining under the light. There was a faint silvery scar running across the top of his head, and I wondered whether he had got it in combat as a young man, or whether he had tripped over a rug at an embassy reception.

Across the desk from him a thin man in a gray pincheck suit was jackknifed on the carpet, half-supported by a chair-leg, rump higher than his head.

There were two six-foot filing cabinets in the right-hand corner behind the desk. Both were locked; the drawers of the first one were labeled alphabetically, the other was unmarked.

I unhooked Parst's key-chain from his belt. He had as many keys as a janitor or a high-school principal, but not many of them were small enough to fit the filing cabinets. I got the second one unlocked and began going through the drawers. I found what I wanted in the top one—seven fat manila folders labeled "Aza-Kra—Armor," "Aza-Kra —General information," Aza-Kra—Power sources," "Aza-Kra—Spaceflight" and so on; and one more labeled "Directives and related correspondence."

I hauled them all out, piled them on Parst's desk and pulled up a chair.

I took "Armor" first because it was on top and because the title puzzled me. The folder was full of transcripts of interviews whose subject I had to work out as I went along. It appeared that when captured, Aza-Kra had been wearing a lightweight bulletproof body armor, made of something that was longitudinally flexible and perpendicularly rigid—in other words, you could pull it on like a suit of winter underwear, but you couldn't dent it with a sledge hammer.

They had been trying to find out what the stuff was and how it was made for almost three months and as far as I could see they had not made a nickel's worth of progress.

I looked through "Power sources" and "Spaceflight" to see if they were the same, and they were. The odd part was that Aza-Kra's answers didn't sound reluctant or evasive; but he kept running into ideas for which there weren't any words in English and then they would have to start all over again, like Twenty Questions. . . . Is it animal? vegetable? mineral? It was a mess.

I put them all aside except "General information" and "Directives." The first, as I had guessed, was a catch-all for nontechnical subjects—where Aza-Kra had come from, what his people were like, his reasons for coming to this planet: all the unimportant questions; or the only questions that had any importance, depending on how you looked at it.

Parst had already given me an accurate summary of it, but it was surprisingly effective in Aza-Kra's words. *You say we want your planet. There are many planets, so many you would not believe. But if we wanted your planet, and if we could kill as you do, please understand, we are very many. We would fall on your planet like snowflakes. We would not send one man alone.*

And later: *Most young peoples kill. It is a law of nature, yes, but try to understand, it is not the only law. You have been a young people, but now you are growing older. Now you must learn the other law, not to kill. That is what I have come to teach. Until you learn this, we cannot have you among us.*

There was nothing in the folder dated later than a month and a half ago. They had dropped that line of questioning early.

The first thing I saw in the other folder began like this:
You are hereby directed to hold yourself in readiness to destroy the subject under any of the following circumstances, without further specific notification:

1, a: If the subject attempts to escape.

1, b: If the subject kills or injures a human being.

1, c: If the landing, anywhere in the world, of other members of the subject's race is reported and their similarity to the subject established beyond a reasonable doubt. . . .

Seeing it written down like that, in the cold dead-aliveness of black words on white paper, it was easy to forget that the alien was a stomach-turning monstrosity, and to see only that what he had to say was lucid and noble.

But I still hadn't found anything that would persuade me to help him escape. The problem was still there, as insoluble as ever. There was no way of evaluating a word the alien said about himself. He had come alone—perhaps—instead of bringing an invading army with him; but how did we know that one member of his race wasn't as dangerous to us as Perry's battleship to the Japanese? He might be; there was some evidence that he was.

My quarrel with the Defense Department was not that they were mistreating an innocent three-legged missionary, but simply that the problem of Aza-Kra belonged to the

35

world, not to a fragment of the executive branch of the
Government of the United States—and certainly not to
me.

. . . There was one other way out, I realized. Instead
of calling Frisbee in Washington, I could call an arm-long
list of senators and representatives. I could call the UN
secretariat in New York; I could call the editor of every
major newspaper in this hemisphere and the head of
every wire service and broadcasting chain. I could stir up a
hornet's nest, even, as the saying goes, if I swung for
it.

Wrong again: I couldn't. I opened the "Directives"
folder again, looking for what I thought I had seen there
in the list of hypothetical circumstances. There it was:

*1, f: If any concerted attempt on the part of any per-
son or group to remove the subject from Defense Department custody, or to aid him in any way, is made; or if the
subject's existence and presence in Defense Department
custody becomes public knowledge.*

That sewed it up tight, and it also answered my question about Aza-Kra. Knocking out the personnel of B
building would be construed as an attempt to escape or as
a concerted attempt by a person or group to remove the
subject from Defense Department custody, it didn't matter which. If I broke the story, it would have the same
result. They would kill him.

In effect, he had put his life in my hands: and that
was why he was so sure that I'd help him.

It might have been that, or what I found just before I
left the office, that decided me. I don't know; I wish I
did.

Coming around the desk the other way, I glanced at
the thin man on the floor and noticed that there was something under him, half-hidden by his body. It turned out to
be two things: a gray fedora and a pint-sized gray-leather
briefcase, chained to his wrist.

So I looked under Parst's folded arms, saw the edge of
a thick white sheet of paper, and pulled it out.

Under Frisbee's letterhead, it said:

By courier.

Dear General Parst:

Some possibility appears to exist that A. K. is responsible for recent disturbances in your area; please give me your thought on this as soon as possible—the decision can't be long postponed.

In the meantime you will of course consider your command under emergency status, and we count on you to use your initiative to safeguard security at all costs. In a crisis, you will consider Lieut. D. as expendable.

Sincerely yours,
CARLTON FRISBEE

cf/cf/enc.

"Enc." meant "enclosure"; I pried up Parst's arms again and found another sheet of stiff paper, folded three times, with a paperclip on it.

It was a First Lieutenant's commission, made out to Robert James Dahl, dated three days before.

If commissions can be forged, so can court-martial records.

I put the commission and the letter in my pocket. I didn't seem to feel any particular emotion, but I noticed that my hands were shaking as I sorted through the "General information" file, picked out a few sheets and stuffed them into my pocket with the other papers. I wasn't confused or in doubt about what to do next. I looked around the room, spotted a metal locker diagonally across from the filing cabinets, and opened it with one of the General's keys.

Inside were two .45 automatics, boxes of ammunition, several loaded clips, and three odd-looking sets of handcuffs, very wide and heavy, each with its key.

I took the handcuffs, the keys, both automatics and all the clips.

In a storeroom at the end of the corridor I found a two-wheeled dolly. I wheeled it all the way around to Section One and left it outside the center door. Then it struck me that I was still wearing the pinks they had given me when I arrived, and where the hell were my own clothes? I took a chance and went up to my room on the second floor, remembering that I hadn't been back there since morning.

There they were, neatly laid out on the bed. My keys, lighter, change, wallet and so on were on the bedside table. I changed and went back down to Section One.

In the gun room were two sprawled shapes, one beside the machine-gun that poked its snout through the hemispherical blister, the other under a panel set with three switches and a microphone.

The switches were clearly marked. I opened the first two, walked out and around and laid the three sets of handcuffs on the floor in the middle room. Then I went back to the gun room, closed the first two doors and opened the third.

Soft thumping sounds came from the loudspeaker over the switch panel; then the rattling of metal, more thumps, and finally a series of rattling clicks.

I opened the first door and went back inside. Through the panel in the middle door I could see Aza-Kra; he had retreated into the inner room so that all of him was plainly visible. He was squatting on the floor, his legs drawn up. His arms were at full stretch, each wrist manacled to an ankle. He strained his arms outward to show me that the cuffs were tight.

I made one more trip to open the middle door. Then I got the dolly and wheeled it in.

"Thank you," said Aza-Kra. I got a whiff of his "breath"; as Donnelly had intimated, it wasn't pleasant.

Halfway to the airport, at Aza-Kra's request, I held my breath again. Aside from that we didn't speak except when I asked him, as I was loading him from the jeep into a limousine, "How long will they stay unconscious?"

"Not more than twenty hours, I think. I could have given them more, but I did not dare. I do not know your chemistry well enough."

We could go a long way in twenty hours. We would certainly have to.

I hated to go home, it was too obvious and there was a

38

good chance that the hunt would start before any twenty hours were up, but there wasn't any help for it. I had a passport and a visa for England, where I had been planning to go for a publishers' conference in January, but it hadn't occurred to me to take it along on a quick trip to Washington. And now I had to have the passport.

My first idea had been to head for New York and hand Aza-Kra over to the UN there, but I saw it was no good. Extraterritoriality was just a word, like a lot of other words; we wouldn't be safe until we were out of the country, and on second thought, maybe not then.

It was a little after eight-thirty when I pulled in to the curb down the street from my house. I hadn't eaten since noon, but I wasn't hungry; and it didn't occur to me until later to think about Aza-Kra.

I got the passport and some money without waking my housekeeper. A few blocks away I parked again on a side street. I called the airport, got a reservation on the next eastbound flight, and spent half an hour buying a trunk big enough for Aza-Kra and wrestling him into it.

It struck me at the last minute that perhaps I had been counting too much on that atmosphere-plant of his. His air supply was taken care of, but what about his respiratory waste products—would he poison himself in that tiny closed space? I asked him, and he said, "No, it is all right. I will be warm, but I can bear it."

I put the lid down, then opened it again. "I forgot about food," I said. "What do you eat, anyway?"

"At Chillicothe I ate soya bean extract. With added minerals. But I am able to go without food for long periods. Please, do not worry."

All right. I put the lid down again and locked the trunk, but I didn't stop worrying.

He was being too accommodating.

I had expected him to ask me to turn him loose, or take him to wherever his spaceship was. He hadn't brought the subject up; he hadn't even asked me where we were going, or what my plans were.

I thought I knew the answer to that, but it didn't make me any happier. He didn't ask because he already knew —just as he'd known the contents of Parst's office, down to the last document; just as he'd known what I was thinking when I was in the anteroom with Donnelly.

He read minds. And he gassed people through solid metal walls.

What else did he do?

There wasn't time to dispose of the limousine; I simply left it at the airport. If the alarm went out before we got to the coast, we were sunk anyhow; it not, it wouldn't matter.

Nobody stopped us. I caught the stratojet in New York at 12:20, and five hours later we were in London.

Customs was messy, but there wasn't any other way to handle it. When we were fifth in line, I thought: *Knock them out for about an hour*—and held my breath. Nothing happened. I rapped on the side of the trunk again to attract his attention, and did it again. This time it worked: everybody in sight went down like a rag doll.

I stamped my own passport, filled out a declaration form and buried it in a stack of others, put a tag on the trunk, loaded it aboard a handtruck, wheeled it outside and took a cab.

I had learned something in the process, although it certainly wasn't much: either Aza-Kra couldn't, or didn't, eavesdrop on my mind all the time—or else he was simply one step ahead of me.

Later, on the way to the harbor, I saw a newsstand and realized that it was going on three days since I had seen a paper. I had tried to get the New York dailies at the airport, but they'd been sold out—nothing on the stands but a lone copy of the Staten Island *Advance*. That hadn't struck me as odd at the time—an index of my state of mind—but it did now.

I got out and bought a copy of everything on the stand except the tipsheets—four newspapers, all of them together about equaling the bulk of one *Herald-Star*. I felt frustrated enough to ask the newsvendor if he had any papers left over from yesterday or the day before. He gave me a glassy look, made me repeat it, then pulled his face into an indescribable expression, laid a finger beside his nose, and said, " 'Arf a mo'." He scuttled into a bar a few yards down the street, was gone five minutes, and came back clutching a mare's-nest of soiled and bedraggled papers.

" 'Ere you are, guvnor. Three bob for the lot."

I paid him. "Thanks," I said, "very much."

He waved his hand expansively. "Okay, bud," he said. "T'ink nuttin' of it!"

A comedian.

The only Channel boat leaving before late afternoon turned out to be an excursion steamer—round trip, two guineas. The boat wasn't crowded; it was the tag-end of the season, and a rough, windy day. I found a seat without any trouble and finished sorting out my stack of papers by date and folio.

British newspapers don't customarily report any more of our news than we do of theirs, but this week our supply of catastrophes had been ample enough to make good reading across the Atlantic. I found all three of the Chicago stories—trimmed to less than two inches apiece, but there. I read the first with professional interest, the second skeptically, and the third with alarm.

I remembered the run of odd items I'd read in that Washington hotel room, a long time ago. I remembered Frisbee's letter to Parst: *"Some possibility appears to exist that A.K. is responsible for recent disturbances in your area. . . ."*

I found two of the penitentiary stories, half smothered by stop press, and I added them to the total. I drew an imaginary map of the United States in my head and stuck imaginary pins in it. Red ones, a little cluster: Des Moines, Kansas City, Decatur, St. Louis. Blue ones, a scattering around them: Chicago, Leavenworth, Terre Haute.

Down toward the end of the cabin someone's portable radio was muttering.

A fat youth in a checkered jacket had it. He moved over reluctantly and made room for me to sit down. The crisp, controlled BBC voice was saying, ". . . in Commons today, declared that Britain's trade balance is more favorable than at any time during the past fifteen years. In London, ceremonies marking the tenth anniversary of the death . . ." I let the words slide past me until I heard:

"In the United States, the mysterious epidemic affecting

41

stockyard workers in the central states has spread to New York and New Jersey on the eastern seaboard. The President has requested Congress to provide immediate emergency meat-rationing legislation."

A blurred little woman on the bench opposite leaned forward and said, "Serve 'em right, too! Them with their beefsteak a day."

There were murmurs of approval.

I got up and went back to my own seat. . . . It all fell into one pattern, everything: the man who kicked his wife, the prize-fighters, the policeman, the wardens, the slaughterhouse "epidemic."

It was the *lex talionis*—or the Golden Rule in reverse: Be done by as you do to others.

When you injured another living thing, both of you felt the same pain. When you killed, you felt the shock of your victim's death. You might be only stunned by it, like the slaughterhouse workers, or you might die, like the policeman and the schoolboy murderer.

So-called mental anguish counted too, apparently. That explained the wave of humanitarianism in prisons, at least partially; the rest was religious hysteria and the kind of herd instinct that makes any startling new movement mushroom.

And, of course, it also explained Chillicothe: the horrible blanketing depression that settled anywhere the civilian staff congregated—the feeling of being penned up in a place where something frightful was going to happen—and the thing the two psychiatrists had been arguing about, the pseudo-claustrophobia . . . all that was nothing but the reflection of Aza-Kra's feelings, locked in that cell on an alien planet.

Be done by as you do.

And I was carrying that with me. Des Moines, Kansas City, Decatur, St. Louis, Chicago, Leavenworth, Terre Haute—*New York*. After that, England. We'd been in London less than an hour—but England is only four hundred-odd miles long, from John o'Groat's to Lands End.

I remembered what Aza-Kra had said: *Now you must learn the other law, not to kill.*

Not to kill tripeds.

42

My body was shaking uncontrollably; my head felt like a balloon stuffed with cotton. I stood up and looked around at the blank faces, the inward-looking eyes, every man, woman and child living in a little world of his own. I had a hysterical impulse to shout at them, *Look at you, you idiots! You've been invaded and half conquered without a shot fired, and you don't know it!*

In the next instant I realized that I was about to burst into laughter. I put my hand over my mouth and half-ran out on deck, giggles leaking through my fingers; I got to the rail and bent myself over it, roaring, apoplectic. I was utterly ashamed of myself, but I couldn't stop it; it was like a fit of vomiting.

The cold spray on my face sobered me. I leaned over the rail, looking down at the white water boiling along the hull. It occurred to me that there was one practical test still to be made: a matter of confirmation.

A middle-aged man with rheumy eyes was standing in the cabin doorway, partly blocking it. As I shouldered past him, I deliberately put my foot down on his.

An absolutely blinding pain shot through the toes of my right foot. When my eyes cleared I saw that the two of us were standing in identical attitudes—weight on one foot, the other knee bent, hand reaching instinctively for the injury.

I had taken him for a "typical Englishman," but he cursed me in a rattling stream of gutter French. I apologized, awkwardly but sincerely—very sincerely.

When we docked at Dunkirk I still hadn't decided what to do.

What I had had in mind up till now was simply to get across France into Switzerland and hold a press conference there, inviting everybody from Tass to the UP. It had to be Switzerland for fairly obvious reasons; the English or the French would clamp a security lid on me before you could say NATO, but the Swiss wouldn't dare—they paid for their neutrality by having to look *both* ways before they cleared their throats.

I could still do that, and let the UN set up a committee to worry about Aza-Kra—but at a conservative estimate it would be ten months before the committee got its foot out of its mouth, and that would be pretty nearly ten months too late.

Or I could simply go to the American consulate in Dunkirk and turn myself in. Within ten hours we would be back in Chillicothe, probably, and I'd be free of the responsibility. I would also be dead.

We got through customs the same way we'd done in London.

And then I had to decide.

The cab driver put his engine in gear and looked at me over his shoulder. *"Un hôtel?"*

". . . Yes," I said. "A cheap hotel. *Un hôtel à bon marché.*"

"Entendu." He jammed down the accelerator an instant before he let out the clutch; we were doing thirty before he shifted into second.

The place he took me to was a villainous third-rate commercial-travelers' hotel, smelling of urine and dirty linen. When the porters were gone I unlocked the trunk and opened it.

We stared at each other.

Moisture was beaded on his blue-gray skin, and there was a smell in the room stronger and ranker than anything that belonged there. His eyes looked duller than they had before; I could barely see the pupils.

"Well?" I said.

"You are half right," he buzzed. "I am doing it, but not for the reason you think."

"All right; you're doing it. *Stop it.* That comes first. We'll stay here, and I'll watch the papers to make sure you do."

"At the customs, those people will sleep only an hour."

"I don't give a damn. If the gendarmes come up here, you can put them to sleep. If I have to I'll move you out to the country and we'll live under a haystack. But no matter what happens we're not going a mile farther into Europe until I know you've quit. If you don't like that, you've got two choices. Either you knock me out, and see how much good it does you, or I'll take that air-machine off your head."

He buzzed inarticulately for a moment. Then, "I have to say no. It is impossible. I could stop for a time, or pretend to you that I stop, but that would solve nothing. It will be—it will do the greatest harm if I stop; you don't understand. It is necessary to continue."

I said, "That's your answer?"

"Yes. If you will let me explain—"

I stepped toward him. I didn't hold my breath, but I think half-consciously I expected him to gas me. He didn't. He didn't move; he just waited.

Seen at close range, the flesh of his head seemed to be continuous with the black substance of the cone; instead of any sharp dividing line, there was a thin area that was neither one nor the other.

I put one hand over the fleshy bulb, and felt his eyes retract and close against my palm. The sensation was indescribably unpleasant, but I kept my hand there, put the other one against the far side of the cone—pulled and pushed simultaneously, as hard as I could.

The top of my head came off.

I was leaning against the top of the open trunk, dizzy and nauseated. The pain was like a white-hot wire drawn tight around my skull just above the eyes. I couldn't see; I couldn't think.

And it didn't stop; it went on and on. . . . I pushed myself away from the trunk and let my legs fold under me. I sat on the floor with my head in my hands, pushing my fingers against the pain.

Gradually it ebbed. I heard Aza-Kra's voice buzzing very quietly, not in English but in a rhythm of tone and phrasing that seemed almost directly comprehensible; if there were a language designed to be spoken by bass viols, it might sound like that.

I got up and looked at him. Shining beads of blue liquid stood out all along the base of the cone, but the seam had not broken.

I hadn't realized that it would be so difficult, that it would be so painful. I felt the weight of the two automatics in my pockets, and I pulled one out, the metal cold and heavy in my palm . . . but I knew suddenly that I couldn't do that either.

I didn't know where his brain was, or his heart. I didn't know whether I could kill him with one shot.

I sat down on the bed, staring at him. "You knew that

would happen, didn't you," I said. "You must think I'm a prize sucker."

He said nothing. His eyes were half-closed, and a thin whey-colored fluid was drooling out of the two mouths I could see. Aza-Kra was being sick.

I felt an answering surge of nausea. Then the flow stopped, and a second later, the nausea stopped too. I felt angry, and frustrated, and frightened.

After a moment I got up off the bed and started for the door.

"Please," said Aza-Kra. "Will you be gone long?"

"I don't know," I said. "Does it matter?"

"If you will be gone long," he said, "I would ask that you loosen the handcuffs for a short period before you go."

I stared at him, suddenly hating him with a violence that shook me.

"No," I said, and reached for the door-handle.

My body knotted itself together like a fist. My legs gave way under me, and I missed the door-handle going down; I hit the floor hard.

There was no sensation in my hands or feet. The muscles of my shoulders, arms, thighs, and calves were one huge, heavy pain. And I couldn't move.

I looked at Aza-Kra's wrists, shackled to his drawn-up ankles. He had been like that for something like fourteen hours.

"I am sorry," said Aza-Kra. "I did not want to do that to you, but there was no other way."

I thought dazedly, *No other way to do what?*

"To make you wait. To listen. To let me explain."

I said, "I don't get it." Anger flared again, then faded under something more intense and painful. The closest English word for it is "humility"; some other language may come nearer, but I doubt it; it isn't an emotion that we like to talk about. I felt bewildered, and ashamed, and very small, all at once, and there was another component, harder to name. A . . . threshold feeling.

I tried again. "I felt the other pain, before, but not this. Is that because—"

"Yes. There must be the intention to injure or cause

46

pain. I will tell you why. I have to go back very far. When an animal becomes more developed—many cells, instead of one—always the same things happen. I am the first man of my kind who ever saw a man of your kind. But we both have eyes. We both have ears." The feathery spines on his neck stiffened and relaxed. "Also there is another sense that always comes. But always it goes only a little way and then stops.

"When you are a young animal, fighting with the others to live, it is useful to have a sense which feels the thoughts of the enemy. Just as it is useful to have a sense which sees the shape of his body. But this sense cannot come all at once, it must grow by a little and a little, as when a surface that can tell the light from the dark becomes a true eye.

"But the easiest thoughts to feel are pain thoughts, they are much stronger than any others. And when the sense is still weak—it is a part of the brain, not an organ by itself —when it is weak, only the strongest stimulus can make it work. This stimulus is hatred, or anger, or the wish to kill.

"So that just when the sense is enough developed that it could begin to be useful, it always disappears. It is not gone, it is pushed under. A very long time ago, one race discovered this sense and learned how it could be brought back. It is done by a class of organic chemicals. You have not the word. For each race a different member of the class, but always it can be done. The chemical is a catalyst, it is not used up. The change it makes is in the cells of all the body—it is permanent, it passes also to the children.

"You understand, when a race is older, to kill is not useful. With the change, true civilization begins. The first race to find this knowledge gave it to others, and those to others, and now all have it. All who are able to leave their planets. We give it to you, now, because you are ready. When you are older there will be others who are ready. You will give it to them."

While I had been listening, the pain in my arms and legs had slowly been getting harder and harder to take. I reminded myself that Aza-Kra had borne it, probably, at least ten hours longer than I had; but that didn't make it much easier. I tried to keep my mind off it but that wasn't possible; the band of pain around my head was still there, too, a faint throbbing. And both were consequences of things I had done to Aza-Kra. I was suffering with him, measure for measure.

Justice. Surely that was a good thing? Automatic instant retribution, mathematically accurate: an eye for an eye.

I said, "That was what you were doing when they caught you, then—finding out which chemical we reacted to?"

"Yes. I did not finish until after they had brought me to Chillicothe. Then it was much more difficult. If not for my accident, all would have gone much more quickly."

"The walls?"

"Yes. As you have guessed, my air machine will also make other substances and expel them with great force. Also, when necessary, it will place these substances in a—state of matter, you have not the word—so that they pass through solid objects. But this takes much power. While in Chillicothe my range was very small. Later, when I can be in the open, it will be much greater."

He caught what I was thinking before I had time to speak. He said, "Yes. You will agree. When you understand."

It was the same thing he had told me at Chillicothe, almost to the word.

I said, "You keep talking about this thing as a gift but I notice you didn't ask us if we wanted it. What kind of a gift is that?"

"You are not serious. You know what happened when I was captured."

After a moment he added, "I think if it had been possible, if we could have asked each man and woman on the planet to say yes or no, explaining everything, showing that there was no trick, that most would have said yes. For people the change is good. But for governments it is not good."

I said, "I'd like to believe you. It would be very pleasant to believe you. But nothing you can say changes the fact that this thing, this gift of yours could be a weapon. To soften us up before you move in. If you were an advance agent for an invasion fleet, this is what you'd be doing."

"You are thinking with habits," he said. "Try to think with logic. Imagine that your race is very old, with much knowledge. You have ships that cross between the stars. Now you discover this young race, these Earthmen, who only begin to learn to leave their own planet. You decide to conquer them. Why? What is your reason?"

"How do I know? It could be anything. It might be something I couldn't even imagine. For all I know you want to eat us."

His throat-spines quivered. He said slowly, "You are partly serious. You really think . . . I am sorry that you did not read the studies of the physiologists. If you had, you would know. My digestion is only for vegetable food. You cannot understand, but—with us, to eat meat is like with you, to eat excretions."

I said, "All right, maybe we have something else you want. Natural resources that you've used up. Some substance, maybe some rare element."

"This is still habit thinking. Have you forgotten my air machine?"

"—Or maybe you just want the planet itself. With us cleared off it, to make room for you."

"Have you never looked at the sky at night?"

I said, "All *right*. But this quiz was your idea, not mine. I *admit* that I don't know enough even to make a sensible guess at your motives. And that's the reason why I can't trust you."

He was silent a moment. Then: "Remember that the substance which makes the change is a catalyst. Also it is a very fine powder. The particles are of only a few molecules each. The winds carry it. It is swallowed and breathed in and absorbed by the skin. It is breathed out and excreted. The wind takes it again. Water carries it. It is carried by insects and by birds and animals, and by men, in their bodies and in their clothing.

"This you can understand and know that it is true. If I die another could come and finish what I have begun, but even this is not necessary. The amount of the catalyst I have already released is more than enough. It will travel slowly, but nothing can stop it. If I die now, this instant, still in a year the catalyst will reach every part of the planet."

After a long time I said, "Then what did you mean by

49

saying that a great harm would be done, if you stopped now?"

"I meant this. Until now, only your Western nations have the catalyst. In a few days their time of crisis will come, beginning with the United States. And the nations of the East will attack."

IV

I found that I could move, inchmeal, if I sweated hard
enough at it. It took me what seemed like half an hour to
get my hand into my pocket, paw all the stuff out onto the
floor, and get the key-ring hooked over one finger. Then I
had to crawl about ten feet to Aza-Kra, and when I got
there my fingers simply wouldn't hold the keys firmly
enough.

I picked them up in my teeth and got two of the wrist-
cuffs unlocked. That was the best I could do; the other one
was behind him, inside the trunk, and neither of us had
strength enough to pull him out where I could get at it.

It was comical. My muscles weren't cramped, but my
nervous system was getting messages that said they were—
so, to all intents and purposes, it was true. I had no control
over it; the human body is about as skeptical as a God-
smitten man at a revival meeting. If mine had thought it
was burning, I would have developed simon-pure blisters.

Then the pins-and-needles started, as Aza-Kra began to
flex his arms and legs to get the stiffness out of them. Between us, after a while, we got him out of the trunk and
unlocked the third cuff. In a few minutes I had enough
freedom of movement to begin massaging his cramped
muscles; but it was three-quarters of an hour before either
of us could stand.

We caught the mid-afternoon plane to Paris, with Aza-
Kra in the trunk again. I checked into a hotel, left him
there, and went shopping: I bought a hideous black dress
with imitation-onyx trimming, a black coat with a cape, a
feather muff, a tall black hat and the heaviest mourning
veil I could find. At a theatrical costumer's near the Place
de l'Opera I got a reasonably lifelike old-woman mask and
a heavy wig.

51

When he was dressed up, the effect was startling. The tall hat covered the cone, the muff covered two of his hands. There was nothing to be done about the feet, but the skirt hung almost to the ground, and I thought he would pass with luck.

We got a cab and headed for the American consulate, but halfway there I remembered about the photographs. We stopped off at an amusement arcade and I got my picture taken in a coin-operated machine. Aza-Kra was another problem—that mask wouldn't fool anybody without the veil—but I spotted a poorly-dressed old woman and with some difficulty managed to make her understand that I was a crazy American who would pay her fifty francs to pose for her picture. We struck a bargain at a hundred.

As soon as we got into the consulate waiting-room, Aza-Kra gassed everybody in the building. I locked the street door and searched the offices until I found a man with a little pile of blank passport books on the desk in front of him. He had been filling one in on a machine like a typewriter except that it had a movable plane-surface platen instead of a cylinder.

I moved him out of the way and made out two passports; one for myself, as Arthur James LeRoux; one for Aza-Kra, as Mrs. Adrienne LeRoux. I pasted on the photographs and fed them into the machine that pressed the words *"Photograph attached U. S. Consulate Paris, France"* into the paper, and then into the one that impressed the consular seal.

I signed them, and filled in the blanks on the inside covers, in the taxi on the way to the Israeli consulate. The afternoon was running out, and we had a lot to do.

We went to six foreign consulates, gassed the occupants, and got a visa stamp in each one. I had the devil's own time filling them out; I had to copy the scribbles I found in legitimate passports at each place and hope for the best. The Israeli one was surprisingly simple, but the Japanese was a horror.

We had dinner in our hotel room—steak for me, water and soy-bean paste, bought at a health-food store, for Aza-Kra. Just before we left for Le Bourget, I sent a cable to Eli Freeman:

BIG STORY WILL HAVE TO WAIT SPREAD THIS NOW ALL
STOCKYARD SO-CALLED EPIDEMIC AND SIMILAR PHE-
NOMENA DUE ONE CAUSE STEP ON SOMEBODY'S TOE TO
SEE WHAT I MEAN.

Shortly after seven o'clock we were aboard a flight
bound for the Middle East.

And that was the fourth day, during which a number of
things happened that I didn't have time to add to my list
until later.

Commercial and amateur fishermen along the Atlantic
seaboard, from Delaware Bay as far north as Portland,
suffered violent attacks whose symptoms resembled those
of asthma. Some—who had been using rods or poles rather
than nets—complained also of sharp pains in the jaws and
hard palate. Three deaths were reported.

The "epidemic" now covered roughly half the continen-
tal United States. All livestock shipments from the West
had been canceled, stockyards in the affected area were
full to bursting. The President had declared a national
emergency.

Lobster had disappeared completely from east-coast
menus.

One Robert James Dahl, described as the owner and
publisher of a Middle Western newspaper, was being
sought by the Defense Department and the FBI in connection with the disappearance of certain classified documents.

The next day, the fifth, was Saturday. At two in the
morning on a Sabbath, Tel Aviv seemed as dead as Angkor. We had four hours there, between planes; we could
have spent them in the airport waiting room, but I was
wakeful and I wanted to talk to Aza-Kra. There was one
ancient taxi at the airport; I had the driver take us into the
town and leave us there, down in the harbor section, until
plane time.

We sat on a bench behind the sea wall and watched the
moonlight on the Mediterranean. Parallel banks of faintly-
silvered clouds arched over us to northward; the air was
fresh and cool.

After a while I said, "You know that I'm only playing
this your way for one reason. As far as the rest of it goes,
the more I think about it the less I like it."

"Why?"

"A dozen reasons. The biological angle, for one. I don't like violence, I don't like war, but it doesn't matter what I like. They're biologically necessary, they eliminate the unfit."

"Do you say that only the unfit are killed in wars?"

"That isn't what I mean. In modern war the contest isn't between individuals, it's between whole populations. Nations, and groups of nations. It's a cruel, senseless, wasteful business, and when you're in the middle of it it's hard to see any good at all in it, but it works—the survivors *survive*, and that's the only test there is."

"Our biologists do not take this view." He added, "Neither do yours."

I said, "How's that?"

"Your biologists agree with ours that war is not biological. It is social. When so many are killed, no stock improves. All suffer. It is as you yourself say, the contest is between nations. But their wars kill men."

I said, "All right, I concede that one. But we're not the only kind of animal on this planet, and we didn't get to be the dominant species without fighting. What are we supposed to do if we run into a hungry lion—argue with him?"

"In a few weeks there will be no more lions."

I stared at him. "This affects lions, too? Tigers, elephants, everything?"

"Everything of sufficient brain. Roughly, everything above the level of your insects."

"But I understood you to say that the catalyst—that it took a different catalyst for each species."

"No. All those with spines and warm blood have the same ancestors. Your snakes may perhaps need a different catalyst, and I believe you have some primitive sea creatures which kill, but they are not important."

I said, "My God." I thought of lions, wolves, coyotes, housecats, lying dead beside their prey. Eagles, hawks and owls tumbling out of the sky. Ferrets, stoats, weasels . . .

The world a big garden, for protected children.

My fists clenched. "But this is a million times worse than I had any idea. It's insane. You're upsetting the whole natural balance, you're knocking it crossways. Just for a start, what the hell are we going to do about rats and

54

mice? That's—" I choked on my tongue. There were too many images in my mind to put any of them into words. Rats like a tidal wave, filling a street from wall to wall. Deer swarming out of the forests. The sky blackening with crows, sparrows, jays.

"It will be difficult for some years," Aza-Kra said. "Perhaps even as difficult as you now think. But you say that to fight for survival is good. Is it not better to fight against other species than among yourselves?"

"Fight!" I said. "What have you left us to fight with? How many rats can a man kill before he drops dead from shock?"

"It is possible to kill without causing pain or shock. . . . You would have thought of this, although it is a new idea for you. Even your killing of animals for food can continue. We do not not ask you to become as old as we are in a day. Only to put behind you your cruelty which has no purpose."

He had answered me, as always; and as always, the answer was two-edged. It was possible to kill painlessly, yes. And the only weapon Aza-Kra had brought to Earth, apparently, was an anesthetic gas. . . .

We landed at Srinagar, in the Vale of Kashmir, at high noon: a sea of white light under a molten-metal sky.

Crossing the field, I saw a group of white-turbaned figures standing at the gate. I squinted at them through the glare; heat-waves made them jump and waver, but in a moment I was sure. They were bush-bearded Sikh policemen, and there were eight of them.

I pressed Aza-Kra's arm sharply and held my breath.

A moment later we picked our way through the sprawled line of passengers to the huddle of bodies at the gate. The passport examiner, a slender Hindu, lay a yard from the Sikhs. I plucked a sheet of paper out of his hand.

Sure enough, it was a list of the serial numbers of the passports we had stolen from the Paris consulate.

Bad luck. It was only six-thirty in Paris now, and on a Saturday morning at that; we should have had at least six hours more. But something could have gone wrong at any of the seven consulates—an after-hours appointment, or a worried wife, say. After that the whole thing would have unraveled.

"How much did you give them this time?" I asked.

"As before. Twenty hours."

"All right, good. Let's go."

He had overshot his range a little: all four of the hack-drivers waiting outside the airport building were snoring over their wheels. I dumped the skinniest one in the back seat with Aza-Kra and took over.

Not for the first time, it occurred to me that without me or somebody just like me Aza-Kra would be helpless. It wasn't just a matter of getting out of Chillicothe; he couldn't drive a car or fly a plane, he couldn't pass for human by himself; he couldn't speak without giving himself away. Free, with no broken bones, he could probably escape recapture indefinitely; but if he wanted to go anywhere he would have to walk.

And not for the first time, I tried to see into a history book that hadn't been written yet. My name was there, that much was certain, providing there was going to be any history to write. But was it a name like Blondel . . . or did it sound more like Vidkun Quisling?

We had to go south; there was nothing in any other direction but the highest mountains in the world. We didn't have Pakistan visas, so Lahore and Amritsar, the obvious first choices, were out. The best we could do was Chamba, about two hundred rail miles southeast on the Srinagar-New Delhi line. It wasn't on the principal air routes, but we could get a plane there to Saharanpur, which was.

There was an express leaving in half an hour, and we took it. I bought an English-language newspaper at the station and read it backward and forward for four hours; Aza-Kra spent the time apparently asleep, with his cone, hidden by the black hat, tilted out the window.

The "epidemic" had spread to five Western states, plus Quebec, Ontario and Manitoba, and parts of Mexico and Cuba . . . plus England and France, I knew, but there was nothing about that in my Indian paper; too early.

In Chamba I bought the most powerful battery-operated portable radio I could find; I wished I had thought of it sooner. I checked with the airport: there was a flight leaving Saharanpur for Port Blair at eight o'clock.

Port Blair, in the Andamans, is Indian territory; we wouldn't need to show our passports. What we were going to do after that was another question.

I could have raided another set of consulates, but I knew it would be asking for trouble. Once was bad enough; twice, and when we tried it a third time—as we would have to, unless I found some other answer—I was willing to bet we would find them laying for us, with gas masks and riot guns.

Somehow, in the few hours we were to spend at Port Blair, I had to get those serial numbers altered by an expert.

We had been walking the black, narrow dockside streets for two hours when Aza-Kra suddenly stopped.

"Something?"

"Wait," he said. ". . . Yes. This is the man you are looking for. He is a professional forger. His name is George Wheelwright. He can do it, but I do not know whether he will. He is a very timid and suspicious man."

"All right. In here?"

"Yes."

We went up a narrow unlighted stairway, choked with a kitchen-midden of smells, curry predominating. At the second-floor landing Aza-Kra pointed to a door. I knocked.

Scufflings behind the door. A low voice: "Who's that?"

"A friend. Let us in, Wheelwright."

The door cracked open and yellow light spilled out; I saw the outline of a head and the faint gleam of a bulbous eye. "What d'yer want?"

"Want you to do a job for me, Wheelwright. Don't keep us talking here in the hall."

The door opened wider and I squeezed through into a cramped, untidy box of a kitchen. A faded cloth covered the doorway to the next room.

Wheelwright glanced at Aza-Kra and then stared hard at me; he was a little chicken-breasted wisp of a man, dressed in dungarees and a striped polo shirt. "Who sent yer?"

"You wouldn't know the name. A friend of mine in Calcutta." I took out the passports. "Can you fix these?"

He looked at them carefully, taking his time. "What's wrong with 'em?"

"Nothing but the serial numbers."

"What's wrong with *them?*"

"They're on a list."

He laughed, a short, meaningless bark.

I said, "Well?"

"Who'd yer say yer friend in Calcutter was?"

"I haven't any friend in Calcutta. Never mind how I knew about you. Will you do the job or won't you?"

He handed the passports back and moved toward the door. "Mister, I haven't got the time to fool with yer. Perhaps yer having me on, or perhaps yer've made an honest mistake. There's another Wheelwright over on the north side of town. You try him." He opened the door. "Good night, both."

I pushed it shut again and reached for him, but he was a yard away in one jump, like a rabbit. He stood beside the table, arms hanging, and stared at me with a vague smile.

I said, "I haven't got time to play games, either. I'll pay you five hundred American dollars to alter these passports—" I tossed them onto the table—"or else I'll beat the living tar out of you." I took a step toward him.

I never saw a man move faster: he had the drawer open and the gun out and aimed before I finished that step. But the muzzle trembled slightly. "No nearer," he said hoarsely.

I thought, *Five minutes,* and held my breath.

When he slumped, I picked up the revolver. Then I lifted him—he weighed about ninety pounds—propped him in a chair behind the table, and waited.

In a few minutes he raised his head and goggled at me dazedly. "How'd yer do that?" he whispered.

I put the money on the table beside the passports. "Start," I said.

He stared at it, then at me. His thin lips tightened. "Go ter blazes," he said.

I stepped around the table and cuffed him backhand.
I felt the blow on my own face, hard and stinging, but I
did it again. I kept it up. It wasn't pleasant; I was feeling
not only the blows themselves, but Wheelwright's emotional reponses, the shame and wretchedness and anger,
and the queasy writhing fear: Wheelwright couldn't bear
pain.

At that, he beat me. When I stopped, sickened and
dizzy, and said as roughly as I could, "Had enough,
Wheelwright?" he answered, "Not if yer was ter kill me,
yer bloody barstid."

His voice trembled, and his face was streaked with
tears, but he meant it. He thought I was a government
agent, trying to bully him into signing his own prison sentence, and rather than let me do it he would take any
amount of punishment; prison was the one thing he feared
more than physical pain.

I looked at Aza-Kra. His neck-spines were erect and
quivering; I could see the tips of them at the edges of the
veil. Then inspiration hit me.

I pulled him forward where the little man could see
him, and lifted the veil. The feathery spines stood out
clearly on either side of the corpse-white mask.

"I won't touch you again," I said. "But look at this.
Can you see?"

His eyes widened; he scrubbed them with the palms of
his hands and looked again.

"And this," I said. I pulled at Aza-Kra's forearm and
the clawed blue-gray hand came out of the muff.

Wheelwright's eyes bulged. He flattened himself
against the back of the chair.

"Now," I said, "six hundred dollars—or I'll take this
mask off and show you what's behind it."

He clenched his eyes shut. His face had gone yellowish-
pale; his nostrils were white.

"Get it out of here," he said faintly.

He didn't move until Aza-Kra had disappeared behind
the curtain into the other room. Then, without a word, he
poured and drank half a tumblerful of whisky, switched
on a gooseneck lamp, produced bottles, pens and brushes
from the table drawer, and went to work. He bleached
away the first and last digits of both serial numbers, then

painted over the areas with a thin wash of color that matched the blue tint of the paper. With a jeweler's loupe in his eye, he restored the obliterated tiny letters of the background design; finally, still using the loupe, he drew the new digits in black. From first to last, it took him thirty minutes; and his hands didn't begin to tremble until he was done.

V

The sixth day was two days—because we left Otaru at 3:30 p.m. Sunday and arrived at Honolulu at 4:00 a.m. Saturday. We had lost five hours in traversing sixty-one degrees of longitude—but we'd also gained a day by crossing the International Date Line from west to east.

On the sixth day, then, which was two days, the following things happened and were duly reported:

Be Done By As Ye Do was the title of some thousands of sermons and, by count, more than seven hundred front-page newspaper editorials from Newfoundland to Oaxaca. My cable to Freeman had come a little late; the *Herald-Star's* announcement was lost in the ruck.

Following this, a wave of millennial enthusiasm swept the continent; Christians and Jews everywhere feasted, fasted, prayed and in other ways celebrated the imminent Second (or First) Coming of Christ. Evangelistic and fundamentalist sects garnered souls by the million.

Members of the Apostolic Overcoming Holy Church of God, the Pentecostal Fire Baptized Holiness Church and numerous other groups gave away most or all of their worldly possessions. Others were more practical. The Seventh Day Adventists, who are vegetarians, pooled capital and began an enormous expansion of their meatless-food factories, dairies and other enterprises.

Delegates to a World Synod of Christian Churches began arriving at a tent city near Smith Center, Kansas, late Saturday night. Trouble developed almost immediately between the Brethren Church of God (Reformed Dunkers) and the Two-Seed-in-the-Spirit Predestinarian Baptists—later spreading to a schism which led to the establishment of two rump synods, one at Lebanon and the other at Athol.

61

Five hundred Doukhobors stripped themselves mother-naked, burned their homes, and marched on Vancouver.

Roman Catholics in most places celebrated the Feast of the Transfiguration as usual, awaiting advice from Rome.

Riots broke out in Chicago, Detroit, New Orleans, Philadelphia and New York. In each case the original disturbances were brief, but were followed by protracted vandalism and looting which local police, state police, and even National Guard units were unable to check. By midnight Sunday property damage was estimated at more than twenty million dollars. The casualty list was fantastically high. So was the proportion of police-and-National-Guard casualties—exactly fifty per cent of the total. . . .

In the British Isles, Western Europe and Scandinavia, the early symptoms of the Western hemisphere's disaster were beginning to appear: the stricken slaughterers and fishermen, the unease in prisons, the freaks of violence.

An unprecedented number of political refugees turned up on the West-German side of the Burnt Corridor early Saturday morning.

Late the same day, a clash between Sikh and Moslem guards on the India-Pakistan border near Sialkot resulted in the annihilation of both parties.

And on Sunday it hit the fighting in Indo-China.

Allied and Communist units, engaging at sixty points along the eight-hundred-mile front, fell back with the heaviest casualties of the war.

Red bombers launched a successful daylight attack on Luangprabang: successful, that is, except that nineteen out of twenty planes crashed outside the city or fell into the Nam Ou.

Forty Allied bombers took off on sorties to Yen-bay, Hanoi and Nam-dinh. None returned.

Nobody knew it yet, but the war was over.

Still other things happened but were not recorded by the press:

A man in Arizona, a horse gelder by profession, gave up his business and moved out of the county, alleging ill health.

So did a dentist in Tacoma, and another in Galveston.

In Breslau an official of the People's Police resigned

his position with the same excuse; and one in Buda; and one in Pest.

A conservative Tajik tribesman of Indarab, discovering that his new wife had been unfaithful, attempted to deal with her in the traditional manner, but desisted when a critical observer would have said he had hardly begun; nor did this act of compassion bring him any relief.

And outside the town of Otaru, just two hundred and fifty miles across the Sea of Japan from the eastern shore of the Russian Socialist Federated Soviet Republic, Aza-Kra used his anesthetic gas again—on me.

I had been bone-tired when we left Port Blair shortly before midnight, but I hadn't slept all the long dark droning way to Manila; or from there to Tokyo, with the sun rising half an hour after we cleared the Philippines and slowly turning the globe underneath us to a white disk of fire; or from Tokyo north again to Otaru, bleak and windy and smelling of brine.

In all that time, I hadn't been able to forget Wheelwright except for half an hour toward the end, when I picked up an English-language broadcast from Tokyo and heard the news from the States.

The first time you burn yourself playing with matches, the chances are that if the blisters aren't too bad, you get over it fast enough; you forget about it. But the second time, it's likely to sink in.

Wheelwright was my second time; Wheelwright finished me.

It's more than painful, it's more than frightening, to cause another living creature pain and feel what he feels. It tears you apart. It makes you the victor and the victim, and neither half of that is bearable.

It makes you love what you destroy—as you love yourself—and it makes you hate yourself as your victim hates you.

That isn't all. I had felt Wheelwright's self-loathing as his body cringed and the tears spilled out of his eyes, the helpless gut-twisting shame that was as bad as the fear; and that burden was on me too.

Wheelwright was talented. That was his own achievement; he had found it in himself and developed it and

63

trained himself to use it. Wheelwright had courage. That was his own. But who had made Wheelwright afraid? And who had taught him that the world was his enemy?

You, and I, and every other human being on the planet, and all our two-legged ancestors before us. Because we had settled for too little. Because not more than a handful of us, out of all the crawling billions, had ever had the will to break the chain of blows, from father to daughter to son, generation after generation.

So there was Wheelwright; that was what we had made out of man: the artistry and the courage compressed to a needle-thin, needle-hard core inside him, and that only because we hadn't been able to destroy it altogether; the rest of him self-hatred, and suspicion, and resentment, and fear.

But after breakfast in Tokyo, it began to seem a little more likely that some kind of a case could be made for the continued existence of the human race. And after that it was natural to think about lions, and about the rioting that was going on in America.

For all his moral nicety, Aza-Kra had no trouble in justifying the painful extinction of carnivores. From his point of view, they were better off dead. It was regrettable, of course, but . . .

But, *sub specie aeternitatis,* was a man much different from a lion?

It was a commonplace that no other animal killed on so grand a scale as man. The problem had never come up before: could we live without killing?

I was standing with Aza-Kra at the top of a little hill that overlooked the coast road and the bay. The bus that had brought us there was dwindling, a white speck in a cloud of dust, down the highway toward Cape Kamui.

Aza-Kra sat on a stone, his third leg grotesquely bulging the skirt of his coat. His head bent forward, as if the old woman he was pretending to be had fallen asleep, chin on massive chest; the conical hat pointed out to sea.

I said, "This is the time of crisis you were talking about, for America."

"Yes. It begins now."

"When does it end? Let's talk about this a little more.

64

This justice. Crimes of violence—all right. They punish themselves, and before long they'll prevent themselves automatically. What about crimes of property? A man steals my wallet and runs. Or he smashes a window and takes what he wants. Who's going to stop him?"

He didn't answer for a moment; when he did the words came slowly and the pronunciation was bad, as if he were too weary to attend to it. "The wallet can be chained to your clothing. The window can be made of glass that does not break."

I said impatiently. "You know that's not what I mean. I'm talking about the problem as it affects everybody. We solve it by policemen and courts and prisons. What do we do instead?"

"I am sorry that I did not understand you. Give me a moment. . . ."

I waited.

"In your Middle Ages, when a man was insane, what did you do?"

I thought of Bedlam, and of creatures with matted hair chained to rooftops.

He didn't wait for me to speak. "Yes. And now, you are more wise?"

"A little."

"Yes. And in the beginning of your Industrial Revolution, when a factory stopped and men had no work, what was done?"

"They starved."

"And now?"

"There are relief organizations. We try to keep them alive until they can get work."

"If a man steals what he does not need," Aza-Kra said, "is he not sick? If a man steals what he must have to live, can you blame him?"

Socrates, in an onyx-trimmed dress, three-legged on a stone.

Finally I said, "It's easy enough to make us look foolish, but we have made some progress in the last two thousand years. Now you want us to go the rest of the way overnight. It's impossible; we haven't got time enough."

"You will have more time now." His voice was very

faint. "Killing wastes much time. . . . Forgive me, now I must sleep."

His head dropped even farther forward. I watched for a while to see if he would topple over, but of course he was too solidly based. A tripod. I sat down beside him, feeling my own fatigue drag at my body, envying him his rest; but I couldn't sleep.

There was really no point in arguing with him, I told myself; he was too good for me. I was a savage splitting logic with a missionary. He knew more than I did; probably he was more intelligent. And the central question, the only one that mattered, couldn't be answered the way I was going at it.

Aza-Kra himself was the key, not the doctrine of non-violence, not the psychology of crime.

If he was telling the truth about himself and the civilization he came from, I had nothing to worry about.

If he wasn't, then I should have left him in Chillicothe or killed him in Paris; and if I could kill him now, that was what I should do.

And I didn't know. After all this time, I still didn't know.

I saw the bus come back down the road and disappear towards Otaru. After a long time, I saw it heading out again. When it came back from the cape the second time, I woke Aza-Kra and we slogged down the steep path to the roadside. I waved as the bus came nearer; it slowed and rattled to a halt a few yards beyond us.

Passengers' heads popped out of the windows to watch us as we walked toward the door. Most of them were Japanese, but I saw one Caucasian, leaning with both arms out of the window. I saw his features clearly, narrow pale nose and lips, blue eyes behind rimless glasses; sunlight glinting on sparse yellow hair. And then I saw the flat dusty road coming up to meet me.

I was lying face-up on a hard sandy slope; when I opened my eyes I saw the sky and a few blades of tough, dry grass. The first thought that came into my head was, *Now I know. Now I've had it.*

I sat up. And a buzzing voice said, "Hold your breath!" Turning, I saw a body sprawled on the slope just below me. It was the yellow-haired man. Beyond him squatted the gray form of Aza-Kra.

"All right," he said.

I let my breath out. "What—?"

He showed me a brown metal ovoid, cross-hatched with fragmentation grooves. A grenade.

"He was about to arm it. There was no time to warn you. I knew you would wish to see for yourself."

I looked around dazedly. Thirty feet above, the slope ended in a clean-cut line against the sky; beyond it was a short, narrow white stripe that I recognized as the top of the bus, still parked at the side of the road.

"We have ten minutes more before the others awaken."

I went through the man's pockets. I found a handful of change, a wallet with nothing in it but a few yen notes, and a folded slip of glossy white paper. That was all.

I unfolded the paper, but I knew what it was even before I saw the small teleprinted photograph on its inner side. It was a copy of my passport picture—the one on the genuine document, not the bogus one I had made in Paris.

On the way back, my hands began shaking. It got so bad that I had to put them between my thighs and squeeze hard; and then the shaking spread to my legs and arms and jaw. My forehead was cold and there was a football-sized ache in my belly, expanding to a white pain every time we hit a bump. The whole bus seemed to be tilting ponderously over to the right, farther and farther but never falling down.

Later, when I had had a cup of coffee and two cigarettes in the terminal lunchroom, I got one of the most powerful irrational impulses I've ever known: I wanted to take the next bus back to that spot on the coast road, walk down the slope to where the yellow-haired man was, and kick his skull to flinders.

If we were lucky, the yellow-haired man might have been the only one in Otaru who knew we were here. The only way to find out was to go on to the airport and take a chance; either way, we had to get out of Japan. But it didn't end there. Even if they didn't know where we were now, they knew all the stops on our itinerary; they knew

which visas we had. Maybe Aza-Kra would be able to
gas the next one before he killed us, and then again
maybe not.

I thought about Frisbee and Parst and the President—
damning them all impartially—and my anger grew. By
now, I realized suddenly, they must have understood that
we were responsible for what was happening. They would
have been energetically apportioning the blame for the
last few days; probably Parst had already been court-
martialed.

Once that was settled, there would be two things they
could do next. They could publish the truth, admit their
own responsibility, and warn the world. Or they could destroy all the evidence and keep silent. If the world went to
hell in a bucket, at least they wouldn't be blamed for
it. . . . Providing I was dead. Not much choice.

After another minute I got up and Aza-Kra followed
me out to a taxi. We stopped at the nearest telegraph office and I sent a wire to Frisbee in Washington:

HAVE SENT FULL ACCOUNT CHILLICOTHE TO TRUST-
WORTHY PERSON WITH INSTRUCTIONS PUBLISH EVENT
MY DEATH OR DISAPPEARANCE. CALL OFF YOUR DOGS.

It was childish, but apparently it worked. Not only did
we have no trouble at Otaru airport—the yellow-haired
man, as I'd hoped, must have been working alone—but
nobody bothered us at Honolulu or Asuncion.

Just the same, the mood of depression and nervousness
that settled on me that day didn't lift; it grew steadily
worse. Fourteen hours' sleep in Asuncion didn't mend it;
Monday's reports of panics and bank failures in North
America intensified it, but that was incidental.

And when I slept, I had nightmares: dreams of
stifling-dark jungles, full of things with teeth.

We spent twenty-four hours in Asuncion, while Aza-Kra
pumped out enough catalyst to blanket South America's
seven million square miles—a territory almost as big as
the sprawling monster of Soviet Eurasia.

After that we flew to Capetown—and that was it. We
were finished.

We had spiraled around the globe, from the United

States to England, to France, to Israel, to India, to Japan, to Paraguay, to the Union of South Africa, trailing an expanding invisible cloud behind us. Now the winds were carrying it westward from the Atlantic, south from the Mediterranean, north from the Indian Ocean, west from the Pacific.

Frigate birds and locusts, men in tramp steamers and men in jet planes would carry it farther. In a week it would have reached all the places we had missed: Australia, Micronesia, the islands of the South Pacific, the Poles.

That left the lunar bases and the orbital stations. Ours and Theirs. But they had to be supplied from Earth; the infection would come to them in rockets.

For better or worse, we had what we had always said we wanted. Ahimsa. The Age of Reason. The Kingdom of God.

And I still didn't know whether I was Judas, or the little Dutch boy with his finger in the dike.

I didn't find out until three weeks later.

We stayed on in Capetown, resting and waiting. Listening to the radio and reading newspapers kept me occupied a good part of the time. When restlessness drove me out of doors, I wandered aimlessly in the business section, or went down to the harbor and spent hours staring out past the castle and the breakwater.

But my chief occupation, the thing that obsessed me now, was the study of Aza-Kra.

He seemed very tired. His skin was turning dry and rough, more gray than blue; his eyes were blue-threaded and more opaque-looking than ever. He slept a great deal and moved little. The soy-bean paste I was able to get for him gave him insufficient nourishment; vitamins and minerals were lacking.

I asked him why he didn't make what he needed in his air machine. He said that some few of the compounds could be inhaled, and he was making those; that he had had another transmuter, for food-manufacture, but that it had been taken from him; and that he would be all right; he would last until his friends came.

He didn't know when that would be; or he wouldn't tell me.

His speech was slower and his diction more slurred each day. It was obviously difficult for him to talk; but I goaded him, I nagged him, I would not let him alone. I spent days on one topic, left it, came back to it and asked the same questions over. I made copious notes of what he said and the way he said it.

I wanted to learn to read the signs of his emotions; or failing that, to catch him in a lie.

A dozen times I thought I had trapped him into a contradiction, and each time, wearily, patiently, he explained what I had misunderstood. As for his emotions, they had only one visible sign that I was able to discover: the stiffening and trembling of his neck-spines.

Gestures of emotion are arbitrary. There are human tribes whose members never smile. There are others who smile when they are angry. Cf. Dodgson's Cheshire Cat.

He was doing it more and more often as the time went by; but what did it mean? Anger? Resentment? Annoyance? *Amusement?*

The riots in the United States ended on the 9th and 10th when interfaith committees toured each city in loudspeaker trucks. Others began elsewhere.

Business was at a standstill in most larger cities. Galveston, Nashville and Birmingham joined in celebrating Hallelujah Week: dancing in the streets, bonfires day and night, every church and every bar roaring wide open.

Russia's delegate to the United Nations, who had been larding his speeches with mock-sympathetic references to the Western nations' difficulties, arose on the 9th and delivered a furious three-hour tirade accusing the entire non-Communist world of cowardly cryptofascistic biological warfare against the Soviet Union and the People's Republics of Europe and Asia.

The new staffs of the Federal penitentiaries in America, in office less than a week, followed their predecessors in mass resignations. The last official act of the wardens of Leavenworth, Terre Haute and Alcatraz was to report the "escape" of their entire prison populations.

Police officers in every major city were being frantically urged to remain on duty.

Queen Elizabeth, in a memorable speech, exhorted all citizens of the Empire to remain calm and meet whatever might come with dignity, fortitude and honor.

The Scots stole the Stone of Scone again.

Rioting and looting began in Paris, Marseilles, Barcelona, Milan, Amsterdam, Munich, Berlin.

The Pope was silent.

Turkey declared war on Syria and Iraq; peace was concluded a record three hours later.

On the 10th, Warsaw Radio announced the formation of a new Polish Provisional Government whose first and second acts had been, respectively, to abrogate all existing treaties with the Soviet Union and border states, and to petition the UN for restoration of the 1938 boundaries.

On the 11th East Germany, Austria, Czechoslovakia, Hungary, Rumania, Bulgaria, Latvia and Lithuania followed suit, with variations on the boundary question.

On the 12th, after a brief but by no means bloodless putsch, the Spanish Republic was re-established; the British government fell once and the French government twice; and the Vatican issued a sharp protest against the ill-treatment of priests and nuns by Spanish insurgents.

Not a shot had been fired in Indo-China since the morning of the 8th.

On the 13th the Karelo-Finnish S. S. R., the Estonian S. S. R., the Byelorussian S. S. R., the Ukrainian S. S. R., the Azerbaijan S. S. R., the Turkmen S. S. R. and the Uzbek S. S. R. declared their independence of the Soviet Union. A horde of men and women escaped or released from forced-labor camps, the so-called Slave Army, poured westward out of Siberia.

VI

On the 14th, Zebulon, Georgia (pop. 312), Murfrees-
boro, Tennessee (pop. 11,190) and Orange, Texas (pop.
8,470) seceded from the Union.

That might have been funny, but on the 15th peti-
tions for a secession referendum were circulating in Tennessee, Arkansas, Louisiana and South Carolina. Early
returns averaged 61% in favor.

On the 16th Texas, Oklahoma, Mississippi, Alabama,
Kentucky, Virginia, Georgia and—incongruously—Rhode
Island and Minnesota added themselves to the list. Sep-
aratist fever was rising in Quebec, New Brunswick, Newfoundland and Labrador. Across the Atlantic, Catalonia,
Bavaria, Moldavia, Sicily and Cyprus declared themselves
independent states.

And that might have been hysteria. But that wasn't all.

Liquor stores and bars were sprouting like mushrooms
in dry states. Ditto gambling halls, horse rooms, houses of
prostitution, cockpits, burlesque theaters.

Moonshine whisky threatened for a few days to become
the South's major industry, until standard-brand distillers
cut their prices to meet the competition. Not a bottle of
the new stocks of liquor carried a Federal tax stamp.

Mexican citizens were walking across the border into
Arizona and New Mexico, swimming into Texas. The first
shipload of Chinese arrived in San Francisco on the 16th.

Meat prices had increased by an average of 60% for
every day since the new control and rationing law took
effect. By the 16th, round steak was selling for $10.80 a
pound.

Resignations of public officials were no longer news; a
headline in the Portland *Oregonian* for August 15th read:

WILL STAY AT DESK, SAYS GOVERNOR.

It hit me hard.

But when I thought about it, it was obvious enough; it was such an elementary thing that ordinarily you never noticed it—that all governments, not just tyrannies, but *all* governments were based on violence, as currency was based on metal. You might go for months or years without seeing a silver dollar or a policeman; but the dollar and the policeman had to be there.

The whole elaborate structure, the work of a thousand years, was coming down. The value of a dollar is established by a promise to pay; the effectiveness of a law, by a threat to punish.

Even if there were enough jailers left, how could you put a man in jail if he had ten or twenty friends who didn't want him to go?

How many people were going to pay their income taxes next year, even if there was a government left to pay them to?

And who was going to stop the landless people from spilling over into the nations that had land to spare?

Aza-Kra said, "These things are not necessary to do."

I turned around and looked at him. He had been lying motionless for more than an hour in the hammock I had rigged for him at the end of the room; I had thought he was asleep.

It was raining outside. Dim, colorless light came through the slotted window blinds and striped his body like a melted barber pole. Caught in one of the bars of light, the tips of two quivering neck-spines glowed in faint filigree against the shadow.

"All right," I said. "Explain this one away. I'd like to hear you. Tell me why we don't need governments any more."

"The governments you have now—the governments of nations—they are not made for use. They exist to fight other nations."

"That's not true."

"It is true. Think. Of the money your government

73

spends, in a year, how much is for war and how much for use?"

"About sixty per cent for war. But that doesn't—".

"Please. This is sixty per cent now, when you have only a small war. When you have a large war, how much then?"

"Ninety per cent. Maybe more, but that hasn't got anything to do with it. In peace *or* wartime there are things a national government does that can't be done by anybody else. Now ask me for instance, what."

"Yes. I ask this."

"For instance, keeping an industrial country from being dragged down to coolie level by unrestricted immigration."

"You think it is better for those who have much to keep apart from those who have little, and give no help?"

"In principle, no, but it isn't just that easy. What good does it do the starving Asiatics if we turn America into another piece of Asia and starve along with them?"

He looked at me unwinkingly.

"What good has it done to keep apart?"

I opened my mouth, and shut it again. Last time it had been Japan, an island chain a little smaller than California. In the next one, half the world would have been against us.

"The problem is not easy, it is very difficult. But to solve it by helping is possible. To solve it by doing nothing is not possible."

"Harbors," I said. "Shipping. Soil conservation. Communications. Flood control."

"You do not believe these things can be done if there are no nations?"

"No. We haven't got time enough to pick up all the pieces. It's a hell of a lot easier to knock things apart than to put them together again."

"Your people have done things more difficult than this. You do not believe now, but you will see it done."

After a moment I said, "We're supposed to become a member of your galactic union now. Now that you've pulled our teeth. Who's going to build the ships?"

"Those who build them now."

I said, "Governments build them now."

74

"No. Men build ships. Men invent ships and design ships. Government builds nothing but more government."

I put my fists in my pockets and walked over to the window. Outside, a man went hurrying by in the rain, one hand at his hat-brim, the other at his chest. He didn't look around as he passed; his coffee-brown face was intent and impersonal. I watched him until he turned the corner, out of sight.

He had never heard of me, but his life would be changed by what I had done. His descendants would know my name; they would be bored by it in school, or their mothers would frighten them with it after dark. . . .

Aza-Kra said, "To talk of these things is useless. If I would lie, I would not tell you that I lie. And if I would lie about these things, I would lie well; you would not find the truth by questions. You must wait. Soon you will know."

I looked at him. "When your friends come."

"Yes," he said.

And the feathery tips of his neck-spines delicately trembled.

They came on the last day of August—fifty great rotiform ships drifting down out of space. No radar spotted them; no planes or interceptor rockets went up to meet them. They followed the terminator around, landing at dawn: thirteen in the Americas, twenty-five in Europe and Asia, five in Africa, one each in England, Scandinavia, Australia, New Zealand, New Guinea, the Philippines, Japan.

Each one was six hundred feet across, but they rested lightly on the ground. Where they landed on sloping ground, slender curved supporting members came out of the doughnut-shaped rim, as dainty as insect's legs, and the fat lozenge of the hub lowered itself on the five fat spokes until it touched the earth.

Their doors opened.

In twenty-four days I had watched the nations of the Earth melt into shapelessness like sculptures molded of silicone putty. Armies, navies, air forces, police forces lost their cohesion first. In the beginning there were individual desertions, atoms escaping one at a time from the mass;

later, when the pay failed to arrive, when there were no orders or else orders that could not be executed, men and women simply went home, orderly, without haste, in thousands.

Every useful item of equipment that could be carried or driven or flown went with them. Tractors, trucks, jeeps, bulldozers gladdened the hearts of farmers from Keokuk to Kweiyang. Bombers, small boats, even destroyers and battleships were in service as commercial transports. Quartermasters' stores were carried away piecemeal or in ton lots. Guns and ammunition rusted undisturbed.

Stock markets crashed. Banks failed. Treasuries failed. National governments broke down into states, provinces, cantons. In the United States, the President resigned his office on the 18th and left the White House, whose every window had been broken and whose lawn was newly landscaped with eggshells and orange rind. The Vice-President resigned the next day, leaving the Presidency, in theory, to the Speaker of the House; but the Speaker was at home on his Arkansas farm; Congress had adjourned on the 17th.

Everywhere it was the same. The new governments of Asia and Eastern Europe, of Spain and Portugal and Argentina and Iran, died stillborn.

The Moon colonies had been evacuated; work had stopped on the Mars rocket. The men on duty in the orbital stations, after an anxious week, had reached an agreement for mutual disarmament and had come down to Earth.

Seven industries out of ten had closed down. The dollar was worth half a penny, the pound sterling a little more; the ruble, the Reichsmark, the franc, the sen, the yen, the rupee were waste paper.

The great cities were nine-tenths deserted, gutted by fires, the homes of looters, rats and roaches.

Even the local governments, the states, the cantons, the counties, the very townships, were too fragile to stand. All the arbitrary lines on the map had lost their meaning.

You could not say any more, "Japan will—" or "India is moving toward—" It was startling to realize that; to have to think of a sprawling, amorphous, unfathomable mass of infinitely varied human beings instead of a single inclusive symbol. It made you wonder if the symbol had ever had any connection with reality at all: whether there had ever been such a thing as a nation.

Toward the end of the month, I thought I saw a flicker of hope. The problem of famine was being attacked vigorously and efficiently by the Red Cross, the Salvation Army, and thousands of local volunteer groups: they commandeered fleets of trucks, emptied warehouses with a calm disregard of legality, and distributed the food where it was most needed. It was not enough—too much food had been destroyed and wasted by looters, too much had spoiled through neglect, and too much had been destroyed in the field by wandering, half-starved bands of the homeless—but it was a beginning; it was something.

Other groups were fighting the problem of these wolf-packs, with equally encouraging results. Farmers were forming themselves into mutual-defense groups, "communities of force." Two men could take any property from one man of equal strength without violence, without the penalty of pain; but not from two men, or three men.

One district warned the next when a wolf-pack was on the way, and how many to expect. When the pack converged on a field or a storehouse, men in equal or greater numbers were there to stand in the way. If the district could absorb, say, ten workers, that many of the pack were offered the option of staying; the rest had to move on. Gradually, the packs thinned.

In the same way, factories were able to protect themselves from theft. By an extension of the idea, even the money problem began to seem soluble. The old currency was all but worthless, and an individual's promise to pay in kind was no better as a medium of exchange; but promissory notes obligating whole communities could and did begin to circulate. They made an unwieldy currency, their range was limited, and they depreciated rapidly. But it was something; it was a beginning.

Then the wheel-ships came.

In every case but one, they were cautious. They landed in conspicuous positions, near a city or a village, and in the dawn light, before any man had come near them, oddly-shaped things came out and hurriedly unloaded boxes and bales, hundreds, thousands, a staggering array. They set up sun-reflecting beacons; then the ships rose again and disappeared, and when the first men came hesitantly out to investigate, they found nothing but the beacon, the acre of carefully-stacked boxes, and the signs, in the language of the country, that said:

THIS FOOD IS SENT BY THE PEOPLES OF OTHER WORLDS TO HELP YOU IN YOUR NEED. ALL MEN ARE BROTHERS.

And a brave man would lift the top of a box; inside he would see other boxes, and in them oblong pale shapes wrapped in something transparent that was not cellophane. He would unwrap one, feel it, smell it, show it around, and finally taste it; and then his eyebrows would go up.

The color and the texture were unfamiliar, but the taste was unmistakable! Tortillas and beans! (Or taro; or rice with beansprouts; or stuffed grape leaves; or herb omelette!)

The exception was the ship that landed outside Capetown, in an open field at the foot of Table Mountain.

Aza-Kra woke me at dawn. "They are here."

I mumbled at him and tried to turn over. He shook my shoulder again, buzzing excitedly to himself. "Please, they are here. We must hurry."

I lurched out of bed and stood swaying. "Your friends?" I said.

"Yes, yes." He was struggling into the black dress, pushing the peaked hat backward onto his head. *"Hurry."*

I splashed cold water on my face, and got into my clothes. I pulled out the top dresser drawer and looked at the two loaded automatics. I couldn't decide. I couldn't figure out any way they would do me any good, but I didn't want to leave them behind. I stood there until my legs went numb before I could make up my mind to take them anyhow, and the hell with it.

There were no taxis, of course. We walked three blocks along the deserted streets until we saw a battered sedan nose into view in the intersection ahead, moving cautiously around the heaps of litter.

"Hold your breath!"

The car moved on out of sight. We found it around the corner, up on the sidewalk with the front fender jammed against a railing. There were two men and a woman in it, Europeans.

"Which way?"

"Left. To the mountain."

When we got to the outskirts and the buildings began to thin out, I saw it up ahead, a huge silvery-metal shelf jutting out impossibly from the slope. I began to tremble. *They'll cut me up and put me in a jar,* I thought. *Now is the time to stop, if I'm going to.*

But I kept going. Where the road veered away from the field and went curving on up the mountain the other way, I stopped and we got out. I saw dark shapes and movements under that huge gleaming bulk. We stepped over a broken fence and started across the dry, uneven clods in the half-light.

Light sprang out: a soft, pearl-gray shimmer that didn't dazzle the eye although it was aimed straight toward us, marking the way. I heard a shrill wordless buzzing, and above that an explosion of chirping, and under them both a confusion of other sounds, humming, droning, clattering. I saw a half-dozen nightmare shapes bounding forward.

Two of them were like Aza-Kra; two more were squat things with huge humped shells on top, like tortoise-shells the size of a card table, with six long stump-ended legs underneath, and a tangle of eyes, tentacles, and small wriggly things peeping out in front; one, the tallest, had a long sharp-spined column of a body rising from a thick base and four startlingly human legs, and surmounted by four long whiplike tentacles and a smooth oval head; the sixth looked at first glance like an unholy cross between a grasshopper and a newt.

They crowded around Aza-Kra, humming, chirping, droning, buzzing, clattering. Their hands and tentacles went over him, caressingly; the newt-grasshopper thing hoisted him onto its back.

They paid no attention to me, and I stayed where I was, with my hands tight and sweating on the grips of my guns. Then I heard Aza-Kra speak, and the tallest one turned back to me.

It reeked: something like brine, something like wet fur, something rank and indescribable. It had two narrow red eyes in that smooth knob of a head. It put one of its tentacles on my shoulder, and I didn't see a mouth open anywhere, but a droning voice said, "Thank you for caring for him. Come now. We go to ship."

I pulled away instinctively, quivering, and my hands came out of my pockets. I heard a flat, echoing *crack* and a yell, and I saw a red wetness spring out across the smooth skull; I saw the thing topple and lie in the dirt, twitching.

I thought for an instant that I had done it, the shot, the yell and all. Then I heard another yell, behind me: I whirled around and heard a car grind into gear and saw it bouncing away down the road into town, lights off, a black moving shape on the dimness. I saw it veer wildly and slew into the fence at the first turn; I heard its tires popping as it went through and the muffled crash as it turned over.

Dead, I thought. But the next time I looked I saw two figures come erect beyond the overturned car and stagger toward the road. They disappeared around the turn, running.

I looked back at the others, bewildered. They weren't even looking that way; they were gathered around the body, lifting it, carrying it toward the ship.

The feeling—the black depression that had been getting stronger every day for three weeks—tightened down on me as if somebody had turned a screw. I gritted my teeth against it, and stood there wishing I were dead.

They were almost to that open hatch in the oval hub that hung under the rim when Aza-Kra detached himself from the group and walked slowly back to me. After a moment one of the others—a hump-shelled one—trundled along after him and waited a yard or two away.

"It is not your fault," said Aza-Kra. "We could have prevented it, but we were careless. We were so glad to meet that we did not take precautions. It is not your fault. Come to the ship."

The hump-shelled thing came up and squeaked something, and Aza-Kra sat on its back. The tentacles waved at me. It wheeled and started toward the hatchway. "Come," said Aza-Kra.

I followed them, too miserable to care what happened. We went down a corridor full of the sourceless pearl-gray light until a doorway suddenly appeared, somehow, and we went through that into a room where two tripeds were waiting.

Aza-Kra climbed onto a stool, and one of the tripeds began pressing two small instruments against various parts of his body; the other squirted something from a flexible canister into his mouth.

And as I stood there watching, between one breath and the next, the depression went away.

I felt like a man whose toothache has just stopped; I probed at my mind, gingerly, expecting to find that the feeling was still there, only hiding. But it wasn't. It was gone so completely that I couldn't even remember exactly what it had been like. I felt calm and relaxed—and safe.

I looked at Aza-Kra. He was breathing easily; his eyes looked clearer than they had a moment before, and it seemed to me that his skin was glossier. The feathery neck-spines hung in relaxed, graceful curves.

. . . It was all true, then. It had to be. If they had been conquerors, the automatic death of the man who had killed one of their number, just now, wouldn't have been enough. An occupying army can never be satisfied with an eye for an eye. There must be retaliation.

But they hadn't done anything; they hadn't even used the gas. They'd seen that the others in the car were running away, that the danger was over, and that ended it. The only emotions they had shown, as far as I could tell, were concern and regret—

Except that, I remembered now, I had seen two of the tripeds clearly when I turned back to look at them gathering around the body: Aza-Kra and another one. And their neck-spines had been stiff. . . .

Suddenly I knew the answer.

Aza-Kra came from a world where violence and cruelty didn't exist. To him, the Earth was a jungle—and I was one of its carnivores.

I knew, now, why I had felt the way I had for the last three weeks, and why the feeling had stopped a few minutes ago. My hostility toward him had been partly responsible for his fear, and so I had picked up an echo of it. Undirected fear is, by definition, anxiety, depression, uneasiness—the psychologists' *Angst*. It had stopped because Aza-Kra no longer had to depend on me; he was with his own people again; he was safe.

I knew the reason for my nightmares.

I knew why, time and again when I had expected Aza-Kra to be reading my mind, I had found that he wasn't. He did it only when he had to; it was too painful.

And one thing more:

I knew that when the true history of this time came to be written, I needn't worry about my place in it. My name would be there, all right, but nobody would remember it once he had shut the book.

Nobody would use my name as an insulting epithet, and nobody would carve it on the bases of any statues, either.

I wasn't the hero of the story.

It was Aza-Kra who had come down alone to a planet so deadly that no one else would risk his life on it until he had softened it up. It was Aza-Kra who had lived for nearly a month with a suspicious, irrational, combative, uncivilized flesh-eater. It was Aza-Kra who had used me, every step of the way—used my provincial loyalties and my self-interest and my prejudices.

He had done all that, weary, tortured, half-starved ... and he'd been scared to death the whole time.

We made two stops up the coast and then moved into Algeria and the Sudan: landing, unloading, taking off again, following the dawn line. The other ships, Aza-Kra explained, would keep on circling the planet until enough food had been distributed to prevent any starvation until the next harvests. This one was going only as far as the middle of the North American continent—to drop me off. Then it was going to take Aza-Kra home.

I watched what happened after we left each place in a vision device they had. In some places there was more hesitation than in others, but in the end they always took the food: in jeep-loads, by pack train, in baskets balanced on their heads.

Some of the repeaters worried me. I said, "How do you know it'll get distributed to everybody who needs it?"

I might have known the answer: "They will distribute it. No man can let his neighbor starve while he has plenty."

The famine relief was all they had come for, this time. Later, when we had got through the crisis, they would come back; and by that time, remembering the food, people would be more inclined to take them on their merits instead of shuddering because they had too many eyes or fingers. They would help us when we needed it, they would show us the way up the ladder, but we would have to do the work ourselves.

He asked me not to publish the story of Chillicothe and the month we had spent together. "Later, when it will hurt no one, you can explain. Now there is no need to make anyone ashamed; not even the officials of your government. It was not their fault; they did not make the planet as it was."

So there went even that two-bit chance at immortality.

It was still dawn when we landed on the bluff across the river from my home; sky and land and water were all the same depthless cool gray, except for the hairline of scarlet in the east. Dew was heavy on the grass, and the air had a smell that made me think of wood smoke and dry leaves.

He came out of the ship with me to say good-by.

"Will you be back?" I asked him.

He buzzed wordlessly in a way I had begun to recognize; I think it was his version of a laugh. "I think not for a very long time. I have already neglected my work too much."

"This isn't your work—opening up new planets?"

"No. It is not so common a thing, that a race becomes ready for space travel. It has not happened anywhere in the galaxy for twenty thousand of your years. I believe, and I hope, that it will not happen again for twenty thousand more. No, I am ordinarily a maker of—you have not the word, it is like porcelain, but a different material. Perhaps some day you will see a piece that I have made. It is stamped with my name."

He held out his hand and I took it. It was an awkward grip; his hand felt unpleasantly dry and smooth to me, and I suppose mine was clammy to him. We both let go as soon as we decently could.

Without turning, he walked away from me up the ramp. I said, "Aza-Kra!"

"Yes?"

"Just one more question. The galaxy's a big place. What happens if you miss just one bloodthirsty race that's ready to boil out across the stars—or if nobody has the guts to go and do to them what you did to us?"

"Now you begin to understand," he said. "That is the question the people of Mars asked us about you . . . twenty thousand years ago."

The story ends there, properly, but there's one more thing I want to say.

When Aza-Kra's ship lifted and disappeared, and I walked down to the bottom of the bluff and across the bridge into the city, I knew I was going back to a life that would be a lot different from the one I had known.

For one thing, the *Herald-Star* was all but done for when I came home: wrecked presses, half the staff gone, supplies running out. I worked hard for a little over a year trying to revive it, out of sentiment, but I knew there were more important things to be done than publishing a newspaper.

Like everybody else, I got used to the changes in the world and in the people around me: to the peaceful, un-worried feel of places that had been electric with tension; to the kids—the wonderful, incredible kids; to the new kind of excitement, the excitement that isn't like the night before execution, but like the night before Christmas.

But I hadn't realized how much I had changed, myself, until something that happened a week ago.

I'd lost touch with Eli Freeman after the paper folded; I knew he had gone into pest control, but I didn't know where he was or what he was doing until he turned up one day on the wheat-and-dairy farm I help run, south of the Platte in what used to be Nebraska. He's the advance man for a fleet of spray planes working out of Omaha, aborting rabbits.

He stayed on for three days, lining up a few of the stiff-necked farmers in this area that don't believe in hormones or airplanes either; in his free time he helped with the harvest, and I saw a lot of him.

On his last night we talked late, working up from the old times to the new times and back again until there was nothing more to say. Finally, when we had both been quiet for a long time, he said something to me that is the only accolade I am likely to get, and oddly enough, the only one I want.

"You know, Bob, if it wasn't for that unique face of yours, it would be hard to believe you're the same guy I used to work for."

I said, "Hell, was I that bad?"

"Don't get shirty. You were okay. You didn't bleed the help or kick old ladies, but there just wasn't as much to you as there is now. I don't know," he said. "You're—more human."

More human.

Yes. We all are.

Natural State

I

The most promising young realie actor in Greater New York, everyone agreed, was a beetle-browed Apollo named Alvah Gustad. His diction, which still held over-tones of the Under Flushing labor pool, the unstudied animal grace of his movements and his habitually sullen expression enabled him to dominate any stage not oc-cupied by an unclothed woman at least as large as him-self. At twenty-six, he had a very respectable following among the housewives of Manhattan, Queens, Jersey and the rest of the seven boroughs. The percentage of blown fuses resulting from subscribers' attempts to clutch his realized image was extraordinarily low—Alvah, his press agents explained with perfect accuracy, left them too numb.

Young Gustad, who frequently made his first entrance water-beaded as from the shower, with a towel girded chastely around his loins, was nevertheless in his private life a modest and slightly bewildered citizen, much given to solitary reading, and equipped with a perfect set of the conventional virtues.

These included cheerful performance of all municipal duties and obligations; like every right-thinking citizen, Gustad held down two jobs in summer and three in win-ter. At the moment, for example, he was an actor by day and a metals-reclamation supervisor by night.

Chief among his less tangible attributes was that emo-tion which in some ages has been variously described as civic pride or patriotism. In A.D. 2064, as in B.C. 400, they amounted to the same thing.

Behind the Manager's desk, the wall was a single huge slab of black duroplast, with a map of the city picked out in pinpoints of brilliance. As Gustad entered with his manager and his porter, an unseen chorus of basso profundos broke into the strains of *The Slidewalks of New York.* After four bars, it segued to *New York, New York, It's a Pip of a Town,* and slowly faded out.

The Manager himself, the Hon. Boleslaw Wytak, broke the reverent hush by coming forward to take Alvah's hand and lead him toward the desk. "Mr. Gustad—and Mr. Diamond, isn't it? Great pleasure to have you here. I don't know if you've met all these gentlemen. Commissioner Laurence, of the Department of Extramural Relations—Director Ostertag, of the Bureau of Vital Statistics—Chairman Neddo of the Research and Development Board."

Wytak waited until everyone was comfortably settled in one of the reclining chairs which fitted into slots in the desk, with cigars, cigarettes, liquor capsules and cold snacks at each man's elbow. "Now, Mr. Gustad—and Mr. Diamond—I'm a plain blunt man and I know you're wondering why I asked you to come here today. I'm going to tell you. The City needs a man with great talent and great courage to do a job that, I tell you frankly, I wouldn't undertake myself without great misgivings." He gazed at Gustad warmly, affectionately but sternly. "You're the man, Alvah."

Little Jack Diamond cleared his throat nervously. "What kind of a job did you have in mind, Mr. Manager? Of course, anything we can do for our city . . ."

Wytak's big face, without perceptibly moving a muscle, somehow achieved a total change of expression. "Alvah, I want you to go to the Sticks."

Gustad blinked and tilted upright in his chair. He looked at Diamond.

The little man suddenly seemed two sizes smaller inside his box-cut cloth-of-silver tunic. He gestured feebly and wheezed, *"Wake-me-up!"* The porter behind his chair stepped forward alertly, clanking, and flipped open one of the dozens of metal and plastic boxes that clung to him all over like barnacles. He popped a tiny capsule into his palm, rolled it expertly to thumb-and-finger position, broke it under Diamond's nose.

A reeking-sweet green fluid dripped from it and ran stickily down the front of Diamond's tunic.

"Dumbhead!" said Diamond. "Not cream de menthy, a wake-me-up!" He sat up as the abashed servant produced another capsule. "Never mind." Some color was beginning to come back into his face. *"Blotter!"* A wad of absorbent fibers. *"Vacuum!"* A lemon-sized globe with a flaring snout. *"Gon-Stink! Presser!"*

Gustad looked back at the Manager. "Your Honor, you mean you want me to go into the Sticks? I mean," he said, groping for words, "you want me to play for the *Muckfeet?*"

"That is just exactly what I want you to do." Wytak nodded toward the Commissioner, the Director and the Chairman. "These gentlemen are here to tell you why. Suppose you start, Ozzie."

Ostertag, the one with the fringe of yellowish white hair around his potato-colored pate, shifted heavily and stared at Gustad. "In my bureau, we have records of population and population density, imports and exports, ratio of births to deaths and so on that go back all the way to the time of the United States. Now this isn't known generally. Mr. Gustad, but although New York has been steadily growing ever since its founding in 1646, our growth in the last thirty years has been entirely due to immigration from other less fortunate cities.

"In a way, it's fortunate—I mean to say that we can't expand *horizontally,* because it has been found impossible to eradicate the soil organisms—" a delicate shudder ran around the group—"left by our late enemies. And as for continuing to build vertically—well, since Pittsburgh fell, we have been dependent almost entirely on salvaged scrap for our steel. To put it bluntly, unless something is done about this situation, the end is in sight. Not alone of this administration, but of the city as well. Now the *reasons* for this—ah—what shall I say . . ."

With his head back, staring at the ceiling, Wytak began to speak so quietly that Ostertag blundered through another phrase and a half before he realized he had been superseded as interlocutor.

"Thirty years ago, when I first came to this town, an immigrant kid with nothing in the whole world but the tunic on my back and the gleam in my eye, we had just got through with the last of the Muckfeet Wars. According to your history books, we won that war. I'll tell you something—we were licked!"

Alvah squirmed uncomfortably as Wytak raised his head and glanced defiantly around the desk, looking for contradiction. The Manager said, "We drove them back to the Ohio, thirty years ago. And where are they now?" He turned to Laurence. "Phil?"

Laurence rubbed his long nose with a bloodless forefinger. "Their closest settlement is twelve miles away. That's to the southwest, of course. In the west and north—"

"Twelve miles," said Wytak reflectively. "But that isn't the reason I say they licked us. They licked us because there are twenty million of us today . . . and about one hundred fifty million of them. Right, Phil?"

Laurence said, "Well, there aren't any accurate figures, you know, Boley. There hasn't been any census of the Muckfeet for almost a century, but—"

"About one hundred fifty million," interrupted Wytak. "Even if we formed a league with every other city on this continent, the odds would be heavily against us—and they breed like flies." He slapped the desk with his open palm. "So do their filthy animals!"

A shudder rippled across the group. Diamond shut his eyes tight.

"There it is," said Wytak. "Rome fell. Babylon fell. The same thing can happen to New York. Those illiterate savages will go on increasing year by year, getting more ignorant and more degraded with every generation . . . and a century from now—or two, or five—*they'll be the human race*. And New York . . ."

Wytak turned to look at the map behind him. His hand touched a button and the myriad tiny lights went out.

Gustad was not an actor who wept readily, but he felt tears welling over his eyelids. At the same time, the thought crossed his mind that, competition being what it was in the realies, it was a good thing that Wytak had gone into politics instead of acting.

"Sir," he said, "what can we do?"

Wytak's eyes were focused far away. After a moment,

Natural State

his head turned heavily on his massive shoulders, like a gun turret. "Chairman Neddo has the answer to that. I want you to listen carefully to what he's going to tell you, Alvah."

Neddo's crowded small face flickered through a complicated series of twitches, all centripetal and rapidly executed. "Over the past several years," he said jerkily, "under Manager Wytak's direction, we have been developing certain devices, certain articles of commerce, which are designed, especially designed, to have an attraction for the Muckfeet. Trade articles. Most of these, I should say all of—"

"Trade articles," Wytak cut in softly. "Thank you, Ned. That's the phrase that tells the story. Alvah, we're going to go back to the principles that made our ancestors great. Trade—expanding markets—expanding industries. Think about it. From the Arctic Ocean to the Gulf of Mexico, there are some 150 million people who haven't got a cigarette lighter or a wristphone or a realie set among them. Alvah, we're going to civilize the Muckfeet. We've put together a grab-bag of modern science, expressed in ways their primitive minds can understand—and *you're* the man who's going to sell it to them! What do you say to that?"

This was a familiar cue to Gustad—it had turned up for the fiftieth or sixtieth time in his last week's script, when he had played the role of a kill-crazy sewer inspector, trapped by flood waters in the cloacae of Under Brooklyn. "I say—" he began, then realized that his usual response was totally inappropriate. "It sounds wonderful," he finished weakly.

Wytak nodded in a businesslike way. "Now here's the program." He pressed a button, and a relief map of the North American continent appeared on the wall behind him. "Indicator." Wytak's porter put a metal tube with a shaped grip into his hand; a tiny spot on the map fluoresced where he pointed it.

"You'll swing down to the southwest until you cross the Tennessee, then head westward about to here, then up through the Plains, then back north of the Great Lakes and home again. You'll notice that this route keeps you well clear of both Chicago and Toronto. Remember

93

that—it's important. We know that Frisco is working on a project similar to ours, although they're at least a year behind us. If we know that, the chances are that the other cities know it too, but we're pretty sure there's been no leak in our own security. There isn't going to be any."

He handed the indicator back. "You'll be gone about three months . . ."

Diamond was having trouble with his breathing again.

". . . You'll have to rough it pretty much—there'll be room in your floater for you and your equipment, and that's all."

Diamond gurgled despairingly and rolled up his eyes. Gustad himself felt an unpleasant sinking sensation.

"You mean," he asked incredulously, "I'm supposed to go all by myself—without even a *porter?*"

"That's right," said Wytak. "You see, Alvah, you and I are civilized human beings—we know there are so many indispensable time and labor saving devices that nobody could possibly carry them all himself. But could you explain that to a Muckfoot?"

"I guess not."

"That's why only a man with your superb talents can do this job for the City. Those people actually live the kind of sordid brutal existence you portray so well in the realies. Well, you can be as rough and tough as they are —you can talk their own language, and they'll respect you."

Gustad flexed his muscles slightly, feeling pleased but not altogether certain. Then a new and even more revolting aspect of this problem occurred to him. "Your Honor, suppose I got along *too* well with the Muckfeet? I mean suppose they invited me into one of their houses to—" he gagged slightly—"eat?"

Wytak's face went stony. "I am surprised that you feel it necessary to bring that subject up. All that will be covered very thoroughly in the briefing you will get from Commissioner Laurence and Chairman Neddo and their staffs. And I want you to understand, Gustad, that no pressure of any kind is being exerted on you to take this assignment. This is a job for a willing, cooperative volunteer, not a draftee. If you feel you're not the man for it, just say so now."

Gustad apologized profusely. Wytak interrupted him, with the warmest and friendliest smile imaginable. "That's all right, son, I understand. I understand perfectly. Well, gentlemen, I think that's all."

As soon as they were alone, Diamond clutched Gustad's sleeve and pulled him over to the side of the corridor. "Listen to me, Al boy. We can still pull you out of this. I know a doctor that will make you so sick you couldn't walk across the street. He wouldn't do it for everybody, but he owes me a couple of—"

"No, wait a minute, I don't—"

"I know, I *know*," said Diamond impatiently. "You'll get your contract busted with Seven Boroughs and you'll lose a couple months, maybe more, and you'll have to start all over again with one of the little studios, but what of it? In a year or two, you'll be as big as—"

"Now wait, Jack. In the first—"

"Al, I'm not just thinking about my twenty per cent of you. I don't even *care* about that—it's just money. What I want, I want you should still be alive next year, you understand what I mean?"

"Look," said Gustad, "you don't understand, Jack. I *want* to go. I mean I don't exactly want to, but—" He pointed down the corridor to the window that framed a vista of gigantic columns, fiercely brilliant below, fading to massive darkness above, with a million tiny floater-lights like a river of stardust down the avenue. "Just look at that. It took hundreds of years to build! I mean if I can keep it going just by spending three months . . .

"And besides," he added practically, "think of the publicity."

II

The foothill country turned out to be picturesque but not very rewarding. Alvah had bypassed the ancient states of Pennsylvania and Maryland as directed, since the tribes nearest the city were understood to be still somewhat rancorous. By the end of his first day, he was beginning to regard this as a serious understatement.

He had brought his floater down, with flags flying, loudspeakers blaring, colored lights flashing and streamers flapping gaily behind him, just outside an untidy collection of two-story beehive huts well south of the former Pennsylvania border. He had seen numerous vaguely human shapes from the air, but when he extruded his platform and stepped out, every visible door was shut, the streets were empty, and there was no moving thing in sight, except for a group of singularly unpleasant-looking animals in a field to his right.

After a few moments, Gustad shut off the loudspeakers and listened. He thought he heard a hum of voices from the nearest building. Suppressing a momentary qualm, he lowered himself on the platform stair and walked over to the building. It had a single high window, a crude oval in shape, closed by a discolored pane.

Standing under this window, Alvah called, "Hello in there!"

The muffled voices died away for a moment, then buzzed as busily as ever.

"Come on out—I want to talk to you!"

Same result.

"You don't have to be afraid! I come in peace!"

The voices died away again, and Alvah thought he saw a dim face momentarily through the pane. A single voice rose on an interrogative note.

"Peace!" Alvah shouted.

The window slid abruptly back into the wall and, as Alvah gaped upward, a deluge of slops descended on him, followed by a gale of coarse laughter.

Alvah's immediate reaction, after the first dazed and gasping instant, was a hot-water-and-soap tropism, carrying with it an ardent desire to get out of his drenched clothes and throw them away. His second, as imperious as the first, had the pure flame of artistic inspiration—he wanted to see how many esthetically satisfying small pieces one explosive charge would make out of that excrescence-shaped building.

Under no conditions, said the handbook he had been required to memorize, *will you commit any act which might be interpreted by the Muckfeet as aggression, nor will you make use of your weapons at any time, unless such use becomes necessary for the preservation of your own life.*

Alvah wavered, grew chilly and retired. Restored in body, but shaken in spirit, he headed south.

Then there had been his encounter with the old man and the animal. Somewhere in the triangle of land between the Mississippi and the Big Black, at a point which was not on his itinerary at all, but had the overwhelming attraction of being more than a thousand air-miles from New York, he had set the floater down near another sprawling settlement.

As usual, all signs of activity in and around the village promptly disappeared. With newly acquired caution, Alvah sat tight. Normal human curiosity, he reasoned, would drive the Muckfeet to him sooner or later—and even if that failed, there was his nuisance value. How long could you ignore a strange object, a few hundred yards from your home, that was shouting, waving flags, flashing colored lights and sending up puffs of pink-and-green smoke?

Nothing happened for a little over an hour. Then, half dozing in his control chair, Alvah saw two figures coming toward him across the field.

Alvah's ego, which had been taking a beating all day, began to expand. He stepped out onto the platform and waited.

The two figures kept coming, taking their time. The tall one was a skinny loose-jointed oldster with a conical hat on the back of his head. The little one ambling along in front of him was some sort of four-footed animal.

In effect, an audience of one—at any rate, it was Alvah's best showing so far. He mentally rehearsed his opening lines. There was no point, he thought, in bothering with the magic tricks or the comic monologue. He might as well go straight into the sales talk.

The odd pair was now much closer, and Gustad recognized the animal half of it. It was a so-called watchdog, one of the incredibly destructive beasts the Muckfeet trained to do their fighting for them. It had a slender, supple body, a long feline tail and a head that looked something like a terrier's and something like a housecat's. However, it was not half as large or as frightening in appearance as the pictures Alvah had seen. It must, he decided, be a pup.

Two yards from the platform, the oldster came to a halt. The watchdog sat down beside him, tongue lolling wetly. Alvah turned off the loudspeakers and the color displays.

"Friend," he began, "I'm here to show you things that will astound you, marvels that you wouldn't believe unless you saw them with your own—"

"You a Yazoo?"

Thrown off stride, Alvah gaped. "What was that, friend?"

"Ah *said*—you a Yazoo?"

"No," said Alvah, feeling reasonably positive.

"Any kin to a Yazoo?"

"I don't think so."

"Git," said the old man.

Unlikely as it seemed, a Yazoo was apparently a good thing to be. "Wait a second," said Alvah. "Did you say *Yazoo?* I didn't understand you there at first. Am I a *Yazoo!* Why, man, my whole family on both sides has been—" what was the plural of Yazoo?

"Ah'll count to two," said the old man. *"One."*

"Now wait a minute," said Alvah, feeling his ears getting hot. The watchdog, he noticed, had hoisted its rump a fraction of an inch and was staring at him in a marked manner. He flexed his right forearm slightly and felt the reassuring pressure of the pistol in its pop-out holster. "What makes you Muckfeet think you can—"

"Two," said the oldster, and the watchdog was a spread-eagled blur in midair, seven feet straight up from the ground.

Instinct took over. Instinct had nothing to do with pistols or holsters, or with the probable size of a full-grown Muckfoot watchdog. It launched Alvah's body into a backward standing broad jump through the open floater door, and followed that with an economical underhand punch at the control button inside.

The door slammed shut. It then bulged visibly inward and rang like a gong. Sprawled on the floor, Gustad stared at it incredulously. There were further sounds—a thunderous growling and a series of hackle-raising skreeks, as of hard metal being gouged by something even harder. The whole floater shook.

Alvah made the control chair in one leap, slammed on the power switch and yanked at the steering bar. At an altitude of about a hundred feet, he saw the dark shape of the watchdog leap clear and fall, twisting.

A few seconds later, he put the bar into neutral and looked down. Man and watchdog were moving slowly back across the field toward the settlement. As far as Alvah could tell, the beast was not even limping.

Alvah's orders were reasonably elastic, but he had already stretched them badly in covering the southward leg of his route in one day. Still, there seemed to be nothing else to do. Either there was an area somewhere on the circuit where he could get the Muckfeet to listen to him, or there wasn't. If there was, it would make more sense to hop around until he found it, and then work outward to its limits, than to blunder straight along, collecting bruises and insults.

And if there wasn't—and this did not bear thinking about—then the whole trip was a bust.

Alvah switched on his communicator and tapped out the coded clicks that meant, "Proceeding on schedule"—which was a lie—"no results yet"—which was true. Then he headed north.

Nightfall overtook him as he was crossing the Ozark

Plateau. He set the floater's controls to hover at a thousand feet, went to bed and slept badly until just before dawn. With a cup of kaffin in his hand, he watched this phenomenon in surprised disapproval: the scattered lights winking out below, the first colorless hint of radiance, which illuminated nothing, but simply made the universe seem more senselessly vast and formless than before; finally, after an interminable progression of insignificant changes, the rinds of orange and scarlet, and the dim sun bulging up at the rim of the turning earth.

It was lousy theater.

How, Alvah asked himself, could any human being keep himself from dying of sheer irrelevance and boredom against a background like that? He was aware that billions had done so, but his general impression of history was that people who didn't have a city always got busy improving themselves until they could build one or take one away from somebody else. All but the Muckfeet . . .

Once their interest has been engaged, said the handbook at one point, *you will lay principal stress upon the competitive advantages of each product. It will be your aim to create a situation in which ownership of one or more of our products will be not only an economic advantage, but a mark of social distinction. In this way, communities which have accepted the innovations will, in order to preserve and extend the recognition of their own status, be forced to convert members of neighboring communities.*

Well, maybe so.

Alvah ate a Spartan breakfast of protein jelly and citron cakes, called in the coordinates and the time to the operator in New York, and headed the floater northward again.

The landscape unrolled itself. If there were any major differences between this country and the districts he had seen yesterday, Alvah was unable to discern them. In the air, he saw an occasional huge flapping shape, ridden by human figures. He avoided them, and they ignored him. Below, tracts of dark-green forest alternated predictably with the pale green, red or violet of cultivated fields. Here and there across the whole visible expanse, isolated buildings stood. At intervals, these huddled closer and closer together and became a settlement. There were perhaps more roads as he moved northward, dustier ones. That was all.

The dustiness of these roads, it occurred to Alvah, was a matter that required investigation. The day was cloudless and clear; there was no wind at Alvah's level, and nothing in the behavior of the trees or cultivated plants to suggest that there was any farther down.

He slowed the floater and lowered it toward the nearest road. As he approached, the thread of ocher resolved itself into an irregular series of expanding puffs, each preceded by a black dot, the overall effect being that of a line of black-and-tan exclamation points. They seemed to be moving barely perceptibly, but were actually, Alvah guessed, traveling at a fairly respectable clip.

He transferred his attention to another road. It, too, was filled with hurrying dots, as was the next—and all the traffic was heading in approximately the same direction, westward of Alvah's course.

He swung the control bar over. The movement below, he was able to determine after twenty minutes' flying, converged upon a settlement larger than any he had yet seen. It sprawled for ten miles or more along the southern shore of a long and exceedingly narrow lake. Most of it looked normal enough—a haphazard arrangement of cone-roofed buildings—but on the side away from the lake, there was a fairly extensive area filled with what seemed to be long, narrow sheds. This, in turn, was bounded on two sides by a strip of fenced-in plots in which, as nearly as Alvah could make out through the dust, animals of all sizes and shapes were penned. It was this area which appeared to be the goal of every Muckfoot in the central Plains.

The din was tremendous as Alvah floated down. There were shouts, cries, animal bellowings, sounds of hammering, occasional blurts of something that might be intended to be music, explosions of laughter. The newcomers, he noted, were being herded with much confusion to one or another of the fenced areas, where they left their mounts. Afterward, they straggled across to join the sluggish river of bodies in the avenues between the sheds.

No one looked up or noticed the dim shadow of the floater. Everyone was preoccupied, shouting, elbowing, blowing an instrument, climbing a pole. Alvah found a clear space at some distance from the sheds—as far as he could conveniently get from the penned animals—and landed.

He had no idea what this gathering was about. For all he knew, it might be a war council or some kind of religious observance, in which case his presence might be distinctly unwelcome. But in any case, there were customers here.

He looked dubiously at the stud that controlled his attention-catchers. If he used them, he would only be following directives, but he had a strong feeling that it would be a faux pas to do so in this situation. At the other extreme, the obvious thing to do was to get out and go look for someone in authority. This would involve abandoning the protection of the floater, however, and he might blunder into some taboo place or ceremony.

Evidently his proper course was to wait unobtrusively until he was discovered. On the other hand, if he stayed inside the floater with the door shut, the Muckfeet might take more alarm than if he showed himself. Still, wasn't it possible that they would be merely puzzled by a floater, whereas they would be angered by a floater with a man on its platform? Or, taking it from another angle . . .

The hell with it.

Alvah ran the platform out, opened the door and stepped out. He was relieved when, as he was considering the delicate problem of whether or not to lower the stair, a small group of men and urchins came into view around the corner of the nearest shed, a dozen yards away from him.

They stopped when they saw him, and two or three of the smallest children scuttled behind their elders. They exchanged looks and a few words that Alvah couldn't hear. Then a pudgy little man with a fussed expression crowded forward, and the rest followed him at a discreet distance.

"Hello," said Alvah tentatively.

The little man came to a halt a yard or so from the platform. He had a white badge of some kind pinned to his shapeless brown jacket, and carried a sheaf of papers in his hand. "Who might *you* be?" he asked irritably.

"Alvah Gustad is my name. I hope I'm not putting you people out, parking in your area like this, Mr.—"

"Well, I should hope to spit you *is*, though. Supposed to be a tent go up right *there*. Got to be one by noon. What did you say your name was, Gus what?"

"Gustad. I don't believe I caught your name, Mr.—"

"Don't signify what *my* name is. We talking about *you*. What clan you belong to?"

"Uh—Flatbush," said Alvah at random. "Look, as long as I'm in the way here, you just tell me where to move to and—"

"Some little backwoods clan, I never even *heard* of it," said the pudgy man. "*I'll* tell you where you can *move* to. You can just haul that thing back where you come from. Gustad—Flatbush! *You* ain't on my list, I know *that*."

The other Muckfeet had moved up gradually to surround the little man. One of them, a lanky sad-faced youngster, nudged him with his elbow. "Might just check and see, Jake."

"Well, I ought to know. My *land*, Artie, I got my *work* to do. *I* can't spend all day standing here."

Artie's long face grew more mournful. "You thought them Keokuks wasn't on the list, either."

"Well—all right then, rot it." To Alvah: "What's your marks?"

Alvah blinked. "I don't—"

"Come *down* offa there." Jake turned impatiently to a man behind him. "Give'm a stake." As Alvah came hesitantly down the stair, he found he was being offered a sharpened length of wood by a seamy-faced brown man, who carried a bundle of others like it under his arm.

Alvah took it, without the least idea of what to do next. The brown man watched him alertly. "You c'n make your marks with that," he volunteered, and pointed to the ground between them.

The others closed in a little.

"Marks?" said Alvah worriedly.

The brown man hesitated, then took another stake from his bundle. "Like these here," he said. "These is mine." He drew a shaky circle and put a dot in the center of it. "George." A figure four. "Allister—that's me." A long rectangle with a loop at each end. "Coffin—that's m'clan."

Jake burst out, "Well, crying in a bucket, *he* knows that! You know how to sign your *name,* don't you?"

"Well," said Alvah, "yes." He wrote *Alvah Gustad* and, as an afterthought, added *Flatbush.*

There were surprised whistles. "Wrote it just as slick as Doc!" said a ten-year-old tow-headed male, bug-eyed with awe.

Jake stared at Alvah, then spun half around to wave his papers under Artie's nose. "Well, you satisfied now, Artie Brumbacher? I guess *that* ain't on my list, is it?"

"No," Artie admitted, "I guess it ain't—not if you can read the lisf, that is."

Everybody but Alvah laughed, Jake louder than anyone. "All right," he said, turning back to Alvah, "you just hitch up your brutes and get that thing *out* of here. If you ain't gone by the time I—"

"Jake!" called a businesslike female voice, and a small figure came shouldering through the crowd. "They need you over in the salamander shed—the Quincies is ready to move in, but there's some Sullivans ahead of them." She glanced at Alvah, then at the floater behind him. "You having any trouble here?"

"All settled *now,*" Jake told her. "This feller ain't on the list. I just give him his *marching* orders."

"Look, if I can say something—" Alvah began.

The girl interrupted him. "Did you want to exhibit something at the Fair?"

"That's right," said Alvah gratefully. "I was just trying to explain—"

"Well, you late, but maybe we can squeeze you in. You won't sell anything, though, if it's what I think it is. Let me see that list, Jake."

"Now *wait* a minute," said Jake indignantly. "You know we ain't got room for nobody that ain't on the *list.* We got enough trouble—"

"The earth-movers won't be here from Butler till tomorrow," said the girl, examining the papers. "We can put him in there and move him out again when they get here. You need any equipment besides what you brought?"

"No," said Alvah. "That would be fine, thanks. All I need is a place—"

"All right. Before you go, Jake, did you tell those Sullivans they could have red, green and yellow in the salamander shed?"

"Well, *sure* I did. That what it says right there."

She handed him back the papers and pointed to a line. "That's Quincy, see? Dot instead of a cross. Sullivans is supposed to have that corner in the garden truck shed, keep the place warm for the seedlings, but they won't budge till you tell them it was a mistake. Babbishes and Stranahans is fit to be tied. You get over there and straighten them out, will you? And don't worry too much about *him*."

Jake snorted and moved away, still looking ruffled. The girl turned to Alvah. "All right, let's go."

Unhappy but game, Alvah turned and climbed back into the floater with the girl close behind him. The conditioning he'd had just before he left helped when he was in the open air, but in the tiny closed cabin of the floater the girl's triply compounded stench was overpowering.

How did they live with themselves?

She leaned over the control chair, pointing. "Over there," she said. "See that empty space I'm pointing at?"

Alvah saw it and put the floater there as fast as the generator would push it. The space was not quite empty —there were a few very oddly assorted Muckfeet and animals in it, but they straggled out when they saw him hovering, and he set the floater down.

To his immense relief, the girl got out immediately. Alvah followed her as far as the platform.

III

In a tailor shop back in Middle Queens, the proprietors, two brothers named Wynn, whose sole livelihood was the shop, stared glumly at the bedplate where the two-hundred-gallon Klenomatic ought to have been.

"He say anything when he took it away?" Clyde asked. Morton shrugged and made a sour face.

"Yeah," said Clyde. He looked distastefully at a dead cigar and tossed it at the nearest oubliette. He missed.

"He said a month, two months," Morton told him. "You know what that means."

"Yeah."

"So I'll call up the factory," Morton said violently. "But I know what they're gonna tell me. Give us a deposit and we'll put you on a waiting list. *Waiting* list!"

"Yeah," said Clyde.

In a factory in Under Bronnix, the vice president in charge of sales shoved a thick folder of coded plastic slips under the nose of the vice president in charge of production. "Look at those orders," he said.

"Uh-huh," said Production.

"You know how far back they go? *Three years.* You know how much money this company's lost in unfilled orders? Over two million—"

"I *know.* What do you expect? Every fabricator in this place is too old. We're holding them together with spit and string. Don't bother me, will you, Harry. I got my own—"

"Listen," said Sales. "This can't go on much longer. It's up to us to tell the Old Man that he's got to try a bigger bribe on the Metals people. Mortgage the plant if we have to."

106

"We have more mortgages now than the plant is worth."

Sales reddened. "Nick, this is serious. Last fall, it looked like we might squeeze through another year, but now . . . You know what's going to happen in another eight, ten months?" He snapped his fingers. "Right down the drain."

Production blinked at him wearily. "Bribes are no good any more, Harry. You know that as well as I do. They're out."

"Well, then what are we going to *do?*"

Production shook his head. "I don't know. I swear to God, I don't know."

Over in Metals Reclamation Four, in Under and Middle Jersey, the night shift was just beginning. In the blue-lit cavern of Ferrous, this involved two men, one bald and flabby, the other gray and gnarled. They exchanged a silent look, then each in turn put his face into the time clock's retinoscope mask. The clock, which had been emitting a shrill irritating sound, gurgled its satisfaction and shut up.

"Well, that's it," said the gray one. "I'll be your work gang and you be mine, huh?"

The flabby one spat. "Wonder what happened to Turk."

"Who cares? I never liked him."

"Just wondering. Yesterday he's here, today where is he? Labor pool, army—" he spat again, with care— "repair, maintenance . . . He was fifteen years in this department. I was just wondering."

"Scooping dreck, probably. That's about his speed." The gray man shambled over to the control bench opposite and looked at the indicators. Then he lighted a cigarette.

"Nothing in the hoppers?" the flabby one asked.

"Nah. They ought to put Turk in the hoppers. He had metal in his goddam *teeth.*"

"Turk wasn't old," the flabby one said reproachfully. "No more than sixty."

"I never liked him."

"First it was the kid—you know. Pimples. Then, lessee, the next one was that big guy, the realie actor—"

"Gustad. The hell with him."

"Yeah, Gustad. What I mean is, where do they go to? It's the same thing on my three-to-seven shift, over in Yeasts. Guys I knew for ten, fifteen, twenty years on the same job. All of a sudden, they're gone and you never see them. Must be a hell of a thing, starting all over again somewhere else—guys like that—I mean you get set in your ways, kind of."

His eyes were patient and bewildered in their watery pouches. "Guys like me—no kids, nobody that gives a damn about 'em. Kind of gives you the jumps to think about it. You know what I mean?"

The gray one looked embarrassed, then irritated, then defiant. "Aah," he said, and produced a deck of cards from his kit—the grimy coating on the creaseless, frayless plastic as lovingly built and preserved as the patina in a meerschaum. "Cut for deal."

"I'll have to know what you going to exhibit," the girl said. "For the Fair records."

"Labor-saving devices," Alvah told her, "the latest and best products of human ingenuity, designed to—"

"Machines," she said, writing. She added, looking up, "There's a fee for the use of the fairground space. Since you're only going to have it for a day, we'll call it twenty twains."

Alvah hesitated. He had no idea what a twain might be—it had *sounded* like "twain." Evidently it was some sort of crude Muckfoot coinage.

"Afraid I haven't got any of your money," he said, producing a handful of steels from his belt change-meter. "I don't suppose these would do?"

The girl looked at him steadily. "Gold?" she said. "Precious stones, platinum, anything of that kind?" Alvah shook his head. "Sure?" Alvah shrugged despairingly. "Well," she said after a moment, "maybe something can be arranged. I'll let you talk to Doc about it, anyhow. He'll have to decide. Come on."

"Just a minute," Alvah said, and ducked back into the floater. He found what he was looking for and trotted outside again.

"What's that?" asked the girl, looking at the bulky kit at his waist.

"Just a few things I like to have with me."

"Mind showing me?"

"Well—no." He opened the kit. "Cigarette lighter, flashlight, shaver, raincoat, heater, a few medicines over here, jububes, food concentrates, things like that. Uh, I don't know why I put this in here—it's a distress signal for people who get lost in the subway."

"You never can tell," said the girl, "when a thing like that will come in handy."

"That's true. Uh, this thing that looks like two dumb-bells and a corkscrew . . ."

"Never mind," said the girl. "Come along."

The first shed they passed was occupied by things that looked like turtles with glittery four-foot shells. In the nearest stall, a man was peeling off from one of the beasts successive thin layers of this shell-stuff, which turned out to be colorless and transparent. He passed them to a woman, who dipped them into a basin and then laid them on a board to dry. The ones at the far end of the row, Alvah noticed, had flattened into discs.

The girl apparently misread his expression as curiosity. "Glass tortoise," she told him. "For windows and so on. The young ones have more hump to their shells—almost spherical to start with. Those are for bottles and bowls and things."

Alvah blinked noncommittally.

They passed a counter on which metal tools were displayed—knives, axes and the like. Similar objects, Alvah noted automatically, had only approximately similar outlines. There seemed to be no standardization at all.

"These are local," the girl said. "The metal comes from Iron Pits, just a few miles south of here."

In the next shed was a long row of upright rectangular frames, most of them empty. One near the end, however, was filled with some sort of insubstantial film or fabric. A tiny scarlet creature was crawling rapidly up and down this gossamer substance, working its way gradually from left to right.

"Squareweb," the girl informed him. "This dress I'm wearing was made that way."

Alvah verified his previous impression that the dress was opaque. Rather a pity, since it was also quite handsomely filled out. Not, he assured himself, that it made any difference—the girl was a Muckfoot, after all.

Next came a large cleared space. In it were half a dozen animals that resembled nothing in nature or nightmare except each other. They were wide and squat and at least six feet high at the shoulder. They had vaguely reptilian heads, and their scaly hides were patterned in orange and blue, rust and vermilion, yellow and poppyred.

The oddest thing about them, barring the fact that each had three sets of legs, was the extraordinary series of protuberances that sprouted from their backs. First came an upright, slightly hollow shield sort of thing, set crossways behind the first pair of shoulders. Behind that, something that looked preposterously like an armchair—it even had a bright-colored cushion—and then a double row of upright spines with a wide space between them.

"Trucks," said the girl.

Alvah cleared his throat. "Look, Miss—"

"Betty Jane Hofmeyer. Call me B. J. Everybody does."

"All right—uh—B. J. I wonder if you could explain something to me. What's wrong with metal? And plastic, and things like that. I mean why should you people want to go to so much trouble and—and *mess,* when there are easier ways to do things better?"

"Each," she said, "to his own taste. We turn here."

A few yards ahead, the Fair ended and the settlement proper began with an unusually large building—large enough, Alvah estimated, to fill almost an entire wing of a third-class hotel in New York. Unlike the hovels he had seen farther south—which looked as if they had been excreted—it was built of some regular, smooth-surfaced material, seamless and fairly well shaped.

Alvah was so engrossed in these and other considerations that it wasn't until the girl turned three steps inside the doorway, impatiently waiting, that he realized a minor crisis was at hand— he was being invited to enter a Muckfoot dwelling.

"Well, come on," said B. J.

Refuse any offers of food, transportation, etc., said the handbook, *firmly, but as diplomatically as possible. Employ whatever subterfuge the situation may suggest, such as, "Thank you, but my doctor has forbidden me to touch fur," or, "Pardon me, but I have a sore throat and am unable to eat."*

Alvah cleared his throat frantically. The situation did not suggest anything at all. Luckily, however, his stomach did.

"Maybe I'd better not come in," he said. "I don't feel very well. Maybe if I just sit down here quietly—"

"You can sit down inside," said the girl. "If there's anything wrong with you, Doc will look you over."

"Well," Alvah asked desperately, "couldn't you bring him out here for a minute? I really don't think—"

"Doc is a busy man. Are you coming or not?"

Alvah hesitated. There were, he told himself, only two possibilities, after all: (a) he would somehow manage to keep his breakfast, and (b) he wouldn't.

The nausea began as a faint, premonitory twinge when he stepped through the doorway. It increased steadily as he followed B. J. past cages filled with things that chirruped, croaked, rumbled, rustled or simply stared at him. The girl didn't invite comment on any of them, for which Alvah was grateful. He was too busy concentrating on trying not to concentrate on his misery.

For the same reason, he did not notice at what precise point the cages gave way to long rows of potted green plants. Alvah was just beginning to wonder if he would live to see the end of them when, still following B. J., he turned a corner and came upon a cleared space with half a dozen people in it.

One of them was the sad-faced youth, Artie. Another was a stocky man, all chest and paunch and no neck at all, who was talking to Artie while the others stood and listened. B. J. stopped and waited quietly. Alvah, perforce, did the same.

"—just a few seedlings and a couple of one-year-olds for now—we'll see how they go. If you have more room later on . . . What else was I going to tell you?" The stocky man rumpled his hair nervously. "Oh, look, Artie, I had a copy of the specifications for you, but the fool bird got into a fight with a mirror and broke his . . . Wait a second." He turned abruptly. "Hello, Beej. Come along to the library for a second, will you?"

He turned again and strode off, with Artie, B. J., and Alvah in his wake.

The room they entered was, from Alvah's point of view, the worst he had struck yet. It was a hundred feet long by fifty wide, and everywhere—perched on the walls and on multi-leveled racks that ran the length of the room, darting through the air in flutters of brilliance—were tiny raucous birds, feathered in every prismatic shade, green, electric-blue, violet, screaming red.

"Mark seven one-oh-three!" the stocky man shouted. The roomful of birds took it up in a hideous echoing chorus. An instant later, a sudden flapping sound turned itself into an explosion of color and alighted on the stocky man's shoulder, preening its feathers with a blunt green beak. *"Rrk,"* it said and then, quite clearly, "Mark seven one-oh-three."

The stocky man made a perch of one forefinger and handed the thing across to Artie's shoulder. "I can't give you this one. It's the only copy I got. You'll have to listen to it and remember what you need."

"I'll remember." Artie glanced at the bird on his shoulder and said, "Magnus utility tree."

The stocky man looked around, saw B. J. "Now, Beej, is it important? Because—"

"Magnus utility tree," the bird was saying. "Thrives in all soils, over ninety-one per cent resistant to most rusts, scales and other infestations. Edible from root to branch. Young shoots and leaves excellent for salads. Self-fertilizing. Sap can be drawn in second year for—"

"Doc," said the girl clearly, "this is Alvah Gustad. From New York. Alvah, meet Doc Bither."

"—golden orangoes in spring and early summer, Bither aperries in late summer and fall. Will crossbreed with—"

"New York, huh?" said Bither. "You a long way from home, young— Excuse me. Artie?"

"—series five to one hundred fifteen. Trunks guaranteed straight and rectilinear, two-by-four at end of second year, four-by-six at—"

"I all set, Doc."

"—mealie pods and winterberries—"

"Fine, all right." He took B. J.'s arm. "Let's go someplace we can talk."

"—absorb fireproofing and stiffening solutions freely through roots . . ."

Bither led the way into a small, crowded room. "Now," he said, peering intently at Alvah, "what's the problem?"

B. J. explained briefly. Then they both stared at Alvah. Sweat was beaded coldly on his brow and his knees were trembling, but he seemed to have stabilized the nausea just below the critical point. The idea, he told himself, was to convince yourself that the whole building was a realie stage and all the objects in it props. Wasn't there a line to that effect in one of the classics—*The Manager of Copenhagen,* or perhaps *Have It Your Own Way?*

"What do you think?" Bither asked.

"Might try him out."

"Um. Damn it, I wish we hadn't run out of birds. Can you take this down for me, Beej? I'll arrange for the Fair rental fee, Alvah, if you just answer a few questions."

It sounded innocuous enough, but Alvah felt a twinge of suspicion. "What kind of questions?"

"Just personal questions, like how old, what do you do for a living."

"Twenty-six. I'm an actor."

"Always been an actor?"

"No."

"What else you done?"

"Labor."

"What kind?" B. J. asked.

"Worked with his hands, he means," Bither told her. "Parents laborers, too?"

"Yes."

B. J. and Bither exchanged glances. Alvah shifted uncomfortably. "If that's all . . ."

"One or two more. I want you to tell me, near as you can, when was the first time you remember knowing that

113

our clothes and our animals and us and all the things we make smelled bad."

It was too much. Alvah turned and lurched blindly out the door. He heard their voices behind him:

". . . minutes."

". . . alley door!"

Then there were hands on him, steering him from behind as he stumbled forward at a half-run. They turned him right, then left, and finally he was out in the cool air, not a moment too soon.

When he straightened, wiping tears away, he was alone, but a moment later the girl appeared in the doorway.

"That's all," she said distantly. "You can start your exhibition whenever you want."

IV

The magic tricks went over fairly well—at leas nobody yawned. The comic monologue, however, was a flat failure, even though the piece had been expertly slanted for a rural audience and, by all the laws of psychostatics, should have rated at least half a dozen boffs. ("So the little boy came moseying back up the road, and his grandpa said to him, 'Why didn't you drive them hogs out of the corn like I told you?' And the little fellow piped up, 'Them ain't hogs—them's shoats!' ")

Alvah launched hopefully into his sales talks and demonstrations.

The all-purpose fireless lifetime cooker was received with blank stares. When Alvah fried up a savory batch of protein-paste fritters and offered to hand them out, nobody responded but one small boy, and his mother hauled him down off the platform stair by the slack of his pants.

Smiling doggedly, Alvah brought out the pocket-workshop power tools and accessories. This, it appeared, was more like it. An interested hum went up as he drilled three holes of various sizes in a bar of duroplast, then sawed through it from end to end and finally cut a mortise in one piece, a tenon in the other, and fitted them together. A few more people drifted in.

"And now, friends," said Alvah, "if you'll continue to give me your kind attention . . ."

The next item was the little giant power-plant for the home, shop or office. Blank stares again. Alvah picked out one Muckfoot in the front row—a blear-eyed, open-mouthed fellow, with hair over his forehead and a basket under his arm, who seemed typical—and spoke directly to him. He outdid himself about the safety, economy, efficiency and unobtrusiveness of a little giant power-plant.

He explained its operation in words a backward two-year-old could understand.

"A little giant," he concluded, leaning over the platform rail to stare hypnotically into the Muckfoot's eyes, "is the power-plant for *you!*"

The fellow blinked, slowly produced a dark-brown lump of something from his pocket, slowly put it into his inattentive mouth, and as slowly began to chew.

Alvah breathed deeply and clutched the rail. "And now," he said, giving the clincher, "the marvel of the age —the super-speed runabout!" He pressed the button that popped open a segment of the floater's hull and lowered the gleaming little two-wheeled car into view.

"Now, friends," he said, "just to demonstrate the amazing qualities of this miracle of modern science—is there any gentleman in the crowd who has an animal he fancies for speed?"

For the first time, the Muckfeet reacted according to the charts. Shouts rocketed up: "Me, by damn!" "Me!" "Right here, mister!" "Yes, sir!"

"Friends, friends!" said Alvah, spreading his hands. "There won't be time to accommodate you all. Choose one of you to represent the rest!"

"Swifty!" somebody yelped, and other voices took up the cry. A red-haired young man began working his way back out of the crowd, propelled by gleeful shouts and slaps on the back.

Alvah took an indicator and began pointing out the salient features of the runabout. He had not got more than a quarter of the way through when the redhead reappeared, mounted astride an animal which, to Alvah's revolted gaze, looked to be part horse, part lynx, part camel and part pure horror.

To the crowd, evidently, it was one of nature's finest efforts. Alvah swallowed bile and raised his voice again. "Clear a space now, friends—all the way around!"

It took time, but eventually self-appointed deputies began to get the crowd moving. Alvah descended, carrying two bright marker poles, and, followed by the inquisitive redhead, set one up at either side of the enclosure, a few yards short of the boundary.

"This will be the course," he told Swifty. "Around these

116

markers and the floater—that thing I was standing on. We'll do ten laps, starting and finishing here. Is that all right?"

"All right with me," said the redhead, grinning more widely than before.

There were self-appointed time-keepers and starters, too. When Alvah, in the runabout, and the redhead, on his monster, were satisfactorily lined up, one of them bellowed, "On y' marks—Git set . . ." and then cracked a short whip with a noise out of all proportion to its size.

For a moment, Alvah thought Swifty and his horrid mount had simply disappeared. Then he spotted them, diminished by perspective, halfway down the course, and rapidly getting smaller. He slammed the power bar over and took off in pursuit.

Around the first turn, it was Swifty, with Alvah nowhere. In the stretch, Alvah was coming up fast on the outside. Around the far turn, he was two monster lengths behind and, in the stretch again, they were neck and neck. Alvah kept it that way for the next two laps and then gradually pulled ahead. The crowd became a multicolored streak, whirling past him. In the sixth lap, he passed Swifty again—in the eighth, again—in the tenth, still again—and when he skidded to a halt beyond the finish post, fluttering its flags with the wind of his passage, poor old Swifty and his steaming beast were still lumbering halfway down the stretch.

"Now, friends," said Alvah, triumphantly mounting the platform again, "in a moment, I'm going to tell you how you, yourselves, can own this wonderful runabout and many marvels more—but first, are there any questions you'd like to ask?"

Swifty pushed forward, grinless, looking like a man smitten by lightning. "How many to a get?" he called.

Alvah decided he must have misunderstood. "You can have any number you want," he said. "The price is so reasonable—but I'm going to come to that in a—"

"I don't mean how many will you *sell*. How many to a get?" Alvah looked blank. "How many calves, or colts, or whatever, is what I want to know."

There was a general murmur of agreement. This, it would seem, was what everybody wanted to know.

Appalled, Alvah corrected the misapprehension as quickly and clearly as he could.

"Mean to say," somebody called, "they don't *breed?*"

"Certainly not. If one of them ever breaks down—and, friends, they're built to last—you get it repaired or buy another."

"How much?" somebody in the crowd yelled.

"Friends, I'm not here to take your money," Alvah said. "We just want—"

"Then how we going to pay for your stuff?"

"I'm coming to that. When two people want to trade, friends, there's usually a way. You want our products. We want metals—iron, aluminum, chromium—"

"Suppose a man ain't got any metal?"

"Well, sir, there are a lot of other things we can use beside metal. Natural fruits and vegetables, for instance."

The slack-faced yokel in the first row, the one with the basket under his arm, roused himself for the first time. His mouth closed, then opened again. *"What* kind?"

"Natural products, friend. You know, the kind your great-granddad ate. We use a lot every year for table delicacies, and—"

The yokel came halfway up the platform stair. His gnarled fingers dipped into the basket and came up with a smooth red-gold ovoid. He shoved it toward Alvah. "You mean," he said incredulously, "you wouldn' eat *that?*"

Gulping, Alvah backed away a step. The Muckfoot came after him. "Raise 'em myself," he said plaintively, holding out the red fruit. "I tell you, they're just the juiciest, goodest—Go ahead, try one."

"I'm not hungry," Alvah said desperately. "I'm on a diet. Now if you'll just step down quietly, friend, till after the—"

The Muckfoot stared at him, holding the fruit under Alvah's nose. "You mean, you won't *try* it?"

"No," said Alvah, trying not to breathe. "Now go on back down there, friend—don't crowd me."

"Well," said the Muckfoot, "then durn you!" And he shoved the disgusting thing squashily into Alvah's face.

Alvah saw red. Blinking away a glutinous film of juice and pulp, he glimpsed the yokel's face, spread into a hideous grin. Waves of laughter beat about his ears. Retching, he brought up his right fist in an instinctive round-house swing that clapped the yokel's grin shut and toppled him over the platform rail, basket, flying fruit and all.

The laughter rumbled away into expectant silence. Alvah fumbled in his kit for tissues, scrubbed a wad of them across his face and saw them come away daubed with streaky red. He hurled them convulsively into the crowd and, leaning over the rail, shouted thickly, "Lousy stinking filthy *Muckfeet!*"

Muckfoot men in the front ranks turned and looked at each other solemnly. Then two of them marched up the platform stair and, behind them, another two.

Still berserk, Alvah met the first couple with two violent kicks in the chest. This cleared the stair, but he turned to find three more candidates swarming over the rail. He swung at the nearest, who ducked. The next one seized Alvah's arm with both hands and toppled over backward. Alvah followed, head foremost, and landed with a jar that shook him to his toes.

The next thing he knew, he was lying on the ground surrounded by upward of twenty thick seamless boots, choking on dust, and getting the daylights methodically kicked out of him.

Alvah rolled over frantically, climbed the first leg that came to hand, got his back against the platform and, by dint of cracking skulls together, managed in two brisk minutes to clear a momentary space around him. Another dim figure lunged at him. Alvah clouted it under the ear, whirled and vaulted over the rail onto the platform.

His gun popped out into his hand.

For just a moment, he was standing alone, feeling the pistol grip clenched hard in his dirt-caked palm and able to judge exactly how long he had before half a dozen Muckfeet would swarm up the stair and over the rail. The crowd's faces were sharp and clear. He saw Artie and Doc Bither and Jake, his mouth open to howl, and he saw the girl, B. J., in a curious posture—leaning forward, her right arm thrust out and down. She had just thrown something at him.

Alvah saw the gray-white blur wobbling toward him. He tried to dodge, but the thing struck his shoulder and exploded with a papery pop. For a bewildering instant, the air was full of dancing bright particles. Then they were gone.

Alvah didn't have time to wonder about it. He thumbed the selector over to *Explosive,* pointed the gun straight up and squeezed the trigger.

Nothing happened.

There were two Muckfeet half over the rail and three more coming up the stair. Incredulous, still aiming at the air, Alvah tried again—and again. The gun didn't work.

Three Muckfeet were on the platform, four more right behind them. Alvah spun through the open door and slapped at the control button. The door stayed open.

The Muckfeet were massed in the doorway, staring in like visitors at an aquarium. Alvah dived at the power bar, shoved it over. The floater didn't lift.

"Holly! Luke!" called a clear voice outside, and the Muckfeet turned. "Leave him alone. He's got enough troubles now."

Alvah was pawing at the control board.

The lights didn't work.

The air-conditioner didn't work.

The scent-organ didn't work.

The musivox didn't work.

One of the Muckfeet put his head in the door. "Reckon he has," he said thoughtfully and went away again. Alvah heard his voice, more faintly. "You do something, B. J.?"

"Yes," said the girl, "I did something."

Moving warily, Alvah went outside. The girl was standing just below the platform, watching as the Muckfoot men filed down the stair.

"You!" he said to her.

She paid him no attention. "Just one of those things, Luke," she said.

Luke nodded solemnly. "Well, the Fair don't come but once a year." He and the other men moved past her into the crowd, each one acquiring a train of curiosity-seekers as he went. The crowd began to drift away.

A familiar voice yelped, "Ride'm out on a *razorback* is what I say!"

A chorus of "Now, Jake!" went up. There were murmurs of dissent, of inquiry, of explanation. "Time for the poultry judging!" somebody called, and the crowd moved faster.

Alvah went dazedly down and climbed into the run-about. He waggled its power bar. No response.

He tore open his kit and began frantically hauling out one glittery object after another, holding each for an instant and then throwing it on the ground. The razor, the heater, the vacuum cleaner, the sonotube, the vibro-masseur.

Swifty rode by, at ease atop his horse-lynx-camel-horror. He was whistling.

The crowd was almost gone. Among the stragglers was Jake, fists on his pudgy hips, his choleric cheeks gleaming with sweat and satisfaction.

"Well, Mister High-and-Mighty," he called, "what you going to do *now?*"

That was just what Alvah was wondering. He was about a thousand miles from home by air—probably more like fifteen hundred across-country. He had no transportation, no shelter, no power tools, no equipment. He had, he realized with horror, been cut off instantly from everything that made a man civilized.

What *was* he going to do?

V

Manager Wytak had his feet on the glossy desktop. So did the Comptroller, narrow-faced old Mr. Creedy; the Director of Information, plump Mr. Kling; the Commissioner of Supply, blotched and pimpled Mr. Jackson; and the porcine Mr. McArdle, Commissioner of War. With chairs tilted back, they stared through a haze of cigar smoke at each other's stolid faces mirrored on the ceiling.

Wytak's voice was as confident as ever, if a trifle muted, and when the others spoke, he listened. These were not the hired nonentities Alvah had seen; these were the men who had made Wytak, the electorate with whose consent he governed.

"Jack," said Wytak, "I want you to look at it my way and see if you don't think I'm right. It isn't a question of how long we can hold out—when you get right down and look at it, it's a question of *can we do anything.*"

"In time," said Jackson expressionlessly.

"In time. But if we can do anything, there'll be time enough. You say we've got troubles now and you're right, but I tell you we can pull through a situation a thousand times worse than this—*if* we've got an answer. And have we got an answer? We have."

Creedy grunted. "Like to see some results, Boley."

"You'll see them. You can't skim a yeast tank the first day, Will."

"You can see the bubbles, though," said Jackson sourly. "Any report from this Gustad today, while we're talking about it?"

"Not yet. He was getting some response yesterday. He's following it up. I trust that boy—the analyzers picked his card out of five million. Wait and see. He'll deliver."

"If you say so, Boley."

"I say so."

Jackson nodded. "That's good enough. Gentlemen?"

In another soundproof, spyproof office in Over Manhattan, Kling and McArdle met again twenty minutes later.

"What do you think?" asked Kling with his meaningless smile.

"Moderately good. I was hoping he would lie about Gustad's report, but of course there was very little chance of that. Wytak is an old hand."

"You admire him?" Kling suggested.

"As a specimen of his type. Wytak pulled us out of a very bad spot in '39."

"Agreed."

"And he has had his uses since then. There are times when brilliant improvisation is better than sound principles—and times when it is not. Wytak is an incurable romantic."

"And you?"

"We," said McArdle grimly, "are realists."

"Oh, yes. But perhaps we are not anything just yet. Creedy is interested, but not convinced—and until he moves, Jackson will do nothing."

"Wytak's project is a failure. You can't do business with the Muckfeet. But the fool was so confident that he didn't even interfere with Gustad's briefing."

Kling leaned forward with interest. "You didn't . . . ?"

"*No*. It wasn't necessary. But it means that Gustad has no instructions to fake successful reports—and that means Wytak can't stall until he gets back. There was no report today. Suppose there's none tomorrow, or the next day, or the next."

"In that case, of course . . . However, it's always as well to offer something positive. You said you might have something to show me today."

"Yes. Follow me."

In a sealed room at the end of a guarded corridor, five young men were sitting. They leaped to attention when Kling and McArdle entered.

"At ease," said McArdle. "This gentleman is going to ask you some questions. You may answer freely." He turned to Kling. "Go ahead—ask them anything."

123

Kling's eyebrows went up delicately, but he looked the young men over, selected one and said, "Your name?"

"Walter B. Limler, sir."

Kling looked mildly pained. "Please don't call me sir. Where do you live?"

"CFF Barracks, Tier Three, McCormick."

"CFF?" said Kling with a frown. "McCormick? I don't place the district. Where is it?"

The young man, who was blond and very earnest, allowed himself to show a slight surprise. "In the Loop," he said.

"And where is the Loop?"

The young man looked definitely startled. He glanced at McArdle, moistened his lips and said, "Well, right here, sir. In Chicago."

Kling's eyebrows went up and then down. He smiled. "I begin to see," he murmured to McArdle. "Very clever."

It cost Alvah two hours' labor, using tools that had never been designed to be operated manually, to get the inspection plate off the motor housing in the floater. He compared the intricate mechanism with the diagrams and photographs in the maintenance handbook. He looked for dust and grime; he checked the moving parts for play; he probed for dislodged wiring plates and corrosion. He did everything the handbook suggested, even spun the flywheel and was positive he felt the floater lift a fraction of an inch beneath him. As far as he could tell, there was absolutely nothing wrong, unless the trouble was in the core of the motor itself—the force-field that rotated the axle that made everything go.

The core casing had an "easily removable" segment, meaning to say that Alvah was able to get it off in three hours more.

Inside, there was no resistance to his cautious finger. The spool-shaped hollow space was empty.

Under *Motor Force-field Inoperative* the manual said simply: *Remove and replace rhodopalladium nodules.*

Alvah looked. He found the tiny sockets where the nodules ought to be, one in the flanged axle-head, the other facing it at the opposite end of the chamber. The nodules were not there.

Alvah went into the storage chamber. Ignoring the increasingly forceful protests of his empty stomach, he spent a furious twenty minutes locating the spare nodules. He stripped the seal off the box and lifted the lid with great care.

There were the nodules. And there, appearing out of nowhere, was a whirling cloud of brightness that settled briefly in the box and then went back where it came from. And there the nodules weren't.

Alvah stared at the empty box. He poked his forefinger into the cushioned niches, one after the other. Then he set the box down with care, about-faced, walked outside to the platform and sat down on the top step with his chin on his fists.

"You look peaked," said B. J.'s firm voice.

Alvah looked up at her briefly. "Go away."

"Had anything to eat today?" the girl asked.

Alvah did not reply.

"Don't sulk," she said. "You've got a problem. We feel responsible. Maybe there's something we can do to help."

Alvah stood up slowly. He looked her over carefully, from top to bottom and back again. "There is one thing you could do for me," he said. "Smile."

"Why?" she asked cagily.

"I wanted to see your fangs." He turned wearily and went into the floater.

He puttered around for a few minutes, then got cold rations out of the storage chamber and sat down in the control chair to eat them. But the place was odious to him with its gleaming, useless array of gadgetry, and he went outside again and sat down with his back to the hull near the doorway. The girl was still there, looking up at him.

"Look," she said, "I'm sorry about this."

The nutloaf went down his gullet in one solid lump and hit his stomach like a stone. "Please don't mention it," he said bitterly. "It was really nothing at all."

"I had to do it. You might have killed somebody."

Alvah tried another bite. Chewing the stuff, at any rate,

gave him something to do. "What *were* those things?" he demanded.

"Metallophage," she said. "They eat metals in the platinum family. Hard to get them that selective—we weren't exactly sure what would happen."

Alvah put down the remnant of nutloaf slowly. "Who's 'we'? You and Bither?"

"Mostly."

"And you—you bred those things to eat rhodopalladium?"

She nodded.

"Then you must have some to feed them," said Alvah logically. He stood up and gripped the railing. "Give it to me."

She hesitated. "There might be some—"

"*Might* be? There *must* be!"

"You don't understand. They don't actually eat the metal—not for nourishment, that is."

"Then what do they do with it?"

"They build nests," she told him. "But come over to the lab and we'll see."

At the laboratory door, they were still arguing. "For the last time," said Alvah. "I will not come in. I've just eaten half a nutcake and I haven't got food to waste. Get the stuff and bring it out."

"For the last time," said B. J., "get it out of your head that what you want is all that counts. If you want me to look for the metal, you'll come in, and that's flat."

They glared at each other. Well, he told himself resignedly, he hadn't wanted that nutloaf much in the first place.

They followed the same route, past the things that chirruped, croaked, rumbled, rustled. The main thing, he recalled, was to keep your mind off it.

"Tell me something," he said to her trim back. "If I hadn't got myself mixed up with that farmer and his market basket, do you still think I wouldn't have sold anything?"

"That's right."

"Well, why not? Why all this resistance to machinery? Is it a taboo of some kind?"

She said nothing for a moment.

"Is it because you're afraid the Cities will get a hold on you?" Alvah insisted. "Because that's foolish. Our interests are really the same as yours. We don't just want to sell you stuff—we want to help you help yourselves. The more prosperous you get, the better for us."

"It's not that," she said.

"Well, what then? It's been bothering me. You've got all these raw materials, all this land. You wouldn't have to wait for us—you could have built your own factories, made your own machines. But you never have. I can't understand why."

"It's not worth the trouble."

He choked. "*Anything* is worth the trouble, if it helps you do the same work more efficiently, more intel—"

"Wait a minute." She stopped a woman who was passing in the aisle between the cages. "Marge, where's Doc?"

"Down in roundworms, I think."

"Tell him I have to see him, will you? It's urgent. We'll wait in here." She led the way into a windowless room, as small and cluttered as any Alvah had seen.

"Now," she said. "We don't make a fuss about machines because most people simply haven't any need for them."

"That's ridiculous," Alvah argued. "You may think—"

"Be quiet and let me finish. We haven't got centralized industries or power installations. Why do you think the Cities have never beaten us in a war, as often as they've tried? Why do you think we've taken over the whole world, except for twenty-two Cities? You've got to face this sooner or later—in every single respect, *our plants and animals are more efficient than any machine you could build.*"

Alvah inspected her closely. Her eyes were intent and brilliant. Her bosom indicated deep and steady breathing. To all appearance, she was perfectly serious.

"Nuts," he replied with dignity.

B. J. shook her head impatiently. "I know you've got a brain. Use it. What's the most expensive item that goes into a machine?"

"Metal. We're a little short of it, to tell the truth."

"Think again. What are all your gadgets supposed to save?"

"Well, labor."

"Human labor. If metal is expensive, it's because it costs a lot of man-hours."

"If you want to look at it that way—"

"It's true, isn't it? Why is a complicated thing more expensive than a simple one? More man-hours to make it. Why is a rare thing more expensive than a common one? More man-hours to find it. Why is a—"

"All right, what's your point?"

"Take your runabout. You saw that was the thing that interested people most, but I'll show you why you never could have sold one. How many man-hours went into manufacturing it?"

Alvah shifted restlessly. "It isn't in production. It's a trade item."

She sniffed. "Suppose it was in production. Make an honest guess. Figure in everything—amortization on the plant and equipment, materials, labor and so on. You can check your answer against wages and prices in your own money—you'll come pretty close."

Alvah reflected. "Between seven-fifty and a thousand."

"Compare that with Swifty's Morgan Gamma—the thing you raced against. Two man-hours—just two, and I'm being generous."

"Interesting," said Alvah, "if true." He suppressed an uneasy belch.

"Figure it out. An hour for the vet when he was foaled. Call it another hour for amortization on the stable where it happened, but that's too much. It isn't hard to grow a stable and they last a long time."

Alvah, who had been holding his own as long as machines were the topic, wasn't sure he could keep it up—or, more correctly, down. "All right, two hours," he said. "The animals feed themselves and water themselves, no doubt."

"They do, but that comes under upkeep. Our animals forage, most of them—all the big ones. The rest are cheap and easy to feed. Your machines have to be fueled. Our animals repair themselves, like any living organism, only better and faster. Your machines have to be repaired and serviced. More man-hours. Incidentally, if you and Swifty took a ten-hour trip, you in your runabout, him on his Morgan, you'd spend just ten hours steering. Swifty would spend maybe fifteen minutes all told. And now we come to the payoff—"

"Some other time," said Alvah irritably.

"This is important. When your runabout—"

"I'd rather not talk about it any more," said Alvah, raising his voice. "Do you *mind?*"

"When your runabout breaks down and can't be fixed," she said firmly, "you have to buy another. Swifty's mare drops twins every year. There. Think about it."

The door opened and Bither came in, looking more disheveled than ever. "Hello, Beej, Alvah. Beej, I think we shoulda used annelid stock for this job. These F_3 batches no good at—you two arguing?"

Alvah recovered himself with an effort. "Rhodopalladium," he said thickly. "I need about a gram. Have you got it?"

"Not a scrap," said Bither cheerfully. "Except in the nests, of course."

"I told him I didn't think so," B. J. said.

Alvah closed his eyes for a second. "Where," he asked carefully, "are the nests?"

"Wish I knew," Bither admitted. "It's frustrating as hell. You see, we had to make them awful small and quick, the metallophage. Once you let them out of the sacs, there's no holding them. We did so good a job, we can't check to see how good a job we did." He rubbed his chin thoughtfully. "Of course, that's beside the point. Even if we had the metals, how would you get the alloy you need?"

"Palladium," said the girl, "melts at fifteen fifty-three Centigrade. I asked the handbird."

"Best we can get out of a salamander is about six hundred," Bither added. "Isn't good for them, either—they get esophagitis."

"And necrosis," the girl said, watching Alvah intently.

His eyes were watering. It was hard to see. "Are you telling—"

"We're trying to tell you," she said, "that you can't go back. You've got to start getting used to the idea. There isn't a thing you can do except settle down here and learn to live with us."

Alvah could feel his jaw working, but no words were

coming out. The bulge of nausea in his middle was squeezing its way inexorably upward.

Somebody grabbed his arm. "In there!" said Bither urgently.

A door opened and closed behind him, and he found himself facing a hideous white-porcelain antique with a pool of water in it. There was a roaring in his ears, but before the first spasm took him, he could hear the girl's and Bither's voices faintly from the outer room:

"Eight minutes that time."

"Beej, I don't know."

"We can *do* it!"

"Well, I suppose we can, but can we do it before he starves?"

There was a sink in the room, but Alvah would sooner have drunk poison. He fumbled in his disordered kit until he found a condenser canteen. He rinsed out his mouth, took a tonus capsule and a mint lozenge. He opened the door.

"Feeling better?" asked the girl.

Alvah stared at her, retched feebly and fled back into the washroom.

When he came out again, Bither said, "He's had enough, Beej. Let's take him out in the courtyard till he gets his strength back."

They moved toward him. Alvah said weakly, but with feeling, "Keep your itchy hands off me." He walked unsteadily past them, turned when he reached the doorway. "I hate to urp and run, but I'll never forget your hospitality. If there's ever anything I can do for you—anything at all—please hesitate to call on me."

He heard muttering voices and an odd scraping sound behind him, but he didn't look back. He was halfway down the aisle between the cages when something furry and gray scuttled into view and sat up, grinning at him.

It looked like an ordinary capuchin monkey except for its head, which was grotesquely large. "Go away," said Alvah. He advanced with threatening gestures. The thing chattered at him and stayed where it was.

The aisle behind him was deserted. Very well, there were other exits. Alvah followed his nose back into the plant section and turned right.

There was the monkey-thing again.

At the next intersection of aisles, there were two of them. Alvah turned left.

And right.

And left.

And emerged into a large empty space enclosed by buildings.

"This is the courtyard," said Bither, coming forward with the girl behind him. "Now be reasonable, Alvah. You want to get back to New York, don't you?"

This did not seem to call for comment. Alvah stared at him in silence.

"Well," said Bither, "there's just one way you can do it. It won't be easy—I don't even say you got more than a fighting chance. One thing, though—it's up to you just how hard you make it for yourself."

"Get to the point," Alvah said.

"You got to let us decondition you so you can eat our food, ride on our animals. Now *think* about it, don't just—"

Alvah swung around, looking for the fastest and most direct exit. Before he had time to find it, a dizzying thought struck him and he turned back.

"Is that what this whole thing has been about?" he said. He glared at Bither, then at B. J. "Is that the reason you were so helpful? *Did you engineer that fight?*"

Bither clucked unhappily. "Would we admit it if we did? Alvah, I'll admit this much—of course we interested in you for our own reasons. This is the first time in thirty years we had a chance to study a City man. But what I just told you is true. If you want to get back home, this is your only chance."

"Then I'm a dead man," said Alvah.

"You is if you think you is," Bither told him. "Beej, you try."

She looked at Alvah levelly. "You think what we suggesting isn't possible. Right?"

"Discounting Doc's grammar," Alvah said sourly, "that's exactly what I'm thinking."

She said, "Doc's grammar is all right—yours is sixty years out of date. But I guess you already realize that your people are backward compared to us."

131

Half angry, half curious, Alvah demanded, "Just how do you figure that?"

"Easy. You probably don't know much biology, but you must know this much. What's the one quality that makes human beings the dominant race on this planet?"

Alvah snorted. "Are you trying to tell me I'm not as bright as a Muckfoot?"

"Not intelligence. Try again. Something more general —intelligence is only a special phase of it."

Alvah's patience was narrowing to a thin and brittle thread. *"You* tell *me."*

"All right. We like to think intelligence is important, but you can't argue that way. It's special pleading—the way a whale might argue that size is the measuring stick, or a microbe might say numbers. But—"

"Control of environment," Alvah said.

"Right. Another name for it is adaptability. No other organism is so independent of environment, so adaptable as Man. And we could live in New York if we had to, just as we can live in the Arctic Circle or the tropics. And, since you don't dare even try to live here . . ."

"All right," Alvah said bitterly. "When do we start?"

VI

He refused to be hypnotized.

"You promised to help," B. J. said in annoyance. "We can't break the conditioning till we find out how it was done, you big oaf!"

"The whole thing is ridiculous anyhow," Alvah pointed out. "I said I'd let you try and I will—you can prod me around to your heart's content—but not that. I've put in a lot of Required Contribution time in restricted laboratories. Military secrets. How do I know you wouldn't ask me about those if you got me under?"

"We're not *interested* in—" B. J. began furiously, but Bither cut her off.

"We is, though, Beej. Might be important for us to know what kind of defenses New York has built up, and I going to ask him if I got the chance." He sighed. "Well, there other ways to skin a glovebeast. Lean back and relax, Alvah."

"No tricks?" Alvah asked suspiciously.

"No, we just going to try to improve your conscious recall. Relax now; close your eyes. Now think of a room, one that's familiar to you, and describe it to me. Take your time . . . Now we going further back—further back. You three years old and you just dropped something on the floor. What is it?"

Bither seemed to know what he was doing, Alvah had to admit. Day after day they dredged up bits and scraps of memory from his childhood, events he had forgotten so completely that he would almost have sworn they had never happened. At first, all of them seemed trivial and irrelevant, but even so, Alvah found, there was an unexpected fascination in the search through the dusty attics of his mind. Once they hit something that made Bither sit up sharply—a dark figure holding something furry, and an accompanying remembered stench.

Whether or not it had been as important as Bither seemed to think, they never got it back again. But they did get other things—an obscene couplet about the Muck-feet that had been popular in P. S. 9073 when Alvah was ten; a scene from a realie feature called *Nix on the Stix;* a whispered horror story; a frightening stereo picture in a magazine.

"What we have to do," B. J. told him at one point, "is to make you realize that none of this was your own idea. They *made* you feel this way. They did it to you."

"Well, I know that," said Alvah.

She stared at him in astonishment. "You knew it all along—and you don't care?"

"No." Alvah felt puzzled and irritated. "Why should I?"

"Don't you think they should have let you make up your own mind?"

Alvah considered this. "You have to make your children see things the way you do, otherwise there wouldn't be any continuity from one generation to the next. You couldn't keep any kind of civilization going. Where would we be if we let people wander off into the Sticks and become Muckfeet?"

He finished triumphantly, but she didn't react properly. She merely grinned with an exasperating air of satisfaction and said, "Why should they want to—unless we can give them a better life than the Cities can?"

This was absurd, but Alvah couldn't find the one answer that would flatten her, no matter how long and often he mulled it over. Meanwhile, his tolerance of Muckfoot dwellings progressed from ten minutes to thirty, to an hour, to a full day. He didn't like it and nothing, he knew, could ever make him like it, but he could stand it. He was able to ride for short distances on Muckfoot animals, and he was even training himself to wear an animal-hide belt for longer and longer periods each day. But he still couldn't eat Muckfoot food—the bare thought of it still nauseated him—and his own supplies were running short.

Oddly, he didn't feel as anxious about it as he should have. He could sense the resistance within him softening

134

day by day. He was irrationally sure that that last obstacle would go, too, when the time came. Something else was bothering him, something he couldn't even name—but he dreamed of it at night and its symbol was the threatening vast arch of the sky.

After the Fair was over, it seemed that B. J. had very little work to do. As far as Alvah could make out, the same was true for everybody. The settlement grew mortuary-still. For an hour or so every morning, lackadaisical trading went on in the central market place. In the evenings, sometimes, there was music of a sort and a species of complicated ungainly folk-dancing. The rest of the time, children raced through the streets and across the pastures, playing incomprehensible games. Their elders, when they were visible, sat—on doorsteps by ones and twos, grouped on porches and lawns—their hands busy, oftener than not, with some trifle of carving or needlework, but their faces as blank and sleepy as a frog's in the sun.

"What do you do for excitement around here?" he asked B. J. in a dither of boredom.

She looked at him oddly. "We work. We make things, or watch things grow. But maybe that's not the kind of excitement you mean."

"It isn't, but let it go."

"Our simple pleasures probably wouldn't interest you," she said reflectively. "They're pretty dull. We dance, go riding, swim in the lake . . ."

So they swam.

It wasn't bad. It was unsettling to have no place to swim *to*—you had to head out from the shore, gauging your distance, and then turn around to go back—but the lake, to Alvah's considerable surprise, was clearer and better-tasting than any pool he'd ever been in.

Lying on the grass afterward was a novel sensation, too. It was comfortable—no, it was nothing of the sort; the grass blades prickled and the ground was lumpy. Not comfortable, but—comforting. It was the weight, he thought lazily, the massive mother-weight of the whole Earth cradling you—the endless slow pendulum-swing you felt when you closed your eyes.

He sat up, feeling cheerfully torpid. B. J. was lying on her back beside him, eyes shut, one arm flung back behind her head. It was a graceful pose. In a detached way, he admired it, first in general and then in particular—the fine texture of her skin, the firmness of her bosom under the halter that half-covered it, the delicate tint of her closed eyelids—the catalogue prolonged itself, and he realized that B. J., when you got a good look at her, was a uniquely lovely girl. He wondered, in passing, how he had missed noticing it before.

She opened her eyes and looked at him. There was a groundswell of some sort and, without particular surprise, Alvah found himself leaning over and kissing her.

"Beej," he said sometime later, "when I go back to New York—I don't suppose you'd want to come with me? I mean—you're different from the others. You're educated, you can read; even your grammar is good."

"I know you mean it as a compliment and I'm doing my best not to sound ungrateful or hurt your feelings, but . . ." She made a frustrated gesture. "Take the reading—that's a hobby of Doc's and I picked it up from him. It's a primitive skill, Alvah, something like manuscript illuminating. We have better ways now. We don't *need* it any more. Then the grammar—didn't it ever strike you that I might be using your kind just to make things easier for you?"

She frowned. "I guess that was a mistake. As of now, I quit. No, listen a minute! The only difference between your grammar and ours is that yours is sixty years out of date. You still use 'I am, you are, he is' and all that archaic nonsense of tenses, case and number. What for? If that's good, suppose we hunted up somebody who said 'I am, thou art, he is,' would his grammar be better than yours?"

"Well—" said Alvah.

"And about New York, I appreciate that. But the Cities are done for, Alvah. In ten years there won't be one left. They're *finished*."

Alvah stiffened. "That's the most ridiculous—"

"*Is* it? Then why you here?"

"Well, we're in a crisis period now, but we've come through them before. You can't—"

"This *crisis* of yours started a long while ago. If I remember, it was around 1927 that Muller first changed the genes in fruit flies with X-ray bombardment. That was the first step—over a hundred years before you was even born. Then came colchicine and the electron microscope and microsurgery, all in the next thirty years. But the day biological engineering really grew up—1962, Jenkins' and Scripture's gene charts and techniques—the Cities began to go. Little by little, people drifted out to the land again, raising the new crops, growing the new animals.

"The big Cities cannibalized the little ones, like an insect eating its own body when its food supply runs out. Now that's gone as far as it can, and you think it's just another crisis, but it isn't. It's the end."

Alvah heard a chill echo of Wytak's words: *"Rome fell. Babylon fell. The same thing can happen to New York . . ."*

He said, "What am I supposed to be, the rat that leaves the sinking ship?"

She sighed. "Alvah, you got a better brain than that. You don't *have* to think in metaphors or slogans, like a moron. I'm not asking you to join the winning side. That doesn't *matter*. In a few years there won't be but one side, no matter which way you jump."

"What do you want then?" he asked.

She looked dispirited. "Nothing, I guess. Let's go home."

It was a series of little things after that. There was the time he and Beej, out walking in the cool of the morning, stopped to rest at an isolated house that turned out to be occupied by George Allister of the Coffin clan, the shy little man who'd tried to show Alvah how to make his marks the day he landed.

George, Alvah believed—and questioning of Beej afterward confirmed it—was about as low on the social scale as a Muckfoot could get. But he was his own master. He had a wife and three children and neat fields, with his own animals grazing in them. His house was big and cool and clean. He poured them lemonade—which Alvah wistfully had to decline—from a sweating peacock-blue pitcher, while sitting at his ease on the broad front porch.

There were no servants among the Muckfeet. Alvah remembered an ancient fear of his, something that had cropped up in the old days every time he got seriously interested in a girl—that his children, if any, might relapse into the labor-pool category from which he had risen, or—it was hard to say which would be worse—into the servants' estate.

He went back from that outing very silent and thoughtful.

There was the time, a few days later, when Beej was working, and Alvah, at loose ends, wandered into a room in the laboratory building where two of Bither's assistants, girls he knew by sight, were sitting with two large, leathery-woody, pod-shaped boxes open on the bench between them.

Being hungry for company and preoccupied with himself at the same time, he didn't notice what should have been obvious, that the girls were busy at something private and personal. Even when they closed the boxes between them, he wasn't warned. "What's this?" he said cheerfully. "Can I see?"

They glanced at each other uncertainly. "These is our bride boxes," said the brunette. "We don't usual show them to singletons—"

They exchanged another glance.

"He's spoke for anyhow," said the redhead, with an enigmatic look at Alvah.

They opened the boxes. Inside each was a multitude of tiny compartments, each with a bit of something wrapped in cloth or paper tissue. The brunette chose one of the largest and unwrapped it with exaggerated care— an amorphous reddish-brown lump.

"Houseplant," she said, and wrapped it up again.

The redhead showed him a vial full of minuscule white spheres. "Weaver eggs. Two hundred of them. That's a lot, but I like more curtains and things than most."

"Wait a minute," said Alvah, perplexed. "What does a houseplant do?"

"Grow a house, of course," the brunette said. She held up another vial full of eggs. "Scavengers."

The redhead had a translucent sac with dark specks in it. "Utility trees."

138

"Garbage converter."

"This grows into a bed and these is chairbushes."

And so on, interminably, while the girls' eyes glittered and their cheeks flushed with enthusiasm.

The boxes, Alvah gathered, contained the germs of everything that would be needed to set up a Muckfoot household—beginning with the house itself. A thought struck him: "Does Beej have one of these outfits?"

Wide-eyed stares from both girls. "Well, of course!"

Alvah shifted uncomfortably. "Funny, she never mentioned it."

The girls exchanged another of those enigmatic glances and said nothing. Alvah, for some reason, grew more uncomfortable still. He tried once more. "What about the man—doesn't he have to put up anything?"

Yes, the man was expected to supply all the brutes and the seeds for outbuildings and all the crops except the bride's kitchen-garden. Everything in and around the home was her province, everything outside was his.

"Oh," said Alvah.

"But if a young fellow don't have all that through no fault of his own, his clan put up for him and let him pay back when he able."

"Ah," said Alvah, and turned to make his escape.

The redhead called after him, "You thought any about what clan you like to get adopted into, Alvah?"

"Uh, no," said Alvah. "I don't think—"

"You talk to Doc Bither. He a elder of the Steins. Mighty good clan!"

Alvah bolted.

Then there was the Shakespeare business. It began in his third week in the Sticks, when he was already carrying a fleshy Muckfoot vegetable around with him—a radnip, B. J. called it. He hadn't had the nerve yet to bite into it, but he knew the time was coming when he would. Beej came to him and said, "Alvah, the Rinaldos' drama group is doing *Hamlet* next Saturday, and they're short a Polonius. Do you think you could study it up by then?"

"What's Hamlet? And who's Polonius?"

She got the bird out of the library for him and he listened to the play, which turned out to be an archaic version of *The Manager of Copenhagen*. The text was nothing like the modernized abridgment he was used to, or the Muckfeet's slovenly speech either. It was full of words like *down-gyved* and *unkennel*. It was three-quarters incomprehensible until he began to get the hang of it, but it had a curious power. *For who would bear the whips and scorns of time, the oppressor's wrong, the proud man's contumely, the pangs of despised love,* and so on and so on. It rumbled, but it rumbled well.

Polonius, however, was the character Alvah knew as Paul Arnson, an inconsequential old man who only existed in the play to foul up the love affair between the principals and got killed in the third act. Alvah ventured to suggest that he might be of more use as Hamlet, but the director, a dry little man with a surprising boom to his voice, stubbornly insisted that all he needed was a Polonius—and seemed to intimate, without actually saying so, that Alvah was a dim prospect even for that.

Alvah, with blood in his eye, accepted the part.

The rehearsals were a nightmare. The lines themselves gave him no trouble—Alvah was a quick study; in the realies, you had to be—and neither, at first, did the rustic crudity of the stage he was asked to perform on. Letter-perfect when the other actors were still stuttering and blowing their lines, he walked through the part with quiet competence and put the director's sour looks down to a witless hayseed hostility—until, three days before the performance, he suddenly awoke to the realization that everyone else in the cast was acting rings around him.

This wasn't the realies. There were no microphones to amplify his voice, no cameras to record every change in his expression. And the audience, what there was of it, was going to be *right—out—there.*

Alvah went to pieces. Trying to emulate the others' wide gestures and declamatory delivery only threw him further off his stride. He had never had stage-fright in his life, but by curtain time on Saturday night, he was a pale and quivering wreck.

Dead and dragged off the stage at the end of act three, he got listlessly back into his own clothes and headed for an inconspicuous exit, but the director waylaid him. "Gustad," he said abruptly, "you ever thought of yourself as a professional actor?"

"I had some such idea at one time," Alvah said. "Why?"

"Well, I don't see why you shouldn't. If you work at it. I never see a man pick up so fast."

"What?" cried Alvah, thunderstruck.

"You wasn't bad," said the director. "A few rough edges, but a good performance. Now I happen to know some people in a few repertory companies—the Mondrillo Troupe, the Kalfoglou Repertory, one or two more. If you interested, I'll bird them and see if there's an opening. Don't thank me, don't thank me." He moved off a few steps, then turned. "Oh, and, Gustad—get back into your costume, will you?"

"Uh," said Alvah. "But I'm dead. I mean—"

"For the curtain calls," said the director. "You don't want to miss those." He waved and walked back into the wings.

Alvah absently drew out his radnip and crunched off a bite of it. The taste was faintly unpleasant, like that of old protein paste or the wrong variety of culture-cheese, but he chewed and swallowed it.

That was when he realized that he had to get out. He didn't put on his costume again. Instead, he rummaged through the property boxes until he found an old pair of moleskin trousers and a stained squareweb shirt. He put them on, left by the rear door and headed south.

South for two reasons. First, because, he hoped, no one would look for him in that direction. Second, because he remembered what Beej had said that first day when they passed the display of tools: *"The metal comes from Iron Pits, just a few miles south of here."*

There might be some slender chance still that he could get the metal he needed, delouse the floater and go home in style—without the painful necessity of explaining to Wytak what had happened to the floater and all his goods and equipment. If not, he would simply keep on walking.

He had to do it now. He had almost waited too long as it was.

They had laid out the pattern of a life for him—to marry Beej, settle down in a house that would grow from a seed Beej kept in a pod-shaped box, be a rustic repertory actor, raise little Muckfeet. And the devil of it was, some unreasonable part of him wanted all of that!

A good thing he hadn't stayed for the curtain calls . . .

The sun declined as he went, until he was walking down a ghost-dim road under the stars, with all the cool cricket-shrill world to himself.

He spent the night uncomfortably huddled under a hedge. Birds woke him with a great clamor in the tree-tops shortly after dawn. He washed himself and drank from a stream that crossed the fields, ate a purplish-red fruit he found growing nearby, then moved on.

Two hours later, he topped a ridge and found his way barred by a miles-long shallow depression in the earth. Like the rest of the visible landscape, it was filled with an orderly checkerwork of growing plants.

There was nothing for it but to go through if he could. But surely he had gone more than "a few miles" by now?

The road slanted down the embankment to a gate in a high thorn hedge. Behind the gate was a kind of miniature domed kiosk, and in the kiosk a sunburned man was dozing with a green-and-purple bird on his shoulder.

Alvah inspected a signboard that was entangled somehow in the hedge next to the gate. He was familiar enough by now with the Muckfeet's picture-writing to be fairly sure of what it said. The first symbol was a nail with an ax-head attached to it. That was *iron*. The second was a few stylized things that resembled fruit seeds. *Pits?*

He stared through the gate in mounting perplexity. You might call a place like this "Pits," all right, but imagination boggled at calling it a mine. Still . . .

The kiosk, he noticed now, bore a scrawled symbol in orange pigment. He recognized that one, too; it was one of the common name-signs.

"Jerry!" he called.

"*Rrk,*" remarked the bird on the sleeping man's shoulder. "Kerry brogue; but the degradation of speech that occurs in London, Glasgow—"

"Oh, damn!" said Alvah. "You, there. *Jerry!*"

"*Rrk.* Kerry brogue; but the—"

"Jerry!"

"*Kerry brogue!*" shrieked the bird. The sunburned man

sat up with a start and seized it by the beak, choking it off in the middle of *"degradation."*

"Oh, hello," he said. "Don't know what it is about a Shaw bird, but they all alike. Can't shut them up."

"I'd like," said Alvah, "to look through the—uh—Pits. Would that be all right?"

"Sure," the man said cheerfully. He opened the gate and led the way down a long avenue between foot-high rows of plants.

"I Jerry Finch," he said. "Littleton clan. Don't believe you said your name."

"Harris," Alvah said at random. "I visiting from up north."

"Yukes?" the man inquired.

Alvah nodded, hoping for the best, and pointed at the plants they were passing. "What these?"

"Hinge blanks. Let them to forage last month. Won't have another crop here till August, and a poor one then. I tell Angus—he's the Pit boss—I tell him this soil's wore out, but he a pincher—squeeze the last ton out and then go after the pounds and ounces. You should of saw what come off the ringbushes in the east hundred this April. Pitiful. Had to sell them for eyelets."

A cold feeling was running up Alvah's spine. He cleared his throat. "Got any knife blades?" he inquired with careful casualness.

"Mean bowies? Well, sure—right over yonder."

Alvah followed him to the end of the field and down three steps into the next. The plants here were much taller and darker, with stems thick and gnarled out of all proportion to their height. Here and there among the glossy leaves were incongruous glints of silvery steel.

Alvah stooped and peered into the foliage.

The silvery glints were perfectly formed six-inch chrome-steel knife blades. Each was attached to—*growing* from—the plant by way of a hard brown stem, exactly the right size and shape to serve as a handle.

He straightened carefully. "We do things a little different up north. You mind explaining briefly how the Pits works?"

Jerry looked surprised, but began readily enough. "These like any other ferropositors. They extract the metal from the ores and deposit it in the bowie shape, or whatever it might be. Work from the outside in, of course, so you don't have no wood core to weaken it. We get a year's crops, average, before the ore used up. Then we bring the earth-movers in, deepen the Pit a few feet, reseed and start over. Ain't much more to it."

Alvah stared at the fantastic growths. Well, why not? Plants that grew into knives or doorknobs or . . .

"What about alloys?" he asked.

"We got iron, lead and zinc. Carbon from the air. Other metals we got to import in granules. Like we get chrome from the Northwest Federation, mostly. They getting too big for their britches, though. Greedy. I think we going to switch over to you Yukes before long. Not that you fellows is any better, if you ask me, but at least—"

"Rhodium," said Alvah. "Palladium. What about them?"

"How that?"

"Platinum group."

"Oh, sure, I know what you mean. We never use them. No call to. We could get you some, I guess—I think the Northwests got them. Take a few months, though."

"Suppose you wanted to make something out of a rhodopalladium alloy. How long would it take after you got the metals?"

"Well, you have to make a bush that would take and put them together, right proportions, right size, right shape. Depends. I guess if you was in a hurry—"

"Never mind," said Alvah wearily. "Thanks for the information." He turned and started back toward the gate. When he was halfway there, he heard a hullabaloo break out somewhere behind him.

"Waw!" the voices seemed to be shouting. *"Waw! Waw!"*

He turned. A dozen paces behind him, Jerry and the bird on his shoulder were in identical neck-straining attitudes. Beyond them, on the near side of a group of low buildings three hundred yards away, three men were waving their arms madly and shouting, *"Waw! Waw!"*

"Wawnt to know what it is," the bird squawked. "I wawnt to be a Mahn. Violet: you come along with me, to your own—"

144

"Shut up," said Jerry, then cupped his hands and yelled, "Angus, what is it?"

"Chicagos," the answer drifted back. "Just got word! They dusting Red Pits! Come *on!*"

Jerry darted a glance over his shoulder. "Come *on!*" he repeated and broke into a loping run toward the buildings.

Alvah hesitated an instant, then followed. With strenuous effort, he managed to catch up to the other man. "Where are we running to?" he panted. "Red Pits?"

"Don't talk foolish," Jerry gasped. "We running to shelter." He glanced back the way they had come. "Red Pits over that way."

Alvah risked a look and then another. The first time, he wasn't sure. The second time, the dusting of tiny particles over the horizon had grown to a cluster of visibly swelling black dots.

Other running figures were converging on the buildings as Angus and Jerry approached. The dots were capsule shapes, perceptibly elongated, the size of a fingernail, a thumbnail, a thumb . . .

And under them on the land was a hurtling streak of golden-dun haze, like dust stirred by a huge invisible finger.

Rounding the corner of the nearest building, Jerry popped through an open doorway. Alvah followed—

And was promptly seized from either side, long enough for something heavy and hard to hit him savagely on the nape of the neck.

VII

Bither was intent over a shallow vessel half full of a viscous clear liquid, with a great rounded veined-and-patterned glistening lump immersed in it, transparent in the phosphor-light that glowed from the sides of the container—a single living cell in mitosis, so grossly enlarged that every gene of every paired chromosome was visible. B. J. watched from the other side of the table, silent, breathing carefully, as the man's thick fingers dipped a hair-thin probe with minuscule precision, again and again, into the yeasty mass, excising a particle, splitting another, delicately shaving a third.

From time to time, she glanced at a sheet of horn intricately inscribed with numbers and genetic symbols. The chart was there for her benefit, not for Bither's—he never paused or faltered.

Finally, he sat back and covered the pan. "Turn on the lights and put that in the reduction fluid, will you, Beej? I bushed."

She whistled a clear note, and the dark globes fixed to the ceiling glowed to blue-white life. "You going to grow it right away?"

"Have to, I guess. Dammit, Beej, I hate making weapons."

"Not our choice. When you think it be?"

He shrugged. "War meeting this afternoon over at Council Flats. They let us know when it be."

She was silent until she had transferred the living lump from one container to another and put it away. Then, "Hear anything more?"

"They dusting every ore-bed from here to the Illinois, look like. Crystal, Butler's—"

"*Butler's!* That worked out."

146

"I know it. We let them land there. They find out."
After another pause, Bither said, "No word about Alvah, Beej. I sorry."

She nodded. "Wouldn't be, this early."

He looked at her curiously. "You still think he be back?"

"If the dust ain't got him. Lay you odds."

"Well," said Bither, lifting the cover of another pan to peer into it, "I hope you—"

"Ozark Lake nine-one-two-five," said a reedy voice from the corner. "Ozark Lake nine—"

"Get that, will you, Beej?"

B. J. picked up the ocher spheroid from its shelf and said into its tympanum, "Bither Laboratories."

"This Angus Littleton at Iron Pits," the thing said. "Let me talk to Bither."

She passed it over, holding a loop of its rubbery cord —the beginning of a miles-long sheathed bundle of cultivated neurons that linked it, via a "switchboard" organism, with thousands like it in this area alone, and with millions more across the continent.

"This Doc Bither. What is it, Angus?"

"Something funny for you, Doc. We got a couple prisoners here, one a floater pilot, other a Chicago spy."

"Well, what you want me to—"

"*Wait*, can't you? This spy claim he know you, Doc. Say his name Custard. Alvah Custard."

Alvah stared out through the window, puzzled and angry. He had been in the room for about half an hour, while things were going on outside. He had tried to break the window. The pane had bent slightly. It was neither glass nor plastic, and it wasn't breakable.

Outside, the last of the invading floaters was dipping down toward the horizon, pursued by a small darting black shape. Golden-dun haze obscured all the foreground except the first few rows of plants, which were drooping on their stems. The squadron had made one grand circle of the mine area, dusting as they went, before the Muckfeet on their incredibly swift flyers—birds or reptiles, Alvah couldn't tell which—had risen to engage them. Since then, a light breeze from the north had carried the stuff dropped over the Pits: radioactive dust with a gravitostatic charge to make it rebound and spread—and then, with its polarity reversed, cling like grim death where it fell.

He turned and looked at the other man, sitting blank-faced and inattentive, wearing a rumpled sky-blue uniform, on the bench against the inner wall. Most of the squadron had flown off to the west after that first pass, and had either escaped or been forced down somewhere beyond the Pits. This fellow had crash-landed in the fields not five hundred yards from Alvah's window. Alvah had seen the Muckfeet walking out to the wreck—strolling fantastically through the deadly haze—and turkey-trotting their prisoner back again. A little later, someone had opened the door and shoved the man in, and there he had sat ever since.

His skin-color was all right. He was breathing evenly and seemed in no discomfort. As far as Alvah could see, there was not a speck of the death-dust anywhere on his skin, hair or clothing. But mad as it was, this was not the most incongruous thing about him.

His uniform was of a cut and pattern that Alvah had seen only in pictures. There was a C on each gleaming button and, on the bar of the epaulette, CHICAGOLAND. In short, he was evidently a Floater Force officer from Chicago. The only trouble was that Alvah recognized him. He was a grip by day at the Seven Boroughs studios, famous for his dirty jokes, which he acquired at his night job in the Under Queens Power Station. He was a lieutenant j.g. in the N. Y. F. F. Reserve, and his name was Joe *"Dimples"* Mundry.

Alvah went over and sat down beside him again. Mundry's normally jovial face was set in wooden lines. His eyes focused on Alvah, but without recognition.

"Joe—"

"My name," said Mundry obstinately, "is Bertram Palmer, Float Lieutenant, Windy City Regulars. My serial number is 79016935."

That was the only tune he knew. Alvah hadn't been able to get another word out of him. Name, rank and serial number—that was normal. Members of the armed services were naturally conditioned to say nóthing else if captured. But why throw in the name of his outfit?

One, that was the way they did things in Chicago, and there just happened to be a Chicago soldier who looked and talked exactly like Joe Mundry, who had the same scars on his knuckles from brawls with the generator monkeys. Two, Alvah's mind had snapped. Three, this was a ringer foisted on Alvah for some incomprehensible purpose by the Muckfeet. And four—a wild and terrible suspicion . . .

Alvah tried again. "Listen, Joe, I'm your friend. We're on the same side. *I'm not a Muckfoot.*"

"My name is Bertram Palmer, Float Lieutenant—"

"Joe, I'm leveling with you. Listen—remember the Music Hall story, the one about the man who could . . ." Alvah explained in detail what the man could do. It was obscenely improbable and very funny, if you liked that sort of thing, and it was a story Joe had told him two days before he left New York.

A gleam of intelligence came into Joe's eyes. "What's the punchline?" he demanded.

"What the hell did you change the key on me for?" Alvah replied promptly.

Joe looked at him speculatively. "That might be a old joke. Maybe they even know it in the Sticks. And my name isn't Joe."

He really believed he was Bertram Palmer of the Windy City Regulars, that much seemed clear. Also, if it was possible that the Muckfeet knew that story, it was likelier still that the Chicagolanders knew it.

"All right," said Alvah, "ask me a question—something I couldn't know if I were a Muckfoot. Go ahead, anything. A place, or something that happened recently, or whatever you want."

A visible struggle was going on behind Joe's face. "Can't think of anything," he said at last. "Funny."

Alvah had been watching him closely. "Let's try this. Did you see *Manhattan Morons?*"

Joe looked blank. "What?"

"The realie. You mean you missed it? *Manhattan Morons?* Till I saw that, I never really knew what a comical bunch of weak-minded, slobber-mouthed, monkey-faced drooling idiots those New Yorkers—"

Joe's expression had not changed, but a dull red flush had crept up over his collar. He made an inarticulate sound and lunged for Alvah's throat.

When Angus Littleton opened the door, with Jerry and B. J. behind him, the two men were rolling on the floor.

"What made you think he was a spy?" B. J. demanded. They were a tight self-conscious group in the corridor. Alvah was nursing a split lip.

"Said he a Yuke," Jerry offered, "but didn't seem too sure, so I said the Yukes greedy. He never turned a hair. And he act like he never see a mine before. Things like that."

B. J. nodded. "It was a natural mistake, I guess. Well, thanks for calling us, Angus."

"Easy," said Angus, looking glum. "We ain't out of the rough yet, Beej."

"What do you mean? He didn't have anything to do with this attack—he's from New York."

"He *say* he is, but how you know? What make you think he ain't from Chicago?"

Alvah said, "While you're asking that, you might ask another question about him." He jerked a thumb toward the closed door. "What makes you think he *is?*"

The other three stared at him thoughtfully. "Alvah," Beej began, "what are you aiming at? Do you think—"

"I'm not sure," Alvah interrupted. "I mean I'm sure, but I'm not sure I want to tell you. Look," he said, turning to Angus, "let me talk to her alone for a few minutes, will you?"

Angus hesitated, then walked away down the hall, followed by Jerry.

"You've got to explain some things to me about this raid," said Alvah when they were out of hearing. "I *saw* those floaters dusting and it was the real thing. I can tell by the way the plants withered. But your people were walking around out there. Him, too—the prisoner. How come?"

"Antirads," said the girl. "Little para-insects, like the metallophage—the metallophage was developed from them. When you've been exposed, the antirads pick the dust particles off you and deposit them in radproof pots. They die in the pots, too, and we bury the whole—"

"All right," Alvah said. "How long have you had those things? Is there any chance the Cities knew about it?"

"The antirads were developed toward the end of the last City war. That was what ended it. At first we stopped the bombing, and then when they used dust—You never heard of any of this?"

"No," Alvah told her. "Third question, what are you going to do about Chicago now, on account of this raid?"

"Pull it down around their ears," B. J. said gravely. "We never did before, partly because it wasn't necessary. We knew for the last thirty years that the Cities could never be more than a nuisance to us again. But this isn't just a raid. They've attacked us all over this district—ruined the crops in every mine. We must put an end to it now—not that it makes much difference, this year or ten years from now. And it isn't as if we couldn't save the people . . ."

"Never mind that," said Alvah abstractedly. Then her last words penetrated. "No, go ahead—what?"

"I started to say, we think we'll be able to save the people, or most of them—partly thanks to what we learned from you. It's just Chicago we're going to destroy, not the—"

"Learned from *me?*" Alvah repeated. "What do you mean?"

"We learned that, when it's a question of survival, a City man can overcome his conditioning. You proved that. Did you eat the radnip?"

"Yes."

"There, you see? And you'll eat another and, sooner or later, you'll realize they taste good. A human being can learn to like anything that's needful to him. We're adaptable—you can't condition that out of us without breaking us."

Alvah stared at her. "But you spent over two weeks on me. How are you going to do that with fifteen or twenty million people all at once?"

"We can do it. You were the pilot model—two weeks for you. But now that we know how, we're pretty sure we can do it in three days—the important part, getting them to eat the food. And it's a good thing the store-houses are full, all over this continent."

They looked at each other silently for a moment. "But the Cities have to go," B. J. said.

"Fourth and last question," he said. "If a City knew about your radiation defenses all along, what would be their reason for attacking you this way?"

"Our first idea was that it was just plain desperation—they had to do something and there wasn't anything they could do that would work, so they just did something that wouldn't. Or maybe they hoped they'd be able to hold the mines long enough to get some metal out, even though they knew it was foolish to hope."

"That was your first idea. What was your second?"

She hesitated. "You remember what I told you, that the Cities cannibalized each other for a while, the big ones draining population away from the little ones and reclaiming their metals—and you remember I said that had gone as far as it could?"

"Yes."

"Well, when the big fish have eaten up all the little fish, they can eat each other till there's just one big fish left."

"And?" asked Alvah tensely.

"And maybe one City might think that, if they got us to make war on another, they could step in when the fighting was over and get all the metals they'd need to keep them going for years. So they might send raiding parties out in the other City's uniforms, and condition them to think they really were from that City. Was that what happened, Alvah?"

Alvah nodded reluctantly. "I don't understand it. They must have started planning this as soon as I stopped communicating. It doesn't make sense. They couldn't be that desperate—or maybe they could. Anyway, it's a dirty stunt. It isn't like New York."

She said nothing—too polite to contradict him, Alvah supposed.

Down at the end of the hall, Angus was beginning to look impatient. Alvah said, "So now you'll pull New York down?"

"Alvah, it may sound funny, but I think you know this, really—you're doing your people a favor."

"If that's so," he said wryly, "then New York was 'really' trying to do one for Chicago."

"I was hoping you'd see that it doesn't matter. It might have been Chicago that went first, or Denver, or any of the others, but that isn't important—they all have to go. What's important is the people. This may be another thing that's hard for you to accept, but they're going to be happier, most of them."

And maybe she was right, Alvah thought, if you counted in everybody, labor pool, porters and all. Why shouldn't you count them, he asked himself defiantly—they were people, weren't they? Maybe the index of civilization was not only how much you had, but how hard you had to work for it—incessantly, like the New Yorkers, holding down two or three jobs at once, because the City's demands were endless—or, like the Muckfeet, judiciously and with honest pleasure.

"Alvah?" said the girl. She put her question no more explicitly than that, but he knew what she meant.

"Yes, Beej," replied Alvah Gustad, Muckfoot.

VIII

On the Jersey flats, hidden by a forest of traveler trees, a sprawling settlement took form—mile after mile of forced-growth dwellings, stables, administration buildings, instruction centers. It was one of five. There was another farther north in Jersey, two in the Poconos and one in the vestigial state of Connecticut.

They lay empty, waiting, their roofs sprouting foliage that perfectly counterfeited the surrounding forests. Roads had been cleared, converging toward the City, ending just short of the half-mile strip of wasteland that girdled New York, and it was there that Alvah stood.

He found it strange to feel himself ready to walk un-protected across that stretch of country, knowing it to be acrawl with tiny organisms that had been developed not to tolerate Man's artificial buildings, whether of stone, metal, cement or plastics, but crumbled them all to the ground. Stranger still to be able to visualize the crawling organisms without horror or disgust.

But the strangest of all was to be looking at the City from this viewpoint. The towers stared back at him across the surrounding wall, tall and shining and proud, the proudest human creation—a century ago. Pitifully out-dated today, the gleaming Cities fought back, unaware that they had lost long ago, that their bright spires and ela-borate gadgets were as antiquated as polished armor would have been against a dun-painted motorized army.

"I wish I could go with you," said Beej from the breathing forest at his back.

"You can't," Alvah said without turning. "They wouldn't let you through the gate alive. They know me, but even so, I'm not sure they'll let me in after all this time. Have to wait and see."

154

"You know you don't have to go. I mean—"

"I know what you mean," said Alvah unhappily, "and you're right. But all the same, I do have to go. Look, Beej, you've got that map I drew. It's a ten to one chance that, if I don't make the grade, they'll put me in the quarantine cells right inside the wall. So you're not to worry. Okay?"

"Okay."

He kissed her and watched her fade back into the forest where the others were—Bither and Artie Brumbacher and a few others from home, the rest Jerseys and other clansmen from the Seaboard Federation—cheerful, matter-of-fact people who were going to bear most of the burdens of what was coming, and never tired of reminding the inlanders of the fact.

He turned and walked out across the wasteland, crunching the dry weeds under his feet.

There was a flaming moat around the City and, beyond the moat, high in the wall, a closed gateway—corroded tight, probably; it was a very long time since the City had had any traffic except by air. But there was a spy tower above the gate. Alvah walked up directly opposite its bulbous idiot eyes, waved, and then waited.

After a long time, an inconspicuous port in the tower squealed open and a fist-sized dark ovoid darted out across the flames. It came to rest in midair, two yards from Alvah, clicked and said crisply, "State your name and business."

"Alvah Gustad. I just got back from a confidential mission for the City Manager. Floater broke down, communicator, everything. I had to walk back. Tell him I'm here."

The ovoid hovered exactly where it was, as if pinned against the air. Alvah waited. When he got tired of standing, he dropped his improvised knapsack on the ground and sat on it. Finally the ovoid said harshly, in another voice, "Who are you and what do you want?"

Alvah patiently gave the same answer.

"What do you mean, broke down?"

"Broke *down*," said Alvah. "Wouldn't run any more."

Silence. He settled himself for another long wait, but it was only five minutes or thereabouts before the ovoid said, "Strip."

When he had done so, the gate opposite broke open with a scream of tortured metal and ground itself back into a recess in the wall. The drawbridge, a long rust-pitted tongue of metal, thrust out and down to span the moat, a wall of flame on either side of it.

Alvah walked across nimbly, the metal already hot against his naked soles, and the drawbridge whipped back into its socket. The gate screamed shut.

The room was the same, the anthems were the same. Alvah, disinfected, shaved all over and clad in an airtight glassine coverall with its own air supply, stopped short two paces inside the door. The man behind the Manager's desk was not Wytak. It was jowly, red-faced Ellery McArdle, Commissioner of the Department of War.

One of the guards prodded Alvah and he kept going up to the desk. "Now I think I get it," he said, staring at McArdle. "When—"

McArdle's cold gaze flickered toward the guards. Then his heavy head dropped forward a trifle, and he said, "Finish what you were saying, Gustad."

"I was about to remark," Alvah said, "that when Wytak's pet project flopped, he lost enough support to let you impeach him. Is that right?"

McArdle nodded and seemed to lose interest. "Your feet are not swollen or blistered, Gustad. You didn't walk back from the Plains. How did you get here?"

Alvah took a deep breath. "We flew—on a passenger roc—as far as the Adirondacks. We didn't want to alarm you by too much air traffic so near the City, so we joined a freight caravan there."

McArdle's stony face did not alter, but all the meaning went suddenly out of it. It was as if the man himself had stepped back and shut a door. The porter behind his chair swayed and looked as if he were about to faint. Alvah heard one of the guards draw in his breath sharply.

"*Fthuh!*" said McArdle abruptly, his face contorting. "Let's get this over. What do you know about the military plans of the Muckfeet? Answer me fully. If I'm not satisfied that you do, I'll have you worked over till I am satisfied."

Alvah, who had been feeling something like St. George

156

and something like a plucked chicken, discovered that anger could be a very comforting thing. "That's what I came here to do." he said tightly. "The Muckfeets' military plans are about what you might have expected, after that lousy trick of yours. They know it wasn't Chicago that raided them."

McArdle started and made as if to rise. Then he sank back, staring fixedly at Alvah.

"They've had a gutful. They're going to finish New York."

"When?" said McArdle, biting the word off short.

"That depends on you. If you're willing to be reasonable, they'll wait long enough for you to dicker with them. Otherwise, if I'm not back in about an hour, the fun starts."

McArdle touched a stud, said "Green alert," pressed the stud again and laced his fingers together on the desk. "Hurry it up," he said to Alvah. "Let's have the rest."

"I'm going to ask you to do something difficult," said Alvah. "It's this—think about what I'm telling you. You're not thinking now, you're just reacting—"

He heard a slight movement behind him, saw McArdle's eyes flicker and his hand make a *Not now* gesture.

"You're in the same room with a man who's turned Muckfoot and it disgusts you. You'll be cured of that eventually—you can be, I'm the proof—but all I want you to do now is put it aside and use your brains. Here are the facts. Your raiding parties got the shorts beat off them. I saw one of the fights—it lasted about twenty minutes. The Muckfeet could have polished off the Cities any time in the last thirty years. They haven't done it till now, because—"

McArdle was beating time with his fingertips on the polished ebonite. He wasn't really listening, Alvah saw, but there was nothing for it except to go ahead.

"—they had the problem of deconditioning and re-educating more than twenty million innocent people, or else letting them starve to death. Now they have the knowledge they need. They can—"

"The terms," said McArdle.

"They're going to close down this—this reservation," Alvah said. "They'll satisfy you in any way you like that they can do it by force. If you help, it can be an orderly process in which nobody gets hurt and everybody gets the best possible break. And they'll keep the City intact as a museum. I talked them into that. Or, if they have to, they'll take the place apart slab by slab."

McArdle's mouth was working violently. "Take him out and kill him, for City's sake! And, Morgan!" he called when Alvah and his guards were halfway to the door.

"Yes, Mr. Manager."

"When you're through, paint him green and dump him out the gate he came in."

It was a pity about Wytak, Alvah's brain was telling him frozenly. Wytak was a scoundrel or he could never have got where he was—had been—but he wasn't afraid of a new idea. It might have been possible to deal with Wytak.

"Where we going to do it?" the younger one asked nervously. He had been pale and sweating in the floater all the way across Middle Jersey.

"In the disinfecting chamber," Morgan said, gesturing with his pistol. "Then we paint him and haul him straight out. In there, you."

"Well, let's get it over with," the younger one said. "I'm sick."

"You think *I'm* not sick?" said Morgan in a strained voice. He gave Alvah a final shove into the middle of the room and stood back, adjusting his gun.

Alvah found himself saying calmly, "Not that way, Morgan, unless you want to turn black and shrivel up a second after."

"What's he talking about?" the boy whispered shakily.

"Nothing," said Morgan. The hand with the gun moved indecisively.

"To puncture me," Alvah warned, "you've got to puncture the suit. And I've been eating Muckfoot food for the last month and a half. I'm full of microorganisms—swarming with them. They'll bloop out of me straight at *you*, Morgan."

Both men jerked back as if they had been stung. "I'm getting outa here!" said the boy, grabbing for the door stud.

Morgan blocked him. "Stay here!"

"What're you going to do?" the younger one asked.

He swore briefly. "We'll tell the O. D. Come on."

The door closed and locked solidly behind them. Alvah looked to see if there was a way to double-lock it from his side, but there wasn't. He tried the opposite door to make sure it was locked, which it was. Then he examined the disinfectant nozzles, wondering if they could be used to squirt corrosive in on him. He decided they probably couldn't and, anyhow, he had no way to spike the nozzles. Then there was nothing to do but sit in the middle of the bare room and wait, which he did.

The next thing that happened was that he heard a faint far-off continuous noise through the almost soundproof door. He stood up and went over and put his ear against the door, and decided it was his imagination.

Then there *was* a noise, and he jumped back, his skin tingling all over, just before the door slid open. The sudden maniacal clangor of a bell swept Morgan into the room with it, wildeyed, his cap missing, drooling from a corner of his mouth, his gun high in one white-knuckled fist.

"*Glah!*" said Morgan and pulled the trigger.

Alvah's heart went *bonk* hard against his ribs, and the room blurred. Then he realized that there hadn't been any hiss of an ejected pellet. And he was still on his feet. And Morgan, with his mouth stretched open all the way to the uvula, was standing there a yard away, staring at him and pulling the trigger repeatedly.

Alvah stepped forward half a pace and put a straight left squarely on the point of Morgan's jaw. As the man fell, there were shrieks and running footsteps in the outer room. Somebody in Guard uniform plunged past the doorway, shouting incoherently, caromed off a wall, dwindled down a corridor. Then the room was full of leaping men in motley.

The first of them was Artie Brumbacher, almost unrecognizable because he was grinning from ear to ear. He handed Alvah a four-foot knobkerrie and a bulging skin bag and said, "Le's go!"

The streets were full of grounded floaters and stalled surface cars. The bells had fallen silent, and so had the faint omnipresent vibration that was like silence itself until it was gone. Not a motor was turning in the Borough of Jersey. Occasional chittering sounds floated on the air, and muffled buzzings and other odd sounds, all against the background chorus of faraway shrieks that rose and fell, rose and fell.

At the corner of Middle Orange and Weehawken, opposite the Superior Court Building, they came upon a squad of Regulars who had thrown away their useless guns and picked up an odd lot of assorted bludgeons—lengths of pipe, tripods and the like.

"Now you'll see," said Artie.

The Regulars set up a ragged yell and came running forward. The two Muckfeet on either side of Alvah, Artie and the bucktoothed one called Lafe, dipped heaping dark-brown handfuls out of the bags they carried slung from their shoulders. Alvah followed suit, and recognized the stuff at last—bran meal, soaked in some fragrant syrup until it was mucilaginous and heavy.

Artie swung first, then Lafe, and Alvah last—and the soggy lumps smacked the foremost faces. The squad broke, wiping frenziedly. But you couldn't wipe the stuff off. It clung coldly and grainily to the hair on the backs of your hands and your eyelashes and the nap of your clothing. All you could do was move it around.

One berserker with a smeared face didn't stop, and Lafe dropped him with a knobkerrie between the eyes. One more, a white-faced youth, stood miraculously untouched, still hefting his club. He took a stride forward menacingly.

Grinning, Artie raised another glob of the mash and ate it, smacking his lips. The youth spun around, walked drunkenly to the nearest wall and was rackingly sick.

An hour later, Knickerbocker Circle in Over Manhattan was littered with amoeba-shaped puddles of clear plastic. Overhead, the stuff was hanging in festoons from the reticulated framework of the Roof and, for the first time in a century, an unfiltered wind was blowing into New York. Halfway up the sheer facade of the Old Movie House, the roc that had brought Alvah from Jersey was flapping along, a wingtip almost brushing the louvers, while its rider sprinkled pale dust from a sack. Farther down the street, a sickly green growth was already visible on cornices and window frames.

The antique neon sign of the Old Movie dipped suddenly, its supports softening visibly. It swung, nodded and crashed to the pavement.

Three hours later, a little group of whey-faced men in official dress was being loaded aboard a freight roc opposite the underpass to the Cauldwell Floatway in Over Bronnix. Alvah thought he saw McArdle among them, but he couldn't be sure.

Twilight—all the streets that radiated from the heart of the City were afloat with long, slowly surging tides of humanity, dim in the weak glow from the lumen globes plastered haphazardly to the flanks of the buildings. At the end of every street, the Wall was crumbled down and the moat filled, its fire long gone out. And down the new railed walkways from all three levels came the men, women and children, stumbling out into the alien lumen-lit night and the strange scents and the wide world.

Watching from the hilltop, with his arm around his wife's waist, Alvah saw them being herded into groups and led away, unprotesting—saw them in the wains, rolling off toward the temporary shelters where, likely as not, they would sleep the night through, too numbed to be afraid of the morrow.

In the morning, their teaching would begin.

Babylon, Alvah thought, *Thebes, Angkor, Lagash, Agade, Tyre, Luxor, and now New York.*

A City grew out and then in—it was always the way, whether or not it had a Wall around it. Growing, it crippled itself and its people—and died. The weeds overleaped its felled stones.

"Like an egg," B. J. said, although he had not spoken. *"Omne ex ovo*—but the eggshell had to break."

"I know," said Alvah, discovering that the empty ache in his belly was not sentiment but hunger. "Speaking of eggs—"

B. J. gave his arm a reassuring squeeze. "Anything you want, dear. Radnip, orangoe, pearots, fleetmeat—*you* pick the menu."

Alvah's mouth began to water.

Double Meaning

I

Somewhere in the city, a monster was hiding. . . .

Lying back against the limousine's cushions, Thorne
Spangler let his mind dwell on that thought, absorbing it
with the deliberate enjoyment of a small boy sucking a
piece of candy. He visualized the monster, walking down
a lighted street, or sitting in a cheap hired room; tentacles
coiled, waiting, under the shell that made it look like a
man—or a woman. And all around it, the life of the city
going on: *Hello, Jeff. Have you heard? They're stopping
all the cars. Some sort of spy case . . . My sister tried to
fly out to Tucson, and they turned her back . . . My cousin
at the spaceport says nothing is coming in or leaving except military ships. It must be something big. . . .*

And the monster, listening, feeling the net tighten
around it.

The tension was growing, Spangler thought; it hung in
the air, in the abnormally empty streets. You could hear
it: a stillness that welled up under the beehive hum—a
waiting stillness, that made you want to stop and hold
your breath.

Spangler glanced at Pembun, sitting quietly beside him.
Does he feel it? he wondered. It was hard to tell. You
never knew what, if anything, a colonial was thinking.
Probably, Spangler decided, he's most heartily wishing
himself back on his own sleepy little planet, far from all
this commotion at the hub of the Universe.

For Spangler himself, this moment was the climax of a
lifetime. The monster—the Rithian—was only the catalyst, the stone flung into the pool. The salient fact was that
just now, for as long as the operation lasted, all the interminable workings of the Earth Empire revolved around
one tiny sphere: Earth Security Department, North Amer-

ican District, Southwestern Sector. For this brief time, one man—Spangler—was more important than all the others who administered the Empire.

It was not bad; not at all bad—for a man whose father had been a common draughtsman.

The car decelerated smoothly and stopped. Two tall men in the pearl-grey knee-breeches of the city patrol barred the way, both with automatic weapons at the ready. Behind them, the squat bulk of a Gun Unit covered half the roadway.

Two more patrolmen came forward and flung open all four doors of the car, stepping back smartly into crossfire positions. "All out," said the one with the sergeant's cape. "Security check. Move!"

As Spangler passed him, the sergeant touched his chest respectfully. "Good afternoon, Commissioner."

"Sergeant," said Spangler, in tranquil acknowledgment, smiling but not troubling himself to look at the man directly; and he led Pembun to the end of the queue.

As the line moved on, Spangler turned and found Pembun craning his short neck curiously. "It's a stereoptic fluoroscope," Spangler explained with languid amusement. "That's one test the Rithian can't meet, no matter how good his human disguise may be. One of these check stations is set up at each corner of every twentieth avenue and every tenth cross-street. If the Rithian is fool enough to pass one, we have him. If he doesn't, the house checks will force him out. He doesn't have a chance."

Spangler stepped between the screen and the bulbous twin projectors, and saw the glowing, three-dimensional image of his skeleton appear in the hooded screen. The square blotch at the left wrist and the smaller one near it were his communicator and thumb-watch. The other, odd-shaped ones lower down were metal objects in his belt pouch—key projectors, calculator, memo spools and the like.

The technician perched above the projector said, "Turn around. All right. Next."

Spangler waited at the limousine door until Pembun joined him. The little man's wide, flat-nosed face ex-

pressed surprise, interest, and something else that Spangler
could not quite define.

"Ow did you ever get 'old of so many portable fluoroscopes in such a 'urry?" he asked.

Spangler smiled delightedly. "It's no miracle, Mr. Pembun, just adequate preparation. Those 'scopes have been
stored and maintained, for exactly this emergency, since
twenty-one eighteen."

"Four 'undred years," said Pembun wonderingly. "My!
And this is the first time you've 'ad to use them?"

"The first time." Spangler waved Pembun into the car.
Following him, he continued, "But it took just under half
an hour to set up the complete network. Not only the
fluoroscopes were ready, but complete, detailed plans of
the entire operation. All I had to do was to take them out
of the files."

The car moved past the barrier.

"My!" said Pembun again. "I feel kind of like an extra
nose." His eyes gleamed faintly in the half-dark as Spangler turned to look at him.

"I ask your pardon?"

"I mean," said Pembun, "it doesn't seem to me as if
you rilly need me very much."

That expressionless drawl, Spangler thought, could become irritating in time. The man had been educated on
Earth; why couldn't he speak properly?

"I'm sure your advice will prove invaluable, Mr. Pembun," he said smoothly. "After all, we have no one here
who's actually had . . . friendly contact with the Rithians."

"That's right," said Pembun, "I almost forgot. We're
so used to the Rithi, ourselves, it's kind of 'ard to remember that Earth never did any trading with them." He
pronounced "Rithi" with a curious whistling fricative,
something between *th* and *s*, and an abrupt terminal
vowel. It was not done for swank, Spangler thought; it
simply came more naturally to the man than the standard-
ized "Rithians." Probably Pembun spoke the Rithian
tongue at least as well as he spoke Standard English.

Spangler half-heartedly tried to imagine himself a part of
Pembun's world. A piebald rabble, spawned by half a
dozen substandard groups that had left five Earth centu-

167

ries before. Haitians, French West Africans, Jamaicans, Puerto Ricans. Low-browed, dull-eyed loafers, breeders, drinkers and brawlers, mouthing an unbelievable tongue degraded from already corrupt English, French and Spanish. *Colonials*—in fact, if not in name.

"We couldn't do any trading with the Rithians, Mr. Pembun," he said at last, coolly. "They're are not human."

"Yes, I recollec' now, Commissioner," the little man replied humbly. "It jus' slipped my mind for a minute. Shoo, I was taught about that in school. Earth's 'ad the same policy toward non-yuman cultures for the last four 'undred years. If they 'aven't got to the spaceship stage yet, put them under surveillance and make sure they don't. If they 'ave, and they're weak enough, a quick preventive war. If they're too strong, like the Rithi—delaying tactics, subversion, sabotage, divide-and-rule. *Then* war." He chuckled. "It makes my 'ead ache jus' thinking about it."

"That policy," Spangler informed him, "has withstood the only meaningful test. Earth survives."

"Yes, sir," said Pembun vacuously. "She certainly does."

The things, Spangler thought half in mockery, half in real annoyance, that I do for the Empire!

A touch of his forefinger at the base of the square, jeweled thumbwatch produced a soft chime and then a female voice: "Fourteen-ten and one quarter."

Spangler hesitated. It was an awkward time to call Joanna; the afternoon break, in her section, came at fourteen thirty. But if he waited until then he would be back at the Hill himself, tied up in a conference that might not end until near quitting time. It was irritating to have to speak to her in Pembun's presence, too, but there was no help for it now. He had been too busy to call earlier in the afternoon—Pembun's arrival had upset his schedule —and his superior, Keith-Ingram, had chosen to call him while he was on his way to the spaceport, occupying the whole journey with fruitless discussion.

He could have called her at any other time during the past three days, of course; he had not done so. That had been deliberate; this Rithian affair was only a convenient pretext. It was good strategy. But Spangler knew his antagonist, knew the limits of her curiosity and pride almost to the hour. Any longer delay would be dangerous.

Spangler reached for the studs of the limousine's communicator, set into the front wall of the compartment. His wristphone would have been easier and more private, but he wanted to see her face.

"You'll excuse me?" he said perfunctorily.

"Of cawse." The little man turned toward the window on his side of the car, presenting his back to Spangler and the communicator screen.

Spangler punched the number. After a moment the screen lighted and Joanna's face came into view.

"Oh—Thorne."

Her tone was poised, cool, almost expressionless—which was to say, normal. She looked at him, out of the screen's upholstered frame, with the expression that almost never altered: direct, gravely intent, receptive. Her skin and eyes were so clear, her emotional responses so deliberate and pallid, that she seemed utterly, almost abstractly normal: a type personified, a symbol, a mathematical fiction. Everything about her was refined and subdued: her gestures, movements, her rare laughter. Her face itself might have been modeled to fit the average man's notion of "Aristocracy."

That, of course, was why Spangler had to have her.

In this one respect, she was precisely what she looked— the Planters were one of the oldest, most powerful, and most unassailably patrician families in the Empire. Without such an alliance, Spangler knew painfully well, he had gone as far as he could, and a good deal farther than a less determined man could have hoped. With her, he would only have begun—and his children would receive, by right of birth, all that he had fought to gain.

In nearly all other ways, Joanna was a mirror of deceptions. She seemed cool and self-possessed, but was neither; she was only afraid. It was fear that delayed and censored every word she spoke, every motion: fear of betraying herself, fear of demanding too much, fear of giving too much.

He let the silence lengthen until, in another second, it

would have been obvious that he was hesitating for effect. Then he said politely, "I'm not disturbing you?"

". . . No, of course not." The pause before she answered had been a trifle longer than normal.

She's hurt, Spangler thought with satisfaction.

"I would have called earlier, if I could," he said soberly. "This is the first free moment I've had in three days."

It was a lie, and she knew it; but it was so plausible that she could accept it, if she chose, without loss of dignity. That was the knife-edge on which Spangler had hung his fortunes. Deliberately, knowing the risk, he had drawn their relationship so thin that a touch would break it.

Had there been any other course he could have taken? Despite himself, Spangler's anxiety led him through each stage of the logic again, seeking a flaw.

Cancel the approach direct. He had asked her to marry him, for the first time, a week after they had become lovers. She had refused without hesitation and without coyness; she meant it.

Cancel the approach dialectical. Joanna had a keen and capable mind, but she could be as stubborn as any dullard. There is no argument that can wear down a woman's "I don't want to."

Cancel the approach violent: tentatively. Four days ago, at the end of a long weekend they had spent together in the Carpathians, he had tried brutality—not on impulse, but with calculated design which had achieved its primary object: he had reduced her to tears.

After that, apology and reconciliation. After that, silence: three days of it. Silence wounds more than a blow, and wounds more deeply.

Joanna had spent her whole life in retreating from things that had injured her.

But Spangler had three things on his side: Joanna's affection and need for him; ordinary human perversity, which desires a thing, however often refused, the instant it is withdrawn; and the breaking of the rhythm. Rhythm, however desirable in some aspects of the relations between sexes, is fatal in most others. Request, argument, violence . . . if he had begun the cycle again, as both of them subconsciously expected, he would simply have made his own defeat more certain.

As it was, he had weakened her resistance by making her gather it against a thrust that never came. . . .

Joanna said, "I understand. You do look tired, Thorne. You're all right, though, aren't you?"

Spangler said abruptly, "Joanna, I want to see you. Soon. Tonight. Will you meet me?"

Before, his tone had been almost as casual as hers, and he had watched the minuscule changes in her expression that meant she was softening toward him. Now he spoke urgently, and saw her stiffen again.

Never let her rest, he thought. Never let her get her balance. . . . He spoke softly again: "It will be the last time, if you decide it that way. But let me see you tonight."

". . . All right."

"Shall I send a car for you?"

She nodded, and then her image dissolved. Spangler leaned back, with a sigh, into the cushions.

"My," said Pembun, "look at awl the tawl buildings!"

II

They were stopped twice more before they reached Administration Hill, and went through a routine search at the entrance. From there, the trip to Security Section took less than a minute. The limousine let them out at Spangler's office door and returned automatically to the motor pool three levels below.

Contrasted with the group that was waiting at the conference table, under the hard, clear glow-lights, Pembun looked like a shabby mongrel that had somehow crawled into a thoroughbred kennel. His skin was yellowish under the brown; his jowls were wider than his naked cranium; his enormous ears stuck straight out from his head. His tunic and pantaloons were correctly cut, but he looked hopelessly awkward in them.

After all, Spangler reminded himself carefully, the man could not help being what he was.

"Gentlemen," he said, "allow me to present Mr. Jawj Pembun of Manhaven. Mr. Pembun was a member of the colonial government before his planet gained its independence, and since that time has been of service to the Empire in various capacities. He brings us expert knowledge of the Rithians. Lieutenant Colonel Cassina, who is our liaison with Space Navy—his new aide, Captain Wei —Dr. Baustian of the Bureau of Alien Physiology—Mr. Pemberton of the Mayor's staff—Miss Timoney and Mr. Gordon, of this office."

Pembun shook hands with all of them without any noticeable sign of awe. To the Mayor's spokesman he said affably, "You know, Pemberton was origin'ly my family's name. They just gradually shortened it to Pembun. That's a coincidence, isn' it?"

Pemberton, a fine-boned young man with pale eyes and hair, stiffened visibly.

172

"I hardly think there is any relation," he said.

Spangler picked up a memo spool that lay before him and tapped it sharply against the table. "At the suggestion of the Foreign Relations Department," he said delicately, "Mr. Pembun was brought in from Ganymede especially for this emergency. I arranged for his passage through the cordon and met him personally at the spaceport." In short, gentlemen, he thought, this yokel has been wished on us by the powers that be, and we shall have to put up with him as best we can.

"Now," he said, "I imagine Mr. Pembun would like to be brought up to date before we proceed." There was a snort from Colonel Cassina which Spangler pointedly ignored. He began the story, covering the main points quickly and concisely. Pembun stopped him only once to ask a question.

"Are you sure that's all the Rithi there were to begin with—just seven?"

"No, Mr. Pembun," Spangler admitted. "We don't yet know how or by whom they were smuggled through to Earth, therefore we must consider the possibility that others are still undetected. To deal with that possibility, Security is patrolling the entire planet, using a random-based spot check system. But we know that these seven were here, and that one of them is still at large. When we find him, we hope to get all the information we need. The idea of suicide is repugnant to these Rithians, I understand."

"That's right," said Pembun soberly. "I guess you can take him alive, all right. Prob'ly could 'ave taken all seven after the accident, if your patrolmen 'adn' shot so quick."

"Those were city patrolmen," said Pemberton acidly, with a flush on his cheekbones, "not Security men. Their conduct was perfectly in order. When they arrived on the scene of the accident, and saw three men attempting to aid four others whose bodies were torn open, exposing the alien shapes underneath, they instantly fired on the whole group. Those were their orders; that was what they had been trained to do in any such event. They would have been right, even if one of the Rithians had not escaped into the crowd."

Smiling, Pembun shook his head.

"I'm not so good at paradoxes," he said. "They jus' mix me up."

"There is no paradox, Mr. Pembun," said Spangler gently. "A fully equipped Security crew can take chances with an unknown force which a municipal patrol cannot. A patrolman, discovering an alien on this planet, must kill first and investigate afterwards—because an alien spy or saboteur, by definition, has unknown potentialities. Planning centuries in advance, as we must, we obviously can't foresee every possible variant of a basic situation; but we can and do lay down directives which will serve our best interests in the vast majority of cases. And we can't, Mr. Pembun, we can*not* allow crucial decisions to be made on the spot by non-executive personnel."

Colonel Cassina cleared his throat impatiently. "Shall we get on?"

"Just one moment. Mr. Pembun, I want to make this point clear to you if I can. *Interpretation is the dry rot of law.* One interpretation, and the law is modified; two, the law is distorted—three hundred million, and there is no law at all, there is pure anarchy. In a small system, of course—a single planet, for example—there are only a few intermediate stages between planning and execution. But when you consider that we're dealing here with an empire of two hundred sixty planets, an aggregate of more than *eight hundred billion* people, you'll realize that directives must be rigid and policy unified.

"In an emergency, the lower-echelon official who acts according to his own personal interpretation may be right or wrong. The similar official who follows a rigid policy, prepared to meet the widest possible variety of actual situations, *will* be right—in nine hundred ninety-nine out of a thousand cases. We take the long view; we can't afford to do otherwise."

Pembun nodded seriously. He said, "We 'ad the same trouble at 'ome—on a smaller scale, of course. Right after we declared our independence, we formed a federation with the two other planets in our system, Novaya Zemlya and Reunion. It seemed like a good idea—you know, for mutual defense and so on. But we found out that to keep that big a gover'ment running we 'ad to stiffen it up something dreadful, an' some'ow or other it didn' seem to be as cheap to run as three diff'rent gover'ments, either. So we split up ag'in."

Spangler maintained his urbane expression with difficulty. Colonel Cassina's neck was brick red, and Dr. Baustian, Captain Wei and Miss Timoney were staring at Pembun in frank amazement. The others merely looked embarrassed.

Really, it was a waste of time to take any pains with a barbarian like this. Try to explain the philosophy behind the workings of the greatest empire of all time, and all Pembun got out of it was a childish analogy to the history of his own pipsqueak solar system!

He regarded the little man through narrowed lids. Come to think of it, was Pembun really as simple as he appeared, or was he snickering to himself behind that stolid yellow-brown face?

He had said several things which could only be explained by the worst of bad taste or the sheerest blind ignorance. After Spangler's reference to Manhaven's "gaining its independence"—surely a polite way of putting it, since Manhaven had seceded from the Empire only on Earth's sufferance, at a time when she was occupied elsewhere—Pembun had said, "After we *declared* our independence—"

Carelessness, or deliberate, subtly pointed insult?

Was Pembun saying, "There are two hundred sixty planets and eight hundred billion people in your Empire, all right—but there used to be a lot more, and a century from now there'll be a lot less?"

Insufferable little planet-crawler. . . .

Colonel Cassina said, "Mr. Pembun, do I understand you to suggest that we too should *split up* as you put it? That the Empire should be *liquidated?*"

"Why, no, Colonel," said Pembun. "That wouldn' be any business of mine, you know. That would be up to the people that still live in the Empire to decide."

Cassina snorted and sputtered. Pemberton's face was white with indignation. It was remarkable, Spangler thought with one corner of his mind, how readily Pembun could rub them all the wrong way. If it could possibly be arranged, future meetings had better be held without him.

"Gentlemen," he said, raising his voice a trifle, "shall we continue?"

After they had left, Spangler sat alone in his inner office, toying absently with the buttons that controlled the big information screen opposite his desk. He switched on one multi-colored, three-dimensional organization chart after another, without seeing any of them.

Pembun had behaved himself, in a manner of speaking, after that clash with Cassina. But the things he had said had become not merely irritating, but—disquieting.

It had begun with the usual complaint from Pemberton, speaking for the mayor. Like almost every planetary and local government department except Security, the city administration wanted to know when the Rithian would be captured and the planet-wide blockade ended.

Spangler had assured him that the Rithian could not possibly remain concealed for more than a week at the utmost.

And then Pembun had remarked, "Excuse me, Commissioner, but I b'lieve it would be safer if you said two months."

"Why, Mr. Pembun?"

"Well, because Rithi got to 'ave a lot of beryllium salts in their food. The way I see it, this one Rithch wouldn' 'ave more than six or eight weeks' supply with 'im. After that, you can either tie up all the supplies of beryllium salts, so 'e 'as to surrender or starve, or jus' watch the chemical supply 'ouses an' arrest anybody 'oo buys them. Either way, you got 'im. Might take a little more than two months. Say two and a 'alf or three."

"Mr. Pembun," Spangler said with icy patience, "that's an admirable plan, but we're not going to need it. The house checks will get our Rithian before a week is up."

"Clear ever'body out of a building, an' wawk them all past one of those fluoroscopes?"

"That's it," Spangler told him. "One area at a time, working inward from the outskirts of the city to the center."

"Uh-mm," said Pembun. "Only thing is, the Rithi got no bones."

Spangler raised his brows and glanced at Dr. Baustian. "Is that correct, doctor?"

"Well, yes, so I understand," said the physiologist tolerantly, "but I assume that would be indication enough—if the fluoroscope showed a very small cartilage and no bones at all?"

Laughter rippled around the table.

"Not," said Pembun, "if 'e swallowed a skel'ton."

Cassina said something rude in an explosive voice. Spangler, incredulous amusement bubbling up inside him, stared at Pembun. *"Swallowed* a skeleton?"

"Uh-mm. You people wouldn't know about it, I guess, because you 'aven' done any trading with the Rithi—scientific trading least of awl—but the Rithi got—" He hesitated. "Our name for it is *mudabs boyó;* I guess in Standard that would be 'protean insides.' "

"Protean!" from Dr. Baustian.

"Yes, sir. Their outside shape is fixed, almos' as much as ours, or they wouldn't need any disguises to look like a man; but the insides is pretty near all protean flesh—make it into a stomach, or a bowel, or a bladder, or w'atever they 'appen to need. They could swallow a yuman skel'ton all right—it wouldn' inconvenience them at awl. An' they could imitate the rest of a man's insides well enough to fool you. They could make it move natural, too. That means they wouldn't need any braces or anything, jus' a plastic shell for a disguise.

"I 'ate to say it, but I don't believe those fluoroscopes are going to do much good."

In a moment, the table had been in an uproar again.

Spangler grunted, switched on his speakwrite and began to dictate a report of the conference. "To Claude Keith-Ingram, Chief Comm Dept-Secur," he said. "Most Secret. Most Urgent." He thought for a moment, then rapidly gave an account of Pembun's statement, adding that Dr. Baustian doubted the validity of his information, and that Pembun admitted he had never seen any actual evidence of the Rithians' alleged protean ability.

He read it over, then detached the spool and tossed it into the out tube.

He was still unsatisfied.

He had done everything he could be expected to do,

exactly according to regulations. If policy were to be changed, it was not for him to change it. Logic and instinct both assured him that Pembun was not to be taken seriously.

But there was something else Pembun had said that still bothered him, for a reason he could not explain. He had not included it in his report; it would have seemed—to put it mildly—frivolous.

Pembun had said:

"There's one more thing you got to watch out for—those Rithi got a 'ell of a sense of yumor."

It was fifteen-twenty; there would be time before he met Joanna.

Spangler passed his hand over the intercom. "Gordon," he said.

"Yes, sir?"

"Did you find quarters for Mr. Pembun?"

"Yes, sir."

"Where is he?"

"G level, section seven, suite one eleven."

"Right," said Spangler, flicking his hand over the intercom to break the connection. He stood up, walked out of the office, and buzzed a scooter.

"G level," he said into its mechanical ear.

III

The door of suite 111 was ajar. Inside, a baritone voice
was singing to the accompaniment of some stringed instrument. Spangler paused and listened.

   Odum Páwkee mónt a mút-ting
   Vágis cásh odúm Paw-kée
   Odum Páwkee mónt a mút-ting
   Tóuda por tásh o cáw-fée!

There was a final chord, then a hollow wooden thump
and jangle as the instrument was set down; then the clink
of ice cubes in a glass.

Spangler put his hand over the doorplate. The chime
was followed by Pembun's voice calling, "Come awn in!"

Pembun was comfortably slumped in a recliner, with his
collar undone and his feet high. The glass in his hand,
judging by color, contained straight whiskey. On a low table at his side were the remains of a man-sized meal, a
decanter, an ice bucket and several clean glasses, and the
instrument—a tiny, round-bellied thing with three strings.

The little man swung himself lithely around and rose. "I
was 'oping somebody would cawl," he said happily. "Gets
kind of lonesome in this place—lonesomer than the mountings a thousand miles from anybody, some'ow. 'Ere, take
the company seat, Commissioner. A glawss of w'iskey?"

Spangler took an upright chair. "This will do nicely," he
said. "No thanks to the whiskey—I haven't your stomach."

Pembun looked startled, then smiled. "I'll get them to
sen' up some soda," he said. He swung himself into the
recliner again, reached for the intercom and gave the
order.

"W'y I looked surprised for a minute w'en you said
that," he explained, turning sidewise on the recliner, "is
becawse we got an expression on Man'aven. W'en we say,

179

'I 'aven' got your stomach,' that means I don' like you, we're not sympathetic. *'E no ay to stomá.'*"

Spangler felt an unexpected twinge of guilt—of course Pembun knew he wasn't liked—and then a wave of irritation. Damn the man! How did he always manage to put one in the wrong?

He kept his voice casual and friendly. "What was that you were singing, just before I came in?"

"Oh, that—'Odum Páwkee Mónt a Mutting.'" He picked up the instrument and sang the chorus Spangler had heard. Spangler listened, charmed in spite of himself. The melody was simple and jaunty—the kind of thing, he told himself, that would go well sung on muleback . . . or the backs of whatever ill-formed beasts the Manhavenites used instead of mules.

Pembun put the instrument down. "In Standard, that means, 'Old Man Pawkey climbs a mounting, clouds 'ide Old Man Pawkey. Old Man Pawkey climbs a mounting, all for a cup of coffee!'"

"Is there more?"

Pembun made his eyes comically wide. "Oh, shoo! There's 'bout a trillion verses. I only know every tenth one, about, but we'd be 'ere all night if I sang 'em. It's kind of a saga. Old Man Pawkey was a settler who lived up in the Desperation Mountings in the early days. That's in the temperate zone, but even so it's awful wild country, all straight up and straight down. 'E loved coffee, you know, but of course there wasn' any. Well, 'e 'eard there was some in the spaceport town, Granpeer, down in the plateau country, and 'e went there, on foot. Twenty-two 'undred kilometers. Or so they say."

The conveyor door popped open, Pembun went over to get the soda and pour Spangler a drink. "There were some big things done in those days," he added, "but there were some big lies told, too."

Spangler felt an obscure shock that left him jumpy again. In the conscious effort to sympathize with Pembun, to understand the man in his own terms, he had managed to build up a picture which was really not too hard to admire: the wild, colorful, free life of the frontier, the hardships accepted and conquered, the deeds of heroism casually done, et cetera, et cetera. It was the sort of life Spangler himself had dreamed of in his early youth, before he had realized that it was a hopeless anachronism; that the only career for an ambitious man was not adventure, not discovery, but control.

And then Pembun himself, in half a sentence, had indifferently rejected that picture. "There were some big lies told, too."

Pembun didn't believe in the Empire; all right. But—if he had no respect for his own planet's traditions, then what in the name of sanity *did* he believe in?

Spangler was a man who tried hard to be liberal. But now, staring at Pembun's round brown face, the yellowish whites of his eyes, he thought once more: It's a waste of time to try to understand this man. He's not civilized; he thinks like an animal. There's simply *no point of contact*.

He said abruptly, "At the meeting, you mentioned something about the Rithian's 'sense of humor.' What, exactly, did you mean?"

He was thinking: In a few minutes I'll be back in my office. I'll drink half of this highball, precisely, and then go.

Pembun leaned back in the relaxer, head turned slightly, eyes alert on Spangler. "Well," he said, "they're kind of peculiar, in this way. They're a real 'ighly-advanced people, technologically—you know that. But the things that strike them funny remind you more of a kind of backwoods planet, like Man'aven. Maybe that's w'y we got along so well with them—Man'aven yumor is kind of primitive. Pulling out a chair w'en a man goes to sit down. That kind of thing. But they beat us.

"They'll go forty kilos out of their way to play a joke, even w'en it isn' good business. I've 'eard a novel written by one of their big authors—twelve spools, mus' be more than five 'undred thousan' words long—jus' so 'e could build up to a dirty joke at the end. It was a bes'-seller in their solar system. An' they're crazy about puns—plays on words. Some of their sentences you're suppose' to read as many as fifteen, twenty different ways."

Spangler's memory groped uneasily for a moment and then produced a relevant fact. "Like Joyce," he said. "The twentieth-century decadent."

"Uh-mm," Pembun agreed. "I use' to be able to quote

pages of *Finnegans Wake*. 'riverrun, past Eve and Adam's, from swerve of shore to bend of bay, brings us by a commodious vicus of recirculation. . . .' That's primer talk, compared to Rithi literature."

Spangler swallowed deliberately and set his glass down on the wide arm of his chair. He felt the vast, cool, good-humored patience of a man who knows how to retreat from his own petty emotions. "I don't want to seem obtuse," he said, "but has this got anything to do with my problem?"

Pembun's brows creased delicately. He looked anxious, searching for words. "Nothing, *specifically*," he said earnestly. "W'at I mean is jus' that in general, you got to watch out for that sense of yumor. I mean, you already know that this Rithi is going to 'urt you bad if 'e can. But you got to remember also that if 'e can, 'e's going to do it some way that'll be side-splittingly funny to 'im. It isn't easy to figure out w'ich way a Rithch is going to jump, but you can do it sometimes if you know w'at makes them lahf."

Spangler swallowed again, leaving exactly half the drink behind, and stood up. He was a trifle impatient with himself for having come here at all, but at least he had the satisfaction of knowing that a lead had been explored and canceled out: that an *x* had been corrected to a zero.

"Thank you, Mr. Pembun," he said from the doorway; "for the drink and the information. Good evening."

"You got to look out for that 'ypnotism, too," said Pembun as an afterthought.

Spangler stood in the doorway, strangling. Pembun looked at him with a politely inquiring expression.

"Hypnotism!" Spangler said, and started back into the room. "What hypnotism?"

"My goodness," cried Pembun, "didn' you know about *that*?"

IV

They lay together in companionable silence, in a darkened room, facing the huge unscreened window—window in the archaic sense, a simple hole in the wall—
through which a feather-light touch of cool, salt air came
unhindered. On either side, where the shore thrust out an
arm, Spangler could see a cluster of multicolored lights—
Angels proper on the right, St. Monica on the left.
Straight ahead was nothing but silver sea and ghost-grey
cloud, except when the tiny spark of an airship crossed
silently and was gone.

The universe was a huge, half-felt presence that flowed
through the open window to contain them; as if, Spangler
thought, they were two grains of dust sunk in an ocean
that stretched to infinity.

It was soothing, in a way, but there was a touch of un-
pleasantness in it. Spangler shifted his body restlessly,
feeling the breeze fumble at his bare skin. The scale was
too big, he thought; he was too used to the rabbit-warren
of the Hill, perhaps, to be entirely easy outside it. Perhaps he needed a change. . . .

"That wind is getting a little chilly," he said. "Let's
close the window and turn on the lights."

"I thought it was nice," she said. "But go ahead, if you
like."

Now I've insulted her window, Spangler thought wryly.
Nevertheless, he reached forward and found the stud that
rolled a sheet of vitrin down over the opening.

It was a period piece, the window—Twenty-first Century, even to the antique servo mechanism that operated
it. So was everything else in Joanna's tower; the absurd

four-legged chairs, the massive tables, the carpets, even the huge pneumatic couch. There were paper books in the shelves, and not the usual decorator's choices, either, but books that a well-read twenty-first-century citizen might actually have owned—Shakespeare and Sterne, Jones and Joyce, Homer and Hemingway all jumbled in together. If the fashion would let her, Spangler thought, I believe she would wear skirts.

A glow of rose-tinted light sprang up, and he turned to see Joanna with one slender arm around her knees, her head bent solemnly over the lighted cigarette she had just taken from the dispenser. She handed him another.

Spangler pulled himself up beside her and leaned against the back of the couch. The smoke of their cigarettes fanned out, pink in the half-light, and faded slowly into floating haze.

The room's curved walls and ceiling enclosed them snugly, safely. . . .

The Twenty-first Century, the Century of Peace, was a womb, Spangler thought. The image was not his, but Joanna's; she had picked it up in some book or other. "A womb with a view." That was it. A childishly fanciful description, as one would expect of that period, but accurate enough. Self-deception was not one of Joanna's vices—unfortunately.

To win her finally and completely, it would be necessary to break down the clear image she had of herself—cast her adrift in chaos, so that she would turn blindly to him for her lost security. It was not going to be easy.

Joanna said, without moving, "Thorne, I'd like to talk seriously to you, just for a minute."

"Of course."

"You know what I'm going to say, probably; but just to have things clear—do you want us to go on together?"

Matching her tone, Spangler said, "Yes."

". . . I do too. You know I'm fonder of you than I've ever been of anyone. But I won't ever marry you. You've got to believe that, and accept it, or it's no good . . . I'm trying to be fair."

"You're succeeding," Spangler told her lightly. He turned and put his hand on her knee. "Just to be equally clear—I've been insufferable to you, and I was a maniac last weekend, and I'm sorry. Shall we both forget it?"

She smiled. "Yes. We will."

Her lips moved and altered as he leaned toward her: corners turning downward, pink moist flesh swelling up into the blind shape of desire. His free arm sank into the softness of her back, abruptly hard as her body tautened. Eyes closed, he heard the sibilant whisper of her legs slowly straightening against the counterpane. . . .

Afterward, he lay wrapped in a warm lethargy that was like floating in quiet water. It was an effort to force himself out of that mindless content, but it was necessary. As he was vulnerable at this moment, so was she. When she spoke to him lazily, he answered her with increasing constraint, until he felt his tension flow into her.

Then he rolled over abruptly, got up and stood at the window, staring out at the vast, obscene emptiness of sky and sea. Now it was easier. As he had often, in his childhood, worked himself deliberately into white-hot anger—when, if he had not forced himself to be angry, he would have been afraid—now, with equal deliberateness, he opened his mind to despair.

Suppose that I failed, and lost Joanna, he thought. But that was not enough. What would be the most dreadful thing that could possibly happen? The answer came of itself: Pembun, and his Rithians with their boneless bodies and their hypnotism. Shapeless faces staring in from a sea of darkness. *Suppose they won.* Suppose the Empire went down under that insensate wave, and all the walls everywhere crumbled to let smothering Chaos in?

Her voice: "Thorne? Is anything the matter?"

He pulled himself back, shuddering from the cold emptiness that his mind had fastened upon. For an instant it had been real, it had happened, it was *there.* He had been lost and alone, fumbling in an endless night.

When he turned, he knew that his agony showed plainly in his face. He did his best to restrain and suppress it: that would show too.

"Nothing," he said. He walked around the couch, reached past her for a cigarette, then moved to the closet.

"You're going?" she asked uncertainly.

"I've got to be in early tomorrow," he said. "And I've been running a little short of sleep."

". . . All right."

Fastening his cloak, he went to her and took her hand. "Don't mind me, will you? I'm a little jumpy—it's been an unpleasant week. I'll call you tomorrow."

Her lips smiled, but her eyes were wide and unfocused. Caution was in them, and a hint of something else—pleasure, perhaps, touched with guilt?

He rode home with a feeling of satisfaction that deepened into a fierce joy. If she learned that she could hurt him, learned to expect it, learned to like it, then in time she could endure the thought of being hurt in return. It was only necessary to go slowly, advancing and retreating, shifting his ground, stripping her defenses gradually; until at last, whether for guilt or pleasure or love, she would marry him.

For love and pleasure, fear and hatred, honor and ambition were all doors that could be opened or shut.

Pain was the key. . . .

Early the following morning, alone in his inner office, Spangler sat composedly and looked into his desk vision screen, from which the broad, grey face of Claude Keith-Ingram stared back at him.

"You asked Pembun why he hadn't divulged this information earlier?" Keith-Ingram demanded sharply.

"I did," Spangler said. "He answered that he had assumed we already knew of it, since the Empire was known to possess the finest body of knowledge in the field of security psychology in the inhabited Galaxy."

"Hmm," said Spangler's superior, frowning. *"Sarcasm, do you think?"*

Spangler hesitated. "I should like to be able to answer that with a definite no, but I can't be sure. Pembun is not an easy man to fathom."

"So I understand," said Keith-Ingram. "However, he has an absolutely impeccable record in the Outworld service. I don't think there can be any question of actual disloyalty."

Spangler was silent.

"Well, then," said Keith-Ingram testily, "what about this alleged psuedo-hypnotic ability of the Rithians? What does it amount to?"

"According to Pembun, complete control under very favorable conditions. He says, however, that the process is rather slow and limited in extent. In other words, that a Rithian might be able to take control of one or two persons if it could get them alone and unsuspecting, but that it would be unable to control a large group at any time or even a small group in an emergency."

Keith-Ingram nodded. "Now, about this other matter of the protean faculty—" he glanced down at something on his own desk, outside the range of the scanner—"none of the available agents who have served in the Rithian system have anything even suggestive to report in that regard."

Spangler nodded. "That could mean anything or nothing."

"Yes," said the grey man. "On the whole, I'm inclined to feel as you evidently do, that there's nothing in it. Pembun may be competent and so on, but he's not Earth and he's not Security. Still, I don't have to remind you that if he's right on all counts, we've got a *very* serious situation on our hands."

Spangler smiled grimly and nodded again. Keith-Ingram was noted for his barbed understatements. *If* Pembun was right, then it followed that the Empire's agents in the Rithian system had carried back no more information than the Rithians wanted them to have. . . .

Keith-Ingram rubbed his chin with a square, well-manicured hand. "Now, to date the normal procedures haven't produced any result."

"That's correct," Spangler admitted. Using all available personnel, it would take another four days to complete the house checks. Before that time, negative results would prove nothing.

"And according to Pembun, those procedures are no good. Now, has he proposed any alternate method, other than that beryllium-salts scheme of his?"

"No, sir. He held out no hope of results from that one under two and a half months."

"Well, he may have something more useful to suggest. Ask him. If he does—try it."

"Right," said Spangler.

"Good," said the grey man, giving Spangler his second-best smile. "Keep in touch, Thorne—and if anything else odd turns up, don't hesitate to call me direct."

The screen cleared.

Spangler stared at the vacant screen for a few moments, pursing his lips thoughtfully, then leaned back, absently fingering the banks of control studs at the edge of his desk. After a moment, he found himself mentally reviewing the film, taken in the Rithian system, which had been used in briefing Security personnel for the spy search.

First you saw only a riotous, bewildering display of green and gold; the shapes were so unfamiliar that the mind took several seconds to adjust. Then you perceived that the green was a swaying curtain of broad-leafed vines; the splashes of gold were intricate, many-petaled blossoms. Behind, barely noticeable, was a spidery framework of metal, and beyond that, an occasional glimpse of mist-blue that suggested open space.

Then the Rithian moved into view.

At first you thought "Spiders!" and Spangler remembered that he had jumped; spiders were a particular horror of his. Then, when the thing stopped in front of the camera, you saw that it was no more like a spider than like an octopus or a monkey.

Curiously, its outline most resembled those of the great golden blossoms. There was a circlet of tentacles, lying in gentle S-curves, and below that another. The thing's body was a soft sac that dangled beneath the lower set of tentacles; there was a head, consisting almost entirely of two huge, dull-red eyes. The creature's body was covered with short, soft-looking ochre fur or spines.

To some people, Spangler supposed, it would be beautiful: the sort of people who professed to find beauty in the striped, oval bodies of big beetles.

The thing turned quickly, hung still for another moment, and then clambered in a blur of limbs up the vine again.

Then there was another scene: darker green, this time —the gloom of a forest rather than a garden city. A Rithian moved into view, clinging to the slick purplish bole of a tree. Three of its fore-tentacles held a long, slender object that was obviously a weapon. It hung motionless for some minutes; then the gun moved slightly and a brilliant thread of violet flame lanced out from it. Far in the background something reddish shrieked and plummeted through the branches.

That was all, but that little was impressive enough. The weapon the film showed, evidently the equivalent of a light sporting rifle, compared favorably in performance with a Mark LV Becket.

There were other films; Spangler had not seen them, but he could imagine the kind of thing they must be. Pictures of Rithian factories, Rithian spaceships, Rithian laboratories. No matter what they were like in detail, in mass they had been impressive enough to convince Earth's strategists that making war on the Rithains might be disastrous.

So the slow campaign had begun: economic sabotage, subversion, propaganda. Nothing overt; nothing that could be surely traced to the Earthmen masquerading as Non-Empire traders in the Rithian system. The tiny disruption bombs that had destroyed many another, weaker world would not be planted: the Rithians were a space-faring people, with colonies and a space fleet, and such a people can retaliate if their home world is destroyed. The campaign would be simply one of slow, patient attrition, designed to weaken the Rithians as a race and as a galactic nation; to divide them politically, hamper them economically and intellectually; to enmesh them in so subtle a net of difficulties that eventually, without knowing how it had come about, the Rithians would find that the crest of the wave had passed them by; that they were settling into the trough of history. It would take centuries, but Earth could wait.

Well, the Rithians *had* discovered their enemies. And now the situation was grotesquely changed. No part of

Earth's knowledge of the Rithians could any longer be considered reliable. The Rithians might be stronger or weaker than had been thought; the one thing that appeared certain was that they were not as they appeared in the films and the written reports that had reached Earth.

Even the best planning could not always succeed, Spangler thought. It was conceivable that Earth had finally met an antagonist against whom neither force nor subtlety would be of any use. Wonderingly, Spangler allowed his mind to focus on the idea of a universe in which the human race had been exterminated, like so many other races which had met superior force, superior subtlety. It was like trying to imagine the universe going forward after one's own death; his mind pulled back from it instinctively, shaken and alarmed.

At any rate, the game was not yet played out; and, Spangler reminded himself wryly, he was not charged with the responsibility of revising the Empire's military policy. He had one simple task to perform:

Find the Rithian.

Which brought him inevitably back to Pembun. Spangler's irritation returned, and grew. With a muttered *"Damn* the man!" he stood and began pacing restlessly up and down his office.

Spangler was a career executive, not a Security operative; but he knew himself to be conscientious, thorough, interested in his work—and he had been in the Department for fifteen years. He ought not to feel about anyone as he felt about Pembun: baffled, uneasy, his mind filled with shadowy suspicions that had no source and no direction.

He had been through Pembun's dossier not once but three times: Keith-Ingram was right, the man's record was absolutely clean. But—Spangler stopped pacing. There was one thing which the dossier did not explain, and it was the first thing an agent of Security should want to know about any man.

"What does he *want?*" Spangler asked aloud.

That was it: it located the sore spot that had been bothering Spangler for two days. What was Pembun after, what did he hope to accomplish? His talk was subtly flavored with amused contempt for the Empire and admiration for the Rithians. Then why was he working for one to defeat the other?

That was the thing to find out.

V

The flow chart of Administration Hill was enormously complex. Processions of speedsters, coptercars and limousines merged, mingled and separated again; scooters, for intramural transport, moved in erratic lines among the larger vehicles and darted along the interoffice channels reserved for them alone. Traffic circles and cloverleaves directed and distributed the flow. At every instant vehicles slipped out of the mainstream, discharged or loaded passengers, and were gone again.

The cars, individually, were silent. In the aggregate, they produced a sound that just crossed the threshold of audibility: a single sustained note which blended itself with the hum of a million conversations, the shuffling of a million feet. The resulting sound was that of an enormous, idling dynamo.

Pembun's movements traced a thin, wavering line across all this ordered confusion. And wherever he passed, amusement spread in his wake.

At the intersection of Corridors Baker and One Zero, he tried to dismount from a scooter before it had come to a complete stop. The scooter's safety field caught him, half on and half off, and held him, his limbs waving like an angry beetle's, until it was safe to put him down.

A ripple of laughter spread, and some of the recordists and codex operators, with nothing better to do in their morning break, followed him into the Section D commissary.

His experience with the scooter seemed to have dazed the little man. He boarded the moving strip inside the commissary and then simply stood there, watching the room swing past him. He made a complete circuit, passing

192

a dozen empty tables, and began another. The recordists and codex girls nudged their friends and pointed him out.

On the third circuit, Pembun appeared to realize that he would eventually have to get off. He put out a foot gingerly, then drew it back. He faced in the other direction, decided that was worse, and turned around again. Finally, with desperate resolution, he stepped off the slowly-moving strip. His feet somehow got tangled. Pembun sat down with a thud that shook the floor.

The laughter spread again. A man at a stripside table got something caught in his windpipe and had to have his back pounded. Diners at more distant locations stood up to see what was happening. Half a dozen people, trying to hide their smiles, helped Pembun to his feet.

Pembun wandered out again. A blue-capped official guide came forward, determinedly helpful, but Pembun, with vehement gestures, explained that he was all right and knew where he was going.

His bones ached, from his coccyx all the way up to his cranium. That had been his sixth pratt-fall of the morning, and there were others still to come.

He felt more than a little foolish—this place was so *big!*—but he plowed through the press at the commissary entrance, signaled for another scooter and rode it half a kilometer down the corridor.

On the walkway, just emerging from one of the offices, was a group which included two people he knew: the darkly mustachioed Colonel Cassina and his expressionless aide, Captain Wei. Pembun waved happily and once more tried to get off the scooter before it had stopped.

He writhed frantically in the tingling, unpleasant grip of the safety field. When it set him down at last, he charged forward, slipped, lost his balance, and—

The jar traveled all the way up his spine and exploded against the back of his head. He looked up dazedly.

The group wore a collective expression of joyful disbelief. There were suppressed gurglings, as of faulty plumbing; a nervous giggle or two from the feminine contingent; snickers from the rear. Colonel Cassina allowed himself a single snort of what passed with him for laughter. Even the impassive Captain Wei emitted a peculiar, high-pitched series of sounds which might be suggested by *"Tcheel tcheel tcheel"*

Helpful hands picked Pembun up and dusted him off. Cassina, his face stern again, said gruffly, "Don't get off before the thing stops, man. That way you won't get hurt." He turned away, then came back, evidently feeling the point needed more stress. *"Don't get off before the thing stops.* Understand?"

Pembun nodded, wordless. Mouth half open, he watched Cassina and Wei as they boarded a tandem scooter and swung off up Corridor Baker.

When he turned around, a disheveled Gordon was looming over him. "There you are!" cried the young man. "Really, Mr. Pembun, I've been looking for you upwards of an hour. Didn't you hear your annunciator buzzing?"

Pembun glanced at the instrument strapped to his right wrist. The movable cover was turned all the way to the left. "My!" he said. "I never thought about it, Mr. Gordon. Looks like I 'ad it turned off all the time."

Gordon smiled with his lips. "Well, I've found you, anyhow, sir. Can you come along to the Commissioner's office now? He's waiting to see you."

Without waiting for an answer, Gordon simultaneously hailed a tandem scooter and spoke into the instrument at his wrist.

"That's fine," said Pembun happily. "That was w'ere I 'ad a mind to go, any'ow."

He boarded the scooter in front of Gordon, and this time followed Cassina's advice. He waited until the scooter had come to a complete stop, got off without difficulty, and strolled cheerfully into Spangler's office.

"Sorry I was 'ard to find," he said apologetically, "I 'ad my mind on w'at I was doing, and I didn't notice I 'ad my communicator turned off."

"Perfectly all right, Mr. Pembun," said Spangler, with iron patience. "Sit down. That's all, Gordon, thanks." He turned to Pembun. "Your suggestions are being followed up," he said curtly. "My immediate superior has directed me to ask you if you can help us still further by suggesting some new line of attack—one, for preference, which won't require two or three months."

"I was working on that," Pembun told him, "and not

getting much of anyw'ere. But it doesn't matter now. I got another idea, and I was lucky. I found your Rithch."

As Spangler's face slowly froze, Pembun added, " 'E's Colonel Cassina's aide, Captain Wei."

Spangler began in a strangled voice, "Are you seriously saying—" He stopped, pressed a stud on the edge of his desk, and began again. "This conversation is being recorded, Mr. Pembun. You have just said that you have found the Rithian, and that he is Captain Wei. Tell me your reasons."

"Well, I better start at the beginning," said Pembun, "otherwise it won't make sense. You see, I 'ad a notion this Rithch might be a little worried. The fluoroscopes wouldn' bother 'im, of cawse, but the planet-wide embargo would. And so far as 'e knew, you might bring up something that would work better than fluoroscopes. So I thought it jus' might be possible that 'e'd 'ide 'imself in the middle of the people that were looking for 'im. That way, 'e'd be able to dodge your search squads, and 'e might stand a chance of getting 'imself out through the cordon. That was w'y 'e picked Colonel Cassina, seemingly. Any'ow, I thought it would strike 'im funny.

"So I went around making people lahf, jus' taking a chance. It was kind of 'ard, because like I told you, the Rithi got a primitive sense of yumor. Now, if you go and fall on your be'ind in front of a Rithch, 'e's going to lahf. 'E can't 'elp 'imself. That's w'at Captain Wei did. I've 'eard the Rithi lahf before. It sounds enough like yuman lahfter to fool you if you're not paying attention, but once you've 'eard it you'll never be mistaken. I'm telling you the truth, Commissioner. Captain Wei is the Rithch."

Spangler, his lips thin, put his hand over the communicator plate. "Dossier on Captain Wei," he said.

"If you'll excuse me, Commissioner, I don' know w'ether 'e knows 'e gave 'imself away or not. If 'e knows we're after 'im and we don' catch 'im pretty quick, 'e's liable to do something we won't like."

Spangler glanced at Pembun, his face sharp with irritation, and started to speak. Then his desk communicator buzzed and he put his hand over it. "Yes?"

Gordon's worried voice said, "There *is* no dossier on Captain Wei, Commissioner. I don't understand how it

195

could have happened. Do you want me to check with District Archives in Denver?"

After a moment Spangler shot another glance at Pembun, a look compounded of excitement, intense dislike and unwilling respect. He said, "Do it later, Gordon. Meanwhile, get me Colonel Cassina, and then call the guardroom. I want all the available counter-Rithian trainees with full equipment, and I want them *now*."

There was no doubt about it: "Captain Wei" was the Rithian spy. Somewhere, somehow, it must have managed to meet Cassina and make friends with him; or, at any rate, contrived to remain in his company long enough to take over control of Cassina's mind—to convince him, probably, that "Wei" was an old and valued friend, with whom Cassina had worked elsewhere; that "Wei" was now free to accept a new assignment, and that Cassina had already arranged for his transfer.

Introduced by Cassina, the supposed Chinese officer had passed without question. But there was no dossier in the files bearing that name. "Captain Wei" did not exist.

All this time, Spangler thought with a shudder, that monster had been living in their midst, sitting at their conferences, hearing everything that was planned against it. It must have been hard for it not to laugh.

The bitterest thing of all was that Pembun had found it. If it ever got out that a moon-faced colonial had solved Spangler's problem for him by falling on his rear all over Administration Hill. . . .

Spangler impatiently put the thought out of his mind. They were at the doorway to Cassina's private office. "Wei" was in the smaller office immediately beyond; it communicated both with Cassina's suite and with the outer offices.

He saw the squad leader raise his watch to his ear. By now the other half of the detail would have reached the outer offices and quietly evacuated them. It must be time to go in.

The squad leader opened the door, and Spangler stepped in past him. Pembun was immediately behind; then came the five operatives, all armed with immobilizing field projectors, and Mark XX "choppers"—energy weapons which, in the hands of a skilled operator, would slice off an arm or leg—or tentacle—as neatly as a surgeon could do it.

The operatives were encased from head to foot in tight, seamless gasproofs. The upper halves of their faces were covered by transparent extensions of the helmets; the rest of the face-coverings, with the flexible tubes that led to oxygen tanks on their backs, dangled open on their chests.

This, at any rate, was according to standard operating procedure. The Rithian was urgently wanted alive, but no chances could or would be taken. "Wei's" room would be shut off by two planar force screens, one projected by the standard equipment in Cassina's desk, the other by a portable projector set up by the squad in the outer offices. At the same instant, the air-conditioning ducts serving the room would be blocked off. Inside that airtight compartment, the operatives would simultaneously gas and immobilize the Rithian; and if anything went wrong, they would use the choppers. It was a maneuver that had been rehearsed by these men a hundred times.

Spangler had told Cassina nothing—had only asked if Wei was in his office, then had hesitated as if changing his mind and promised to call back in a few minutes. Now Cassina stood up behind his desk, eyes bulging. "What's this? What's this?" he said incredulously.

"Wei," Spangler said. "Stand out of the way, please, Colonel. I'll explain in a moment."

"Explain!" said Cassina sharply. "See here, Spangler—"

The squad leader moved forward to the closed door of the inner office. At his signal, three of the remaining men took positions in front of the door; the other moved to herd Cassina out from behind his desk.

Cassina stepped aside, then moved suddenly and violently. Spangler, frozen with shock, saw him stiff-arm the approaching operative and instantly hurl himself into the group at the door. The group dissolved into a maelstrom of motion; then the door was open, Cassina had disappeared, and the others were untangling themselves and streaming in after him.

Spangler found himself running forward. A wisp of something acrid caught his throat; muffled shouts rang in his ears. A man's green-clad back blocked his view for an instant, then he darted to one side and could see.

The Rithian, his back oddly humped, was half-crouched over the dangling, limp body of Colonel Cassina. The monster's hands were clenched around Cassina's throat.

Everything was very clear, highly magnified.

A voice Spangler knew suddenly filled the room. Evidently the loudspeaker system had been turned on, though why they had got Joanna to declaim, *"The quality of mercy is not strained; it droppeth as the gentle rain . . ."* Spangler really could not say.

It was very strange.

Everything had suddenly gone dead still, and the room was tilting very slowly to a vertiginous angle, while the tensed body of the Rithian—or was it really Captain Wei? —collapsed with equal slowness over the body of his victim. Spangler tried languidly to adjust himself to the tilting of the room, but he seemed to be paralyzed. There was no sensation in any part of his body. Then the floor got bigger and bigger, and at last turned into a dazzling mottled display that he watched for a long time before it greyed and turned dark.

"What happened?"

That was just the question Spangler wanted answered; he wished they had let him ask it himself. He tried to say something, but another voice cut in ahead of him.

"He went into the room without a suit. The gas got him."

Whom were they talking about? Slowly it dawned on Spangler that it was himself. That was it; that was why everything had been so strange a moment ago—

He opened his eyes. He was lying on the couch in his own private office. Two medical technicians, in pale-green smocks, were standing near the head of the couch. Farther down were Gordon, Miss Timoney and the squad leader. Pembun was sitting in a chair against the wall.

One of the medics languidly picked up Spangler's wrist and held it for a few seconds, then gently thumbed back one eyelid. "He's all right," he said, turning in Gordon's direction. "No danger at all." He moved away, and the other medic followed him out of the room.

Spangler sat up, swinging his legs over the side of the couch, and drew several deep breaths. He still felt a little dazed, but his head was clearing. He said to the leader, "Tell me what happened."

The leader had removed his gasproof and was standing, bare-headed, in orange tights and high-topped shoes. He had an olive face, with heavy black brows and a stiff brush of greying black hair. He said, "You got a whiff of the gas, Commissioner."

"I know that, man," Spangler said irritably. "Tell me the rest."

"Colonel Cassina attacked us and forced his way into the inner office," the leader said. "We were taken by surprise, but we fired the gas jets and then got inside as fast as we could. When we got inside, we found the Rithian apparently trying to throttle Colonel Cassina. My men and I used the choppers, but, not to excuse ourselves, Commisioner, the Colonel interfered with our aim. The Rithian was killed."

Spangler felt an abrupt wave of nausea, and mastered it with an effort. "Colonel Cassina? How is he?"

"In bad shape, I understand, Commissioner."

"He's in surgery now, sir," Gordon put in. "He's alive, but his throat is crushed."

Spangler stood up a little shakily. "What's been done with the Rithian?"

"I've had the body taken down to the lab, sir," Gordon said. "Dr. Baustian is there now. But they're waiting for your orders before they go ahead."

"All right," said Spangler, "let's get on with it."

He caught a glimpse of Pembun, with a curious expression on his face, trailing along behind the group as they left.

VI

At first the corpse looked like the body of a young Chinese murdered by a meticulously careful axe-fiend: there was a gaping wound straight down from forehead to navel, then a perpendicular cross-cut, and then another gash down each leg.

Then they peeled the human mask away, and underneath lay the Rithian. The worst of it, Spangler thought, was the ochre fur: it was soft-looking, and a darker color where it was rumpled—like the fur of the teddy bear he remembered from his childhood. But this was an obscene teddy bear, a thing of limp tentacles and dull bulging red eyes, with a squashy bladder in the middle. It ought to have been stepped on, Spangler thought, and put into the garbage tube and forgotten.

It filled the human shell exactly. The top ring of tentacles had been divided, three on each side, to fit into "Wei's" arms. In the middle of each clump of tentacles, when the lab men pried them apart, was the white skeleton of a human arm; the shoulder joint emerged just under the ring. The tentacles in the second ring had been coiled neatly around the body, out of the way. The rest of the torso, and the leg spaces, had been filled by a monstrous, muscular bulging of the Rithian's sac-like abdomen.

Then the dissection started . . .

Spangler stayed only because he could not think of a suitable excuse to leave; Cassina was still in shock and could not be seen.

Baustian and the other bio men were like children with new toys: first the muscles, and the nerve and blood and lymph systems in the "legs" the Rithian had formed from its shapeless body; then, when they cut open the torso, one bloody lump after another held up, and prodded, and exclaimed over. "Good Lord, look at this pancreas!" or "this liver!" or "that kidney!"

In the end the resemblance to a teddy bear was nothing at all. The most horrible thing was that the more they cut, the more human the body looked. . . .

Later, he was standing in front of Cassina's door, and Pembun was holding his arm. "Don't tell 'im the Rithi is dead," the little man said urgently. "Tell 'im it was all a mistake. Let 'im think w'at 'e likes of you. It may be important."

"Why?" Spangler asked vacantly.

Pembun looked at him with that same odd, haunted expression Spangler had noticed before, when they had left his office. He ought to be feeling cocky, Spangler thought vaguely, but he isn't. Why, why—

"'E's still in danger, Commissioner. 'E's not responsible for 'is own actions. You've got to convince 'im that you weren't after Wei at all, and that Wei's all right, otherwise I believe 'e'll try to kill 'imself."

"I don't understand you," Spangler said. "How do you know the doctors or nurses haven't already told him?"

"I told them not to say anything," Pembun said, unabashed, "and let them think the order came from you."

Spangler's lips tightened. "We'll talk about this later," he said, and palmed the doorplate.

Cassina's eyes were closed. His face was a dead olive-grey except for a slight flush on either cheekbone. He had the stupid, defenseless look of all sleeping invalids.

His head was supported by a hollow in the bolster; a rigid harness covered his neck. His mouth was slightly open under the coarse black mustachios, and a curved suction tube was hooked over his lower teeth.

The tube emitted a low, monotonous gurgling, which changed abruptly to a dry sucking noise. An attendant stepped forward and joggled the tube with one finger; the gurgling resumed.

As Spangler glanced away from the unconscious man, a medic came forward. He was tall and loose-limbed; his brown eyes gleamed with the brilliance that meant contact lenses. "Commissioner Spangler?"

Spangler nodded.

"I'm Dr. Householder, in charge of this section. You can question this man now, but I want you to avoid exciting him if you can, and don't stay longer than fifteen minutes after the injection. He's got half the pharmacopoeia in him already."

Spangler stepped forward and sat down by the bedside. At Householder's nod, a horse-faced female attendant set the muzzle of a pressure hypodermic against Cassina's bare forearm. She pressed the trigger, then unscrewed the magazine, dropped it into a tray and replaced it with another. In a moment Cassina sighed and opened his eyes.

Another attendant set a metal plate on the bed under Cassina's hand and gently forced a stylus between his fingers. Cables from plate and stylus led back around the foot of the bed to a squat, wheeled machine with a hooded screen. The attendant went to the machine, snapped a switch and then sat down beside it.

Cassina's eyes turned slowly until he discovered Spangler. He frowned, and seemed to be trying to speak. His lips moved minutely, but his jaw still hung open, with the suction tube hooked inside it. The monotonous gurgling of withdrawn sputum continued.

"Don't try to talk," Spangler said. "Your throat and jaws are immobilized. Use the stylus."

Cassina glanced downward, and his hand clenched around the slender metal cylinder. After a moment he wrote, "What have you done to Wei?"

The words crawled like black snakes across the white screen. Spangler nodded, and the attendant turned a knob; the writing vanished.

Spangler looked thoughtfully at Cassina. The question he had been expecting was "What happened?"—meaning "What happened to me?" In the circumstances, the question was almost a certainty—probability point nine nine nine.

But Cassina had asked about Wei instead.

Grudgingly, Spangler said, "Nothing, Colonel. We weren't after Captain Wei, you know. The Rithian spy had concealed itself in his room. We couldn't warn Wei without alerting the Rithian."

Cassina stared gravely at Spangler, as if trying to de-

202

cide whether he was lying. Spangler abruptly found himself gripping his knees painfully hard.

"He's all right?" Cassina scrawled.

"Perfectly," said Spangler. "Everything's all right. We've got the Rithian, and the alert is over."

Cassina drew a deep breath and let it out again. His mouth still hung idiotically slack, but his eyes smiled. He wrote, "What have you got me in this straitjacket for?"

"You were injured in the struggle. You'll be fit again in a few days. We're going to put you back to sleep now." Spangler motioned; the horse-faced girl pressed the hypo against Cassina's arm and pressed the trigger.

After a moment she said, "Colonel Cassina, we want you to write the numbers from one to fifty. Begin, please."

At "15" the scrawled numerals began to grow larger, less controlled; "23" was repeated twice, followed by a wild "17."

The attendant nodded. "He's under."

It was long after office hours, but Spangler still sat behind his desk. He had switched off the overhead illumination; the only light came from the reading screen in front of him. The screen showed a portion of the transcript of his interview with Cassina.

Spangler flipped over a switch and ran the spool back to the beginning. He read the opening lines again:

Q.: Can you hear me, Colonel?
A.: Yes.
Q.: I want you to answer these questions clearly, truthfully and fully to the best of your ability. When and where did you first meet Captain Wei?
A.: In Daressalam, in October, 2501.
Q.: Are you certain of that? Are you telling the truth?
A.: Yes.

Cassina's conscious mind was convinced that he had first met "Wei" twenty years ago in the African District. Several repetitions of the question failed to produce any other answer. Spangler had tried to get around the obstacle by asking for the first meeting after February 18, 2521—

the date of the Rithian agents' discovery by the city patrol.
He skipped a score of lines and read:

Q.: What happened after that dinner?
A.: I invited him to my quarters. We sat and talked.
Q.: What was said?
A.: (2 sec. pause) I don't remember exactly.
Q.: You are ordered to remember. What did Wei
tell you?
A.: (2 sec. pause) He told me—said he was Capt.
Wei, served under me in the African District from
2501 to 2507. He—
Q.: But you knew that already, didn't you?
A.: Yes. No. (2 sec. pause) I don't remember.
Q.: I will rephrase the question. Did you or did you
not know prior to that evening that Wei had served
under you in the African District?
A.: (3 sec. pause) No.
Q.: What else did he tell you that night?
A.: Said he had done Naval Security work. Said he
had applied for transfer, to be attached to me as my
aide.
Q.: Did he tell you anything else, either instructions
or information, other than details of your former ac-
quaintance or details about his transfer, that evening?
A.: No.
Q.: Skip to your next meeting. What did he tell you
on that occasion?

Gradually the whole story had come out, except one
point. Spangler had struck a snag when he came to the
evening of the 20th, two days ago.

Q.: What did Wei tell you that evening?
A.: (4 sec. pause) I don't remember. Nothing.
Q.: You are ordered to remember. What did he tell
you?
A.: (6 sec. pause: subject shows great agitation)
Nothing, I tell you.
Q.: You are ordered to answer, Colonel Cassina.
A.: (subject does not reply; at end of five seconds
begins to weep)

Dr. Householder: The fifteen minutes are up, Commissioner.

End transcript 12.52 hrs 2/22/2521.

Later in the afternoon, after his first report to Keith-Ingram, Spangler had had another session with Cassina under the interrogation machine. He had drawn another blank, and had had to give up after five minutes because of Cassina's increasing distress. On being released from the machine, Cassina had gone into a coma and Householder had declared that it would be dangerous to question him again until further notice.

Half an hour later, while he was talking to Pembun, Spangler had had a report that Cassina, still apparently unconscious, had made a strenuous effort to tear himself free of the protective collar and had gone into massive hemorrhage. He was now totally restrained, drugged, receiving continuous transfusion, and on the critical list.

Pembun. Pembun, Pembun. There was no escaping him: no matter where your thoughts led you, Pembun popped up at the end of the trail, as if you were Alice trying to get out of the looking-glass garden.

Pembun had been right again; Pembun was always right. They had triggered some posthypnotic command in Cassina's mind, and Cassina, twitching to the tug of that string, had done his best to kill himself.

"It seems to me," Pembun had said that afternoon, "that the main question is—*w'y* did Colonel Cassina try so 'ard to get to the Rithch w'en 'e found out you were after 'im? 'E 'ad a command to do it, of course, but w'y? Not jus' to warn the Rithch, becawse 'e didn' get enough warning that way to do 'im any good, an' besides, if it was only that, w'y did the Rithch try to kill Cassina?"

"All right," Spangler had said, keeping his voice level with difficulty. "What is your explanation, Mr. Pembun?"

"Well, the Rithch mus' 'ave left some information buried in Cassina's subconscious that 'e didn' want us to find. I 'ad an idea that was it, and that's w'y I asked you not to tell Cassina the Rithch was dead—I thought 'e might 'ave been given another command, to commit suicide if the Rithch was discovered. I think we're lucky to 'ave Colonel Cassina alive today, Commissioner; I b'lieve 'e's the most important man in the Empire right now."

"That's a trifle strong," Spangler had said. "I won't deny that this buried information, whatever it is, must be valuable. But what makes you assume that it's crucial? Presumably, it's a record of the Rithians' espionage or sabotage activities. . . ."

"Sabotage," Pembun had said quickly. "It couldn' be the other, Commissioner, because the Rithch wouldn' care that much if you found out something you already know. I b'lieve Cassina knows this: 'E knows w'ere the bombs are buried."

"Bombs!" Spangler had said after a moment. The idea was absurd. "They wouldn't be so stupid, Mr. Pembun. We have military installations on two hundred sixty planets, not to mention the fleet in space. We'd retaliate, man. It would be suicide for them to bomb us."

"You don' understand, Commissioner. They don' want to bomb Earth—if they did, there wouldn' 'ave been any need for the Rithch to leave a record of w'ere the bombs were. 'E'd simply set them with a time mechanism, and that would be that. We couldn' do a thing till after they went off. But 'e was the last one alive, an' 'e couldn' be sure 'e'd get back with 'is information, so 'e 'ad to leave a record. That only means one thing. The Rithchi jus' want to be able to say, 'Leave us alone—or else.'"

Spangler's mind had worked furiously. It was terrifyingly possible; he could find no flaw in it. Suitably placed, a few score medium-sized disruption bombs would break a planet apart like a rotten apple. "Medium-sized" meant approximately six cubic centimeters; they would be easy to smuggle, easy to conceal, almost impossible to find. The only defense would be a radio-frequency screen over the whole planet; and if the enemy knew the precise locations of the bombs, even that defense would not work: a tight directional beam, accurately aimed, would get through and trigger the bombs. All it required was a race stubborn enough to say, "Leave us alone—or else"—and mean it. From what Pembun had said about the Rithians, they might well be such a race.

But Earth played the percentages. Earth took only calculated risks. Earth would have to succumb.

That chain of reasoning had taken only a fraction of a

second. Spangler examined it, compared it with the known facts, and discarded it. He smiled.

"But, Mr. Pembun—*we've got* Cassina. It doesn't matter whether we get the information out of him or not; all we care about is that the *Rithians* aren't going to get it."

Pembun had looked absurdly mournful. "No—you're assuming that Cassina is the only one 'oo's got the information. I wish that was so, but I don't see 'ow it can be. Don't you see, giving it to Colonel Cassina was a mistake, becawse 'is mind is the obvious place for us to look. Now, I can see the Rithch making that mistake, deliberately, becawse it struck 'im so funny 'e couldn' resist it—but I can't see 'im making that mistake becawse 'e was stupid. I think Colonel Cassina was just an afterthought; 'e was feeling cocky, and 'e decided to plant the message one more time, right under your noses. I think 'e and 'is friends 'ad *already* planted it a 'undred or two 'undred times, 'owever many they 'ad time for. An' if it was me, I would 'ave picked interstellar travelers—agents for trading companies, executives who travel by spaceship a lot, visitors to Earth from other systems. I think that's w'at they did. If they did, it's practic'ly a mathematical certainty that their agents will eventually reach one of those people. You could keep up the embargo, not let anybody leave, but 'ow long would it take to process everybody 'oo might carry the message?"

"Years," Spangler had said curtly, staring at his desktop.

"That's right. It could be done, and if you were lucky it might work. But it would kill Earth just as sure as blowing it up. . . . We've got to find out w'at Colonel Cassina knows, Commissioner. There isn' any other way."

VII

After that had come the news about Cassina, almost as if it had been timed to underscore Pembun's words. Then the second and more painful interview with Keith-Ingram. Then Spangler had turned to some of the routine matters that had been filling his in-box all day, and quite suddenly it had been quitting time.

Spangler had started to leave, but had stopped at the door, turned to look at the silent, comforting walls, turned around and sat down at his desk again. Acting on an impulse he could hardly explain, he had called Joanna and begged off taking her to dinner. He had been sitting there, hardly moving, ever since.

He pressed the stud of his thumb-watch. "Eighteen eleven and one quarter."

Three hours; and he had had no dinner. There was a sickish taste in his mouth, and he felt a little light-headed, but not at all hungry.

He thumbed open the revolving front of the desk, took out a dispenser vial of pick-me-ups, and swallowed one moodily.

A vast weariness and distaste for his work and everything it implied was rising in him. He suppressed it grimly. He had known such moods before; they passed. Boredom and disgust were like the pangs of dyspepsia: you ignored them, and did your work.

It came down to this, Spangler thought slowly. They had been very nearly beaten; except for one man—Pembun—they would have been beaten. And that was all wrong.

Pembun was uncouth, ill-educated, unmannered. His methods were the merest improvisation. He had intelligence, one was forced to admit, but it was crude, untutored and undirected. But he got results.

208

Why?

It was possible to explain all the events of the past two days simply by saying that Pembun had happened to possess special knowledge, not available to Security, which had happened to be just the knowledge needed. But that was an evasion. The knowledge was not "special"; it was knowledge Earth should have had, and had tried to get, and had failed to get.

Again, *why?*

It seemed to Spangler that since Pembun's arrival the universe had slowly, almost imperceptibly turned over until it was upside down. And yet nothing had changed. Pembun was the same; so were Spangler and the rest of the world he knew.

It was a little like one of those optical illusions that you got in Primary Camouflage—a series of cubes that formed a flight of stairs going upward; and then you blinked, and the cubes were hollow, or the stairs were hanging upside down. Or like the other kind, the silhouettes of two men, with converging perspective lines at the top and bottom: you thought one man was much taller, but when you measured them you found that both were the same—or even that the one that had seemed smaller was larger than the other. . . .

Spangler swore. He had been on the point, he realized, of getting up, taking a scooter to G level, suite 111, and asking Pembun humbly to explain to him why the sun now revolved around the Earth, black was white, and great acorns from little oak trees grew.

He picked up a memocube and flung it violently onto the desk again.

The gesture gave him no relief; the feeling of rebellion passed, depression and bewilderment remained.

Like a moth to the flame—like Mahomet to the mountain—Spangler went to Pembun.

This time the door was closed.

After the space of three heartbeats, the scooter moved off silently down the way he had come, lights winking on ahead of it in the deserted corridor and fading when it passed. It turned the corner at Upsilon and disappeared, heading for the invisible lategoer who had signaled it.

Silence.

Down the corridor for five meters in either direction, glareless overhead lights showed Spangler every detail of the satin-finished walls, the mathematical lines of doors and maintenance hatches, the almost invisible foot-traces that, some time during the night, would be vibrated into molecular dust and then gulped by suction tubes. Beyond was nothing but darkness. Far away, a tiny dot of light flared for an instant, like a shooting star, as someone crossed the corridor.

Spangler had an instant's vision of what it would be like if the whole thing were to stop: the miles of empty corridors, the stagnant air, the darkness, the drifting dust, the slow invasion of insects. The dead weight of the Hill, bearing invisibly down upon you; terrible, insentient weight; weight of a corpse.

Spangler had forced himself into the channel of his ambition, and held himself there without deviation for ten long years. It had not been easy, with the handicap of his birth. He had remade himself with agonizing care, until he was more aristocratic than the aristocrats. He had suppressed everything that did not contribute, emphasized and nurtured everything that did. He had built, he thought, upon a rock.

And now, if that rock crumbled . . .

Swallowing bile, he put his hand over the doorplate. There was a long pause before the door slid open. Pembun, in underblouse and pantaloons, blinked at him as if he had been asleep. "Oh—Commissioner Spangler. Come awn in."

Spangler said roughly, "I'm disturbing you, I'm afraid. It isn't anything urgent; I'll talk with you tomorrow."

"No, please do come in, Commissioner. I'm glad you came. I was getting a little morbid, sitting 'ere by myself."

He closed the door behind Spangler. "Drink? I've still got 'alf the w'iskey left, and all the soda."

The thought of a drink made Spangler's stomach crawl. He refused it and sat down.

On the table beside the recliner were several sheets of paper and an ornate old-fashioned electropen.

"I was jus' writing a letter to my wife," Pembun said, following his glance. "Or trying to." He smiled. "I can't tell 'er anything important without violating security, and

I know I'll prob'ly get back to Ganymede before a letter would, after the embargo is lifted, any'ow, so there rilly wasn' much sense to it. It was jus' something to do."

Spangler nodded. "It's a pity we can't let you leave the Hill. But there's an amusement section right here—cinemas, autochess, dream rooms, baths—"

Pembun shook his head, still smiling. "I wouldn' take any pleasure in those things, Commissioner."

His tone, it seemed to Spangler, was half regretful, half indulgent. No doubt they had other, more vigorous pleasures on Manhaven. Narcotics and mixed bathing would seem to them effete or incomprehensible.

Without knowing what he was about to say, he blurted, "Tell me truthfully, Pembun—do you despise us?"

Pembun's eyes widened slightly, then narrowed, and his whole face subtly congealed. "I try not to," he said quietly. "It's too easy. Did you come 'ere to ask me that, Commissioner?"

Spangler leaned forward, elbows on knees, clasping his hands together, "I think I did," he said. "Forgive my rudeness, Pembun, but I really want to know. What's wrong with us, in your view? What would you change, if you could?"

Pembun said carefully, "W'at would you say was your motive for asking that, Commissioner?"

Spangler glanced up. From this angle, Pembun looked more impressive. Spangler stared at him in a kind of rapture of discovery: the man's face was neither ugly nor ludicrous. The eyes were steady and alive with intelligence; the wide mouth was firm. Even the outsize ears, the heavy cheeks, only gave the face added strength and a curious dignity.

He said, "I want information. I've misjudged you grossly—and I apologize, but that's not enough. I feel that there must be something wrong with my basic assumptions, with the Empire. I want to know why we failed in this Rithian affair, and you succeeded. I think you can help me, if you will."

He waited.

Pembun said slowly, "Commissioner, I think you 'ave another motive, w'ether you rillize it consciously or not.

Let me tell it to you, and see if you agree. Did you ever 'ear of pecking precedence in 'ens?"

"No," said Spangler. "By the way, call me Spangler, or Thorne, won't you?"

"All right—Thorne. You can cawl me Jawj, if you like. Now, about the 'ens. Say there are twelve in a yard. If you watch them, you'll find out that they 'ave a rigid social 'ierarchy. 'En A gets to peck all the others, 'en B pecks all the others but A, C pecks all but A and B, and so on down to 'en L, 'oo gets pecked by everybody and can't peck anybody back."

"Yes," said Spangler, "I see."

Pembun went on woodenly, "You're 'en B or C in the same kind of a system. There are one or two superiors that lord it over you, and you do the same to the rest. Now, usually w'en anybody new comes into the yard, you know right away w'ether it's someone 'oo pecks you or gets pecked. But I'm a diff'rent case. I'm a diff'rent breed of 'en, and I don't rilly belong in your yard at all, so you try not to peck me excep' w'en I provoke you; it would lower your dignity. That's until you suddenly find that *I'm* pecking *you*. Now you've *got* to fit me into the system above yourself, becawse all this pecking wouldn' be endurable if you got it from both directions. So you came 'ere to say, 'I know you're 'igher in the scale than me, so it's all right. Go a'ead—peck me.' "

Spangler stared at him in silence. He was interested to observe that although he felt humiliated, the emotion was not actually unpleasant. It's a species of purge, he thought. It's good for us all to be taken down a peg now and then.

"W'at's more," Pembun said, watching him, "you injoy it. It's a pleasure to you to kowtow to somebody you think is stronger. It gives you a feeling of security. Isn' that true?"

"I won't say you're wrong," Spangler answered, trying to be honest. "I've never heard it expressed just that way before, but it's certainly true that I'm conditioned to accept and exert authority—and you're quite right, I enjoy both acts. It's a necessary state of mind in my profession, or so I've always believed. I suppose it isn't very pretty, looked at objectively."

212

Pembun started to reach for the whiskey decanter, then drew his hand back. He looked at Spangler with a wry smile. "W'at you don' rillize," he said, "is that I get no pleasure out of it. This may be 'ard for you to understand, but it's no fun for me to 'it a man 'oo's not trying to 'it me back. This 'ole conversation 'as been unpleasant to me, but I couldn' avoid it. You put me in a position w'ere no matter w'at I said, I'd be doing w'at you wanted. And this is the funny part, Commissioner—in making me 'urt your self-esteem, you've 'urt mine twice as bad. I expec' I'll 'ave a bad taste in my mouth for days."

Spangler stood up slowly. He took two deep breaths, but his sudden anger did not subside; it grew. He said carefully, "I don't need to have a mountain fall on me. That's a quaint expression we have, Mr. Pembun—it means that one clear and studied insult is enough."

Suddenly Pembun was just what he had seemed in the beginning: an irritating, dirty-faced, ugly little beast of a *colonial.*

Pembun said, "You see, now you're angry. That's becawse I wouldn' play the pecking game with you."

Spangler said furiously, "Mr. Pembun, I didn't come here for insults, or for barnyard psychology either. I came to ask you for information. If you are so far lost to common civility—" The sentence slipped out of his grasp; he started again: "Perhaps I had better remind you that I'm empowered to *demand* your help as an official of the Empire."

Pembun said, unruffled, "I'm 'ere to 'elp if I can, Commissioner. W'at was it you wanted, exactly?"

"I asked you," said Spangler, "to tell me what, in your opinion, were the causes of Security and War Department failure in the Rithian case." As Pembun started to speak, he cut in: "Put your remarks on a spool, and have it on my desk in the morning." His voice sounded unnaturally loud in his own ears; it occurred to him with a shock that he had been shouting.

Pembun shook his head sadly, reprovingly. "I'll be glad to—if you put your request in writing, Commissioner."

Spangler clenched his jaw. "You'll get it tomorrow," he

213

said. He turned, opened the door and strode away down the empty corridor. He did not stop to signal for a scooter until he had turned the corner, and Pembun's doorway was out of sight.

VIII

He found Joanna in the tower room, lying against a section of the couch that was elevated to form a backrest. The room was filled, choked to bursting by a male voice shouting incomprehensible syllables against a strident orchestral background. Spangler's brain struggled futilely with the words for an instant, then rejected them in disgust: the recording was one of Joanna's period collection, sung in one of the dead languages. German; full of long vowels and fruity sibilants.

She waved her hand over the control box, and the volume diminished to a bearable level. She stood up and came to meet him.

"I thought you sounded upset when you called," she said, kissing him. "Sit here. Put your feet up. Have you had anything to eat?"

"No," said Spangler. "I couldn't. I'm too tired for food."

"I'll have something up. You needn't eat it if you don't want to."

"Fine," he said with an effort.

She dialed the antique food-selector at the side of the couch, then came to sit beside him.

The voice was still shouting, but as if it were a long distance away. It rose to a crescendo, there was a dying gasp from the orchestra, a moment's pause, and then another song began.

"Why don't you have that translated?" he said irritably.

"I don't know; I rather like it as it is. Shall I turn it off?"

"That's not the point," said Spangler with controlled impatience. "You like it as it is—why? Because it's incomprehensible? Is that a sane reason?"

The food-selector's light glowed. Joanna opened the hopper, took out a tube of broth and a sandwich loaf, and put them on the table at Spangler's side.

"What are you really angry about, Thorne?" she asked quietly.

"I'll tell you," said Spangler, sitting upright. The words spilled out of him, beyond his control. "Do you think it isn't obvious to me, and to everyone else who knows you, what you're doing to yourself with this morbid obsession? Do you think it's pleasant for me to sit here and watch you wallowing in the past, like a dog in carrion, because you're afraid of anything that hasn't been safely buried for four hundred years?"

Her eyes widened with shock, and Spangler felt an answering wave of pure dark joy. This was what he had come to do, he realized, though he hadn't known it before. It was what he should have done long ago.

She blushed furiously from forehead to breast, then turned ivory-pale.

"Stop it," she said in a tight voice.

"I won't stop," Spangler said, biting the words. "Look at yourself. You're half-alive, half a woman. You let just enough of yourself live to do your work, and answer when you're spoken to, and respond to your lover. The rest is dead and covered with dust. I can taste it when I kiss you. How do you think I feel, wanting you, knowing that you're out of my reach—not because—"

She got up and started toward the door. Spangler reached her in one stride, flung her backward onto the couch and held her there with his whole weight.

"—not because you belong to anyone else, or ever will, but because you're too timid, too selfish, too wrapped up in yourself ever to belong to anybody?"

She struggled ineffectively. Her eyes were unfocused and glazed with tears; her whole body was trembling.

Spangler tore open her robe, pulled it away from her body. "Go ahead, look at yourself! You're a woman, a living human being, not a mummy. Why is that so hateful? Do you get any pleasure from killing yourself and everything you touch?" He shook her. "Answer me."

She gasped, "I can't—"

"What can't you? You can feel, you can speak, you can do anything that a normal human being can do, but you won't. You wouldn't leave that smug little shell of yours

to save a life. You wouldn't leave it to save the Empire—
not even to save yourself."

"Let me go."

"You're not sick, you're not afraid, you're just selfish.
Cold and selfish. Everything for Joanna, and let the rest
of the universe go hang!"

"Let me go."

Her trembling had stopped; she was still breathing hard,
but her pale lips were firm. She raised her lids and looked
at him squarely, without blinking.

Spangler raised his open right hand and struck her in
the face. Her head bobbed. She looked at him incredulously, and her mouth opened.

Spangler hit her again. At the third blow, the tears
started afresh. Her face crumpled suddenly and a series
of short, animal sounds came out of her. At the fourth, she
stopped trying to turn her head aside. Her body was limp,
her eyes closed and without expression. Her sobs were as
mechanical and meaningless as a fit of the hiccoughs.

Spangler rolled away from her, stood up, and went to
the recliner. He felt purged and empty, listless and light.
He said tonelessly, "You can get up now. I won't hit you
again."

After a moment she sat up, spine curved, head hanging.
When she got to her feet and turned toward the bathroom
door, Spangler followed and stepped in front of her,
grasping her arm.

"Listen to me," he said. "You're going to marry me,
and we're going to be happy. Do you understand that?"

She looked up at him without interest.

"You fool," she said.

She stood quietly until he let her go, and then moved
without haste through the doorway. The door closed behind her and Spangler heard the lock click.

Spangler entered his office, as he usually did, half an hour
before the official opening time. He had sat up for a long
time after leaving Joanna's tower the night before, and
had slept badly afterwards. This morning he had a head-
ache which the pick-me-ups would not entirely suppress;
but his mind felt cold and clear. He knew precisely what
he wanted to do.

Last night's blunder was not irreparable. It was all but disastrous; it was criminally foolish; it had set him back at least six months; but it had not beaten him.

His first move would be to send her a present: something she would prize too much to reject—old paintings, or books or recordings. Very likely there would be something of the sort among the property seized by the Department in treason cases; if not, he would get it from a private collector. He had already composed the note to go with the gift: it was humble without servility, regretful without hope. It implied that he would not see her again; and he would not—not for at least a month.

The last three weeks of that time Spangler had allotted to grand strategy—planting rumors, certain to reach Joanna: that he was overworking; that he never smiled; that he was ill but had refused treatment. That sort of thing, details to be worked out later.

The first week was dedicated to an altogether different purpose. His ruinous outburst last night had at least had one salutary effect; it had taught Spangler that he could not fight both battles at once. Commencing today, his total energies would be aimed at one objective: to crush Pembun.

It could be done; it would be done. He had underestimated the man, but that was over. From now on, things would be different.

On his desk was a spool of summarized reports addressed to him from Keith-Ingram.

The activities of the Rithians, it seemed, had now been partially traced: eight of them, traveling together, had reached Earth as passengers aboard a second-rate tramp freighter, docking at Stambul, on the evening of February 10th. From Stambul they were known to have taken the stratosphere express to Paris, but no further trace of their movements had so far turned up until they appeared in Angels on the 18th, with one exception: the eighth Rithian had shipped out aboard a liner leaving for the Capri system on the 12th, only two days after the group had arrived. It had disembarked at Lumi, where its trail ended. Doubtless, Spangler thought, it had changed its disguise there and continued by a devious route. By now it was back in the Rithian system.

Its return before the others' was puzzling. Obviously the group had not finished its collective task, or the others would have got out too; either it had had a separate assignment, which it had completed before the others, or some single item of information had been turned up which the Rithians thought sufficiently important to send a messenger back with it immediately.

He glanced quickly through the conference schedule which Miss Timoney had made up the previous afternoon, then laid it aside and spent the rest of his half-hour in dictating notes to Pembun, Keith-Ingram and Dr. Baustian.

The note to Pembun repeated yesterday's question, word for word.

Keith-Ingram's reported the condition of Colonel Cassina and gave Pembun's analysis of the situation, without comment.

Baustian's requested him to submit, as soon as possible, a reliable procedure for identifying Rithians masquerading as human beings.

Pembun's reply popped into his in-box almost immediately; the man must have prepared it last night and held it ready for Spangler's formal request.

He put the spool viciously into the screen slot and skimmed through it. It was in reasonably good Standard; so good, in fact, that Spangler conceived an instant suspicion that Pembun could speak Standard acceptably when he chose.

The document read, in part:

In my judgment, the most serious weakness of Empire executive personnel is an excessive reliance on prescribed methods and regulations, and inadequate emphasis on original thinking and personal initiative. I am aware that this is in accord with overall policy, which would be difficult if not impossible to alter completely within the framework of the Empire, but it is my feeling that attention should be given to this problem at high policy levels, and efforts made to alter existing conditions if possible.

It is not within my competence to suggest a mode

of procedure, especially since the problem appears to be partly philosophical in nature. The tendency of Empire executive personnel to interpret regulations and directives in a rigid and literal manner is in my opinion clearly related to the increasing tendency toward standardization in Home World art, manners, customs and language. In the final category, I would cite the obsolescence of all Earth languages except Standard, and in Standard the gradual elimination of homonyms and synonyms, as well as the increasing tendency to restrict words to a single meaning, as especially significant. . . .

Spangler removed the spool and tossed it into his "awaiting action" box. A moment later it was time for his first conference.

He had left word with Gordon to give him any message from Baustian as soon as it arrived. Forty-five minutes after the conference began, a spool popped into the in-box in front of him.

Colonel Leclerc, Cassina's replacement, had been giving a long and enthusiastic account of certain difficulties encountered by the Fleet in maintaining the supra-Earth cordon, and the means by which they were being overcome. Medoc was the oldest man at the table, and fairly typical of the holdovers from the last generation but one, when, owing to the shortage of governmental and military personnel caused by the almost-disastrous Cartagellan war, standards had been regrettably lax. He was the sort of man one automatically thought of as "not quite class." His gestures were too wide, his talk imprecise and larded with anachronisms.

Spangler waited patiently until he paused to shrug, then cut in smoothly: "Thank you, Colonel. Now, before we continue, will you all pardon me a moment, please?"

He slipped the spool into place and lighted the reading screen. The note read:

Baustian, G. B., BuAlPhyl
Spangler, T., Dept Secur
MS   MU
2/23/2521

BAP CD18053990
Ref DS CD50347251

1. Recommended procedure for identifying members of the Rithian race masquerading as humans is as follows:

2. Make 1.7 cm. perpendicular incision, using instrument coated with paste of attached composition (Schedule A), in mid-thigh or shoulder region of subject. Reagent, in combination with Rithian body fluids, will produce brilliant purple precipitate. No reaction will take place in contact with human flesh.

3. For convenience of use, it is recommended that incision be made by agency of field-powered blade in standard grip casing, as in attached sketches. (Schedule B.)

4. If desired, blade coating may also contain soporific believed to be effective in Rithian body chemistry. (Schedule C.)

5. End.

    Att BAP CD 18053990A
         BAP CD 18053990B
         BAP CD 18053990C

Spangler smiled and cleared the screen.

"The information is satisfactory, Commissioner?" Colonel Leclerc demanded brightly.

"Quite satisfactory, Colonel." Quickly, so as to give Leclerc no opportunity to launch himself into his subject again, Spangler turned to Pemberton, the mayor's aide. "Mr. Pemberton?"

The young man began querulously, "We don't want to seem impatient, Commissioner, but you know that our office is under considerable pressure. Now, you've given us to understand that the Rithian has already been captured and killed, and what we want to know is, how much longer . . ."

Spangler heard him out as patiently, to all outward appearance, as if he had not heard the same complaint daily since the embargo began. He put Pemberton off smoothly but noncommittally, and adjourned the conference.

Back in his office, Spangler finished reading Baustian's note and dictated an endorsement of paragraphs one to three. Paragraph four was a good notion, but anything with a rider like that on it would take twice as long to go through channels.

Spangler rewound the spool and set the machine to make three copies, one of which he addressed to Keith-Ingram, one to Baustian, and the third to the man in charge of the fabricators assigned to Security, with an AAA priority. Then he took out Pembun's message and read it through carefully:

> With regard to the assumed success of the Rithian pseudo-hypnosis against Empire agents, I would again suggest that the basic fault may be deeply rooted in the social complex of Earth, and in the rigid organization of Empire administration. On most of the outworlds of the writer's experience, good hypnotic subjects are in a minority, but my impression is that this is not the case on Earth, at least among Empire personnel. It may be said that a man who has successfully absorbed all the unspoken assumptions and conditioned attitudes required of him by responsible position in the Empire is already half hypnotized; or to put it differently, that non-suggestible minds tend to be weeded out by the systems of selection and promotion in use. For example, the addressee, Commissioner T. Spangler, is in the writer's opinion suggestible in the extreme. . . .

Spangler grinned angrily and rewound the spool.

How typical of the man that report was!—a solid gelatinous mass of naiveté surrounding one tiny thorn of shrewdness. In Pembun's place, Spangler would simply have disclaimed ability to answer the question. Since Pembun was not employed by any department concerned, the reply would have been plausible and correct; nothing more could ever have come of it.

That must have occurred to Pembun; and yet he had gone stolidly ahead to answer the question fully, and, Spangler was ready to believe, honestly. It was a damaging document; some phrases in it, particularly "within the framework of the Empire," could be interpreted as treasonable. But he had written it; and then he had slipped in that comment about Spangler.

That comment was just damaging enough to Spangler to offset the mildly damaging admissions Pembun had made about himself. Therefore Pembun had actually taken no risk at all. But why had he troubled to dictate a carefully-phrased quarter-spool to be buried in the files, when a disclaimer, in two lines, would have served? Just for "something to do"?

Spangler thought not. There was a curious coherence in Pembun's oddities: they all hung together somehow. Wincing, he forced himself to go back over the recollection of last night. There again, from the normal point of view, Pembun had given himself unnecessary difficulty. Confronted with that inconvenient question of Spangler's, "What's wrong with the Empire?" and the even more embarrassing, "Do you despise us?" any ordinary person would simply have lied.

At any rate, Pembun, by his own statement, had got no pleasure from telling the truth. What was that remark? ". . . a bad taste . . ." Never mind. What emerged from all this, Spangler thought, was the picture of a man who was compulsively, almost pathologically honest. Yes, that expressed it. His frankness was not even ethico-religious in character: it was symbolic, a *gesture*.

Spangler felt himself flushing, and his lips tightened.

The question remained: What did the man want?

He had no answer yet; but he had a feeling that he was getting closer.

IX

At eleven hours a report came from the head of the infirmary's psychiatric section: the information Security wanted from Colonel Cassina was still unavailable and in PsytSec's opinion could not be forced from him without a high probability of destroying the subject's personality. Did Spangler have the necessary priority to list Colonel Cassina as expendable?

At eleven-ten, a call came through from Keith-Ingram.

"On this Cassina affair, Thorne, what progress are you making?"

Spangler told him.

Keith-Ingram rubbed his square chin thoughtfully. "That's unfortunate," he said. "If you want my view, the Empire can spare Colonel Cassina, all right, but I'll have to go to the High Assembly for permission, and the Navy will fight it, naturally. I rather wish there were another way. Have you consulted Pembun about this?"

"The report had just come in when you called."

"Well, let's get this cleaned up now, if we can. Get him on a three-way, will you?"

Face stony, Spangler made the necessary connections. The image of Keith-Ingram dwindled and moved over to occupy one half of the screen. In the other half, Pembun appeared.

Keith-Ingram said, "Now, Mr. Pembun, you've helped us out of the stew right along through this affair. Have you any suggestions that might be useful in this phase of it?"

Pembun's expression was blandly attentive. He said, "My, that would be a 'ard decision to make. Let me think a minute."

Out of screen range, Spangler's fingers moved spasmodically over the control buttons at the edge of his desk.

224

Finally Pembun looked up. "I got one notion," he said. "It's kind of a long chance, but if it works it will get you the information you want without 'urting the Colonel. I was thinking that w'en the Rithi planted that information, they mus' 'ave given their subject some kind of a trigger stimulus to unlock the message. Now if the trigger is verbal, we 'aven't got a chance of 'itting it by accident. But it jus' now struck me that the trigger might be a situation instead of a phrase or a sentence. I mean, it might be a combination of diff'rent kinds of stimuli—a certain smell, say, plus a certain color of the light, plus a certain temperature range, and so on."

"That's doesn't sound a great deal more hopeful, Mr. Pembun," Spangler put in.

"Wait," said Keith-Ingram, "I think I see what he's getting at. You mean, don't you, Mr. Pembun, that the Rithians might have used as a stimulus complex the normal conditions on their home world?"

"That's it," Pembun told him with a smile. "We can't be sure they did, of cawse, but it seems to me there's a fair chance. Any'ow, it isn' as far-fetched as it sounds, becawse those conditions would be available to the Rithi on any planet w'ere any number of them live. You wawk into a Rithch's 'ouse, 'an you think you're on Sirach. They're use' to living in those vine cities of theirs, you know. They 'ate to be penned up. So w'en they 'ave to live in 'ouses, they put up vines in front of illusion screens, an' use artificial light an'. scents, an' fool themselves that way."

"I see," said Keith-Ingram. "That sounds very good, Mr. Pembun; the only question that occurs to me is, can we duplicate those conditions accurately?"

"I should think so," Pembun answered. "It shouldn't be too 'ard."

"Well, I think we'll give it a trial, at any rate. What do you say, Thorne? Do you agree?"

Spangler could tell by the almost imperceptible arch of Keith-Ingram's right eyebrow, and the frozen expression of his mouth, that he knew Spangler didn't, and was enjoying the knowledge.

"Yes, by all means," said Spangler politely.

"That's settled then. I'll leave you and Thorne to work

out the details. Clearing." His image faded out, leaving half the screen blank.

Spangler said coldly, "This is your project, Mr. Pembun, and I'll leave you entirely in charge of it. Requisition any space, materials and labor you need, and have the heads of sections call me for confirmation. I'll want reports twice daily. Are there any questions?"

"No questions, Commissioner."

"Clearing."

Spangler broke the connection, then dialed Keith-Ingram's number again. He got the "busy" response, as he expected, but left the circuit keyed in. Twenty minutes later Keith-Ingram's face appeared on the screen. "Yes, Spangler? What is it now? I'm rather busy."

Spangler said impassively, "There are two matters I wanted to discuss with you, Chief, and I thought it best not to bring them up while Pembun was on the circuit."

"Are they urgent?"

"Quite urgent."

"All right, then, what are they?"

"First," said Spangler, "I've sent you a note on a new testing method of Baustian's, for detecting any future Rithian masqueraders. I'd like to ask you for permission to use it here in the Hill, in advance of final approval, on a provisional test basis."

"Why?"

"Just a precaution. We've found one Rithian here; I want to be perfectly sure there aren't any more."

Keith-Ingram nodded. "No harm in being sure. All right, Thorne, go ahead if you like. Now what else was there?"

"Just one thing more. I'm wondering if it wouldn't be a sound idea to open the question of Cassina's expendability anyhow, regardless of this scheme of Pembun's. If it turns out to be a frost, there'll be less delay before we can go ahead with the orthodox procedure." His stress on the word "orthodox" was delicate, but he knew Keith-Ingram had caught it.

The older man gazed silently at him for a moment. "As a matter of fact," he said, "it happens that I'd already thought of that. However, I may as well say that I have

every confidence in Pembun. If all our personnel were as
efficient as he is, Thorne, things would go a great deal
more smoothly in this department."

Spangler said nothing.

"That's all then? Right. Clearing."

Recalling that conversation before he went to bed that
night, Spangler thought, We'll see how much confidence
you have in Pembun this time tomorrow.

Everything was ready by ten hours.

There was no puzzle, Spangler thought with satisfaction, without a solution. No matter how hopelessly involved
and contradictory a situation might appear on the surface,
or even some distance beneath it, if you kept on relent-
lessly, you would eventually arrive at the core, the quiet
place where the elements of the problem lay exposed in
their basic simplicity.

And this was the revelation that had been vouchsafed
to Spangler:

The real struggle was between savagery and civilization,
between magic and science, between the double meaning
and the single meaning.

Pembun was on the side of ambiguity and lawlessness.
Therefore he was an enemy.

What had blinded Spangler, blinded them all, was the
self-evident fact that Pembun was *human*. Loyalty to a
nation or an idea is conditioned; but loyalty to the race is
bred in the bone. As the old saying had it, "Blood is
thicker than ichor."

Pembun's humanity was self-evident; but was it a fact?

"Wei" had been a human being, too—until the moment
when he was unmasked as a monster.

Pembun belonged to a world so slovenly that Rithians
were allowed to come and go as they pleased. Was it not
more than possible, was it not almost a tactical certainty,
that given opportunity and the made-to-order usefulness
of Pembun's connection with the Empire, they had at the
least made him their agent?

Or, at most, replaced him with one of themselves?

The idea was fantastic, certainly. The picture of Pembun
playing the role of Rithian-killer, deliberately betraying his
own confederate in order to safeguard his position, was

straight out of one of those wild twentieth-century ro-
mances—the kind in which the detective turned out to be
the murderer, the head of the Secret Police was also the
leader of the Underground, and, as often as not, the subordinate hero was a beautiful girl disguised as a boy by the
clever stratagem of cutting her hair.

But that was precisely the kind of world that Pembun
came from, whether he was human or Rithian; that was
the unchanging essence of the ancient Unreason, beaten
now on Earth but not yet stamped out of the Cosmos.
That was the enemy.

"Ten-oh-one," said his watch. In a few moments, now,
one part of the question would be answered.

He glanced at the four men in workmen's coveralls
who stood by an opened section of the wall. One of them
held what appeared to be a cable cutter; the others had
objects that looked like testing instruments and spare-parts
kits. The "cutter," underneath its camouflage shell, was
an immobilizing field projector; the rest were energy
weapons.

The men stood quietly, not talking, until a signal light
flashed on Spangler's desk. He nodded, and they
crouched nearer to the disemboweled wall, beginning a
low-voiced conversation. A moment later, Pembun appeared in the doorway.

Spangler glanced up from his reading screen, frowning.
"Oh, yes—Pembun," he said. "Sit down a moment, will
you?" He gestured to one of the chairs along the far wall.
Pembun sat, hands crossed limply in his lap, idly watching
the workmen.

Spangler thumbed open the front of his desk and
touched a stud; a meter needle swung over and held
steady. The room was now split into two parts by a
planar screen just in front of the desk. Spangler closed
the microphone circuit which would carry his voice
around the barrier.

The intercom glowed; Spangler put his hand over it.
"Yes?"

The man said, as he had been instructed, "Commissioner, is Mr. Pembun in your office?"

"Yes, he is. Why?"

"It's that routine test, sir. You told us to give it to

everybody who'd been in the Hill less than six months, and Mr. Pembun is on our list. If you're not too busy now—"

"Of course, he would be," Spangler said. "That hadn't occurred to me. All right, come in." He turned to Pembun. "You don't mind?"

"W'at is it?" Pembun asked.

"We have a new anti-Rithian test," Spangler explained easily. "We're just making absolutely certain there aren't any more Weis in the Hill. In your case, of course, it's only a formality."

Pembun's expression was hard to read, but Spangler thought he saw a trace of uneasiness there. He watched narrowly, as a white-smocked young man carrying a medical kit came in through the door to Pembun's right.

The workmen separated suddenly, and two of them started toward the door. When they had taken a few steps, one of them turned to call back to the remaining two. "You certain two UBX's will do it?"

"What's the matter, don't you think so?"

"It's up to you, but . . ." The men went on talking, while the medic approached Pembun and opened his kit. "Mr. Pembun?"

"Yes."

"Will you stand up and turn back your right sleeve, please?"

Pembun did as he was told. His upper arm was shapeless with overlaid fat and muscle, like a wrestler's. The medic placed one end of a chromed cylinder against the fleshy part of the shoulder, and pressed the release. Pembun started violently and clapped his hand to the injury. When he took it away, there was a tiny spot of blood on his palm.

The medic extruded the cylinder's narrow blade and showed it to Spangler. "Negative, Commissioner."

Spangler cleared his throat. "Naturally," he said. The medic tore off a swab from his kit and wiped Pembun's wound, then put a tiny patch of bandage on it, closed his kit and went away.

Negative, Spangler thought. Too bad; it would have been gratifying to find out that Pembun had tentacles under that blubber. But it had been a pleasure to watch him jump, anyhow. He opened his desk and cut the field circuit.

The two workmen near the door finished their discussion and left. Spangler said to the remaining pair, "Will you wait outside for a few minutes, please?"

When they had gone, Pembun came forward and took the seat facing the desk. "That's a rough test," he said. " 'Ow does it work?"

Spangler explained. "Sorry if it was unpleasant," he added, "but I believe it's more effective than the old one."

"Well, I'm glad I passed, any'ow," said Pembun, poker-faced.

"To be sure," said Spangler. "Now—your report, Mr. Pembun?"

"Well, I've 'ad a little trouble. I asked Colonel Leclerc to see if 'e couldn' send somebody to Santos in the Shahpur system, to get some Rithian city-vines from the botanical gardens there. 'E gave me to understand that you rifused the request."

"Yes, I'm sorry about that," Spangler said sympathetically. "Until this question is settled, we can't very well relax the embargo, especially not for an Outworld jump."

Pembun accepted that without comment. "Another thing that 'appened, I wanted copies of any Rithi films the War Department might 'ave, in 'opes that one of them would include a sequence of a Rithch I could use to build up the illusion there was a Rithch in the room. That was rifused too; I don' know w'ether it went through your office or not."

"No, this is the first I've heard of it," Spangler lied blandly, "but I'm not surprised. War is extremely touchy about its M. S. files—I'm afraid you'd better give up hope of any help there. Can't you make do without those two items?"

Pembun nodded. "I figured I might 'ave to, so I went a'ead and did the best I could. I don' promise it will work, becawse some of it is awful makeshift, but it's ready."

Spangler felt a muscle jump in his cheek. "It's ready *now?*" he demanded.

"W'enever you like, Commissioner." Pembun got up and turned toward the door.

Spangler made an instant decision. He had not planned to take the second step against Pembun until he had manufactured a plausible opportunity, but he couldn't let Pembun's examination of Cassina proceed. He said sharply, "Just a moment!" and added, "If you don't mind."

As Pembun paused, he put out his hand to the intercom. "Ask those workmen to step in here again, will you?"

The door opened, and all four of the pseudo-workmen trooped in. Pembun looked at them with an expression of mild surprise. "'Aven' you got those UBX's *yet?*" he asked.

No one answered him. Spangler said, "I'll trouble you to come down to the interrogation rooms with me, Mr. Pembun." At his gesture, the four men moved into position around Pembun, one on either side, two behind.

"Interrogation!" said Pembun. "W'y, Commissioner?"

"Not torture, I assure you," Spangler replied, coming around the desk. "Just interrogation, There are a few questions I want to ask you."

"Commissioner Spangler," said Pembun, "am I to understand that I'm suspected of a crime?"

"Mr. Pembun," Spangler answered, "please don't be childish. Security is empowered to question anyone, anywhere, at any time, and for any reason."

After the initial struggle, Pembun had relaxed. He was breathing shallowly now, his eyes half open and unfocused.

"Have you got enough test patterns?" Spangler asked, using a finger-code.

"Yes, I think so, Commissioner," the young technician replied in the same manner. "His basics are very unusual, though. I may have some trouble interpreting when we get into second-orders."

"Do the best you can." He leaned forward, close to Pembun's head. "Can you still hear me, Pembun?" he said aloud.

"Yes."

"State your full name."

"Jawj Pero Pembun."

"How long have you been an agent of the Rithians?"

A pause. "I never was."

Spangler glanced at the technician, who signaled, "Emotional content about point six."

Spangler tried again. "When and where did you last meet a Rithian before coming to Earth?"

"In April, twenty-five fourteen, at the Spring Art Show in Espar, Man'aven."

"Describe that meeting in detail."

"I was standing in the crowd, looking at a big canvas called 'Yeastley and the Tucker.' The Rithch came up and stood beside me. 'E pointed to the painting and said, 'Very amusing.' 'E was looking at the picture through a transformer, so the colors would make sense to 'im. I said, 'I've seen Rithi collages that looked funnier to me.' Then 'e showed me 'ow, by changing the transformer settings, you could make it look like Yeastley 'ad a mouldy face with warts on it, and the Tucker 'ad a long tail. I said . . ."

Pembun went on stolidly to the end of the incident; he and the Rithch, whose name he had never learned, had exchanged a few more remarks and then parted.

The emotional index of his statement did not rise above point nine on a scale of five.

"Before that, when and where was your last meeting with a Rithch?"

"On the street in Espar, early in December, twenty-five thirteen."

"Describe it."

Spangler went grimly on, taking Pembun farther and farther back through innumerable casual meetings. At the end of half an hour, Pembun's breathing was uneven and his forehead was splotched with perspiration. The technician gave him a second injection. Spangler resumed the questioning.

Finally:

". . . Describe the last meeting before that."

"There was none."

Spangler sat rigid for a long moment, then abruptly clenched his fists.

He stared down at Pembun's tortured face. At that moment he felt himself willing to risk the forcing procedures he had planned to use on Cassina, forgetting the consequences; but there would be no profit in it. In Cassina's case, the material was there: it was only a question of applying enough force on the proper fulcrum to get it out. Here, either the material did not exist, or it was so well hidden that the most advanced Empire techniques would never find a hint of it.

But there had to be something: if not espionage, then treason.

Spangler said, "Pembun: In a war between the Rithians and the Empire, which side would you favor?"

"The Empire."

Hoarsely: "But as between the Rithian culture and that of the Empire, which do you prefer?"

"The Rithi."

"Why?"

"Because they 'aven' ossified themselves."

"Explain that."

"They 'aven' overspecialized. They're still yuman, in a sense of the word that's more meaningful than the natural-history sense. They're alive in a way that you can't say the Empire is alive. The Empire is like a robot brain with 'alf the connections soldered shut. It can't adapt, so it's dying, but it's still big enough to be dangerous."

Spangler flicked a glance of triumph toward the technician. He said, "I will repeat, in the event of war between the Rithians and the Empire, which side would you favor?"

Pembun said, "The Empire."

Spangler persisted angrily, "How do you justify that statement, in the face of your admission that you prefer Rithian culture to Empire culture?"

"My personal preferences aren' important. It would be bad for the 'ole yuman race if the Empire cracked up too soon. The Outworlds aren' strong enough. It's too much to expect them to 'urry up and make themselves self-sufficient, w'en they can lean on the Empire through trade agreements. An' if they did, they'd 'ave to overspecialize too; they'd 'ave to subordinate everything else to building

233

up their industrial and war potential. That would be worse than joining the Empire ag'in. The Empire 'as to be kept alive *now*. In another five centuries or so, it won' matter."

Spangler stared a question at the technician, who signaled: "Emotional content one point seven."

One seven: normal for a true statement of a profound conviction. A falsehood, spoken against the truth-compulsion of the drug, would have generated at least 3.0.

So it had all slipped out of his hands again. Pembun's statement was damaging; it would be a black mark on his dossier: but it was not criminal. There was nothing in it to justify the interrogation: it was hardly more than Pembun had given freely in that report of his.

Spangler made one more attempt. "From the time I met you at the spaceport to the present, have you ever lied to me?"

A pause. "Yes."

"How many times?"

"Once."

Spangler leaned forward eagerly.

"Give me the details!"

"I tol' you the song, *Odum Páwkee Mónt a Mutting*, was 'kind of a saga.' That was true in a way, but I said it to fool you. There's an old song with the same name, that dates from the early days on Man'aven, but that's in the old languages. W'at I sang was a modern version. It's not a folk song, or a saga, it's a political song. Old Man Pawkey is the Empire, an' the cup of cawfee is peace. 'E climbs a mounting, and 'e wears 'imself out, and 'e fights a 'undred battles, and 'e lets 'is farm go to forest, just to get a cup of cawfee—instead of growing the bean in 'is own back yard."

A wave of anger towered and broke over Spangler. When it passed, he found himself standing beside the interrogation table, legs spread and shoulders hunched. There was a stinging pain in the knuckles of his right hand; and there was a dark-red blotch oozing a bright drop on Pembun's lip.

The technician was staring at him, but he looked away when Spangler turned.

"Bring him out of it and then let him go," Spangler said, and strode out of the room.

The screen filled one wall of the chamber, so that the three-dimensional orthocolor image appeared to be physically present beyond a wall of vitrin.

Spangler sat a little to right of center, with Gordon at his left. To his right was Colonel Leclerc with his aide; at the far left, sitting a little apart from the others, was Pembun.

Spangler had spoken to Pembun as little as possible since the interrogation; to be in the same room with him was almost physically distasteful.

On the ancillary screen before Spangler, Keith-Ingram's broad grey face was mirrored. The circuit was not two-way, however; Keith-Ingram was receiving the same tight-beam image that appeared on the big wall screen, and so were several heads of other departments and at least one High Assembly member.

The pictured room did not look like a room at all: it looked almost exactly like the Rithian garden-city Spangler had seen in the indoctrination film. There were the bluish light, the broad-leaved green vines and the serpentine blossoms, with the vague feeling of space beyond; and there, supported by a crotch of the vine, was a Rithian.

The reconstruction was uncannily good, Spangler admitted; if he had not seen the model at close hand, he would have believed the thing to be alive.

But something was subtly off-key; some quality of the light, or configuration of the vine stalks, or perhaps even the attitude of the lifelike Rithian simulacrum. The room as a whole was like a museum diorama, convincing only after you had voluntarily taken the first step toward belief.

Leclerc was chatting noisily with his aide: his way of minimizing tension, evidently. The aide nodded and coughed nervously. Gordon shifted his position in the heavily-padded seat, and subsided guiltily when Spangler glanced at him.

Keith-Ingram's lips moved soundlessly; he was talking to one of the high executives on another circuit. Then the sound cut in and he said, "All ready at this end, Spangler. Go ahead."

"Right, sir." Distastefully, Spangler turned his head toward Pembun. "Mr. Pembun?"

Pembun spoke quietly into his intercom. A moment later, the vines at the left side of the room parted and Cassina stepped into view.

His face was pale and he looked acutely uncomfortable. Under forced healing techniques he had made a good recovery, but he still looked unwell. He glanced down at the interlaced vines that concealed the true floor, took two steps forward, turned to face the motionless Rithian, and assumed the "at ease" position, hands behind his back. His face eloquently expressed disapproval and discomfort.

No one in the viewing room moved or seemed to breathe. Even the restless Leclerc sat statue-still, gazing intently at the screen.

How does Cassina feel, Spangler wondered irrelevantly, with a bomb inside his skull?

Leclerc had set his watch to announce seconds. The tiny ticks were distinctly audible.

Three seconds went by, and nothing happened. Presumably, if the buried message in Cassina's brain were triggered by the situation, the buried material would come out verbally, with compulsive force.

Four seconds.

Pembun bent forward over his intercom and murmured. In the room of the image, the Rithian dummy moved slightly; tentacles gripped and relaxed, shifting its weight minutely; the head turned. A high-pitched voice, apparently coming from the dummy, said, "Enter and be at peace."

Six seconds.

The watch ticked once more; then the dummy spoke again, in the sibilants and harsh fricatives of the Rithian language.

Nine seconds. Ten. The dummy spoke once more in Rithian.

Twelve seconds.

The dummy said in Standard, "You will take some refreshment?"

Cassina's expression did not change; his lips remained shut.

Pembun sighed. "It's no use going on," he said. "I'm afraid it's a failure."

"No luck, Chief," said Spangler. "Pembun says that's all he can do."

Keith-Ingram nodded. "Very well. I'll contact you later. Clearing." His screen went blank.

Pembun was speaking into the intercom. A moment later a voice from behind the vines called, "That's all, Colonel." Cassina turned and walked stiffly out. "Clearing," said the voice; and the big screen faded to silvery blankness.

Spangler sat still, savoring his one victory, while the others stood up and moved murmuring toward the door. Vines, he thought mockingly. Dummy monsters. Smells!

When they tried it the next time, it was very different. Cassina lay clipped and swathed in the interrogation harness. His glittering eyes stared with an expression of frozen terror at the ceiling.

Spangler, at the bedside, was only partly conscious of the other men in the room and of the avid bank of vision cameras. He watched Cassina as one who marks the oily ripples of the ocean's surface, knowing that fathoms under, a titanic submarine battle is being fought.

In the submerged depths of Cassina's mind, a three-sided struggle had been going on for more than half an hour without a respite. The field of battle centered around a locked and sealed compartment of Cassina's memory. The three combatants were the interrogation machine, the repressive complex which guarded the sealed memory, and Cassina's own desperate will to survive.

The dynamics of the battle were simple and deadly. First, through normal interrogation, Cassina's attention had been directed to the memory-sector in question. The pattern of that avenue of thought was reproduced in the interrogation machine—its jagged outline performed an endless, shuddering dance in the scope—and fed back rhythmically into Cassina's brain, so that his consciousness was redirected, like a compass needle to a magnet, each time it tried to escape. This technique, without the addition of truth drugs or suggestion, was commonly used to recover material suppressed by neurosis or psychic trauma; the interval between surges of current was so timed that stray bits of the buried memory would be forced out by the repressive mechanism itself—each successive return of attention, therefore, found more of the concealed matter exposed, and complete recall could usually be forced in a matter of seconds.

In Cassina's case, the repressive complex was so strong that these ejected fragments of memory were being reabsorbed almost as fast as they were emitted. The repression was survival-linked, meaning to say that the unreasoning, magical nine-tenths of Cassina's mind was utterly convinced that to give up the buried material was to die. Therefore the battle was being fought two against one: the repressive complex, plus the will to survive, against the interrogation machine.

The machine had two aids: the drugs in Cassina's system, and the tireless, pitiless mechanical voice in his ears: *"Tell! . . . Tell! . . . Tell! . . . Tell! . . ."*

And the power of the machine, unlike that of Cassina's mind, was unlimited.

Cassina's lips worked soundlessly for an instant; then his expression froze again. Spangler waited for another few seconds, and nodded to the technician.

The technician moved his rheostat over another notch.

Seventy times a second, blasting down Cassina's feeble resistance, the feedback current swung his mind back to a single polarity. Cassina could not even escape into insanity, while that circuit was open; there was no room in his mind for any thought but the one, amplified to a mental scream, that tore through his head with each cycle of the current.

The repression complex and the will to survive were constants; the artificial compulsion to remember was a variable.

Spangler nodded again; up went the power.

XI

Cassina's waxen face was shiny with sweat, and so contorted that it was no longer recognizable. Abruptly his eyes closed, and the muscles of his face went slack. The technician darted a glance to one of the dials on his control board, and slammed over a lever. Two signal lights began to flash alternately; Cassina's heart, which had stopped, was being artificially controlled.

An attendant gave Cassina an injection. In a few moments his face contorted again, and his eyes blinked open.

The silence in the room was absolute. Spangler waited while long minutes ticked away, then nodded to the technician again. The power went up. Again: another notch.

Without warning, Cassina's eyes screwed themselves shut, his jaws distended, and he spoke: a single, formless stream of syllables.

Then his face froze into an icy, indifferent mask. The signal lights continued to flash until the technician, with a tentative gesture, cut the heart-stimulating current; then the steady ticking of the indicator showed that Cassina's heart was continuing to beat on its own. But his face might have been that of a corpse.

Spangler felt his body relax in a release of tension that was almost painful. His fingers trembled. At his nod, the technician cut his master switch and the attendant began removing the harness from Cassina's head and body.

Spangler glanced once at the small vision screen that showed Keith-Ingram's intent face, then took the spool the technician handed him, inserted it into the playback in front of him, and ran it through again and again, first at normal speed, then slowed down so that individual words and syllables could be sorted out.

Cassina had shouted, "You will forget what I am about

239

to tell you and will only remember and repeat the message when you see a Rithian and smell this exact odor. If anyone else tries to make you remember, you will die. *Vuyown fowkip tiima Kreth Grana yodg pirup* pet shop *vuyown geckyg odowo coyowod, cpgnvib btui tene* book store *ikpyu. Nobcyeu kivpi cyour myoc. Aoprosu . . .*

There was much more of it, all in outlandish syllables except that "pet shop" was repeated once more. The others crowded around, careful only not to obstruct Keith-Ingram's view, while Spangler, pointedly ignoring Pembun, turned the spool over to Heissler, the rabbity little Rithian expert who had been flown in early that morning from Denver.

Heissler listened to the spool once more, made hieroglyphic notes, frowned, and cleared his throat. "This is what it says, *roughly*," he began. "I don't want to commit myself to an exact translation until I've had time to study the text *thoroughly*." He glanced around, then looked down at his notes.

"On the map we sent you by Kreth Gana you will find a pet shop on a north-south avenue, with a restaurant on one side of it and a book store on the other. The first bomb is at this location. The others will be found as follows: from the first location through the outermost projection of the adjacent coastline—" Heissler paused. "A distance, in Rithian terminology, which is roughly equal to six thousand seven hundred kilometers. I'll work it out exactly in a moment . . . it comes to six seven six eight kilometers, three hundred twenty-nine meters and some odd centimeters—to the second location, which is also a pet shop. From this location, at an interior angle of— let's see, that would be eighty-seven degrees, about eight minutes—yes, eight minutes, six seconds—here's another distance, which works out to . . . ah, nine thousand three hundred seventy-two kilometers, one meter—to the third location. From this location, at an exterior angle of ninety-three degrees, twenty minutes, two seconds . . ."

Spangler had palmed his intercom, got Miss Timoney, and directed her: "Get street maps of all major North American cities and put all the available staff to work on them, starting with those over five million. They are to look for a pet shop—that's right, a *pet shop*—on a north-south avenue, which has a restaurant on one side of it and a book store on the other. This project is to be set up as temporary but has triple-A priority. In the meantime, rough out a replacement project to cover all inhabited areas in this hemisphere, staff to be adequate to finish the task in not over forty-eight hours—and have the outline on my desk for approval when I come back to the office."

". . . seven thousand nine hundred eighty-one kilometers, ninety-eight meters, to the fifth location. Message ends." Heissler folded his hands and sat back.

Spangler glanced at Keith-Ingram. The grey man nodded. "Good work, Thorne! Keep that project of yours moving, and I'll see to it that similar ones are set up in the other Districts. Congratulations to you all. Clearing." His screen faded.

. . . And that was it, Spangler thought. Undoubtedly there were millions of pet shops in the world which had a restaurant on one side and a book store on the other, and were on north-south avenues; but there couldn't be many pairs of them on a line whose exact length was known, and which passed through the salient point of a coastline adjacent to the first. It was just the sort of mammoth problem with which the Empire was superlatively equipped to deal. Within two days, the bombs would have been found and deactivated.

Curiously, it was not his inevitable promotion which occupied Spangler's mind at that moment, not even the certainty that the Empire's most terrible danger had been averted. He was thinking about Pembun.

In more ways than one, he thought, this is the victory of reason over sentiment, science over witchcraft. *This is the historic triumph of the single meaning.*

He glanced at Pembun, still sitting by himself at the end of the room. The little man's face was grey under the brown. He was hunched over, staring at nothing.

Spangler watched him, feeling the void inside himself where triumph should have been. It was always like this, after he had won. So long as the fight lasted, Spangler was a vessel of hatred; when it was over, when his emotions had done their work, they flowed out of him and left him at peace. Sometimes it was difficult to remember how he

241

could have thought the defeated enemy so important, how he could have burned with impotent rage at the very existence of a man so small, so shriveled, so obviously harmless. Sometimes, as now, Spangler felt the intrusive touch of compassion.

It's how we're made, he thought. The next objective is always the important thing, the only thing that exists for us . . . and then, when we've reached it, we wonder why it was so necessary, and sometimes we don't know quite what to do with it. But there's always something else to fight for. It may be childish, but it's the thing that makes us great.

Pembun stood up slowly and walked over to Colonel Leclerc who was talking ebulliently to Gordon. Spangler saw Leclerc turn and listen to something Pembun was saying: then his brows arched roguishly and he shook his head, putting a finger to his pursed lips. Pembun spoke again, and Leclerc grinned hugely, leaned over and whispered something into Pembun's ear, then shouted with laughter.

Pembun walked out of the room, glancing at Spangler as he passed. His face was still grey, but there was a faint, twisted smile on his lips.

He's made a joke, Spangler thought. Give him credit for courage.

He felt suddenly listless, as he had been after the scene with Joanna. He moved toward the door, but a sudden tingling of uneasiness made him hesitate. He turned after a moment and walked over to Leclerc.

"Pardon my curiosity, Colonel," he said. "What was it that Pembun said to you just now?"

Leclerc's eyes glistened. "He was very droll. He asked me if I knew any French, and I said yes—I spoke it as a boy, you know; my family summered in a very backward, very picturesque area. Well, then he asked me if it was not true that in French, 'pet shop' would have an entirely different meaning than in Standard." He snickered.

"And you told him—?" Spangler prompted.

Leclerc made one of his extravagant gestures. "I said yes! That is, if you take the first word to be French, and the second to be Standard, then a pet shop would be—"

he lowered his voice to a dramatic undertone—"a shop that sold impolite noises."

He laughed immoderately, shaking his head. "What a thing to think of!"

Spangler smiled wryly. "Thank you, Colonel," he said, and walked out. That touch of uneasiness had been merely a hangover, he thought; it was no longer necessary to worry about anything that Pembun said, or thought, or did.

Pembun was waiting for him in his outer office.

Spangler looked at him without surprise, and crossed the room to sit beside him. "Yes, Mr. Pembun?" he said simply.

"I 'ave something to tell you," said Pembun, "that you won't like to 'ear. Per'aps we'd better go inside."

"All right," said Spangler, and led the way.

He found himself walking along a deserted corridor somewhere on the recreation level. On one side, the doorways he passed beckoned him with stereos of the tri-D's to be experienced inside—a polar expedition on Nereus VI, an evening with Ayesha O'Shaughnessy, a nightmare, a pantomime, a ballet, a battle in space. On the other, he glimpsed the pale, crystalline shells of empty dream capsules.

He did not know how long he had been walking. He had boarded a scooter, he remembered, but he did not know which direction he had taken, or how long he had ridden, or where he had got off. His feet ached, so he must have been walking quite a long time.

He glanced upward. The ceiling of the corridor was stereo-celled, and the view that was turned on now was that of the night sky: a clear, cold night, by the look of it: a sky of deep jet, each star as brilliant and sharp as a kernel of ice.

Pembun's grey-brown face stared back at him from the sky. He had been watching that face ever since he had left his office; he had seen it against the satin-polished walls of corridors; it was there when he closed his eyes; but it looked singularly appropriate against this background. The stars have Pembun's face, he thought.

A bone-deep shudder passed through his body. He

turned aside and went into one of the dream rooms, and sat down on the robing bench.

The door closed obsequiously behind him.

He looked down into the open capsule, softly padded and just big enough for a man to lie snugly; he dented its midnight-blue lining with his finger. The crystal curve of the top was like ice carved paper-thin; the gas vents were lipped by circlets of rose-tinted metal, antiseptically bright.

No, he thought. At least, not yet. I've got to think. Now of all times, I've got to think.

A pun, a pun, a beastly, moronic pun. . . .

Pembun had said, "I've made a bad mistake, Commissioner. You remember me asking w'y Colonel Cassina tried so 'ard to get to the Rithch w'en 'e saw we'd found 'im out?"

And Spangler, puzzled, uneasy: "I remember."

"An' I answered myself, that Cassina mus' 'ave been ordered to do it so 'e could be killed—becawse of the message in 'is brain that the Rithch wouldn' want us to find."

"You were right, Mr. Pembun."

"No, I was wrong. I ought to 'ave seen it. We know that the Rithch's post-'ypnotic control over Cassina was strong enough to make 'im try to commit suicide; 'e almost succeeded later on, even though we 'ad 'im under close surveillance and were ready for it. So it wouldn' 'ave made any sense for the Rithch to order 'im to come and be killed. If Cassina 'ad tried to kill *imself*, right then, the minute you came into the office, there isn't any doubt that 'e would 'ave been able to do it. You never could 'ave stopped 'im in time."

Spangler's brain had clung to that unanswerable syllogism, and gone around and around with it, and come out nowhere. "What are you getting at?"

"Don't you see, Commissioner? W'at the Rithch rilly wanted was w'at actually 'appened. 'E wanted us to kill *'im*—becawse it was in 'is brain, not in Cassina's, that the rilly dangerous information was."

Pembun had paused. Then: "They love life. 'E couldn' bring 'imself to do it, but 'e could arrange it so that we'd 'ave to kill 'im, not take 'im alive."

And Spangler, hoarsely: "Are you saying that that message we got from Cassina was a fraud?"

"No. It might be, but I don't think so. I think the Rithch left the genuine message in Cassina's mind, all right, for a joke—and becawse 'e knew that even if we found it, it wouldn' do us any good."

Spangler had hardly recognized his own voice. "I don't understand you. What are you trying to—what do you mean, it wouldn't do us any good?"

No triumph in Pembun's voice, only weariness and regret: "I told you you wouldn't like it, Commissioner. Did you notice there were two Standard phrases in that message?"

"Pet shop and book store. Well?"

"You can say the same things in Rochtik—*brutu ka* and *lessi ka*. They're exact translations; there wouldn' 'ave been any danger of confusion at awl."

Spangler had stared at him, silently, for a long moment. Inside him, he had felt as if the solid earth had fallen away beneath him, all but a slender pinnacle on which he sat perched; as if he had to be very careful not to make any sudden motion, lest he slip and tumble down the precipice.

"Did you know," he asked, "that I would ask Colonel Leclerc what you had said to him?"

Pembun nodded slowly. "I thought you might. I thought per'aps it would prepare you, a little. This isn' easy to take."

"What are you waiting for?" Spangler had managed. "Tell me the rest."

"Awl right. . . . *Pet* 'appens to be a sound that's used in a good many yuman languages. In Late Terran French it 'as an impolite meaning. But in Twalaz, w'ich is derived from French, it means 'treasure,' and a pet shop would be w'at you cawl in Standard a jewelry store.

"Then there's Kah-rin, w'ich is the trade language in the Goren system and some others. In Kah-rin, *pet* means a toupee. And as for 'book store,' *book* means 'machine' in Yessuese, 'carpet' in Elda, 'toy' in Baluat—and *bukstor* means 'public urinal' in Perroschi. Those are just a few that I 'appen to know; there's prob'ly a 'undred others that I never 'eard of.

"Prob'ly the Rithi agreed on w'at language or dialect

245

to use before they came 'ere. It's the kind of thing that would amuse them . . . I'm sorry. I told you they liked puns, Commissioner . . . and you know that Earth is the only yuman planet w'ere the language 'asn't evolved to speak of in the last four 'undred years."

Now he understood why Pembun's face was grey: not because Spangler had defeated him in a contest of wills—but because the Empire had had its death-blow.

The Rithians had planned their joke well; they had left a clear message for their enemies saying, "Here are the bombs"—but the message could never be read.

Now Earth's campaign against the Rithians would stop. There would be no check to that alien growth; wherever Man turned, he would find the friendly, pleasure-loving, humorous Rithians. . . . And if other alien empires rose, might not the Rithians send word to say with authority, "Leave our friends alone, too"?

. . . So that somehow, without quite knowing how it had happened, Earth would find that the crest of the wave had passed it by; that it was settling into the trough of history.

Night upon night, deep after endless deep; distance without perspective, relation without order: the universe without the Empire.

One candle, that they had thought would burn forever, now snuffed out and smoking thinly in the darkness.

Another deep shudder racked Spangler's body. Blindly, he crawled into the capsule and closed it over him.

XII

After a long time, he opened his eyes and saw two blurred faces above him. The light hurt his eyes. He blinked until he could see them clearly: one was Pembun and the other was Joanna.

" 'Ow long 'as 'e been in there?" Pembun's voice said.

"I don't know, there must be something wrong with the machine. The dials aren't registering at all." Joanna's voice, but sounding as he had never heard it before. "If the shutoff didn't work—"

"Better cawl a doctor."

"Yes." Joanna's head turned aside and vanished.

"Wait," Spangler said thickly. He struggled to sit up.

Joanna's face reappeared, and both of them stared in at him, as if he were a specimen that had astonishingly come to life. It made Spangler want to laugh.

"Security," he said. "Security has two meanings. I was living a pun, and didn't know it. What do you think of that?"

Joanna choked and turned away. After a moment Spangler realized that she was crying. He shook his head violently to clear it and started to climb out of the capsule. Pembun put a hand on his arm.

"Can you 'ear me, Thorne?" he said anxiously. "Do you understand w'at I'm saying?"

"I'm all right," said Spangler, standing up. "Joanna, what's the matter with you?"

She turned. "You're not—"

"I'm all right. I was tired, and I crawled in there to rest. I stayed there, thinking, for an hour or so. Then I must have fallen asleep."

She took one step and was pressed tight against him, her cheek against his throat, her arms clutching him fiercely.

"You were gone six hours," Pembun said. "I got Miss

247

Planter's name from your emergency listing, and we've been looking for you ever since. I shouldn' 'ave jumped to conclusions, I guess." He turned to go.

"Wait," said Spangler again. He felt weak, but very clear and confident. He had done a lot of thinking, before he fell asleep. There had been time to recast his whole life, to turn it and look at it from new angles, to see meanings that had been hidden from him before. He knew the answer to Pembun, now.

Joanna pulled away from him abruptly and began hunting for a tissue. Spangler got one out of his pouch and handed it to her.

"Thanks," she said in a small voice, and sat down on the bench.

"This is for you, too, Joanna," said Spangler soberly. "Part of it." He turned to Pembun.

"You were wrong," he said clearly.

Pembun's face slowly took on a resigned expression. " 'Ow?"

"You told me, under interrogation, that your only reason for working with the Empire, against its rivals, was that the Empire was necessary to the Outworlds—that if it broke up too soon, the Outworlds would either fall with it, or else become as 'ossified' as the Empire itself, which would be equally bad."

"If you say so, I'll take your word for it, Commissioner."

"You said it. Do you deny it now?"

"No."

"You were wrong. You've given your life to work that must have been distasteful to you, every minute of it." He draw a deep breath. "I can't imagine why, unless you were reasoning on the basis of two assumptions that any twenty-first-century schoolboy could have disproved—that like causes invariably produce like results, and that the end justifies the means."

Pembun's expression had changed from boredom to surprise, to shock, to incredulous surmise. Now he looked at Spangler as if he had never seen him before.

"Go awn," he said softly.

"Instead of staying on Manhaven, where you belonged, you've been bumbling around the Empire, trying to hold together a structure that needed only one push in the right place to bring it down. . . . You've been as wrong as I have. Both of us have been wasting our lives.

"Now see what's happened! Earth is finished as a major power. The Empire is dead this minute, though it may not begin to stink for another century. The Outworlds have *got* to stand alone. If like measures produce like ends, then that's the way it will be, whether you like it or not—but history never repeats itself, Pembun."

"Jawj," said the little man.

"Jawj . . . Incidentally, I know you dislike apologies—"

"You don't owe me any," said Pembun. They smiled at each other for a moment; then Spangler thrust out his hand and Pembun took it.

"Thorne, what are you going to do?" Joanna asked.

He looked at her.

"Resign tomorrow, get a visa as soon as I can, and ship out. If I can find a place that will take me."

"There's a place for you on Man'aven," said Pembun. "If there isn't, we'll make one."

Joanna looked from one to the other, and said nothing.

"Jawj," said Spangler, "wait for us outside a few minutes, will you?"

The little man smiled happily, sketched a bow, and walked out. His voice floated back:

"I'll be with Miss O'Shaughnessy w'en you want me."

Spangler sat down beside Joanna. She looked at him with an expression in which bewilderment and pain were mingled with something else, harder to define.

"Miss O'Shaughnessy?" she asked tentatively.

"One of the tri-D's across the corridor. I wonder if he has any idea of what he's getting into." He paused. It had been easy, with Pembun; nothing had ever been easier to say. This was harder.

"I have something else to tell you, Joanna," he began.

"Thorne, if it's an apology—"

"It isn't. If Pembun told you anything about the last few days, then perhaps you know part of the reason for—what I did."

"Yes."

"But that's nothing. I may beat you again; I doubt if I'll ever apologize for it. What I have to tell you is that I made up my mind to marry you, three months ago . . . not because you're Joanna . . . but because you're a Planter."

"I knew that."

Spangler stared at her.

"You what?"

"Why else do you think I wouldn't?" she demanded, meeting his gaze.

Her cheeks were flushed, her eyes glittering with the last tears. The aloof, icy mask was gone. She looked, Spangler discovered, nothing whatever like a statue of Aristocracy.

His throat ached, and the words came out harshly. "Will you come with me?"

She looked at her hands. "If I were to say no, would you go without me?"

". . . Yes," said Spangler. "I've got a lot to do and a lot of things to make up for. Thirty years. I can't do it here."

Her eyes met his again, and he felt her fingers touch him lightly. "In that case," she said thoughtfully, "you'll have to persuade me, won't you? It may take a long time."

Spangler gripped her arms. "The trip to Manhaven takes five weeks, I believe. We could make a good beginning then."

"Yes," said Joanna.

The Earth Quarter

I

The sun had set half an hour before. Now, through the window of Laszlo Cudyk's garret, the alien city shone frost-blue against the black sky: the tall hive-shapes that no man would have built, glowing with their own light.

Nearer, the slender drunken shafts of lamp-posts marched toward him down the street, each with its prosaic yellow globe. Between them and all around, the darkness had gathered: darkness in angular shapes, the geometry of squalor.

Cudyk liked this view, for at night the blackness of the Earth Quarter seemed to merge with the black sky, as if one were a minor extension of the other—a fist of space held down to the surface of the planet. He could feel, then, that he was not alone, not isolated and forgotten; that some connection still existed across all the light-years of the galaxy between him and what he had lost.

And, at the same time, the view depressed him, for at night the City seemed to press in upon the Quarter like the walls of a prison.

The Quarter: sixteen square blocks, two thousand three hundred human beings of three races, four religions, eighteen nationalities; the only remnant of the human race nearer than Capella.

Cudyk felt the night breeze freshening. He glanced upward once at the frosty blaze of stars, then pulled his head back inside the window. He closed the shutters, turning to the lamplit table with its clutter of unread books, pipes, papers.

Cudyk was a man of middle height, heavy in shoulders and chest, blunt-featured, with a shock of graying black hair. He was fifty-five years old; he remembered Earth.

A drunk stumbled by in the street below, cursing monotonously to himself; paused to spit explosively into the gutter, and faded out of hearing.

Cudyk heard him without attention. He stood with his back to the window, looking at nothing, his square fingers fumbling automatically for pipe and tobacco. *Why do I torture myself with that look out the window every night?* he asked himself. *It's a juvenile sentimentalism.* But he knew he would not give it up.

Other noises drifted up to his window, faint with distance. They grew louder. Cudyk cocked his head suddenly, turned and threw open the shutters again. That had been a scream.

He could see nothing down the street; the trouble must be farther over, on Kwang-Chowfu or Washington. The noise swelled as he listened: the unintelligible wailing of a mob.

Footsteps clicked hurriedly up the stairs. Cudyk went to the door, made sure it was latched, and waited. There was a light tapping on the door.

"Who is it?" he said.

"Lee Far."

He unlatched the door and opened it. The little Chinese blinked at him, his upper lip drawn up over incisors like a rodent's. "Mr. Seu say please, you come." Without waiting for an answer, he turned and tapped his way down into darkness.

Cudyk picked up a jacket from a wall hook, paused for a moment to glance at the locked drawer in which he kept an ancient .32 automatic and two full clips. He shook his head impatiently and went out.

Lee was waiting for him downstairs. When he saw Cudyk emerge, he set off down the street at a dog-trot.

Cudyk caught up with him at the corner of Athenai and Brasil. They turned right for two blocks to Washington, then left again. A block away, at Rossiya and Washington, there was a small crowd of men struggling in the middle of the street. They didn't seem to be very active; as Cudyk approached, he saw that only a few of the rioters were still fighting, and those without a great deal of spirit. The rest were moving aimlessly, some wiping their eyes, others bent almost double in paroxysms of sneezing. A few were motionless on the pavement.

Three slender Chinese were moving through the crowd. Each had a white surgeon's mask tied over his nose and mouth; each carried a plastic bag from which he took handfuls of dark powder and flung them with a motion like a sower's. Cudyk could see now that the air around them was heavy with floating particles. As he watched, the last two fighters in the crowd each took a half-hearted swing at the other and then, coughing and sneezing, moved away in separate directions.

Lee took his sleeve for a moment. "Here, Mr. Cudyk."

Seu was standing in the doorway of Town Hall, his bulk almost filling it. He saluted Cudyk with a lazy, humorous gesture of one fat hand.

"Hello, Min," Cudyk said. "You're efficient, as always. Pepper again?"

"Yes," said Mayor Seu Min. "I hate to waste it, but I don't think the water buckets would have been enough this time. This could have been a bad one."

"How did it start?"

"A couple of Russkies cought Jim Loong sneaking into Madame May's," the fat man said laconically. His shrewd eyes twinkled. "I'm glad you came down, Laszlo. I want you to meet an important visitor who arrived on the Kt-l'ith ship this afternoon." He turned slightly and Cudyk saw that there was a man behind him in the doorway. "Mr. Harkway, may I present Mr. Laszlo Cudyk, one of our leading citizens? Mr. Cudyk, James Harkway, who is here on a mission from the Minority People's League."

Cudyk shook hands with the man. Harkway had a pale, scholarly face, not bad looking, with dark intense eyes. He was young, probably under twenty-five; Cudyk automatically classified him as second generation.

"Perhaps," said Seu, as if the notion had just occurred to him, "you would not mind taking over my duties as host for a short time, Laszlo? If Mr. Harkway would not object? This regrettable occurrence . . ."

"Of course," Cudyk said. Harkway nodded and smiled.

"Excellent." Seu edged past Cudyk, then turned and put a hand on his friend's arm, drawing him closer. "Take care of this fool," he said under his breath, "and for God's sake keep him away from the saloons. Rack is in town too. I've got to make sure they don't meet." He smiled brightly at both of them and walked away. Lee Far appeared from somewhere and trailed after him.

A young Chinese, with blood streaming brightly from a gash in his cheek, was walking dazedly past. Cudyk stepped away from the doorway, turned him around and pointed him down the street, to where Seu's young men were laying out the victims on the pavement and administering first aid.

Cudyk went back to Harkway. "I suppose Seu has found you a place to stay."

"Yes. He's putting me up in his home. Perhaps—I don't want to be in the way—"

"You won't be in the way. What would you like to do?"

"Well, I'd like to meet a few people, if it isn't too late. Perhaps we could have a drink somewhere, where people meet . . . ?" Harkway glanced interrogatively down the street to a phosphorescent sign that announced in Russian and English: THE LITTLE BEAR. WINES AND LIQUORS.

"Not there," said Cudyk. "That's Russky headquarters, and I'm afraid they may be a little short-tempered right now. The best place would be Chong Yin's Tea Room, I think. That's just two blocks up, near Washington and Ceskoslovensko."

"All right," said Harkway. He was still looking down the street. "Who is that girl?" he asked abruptly.

Cudyk glanced that way. The M.D.'s, Moskowitz and Pereira, were on the scene, sorting out the most serious cases to be carted off to the hospital, and so was a slender, dark-haired girl in nurse's uniform.

"That's Kathy Burgess," he said. "Daughter of one of our leading citizens. I'd introduce you, but now isn't the time. You'll probably meet her tomorrow."

"She's very pretty," said Harkway, and suffered himself to be led off up the street. "Married?"

"No. She was engaged to one of our young men, but her father broke it off."

"Oh?" said Harkway. "Political differences?"

"Yes. The young man joined the activists. The father is a conservative."

"That's very interesting," said Harkway. After a moment he asked, "Do you have many of those here?"

"Activists or conservatives? Or pretty girls?"

"I meant conservatives," said Harkway, coloring slightly. "I know the activist movement is strong here—that's why I was sent. We consider them dangerous in the extreme."

"So do I," said Cudyk. "No, there aren't many conservatives. Burgess is the only real fanatic. If you meet him, by the way, you must make certain allowances."

Harkway nodded thoughtfully. "Cracked on the subject, would you say?"

"You could put it that way," Cudyk told him. He said after a moment, "He has convinced himself, in his conscious mind at least, that we are the dominant species on this planet; that the Niori are our social and economic inferiors. He won't tolerate any suggestion that it isn't so."

Harkway nodded again, looking very solemn. "A tragedy," he said. "But understandable, of course. Some of the older people simply can't adjust to the reality of our position in the galaxy."

"Not many people actually like it."

Harkway looked at him thoughtfully. He said, "Mr. Cudyk, I don't want you to take this as a complaint, but I've gathered the impression from your remarks that you're not in sympathy with the Minority Peoples' League."

"No," said Cudyk.

"May I ask what your political viewpoint is?"

"I'm neutral," said Cudyk. "Apolitical."

Harkway said politely, "I hope you won't take offense if I ask why? It's evident, even to me, that you're a man of intelligence and ability."

Everything is evident to you, Cudyk thought wearily, *except what you don't want to see.* "I don't believe our particular Humpty Dumpty can be put back together again, Mr. Harkway."

Harkway looked at him intently, but said nothing. He glanced at the signboard over the lighted windows they were approaching. "Is this the place?"

"Yes."

=J∧ΓγδY INΛ Г/∧/Ʌ\ II˧N

257

Harkway continued to look at the sign. Above the English CHONG YIN'S TEA ROOM, and the Chinese characters, was a legend that read:

"That's a curious alphabet," he said.

"It's a very efficient one. It's based on the design of an X in a rectangle—like this." Cudyk traced it with his finger on the wall. "Counting each arm of the cross as one stroke, there are eight strokes in the figure. Using only two strokes to a character, there are twenty-eight possible combinations. They use the sixteen most graceful ones, and add twenty-seven three-stroke characters to bring it up to forty-three, one for each sound in their language. The written language is completely phonetic, therefore. But there are only eight keys on a Niori typewriter."

He looked at Harkway. "It's also perfectly legible: no character looks too much like any other character. And it has a certain beauty." He paused. "Hasn't it struck you, Mr. Harkway, that anything our hosts do is likely to be a little more sensible and more sensitive than our own version?"

"I come from Reg Otay," said Harkway. "They don't have any visual arts or any written language there. But I see what you mean. What does the sign say—the same thing as the English?"

"No. It says, 'Yungiwo Ren Trakru Rith.' 'Trakru rith' is Niori for 'hospitality house'—it's what they call anything that we would call tea room, or restaurant, or beer garden."

"And 'Yungiwo Ren'?"

"That's their version of 'Chung kuo jen'—the Chinese for 'Chinese.' At first they called us all that, because most of the original immigrants were from China; but they've got over it now—they found out some of us didn't like it."

Cudyk opened the door.

A few aliens were sitting at the round tables in the big outer room. Cudyk watched Harkway's face, and saw his eyes widen with shock. The Niori were something to see, the first time.

They were tall and erect, and their anatomy was not even remotely like man's. They had six limbs each, two

for walking, four for manipulation. Their bodies were covered by a pale, horny integument which grew in irregular
sections, so that you could tell the age of a Niori by the
width of the growth-areas between the plates of his armor.
But you saw none of those things at first. You saw the two
glowing violet eyes, set wide apart in a helmet-shaped
head, and the startlingly beautiful markings on the smooth
shell of the face: blue on pale cream, like an ancient
porcelain tile. And you saw the crest: a curved, lucent
shape that even in a lighted room glowed with its own
frost-blue. No Niori ever walked in darkness.

Cudyk guided Harkway toward the door at the far end
of the room. "We'll see who's in the back room," he said.
"There is usually a small gathering at this hour."

The inner room was more brightly lit than the other.
Down the center, in front of a row of empty booths, was
a long table. Three men sat at one end of it, with teacups
and a bowl of lichee nuts between them. They looked up
as Cudyk and Harkway came in.

"Gentlemen," said Cudyk, "may I present Mr. Harkway, who is here on a mission from the Minority Peoples'
League? Mr. Burgess, Father Exarkos, Mr. Flynn."

The three shook hands with Harkway, Father Exarkos
smiling pleasantly, the other two with more guarded expressions. The priest was in his fifties, grey-haired, hollow-
templed, with high orbital ridges and a square, mobile
mouth. He said, in English oddly accented by a mixture
of French and Greek, "Please sit down, both of you. . . .
I understand that your first evening here has been not too
pleasant, Mr. Harkway. I hope the rest of your stay will
be more so."

Burgess snorted, not quite loudly enough to be deliberately rude. His face had a pleasant, even a handsome
cast except for the expression of petulance he was now
wearing. He was a few years younger than the priest: a
big-boned, big-featured man whose slightly curved back
and hollowed cheeks showed that he had lost bulk since
his prime.

Flynn's face was expressive but completely controlled:
the pale gambler's eyes narrow and unreadable, the lips
and the long muscles of the jaw showing nothing more

259

than surface emotion. He asked politely, "Are you planning to stay long, Mr. Harkway?"

"That all depends, Mr. Flynn, on—to be blunt, on what sort of a reception I get. I won't try to conceal from you that my role here is that of a political propagandist. I want to convince as many people as I can that the Minority Peoples' movement is the best hope of the human race. If I find that there's some chance of succeeding, I'll stay as long as necessary. If not—"

"I'm afraid we won't be seeing much of you, in that case, Mr. Harkway," said Burgess. His tone was scrupulously correct, but his nostrils were quivering with repressed indignation.

"What makes you say that, Mr. Burgess?" Harkway asked, turning his intent, serious gaze on the older man.

"Your program, as I understand it," said Burgess, "aims at putting humanity on an equal basis with various assorted races of lizards, beetles and other vermin. I don't think you will find much sympathy for that program here, sir."

"I'm glad to say that through no fault of your own, you're mistaken," said Harkway. "I think you're referring to the program of the right wing of the League, which was dominant for the last several years. It's true that for that period, the M.P.L.'s line was to work for the gradual integration of human beings—and other repressed races —into the society of the planets on which they live. But that's all done with now; the left wing, to which I belong, has won a decisive victory at the League elections."

Again, thought Cudyk. *I might have expected that this two-rumped beast would have turned upside down again by now.*

"Our program," Harkway was saying earnestly, "rejects the doctrine of assimilation as a biological and cultural absurdity. What we propose to do, and with sufficient help *will* do, is to return humanity to its homeland—to reconstitute Earth as an autonomous, civilized member of the galactic entity. We realize, of course, that this is a gigantic undertaking, and that much aid will be required from the other races of the galaxy— Were you about to say something, Mr. Burgess?"

Burgess said bitterly, "What you mean, in plain words,

260

Mr. Harkway, is that you think we all ought to go home —dissolve Earth's galactic empire, give it all back to the natives. I don't think you'll find much support for *that*, either."

Harkway bit his lip, and cast a glance at Cudyk that seemed to say, "You warned me, but I forgot." He turned to Flynn, who was smiling around his cigar as blandly as if he had heard nothing. "Mr. Flynn?"

The gambler waved his cigar amiably. "You'll have to count me out, Mr. Harkway. I'm doing well as things are. I have no reason to want any changes."

Harkway turned to the little priest. "And you, Father?"

The Greek shrugged and smiled. "I wish you all the luck in the universe, sincerely," he said. "But I am afraid I believe that no material methods can rescue man from his dilemma."

"If I've given any offense," said Burgess suddenly, "I can leave."

Harkway stared at him for a moment, gears almost visibly slipping in his head. Then he said, "Of course not, Mr. Burgess, please don't think that for a moment. I respect your views—"

Burgess looked around him with a wounded expression. "I know," he said with difficulty, "that I am in a minority here—"

Father Exarkos put a hand on his arm and murmured something. Burgess was visibly struggling with his emotions. He stood up and said, "No—no—not tonight. I'm upset. Please excuse me." Head bowed, he walked out.

There was a short silence. "Did I do the wrong thing?" asked Harkway.

"No, no," said Father Exarkos. "It was not your fault; there was nothing you could do. You must excuse him. He is a good man, but he has suffered too much. Since his wife died—of a disease contracted during one of the Famines, you understand—he has not been himself."

Harkway nodded, looking both older and more human than he had a moment before. "If we can only turn back the clock," he said. "Put Humpty Dumpty together again, as you expressed it, Mr. Cudyk." He smiled apologetically at them. "I won't harangue you any more tonight—I'll save that for the meeting tomorrow. But I hope that some of you will come to see it my way."

Father Exarkos' eyebrows lifted. "You are planning to hold a public meeting tomorrow?"

"Yes. There's some difficulty about space—Mayor Seu tells me that Town Hall is already booked for the next six days—but I'm confident that I can find some suitable place. If necessary, I'll make it an open-air meeting."

Rack, thought Cudyk. *Rack usually stays in town for only two or three days at a time. Seu is trying to keep Harkway under cover until he leaves. It won't work.*

Out of the corner of his eye he saw a dark shape in the doorway, and his first thought was that Burgess had come back. But it was not Burgess. It was a squat, bandy-legged man with huge shoulders and arms, wearing a leather jacket and a limp military cap. Cudyk sat perfectly still, warning Exarkos with his eyes.

The squat man walked casually up to the table, nodding almost imperceptibly to Flynn. He ignored the others, except the M.P.L. man. "Your name Harkway?" he asked.

"That's right," said Harkway.

"Got a message for you," said the squat man. "From Commander Lawrence Rack, United Earth Space Navy."

"The Earth Space Navy was dissolved twenty years ago," said Harkway.

The squat man sighed. "You want to hear the message or don't you?"

"Go ahead." Harkway's nostrils were pale, and a muscle stood out at the side of his jaw.

"Here it is. You're planning to hold a meeting of the vermin lovers society, right?"

As Harkway began to reply, the squat man leaned across the table and backhanded him viciously across the mouth. Harkway fell, his chair clattering.

The squat man said: "Don't." He turned and walked out.

Cudyk and Flynn helped Harkway up. The man's eyes were staring wildly out of his pale face, and a thin trickle of blood was running from a pulped lip. "Who was that man?" he asked in a whisper.

"His name is Biff," said Cudyk. "At least that is the only name he has been known to answer to. He's one of

Rack's lieutenants—Rack, as you probably know, is the leader of the activists in this sector. Mr. Harkway, I'm sorrier than I can say. But I must advise you to wait for a week or so before you hold your meeting. There is no question of courage involved: it would be suicide."

Harkway looked at him blindly. "The meeting will be held as planned," he said, and walked out, stiff-legged.

II

The shop was empty except for young Nick Pappageorge dozing behind the long counter, and the pale bluish sunlight that streamed through the plastic window. Most of the counter was in shadow, but stray fingers of light picked out gem trays here and there, turning them into minuscule galaxies of brillance.

Two Niori, walking arm in arm, paused in front of the window display, then went on. Like most of the major fauna of the planet, they were nocturnal, avøiding the full blaze of Palu's blue-white sun. To them, it was late evening," just past the height of the Quarter's business day; the streets were full of Niori tourists and curiosity seekers, pausing gravely to stare at displays of conch shells from America, Oriental pottery, hand-woven fabrics, souvenirs carved in the Quarter from discarded Niori packing boxes. There were other races in the Quarter too: spidery Olada, squat Yuttis, even a hulking, four-footed Weg or two. They dwarfed and outnumbered the few humans on the streets. Even here, it was a Niori planet; the humans stayed in their shops, or in the dark-windowed rooms above.

Two youngsters raced by, shouting. Cudyk caught only a glimpse of them through the pierced screen that closed off the back of his shop, but he recognized them by their voices: Red Gorciak and Stan Eleftheris.

There were few children now, and they were growing up wild. Cudyk wondered briefly what it must be like to be a child born into this microcosm, knowing no other. He dismissed the thought; it was one of the many things that one trained one's mind not to dwell on.

Seu came in, moving quickly. He walked directly to the rear of the shop. His normally bland face looked worried, and there were beads of sweat on his wide forehead, although the morning was cool.

"Sit down," said Cudyk. "You've seen Zydh Oran?"

Seu made a dismissing gesture. "Nothing. Not pleasant, but nothing. The same as usual: he tells me what happened, I deny it. He knows, but under their laws he can't do anything."

"Someday it will be bad," said Cudyk.

"Yes. Someday. Laszlo, you've got to do something about Harkway. Otherwise he's going to be killed tonight, and there will be a stink from here to Sirius. I had to tell him he could use Town Hall—he was all ready to hold a torchlight meeting in the streets."

"I tried," said Cudyk.

"Try again. Please. Your ethnic background is closer to his than mine. He respects you, I think. Perhaps he's even read some of your books. If anyone can persuade him, you can."

"What did he say when you talked to him?"

"An ox. A brain made of soap and granite. He says it is a matter of principle. I knew then that I could do nothing. When an Anglo-Saxon talks about his principles, you may as well go home. He won't accept a weapon; he won't postpone the meeting. I think he wants to be a martyr."

Cudyk winced. "Maybe he does. Have you seen Rack?"

"No. Flynn pretends not to know where he is."

"That's rather odd. What is his motive, do you think?"

Seu said, "Basically, he is afraid of Rack. He cooperates with him—they use each other—but you know that it's not a marriage of minds. Flynn is aware that Rack is stronger than he is, because he is only an amoral egotist, and Rack is a fanatic. I think he believes this business may be Rack's downfall, and he would like that."

He stood up. "I have to go. Will you do it?"

"Of course," Cudyk said. "I'm afraid it won't help, but I'll do it."

"Good. Let me know." Seu walked out.

Nick Pappageorge had roused himself and was polishing a tall, fluted silver vase. Cudyk said, "Nick, go find out where Mr. Harkway is. If he isn't busy, ask him if he'll do me the favor of dropping around to see me. Otherwise, just come back and tell me where he is: I'll go to him."

Nick said, "Sure, Mr. Cudyk," and went out.

Cudyk stared at the tray of unsorted gems on the desk before him. He stirred them with his forefinger, separating out an emerald, two aquamarines, a large turquoise and a star sapphire. That was all he had had to begin with—his dead wife's jewels, carried half across Europe when a loaf of bread was worth more than all the gemstones in the world. The sapphire had bought his passage on the alien ship; the others had been his original stock-in-trade, first at the refugee center on Alfhal, then here on Palu. Now he was a prosperous importer, with a business that netted him the equivalent of ten thousand pounds a year.

But the wealth was ashes; he would have traded all of it for one loaf of bread, eaten in peace, on an Earth that had not sunk back to barbarism.

Momentum, he told himself. *Momentum, and a remnant of curiosity. Those are the only reasons I can think of why I do not blow out my brains. Burgess has his fantasy, though it cracks now and then. Flynn has the sensibility of a jackal. Rack, as Seu said, is a fanatic. But why do the rest of us keep on? For what?*

The doorway darkened again as Harkway came in, followed by Nick. Nick gestured toward the rear of the shop, and Harkway advanced, smiling. His lower lip was stained by a purple substance with a glossy surface.

Cudyk greeted him and offered him a chair. "It was good of you to come over," he said. "I hope I didn't interrupt your work."

Harkway grinned stiffly. "No. I was just finishing lunch when your boy found me. I have nothing more to do until this evening."

Cudyk looked at him. "You got to the hospital after all, I see."

"Yes. Dr. Moskowitz fixed me up nicely."

Cudyk had been asking himself why the M.P.L. man looked so cheerful. Now he thought he understood.

"And Miss Burgess?" he asked, delicately.

"Yes," said Harkway, looking embarrassed. He paused. "She's—an exquisite person, Mr. Cudyk."

Cudyk clasped his square hands together, elbows on the arms of his chair. He said, "Forgive me, I'm going to be personal. Am I right in saying that you now feel more than casually interested in Miss Burgess?"

He added, "Please. I have a reason for asking."

Harkway's expression was guarded. "Yes, that's quite true."

"Do you think she may feel similarly towards you?"

Harkway paused. "I think so. I hope so. Why, Mr. Cudyk?"

"Mr. Harkway, I will be very blunt. Miss Burgess has already lost one lover through no fault of her own, and the experience has not had a good effect on her. She is, as you say, exquisite; she has a beautiful, but not a strong personality. Do you think it is fair for you to give her another such experience, even if the attachment is not fully formed, by allowing yourself to be killed this evening?"

Harkway leaned back in his chair. "Oh," he said, "that's it." He grinned. "I thought you were going to point out that her father broke off the last affair because of the man's politics. If you had, I was going to tell you that Mr. Burgess looked me up this morning and apologized for his attitude yesterday, and breaking down and so on. He's very decent, you know."

He paused. "About this other matter," he said seriously, "I'm grateful for your interest, but I'm afraid I can't concede the validity of your argument." He made an impatient gesture. "I'm not trying to sound noble, but this business is more important than my personal life. That's all, I'm afraid. I'm sorry."

Another fanatic, Cudyk thought. *A liberal fanatic. Now I have seen all kinds.* He said, "I have one more argument to try. Has Seu explained to you how precarious our position is here on Palu?"

"He spoke of it."

"The Niori accepted this one small colony with grave misgivings. Every act of violence that occurs here weakens our position, because it furnishes ammunition for a group which already wants to expel us. Do you understand?"

There was pain in Harkway's eyes. "Mr. Cudyk, it's the same all over the galaxy, wherever these pitifully tiny out-groups exist. My organization is trying to attack that problem on a galaxy-wide scale. I don't say we'll succeed, and I grant you the right to doubt that our program is the right one. But we've got to try. Among other things, we've got to clean out the activists, for just the reason you mention. And pardon me for stressing the obvious, but it's Commander Rack who will be responsible for this particular act of violence if it occurs, not myself."

"And you think that your death at his hands would be a stronger argument than a peaceful meeting, is that it?"

Harkway shook his head ruefully. "I don't know that I have that much courage, Mr. Cudyk. I'm hoping that nothing will happen to me. But I know that the League's prestige here would be enormously hurt if I let Rack bluff me down." He stood up. "You'll be at the meeting?"

"I'm afraid so." Cudyk stood and offered his hand. "The best of luck."

He watched the young man go, feeling very old and tired. He had known it would be this way; he had allowed himself to feel the tug of love and pity toward still another lost soul. Such bonds were destructive—they turned the heart brittle and weathered it away, bit by bit.

The assembly hall in the town building was well filled, although Harkway had made no special effort to advertise the meeting. He had known, Cudyk thought, that Rack's threat would be more than sufficient.

There were no women or children. Flynn was there, and a large contingent of his employees—gamblers, pimps, waiters and strong-arm men—as well as most of the Russian population. All but a few of the Chinese had stayed away, as had Burgess. But a number of men whom Cudyk knew to have M.P.L. leanings, and an even larger number of neutrals, were there. The audience was about evenly divided, for and against Harkway. If he somehow came through this alive, it was just possible that he could swing the Quarter his way. A futile victory, but of course Harkway did not believe that.

There was a murmur and a shuffle of feet as Rack entered with three other men—Biff, the one called Spanner, and young Tom De Grasse, who had once been engaged to Kathy Burgess. The sound dropped almost to stillness for a few moments after the four men took seats

268

at the side of the hall, then rose again to a steady rumble. Harkway and Seu had not yet appeared.

Cudyk saw the man to his right getting up, moving away; he turned in time to see Seu wedge himself through a gap in the line of chairs and sit down in the vacated place.

The fat man's face was blandly expressionless, but Cudyk knew that something had happened. "What is it?" he asked.

Seu's lips barely moved. He looked past Cudyk, inspecting the crowd with polite interest. "I had him kidnapped," he said happily. "He's tied up, in a safe place. There won't be any meeting today."

Seu had been seen. Someone a few rows ahead called, "Where's Harkway, Mayor?"

"I don't know," Seu lied blandly. "He told me he would meet me here—said he had an errand to do. Probably he's on his way now."

Under cover of the ensuing murmur, he turned to Cudyk again. "I didn't want to do it," he said. "It will mean trouble, sooner or later; maybe almost as much trouble as if Harkway had been killed. But I had to make a choice. Do you think I did the right thing, Laszlo?"

"Yes. But I only wish you had told me earlier."

Seu smiled, his heavy face becoming for that instant open and confiding. "If I had, you wouldn't have been so sincere when you talked to Harkway."

Cudyk smiled in spite of himself. He relaxed in his chair, savoring the relief that had come when he'd learned that Harkway was not going to die. The tension built up, day by day, almost imperceptibly; it was a rare, fleeting pleasure when something happened to lower it.

He saw the mayor looking at his watch. The crowd was growing restless; in a few more minutes Seu would get up and announce that the meeting was canceled. Then it would be all over.

Seu was rising, when a new wave of sound traveled over the audience. Out of the corner of his eye Cudyk saw men turning, standing up to see over the heads of their neighbors. Seu spoke a single sharp word, and his hand tightened on the back of his chair.

Cudyk stood. Someone was coming down the center aisle of the room, but he couldn't see who it was.

Those who had stood earlier were sitting down now. Down the aisle, looking straight ahead, with a bruised jaw and a bloody scratch running from cheekbone to chin, came James Harkway.

He mounted the platform, rested both hands on the low speaker's stand, and turned his glance across the audience, once, from side to side. There was a collective scraping of chairs and clearing of throats, then complete stillness. Harkway said:

"My friends—and enemies."

Subdued laughter rippled across the room.

"A few of my enemies didn't want me to hold this meeting," said Harkway. "Some of my friends felt the same way. In fact, it seemed that *nobody* wanted this meeting to take place. But here you all are, just the same. And here I am."

He straightened. "Why is that, I wonder? Perhaps because regardless of our differences, we're all in the same boat—in a lifeboat." He nodded gravely. "Yes, we're all in a lifeboat—all of us together, to live or die, and we don't know which way to turn for the nearest land that will give us harbor.

"Which way shall we turn to find a safe landing? To find peace and honor for ourselves and our children? To find safety, to find happiness?"

He spread his arms. "There are a million directions we could follow. There are all the planets in the galaxy! But everywhere we turn, we find alien soil, alien cultures, alien people. Everywhere, except in one direction only.

"Our ship—our own planet, Earth—is foundering, is sinking, that's true. But *it hasn't yet sunk*. There's still a chance that we can turn back, make Earth what it was, and then, from there—go on! Go on, until we've made a greater Earth, a stronger, happier, more peaceful Earth; till we can take our place with pride in the galaxy, and hold up our heads with any other race that lives."

He had captured only half their attention, and he knew it. They were watching him, listening to what he said; but the heads of the audience were turned slightly, like the heads of plants under a solar tropism, toward the side of the chamber where Rack and his men sat.

Harkway said, "We all know that the Earth's technical civilization is smashed—broken like an eggshell. By ourselves, we could never put it back together. And if we do nothing, no one else is going to put it back together for us. But suppose we went to the other races in the galaxy, and said—"

A baritone voice broke in quietly. *" 'We'll sell our souls to you, if you'll kindly give us a few machines!' "*

Rack stood up—tall, muscular, lean, with deep hollows under his cheekbones, red-gray hair falling over his forehead under the visor of his cap. His short leather jacket was thrown over his shoulders like a cloak. His narrow features were gray and cold, the mouth a straight, hard line. He said, "That's what you want us to tell the vermin, isn't it, Mr. Harkway?"

Harkway seemed to settle himself like a boxer. He said clearly, "The intelligent races of the galaxy are not devils and do not want our souls, Mr. Rack."

Rack ignored the "Mr." He said, "But they'd want certain assurances from us, in return for their help, wouldn't they, Mr. Harkway?"

"Certainly," said Harkway. "Assurances that no sane man would refuse them. Assurances, for example, that there would be no repetition of the Altair Incident—when a handful of maniacs in two ships murdered thousands of peaceful galactic citizens without the slightest provocation. Perhaps you remember that, Mr. Rack; perhaps you were there."

"I was there," said Rack casually. "About five hundred thousand vermin were squashed. We would have done a better job, but we ran out of supplies. Some day we'll exterminate them all, and then there'll be a universe fit for men to live in. Meanwhile"—he glanced at the audience —"we're going to build. We're building now. Not with the vermin's permission, under the vermin's eye. In secret. On a planet they'll never find until our ships spurt out from it like milt from a fish. And when that day comes, we'll squash them down to the last tentacle and the last claw."

"Are you finished?" asked Harkway. He was quivering with controlled rage.

"Yes, I'm finished," said Rack wearily. "So are you. You're a traitor, Harkway, the most miserable kind of a crawling, dirt-eating traitor the human race ever produced. Get down."

Harkway said to the audience, "I came here to try to persuade you to my way of thinking; to ask you to consider the arguments and decide for yourselves. This man wants to settle the question by prejudice and force. Which of us is best entitled to the name 'human'? If you listen to him, can you blame the Niori if they decide to end even this tiny foothold they've given you on their planet? Would you live in a universe drenched with blood?"

Rack said quietly, "Biff."

The squat man stood up, smiling. He took a clasp knife out of his pocket, opened it, and started up the side of the room.

In the dead stillness, another voice said, "No!"

It was, Cudyk saw with a shock, Tom De Grasse. The youngster was up, moving past Rack—who made no move to stop him, did not even change expression—past the squat man, turning a yard beyond, near the front of the room. His square, almost childish face was tight with strain. There was a pistol in one big hand.

Cudyk felt something awaken in him which blossomed only at moments like this, when one of his fellow men did something particularly puzzling: the root, slain but still quasi-living, of the thing that had once been his central drive and his trademark in the world—his insatiable, probing, warmly intelligent curiosity about the motives of men.

De Grasse was committed to Rack's cause twice over, by conviction and by the shearing away of every other tie; and still more important, he worshiped Rack himself with the devotion that only fanatics can inspire. It was as if Peter had challenged Christ.

The three men stood motionless for what seemed a long time. Biff, halted with his weight on one foot, faced De Grasse with his knife hand slightly extended, thumb on the blade. He was visibly tense, waiting for a word from Rack. But Rack stood as if he had forgotten time

272

and space, staring bemused over Biff's shoulder at De Grasse. The fourth man, Spanner—bones and gristle, with a corpse-growth of gray-white hair—stood up slowly. Rack put a hand on his shoulder and pressed him down again.

Cudyk thought, *Kathy Burgess.*

It was the only answer. De Grasse knew, of course, everything that had passed between Harkway and the girl. There was no privacy worth mentioning in the Quarter: pressed in this narrow ghetto, every man swam in the effluvium of every other man's emotions. And De Grasse was willing, apparently, to give up everything that mattered to him, to save Kathy Burgess pain.

It said something for the breed, Cudyk thought—not enough, never enough, for you saw it only in pinpoint flashes, the noble individual who was a part of the bestial mob—but a light in the darkness, nevertheless.

Finally Rack spoke. "You, Tom?"

The youngster's eyes showed sudden pain. But he said, "I mean it, Captain."

There was a slow movement out from that side of the room, men inching away, crowding against their neighbors. Chairs creaked. Someone coughed abruptly, startlingly.

Rack was still looking past Biff's shoulder, into De Grasse's face. He said:

"All right."

He turned, still wearing the same frozen expression, and walked down the side of the room, toward the exit. Biff threw a glance of pure incredulity over his shoulder, glanced back at De Grasse, and then followed. Spanner scrambled after.

De Grasse relaxed slowly, as if by conscious effort. He put away his gun, hesitated a moment, and walked slowly out after the others. His wide shoulders were slumped.

The cougher broke into a renewed spasm, drowned out by the scraping of chairs and boot soles, the rising beehive hum, as the audience stood up and began to move out. Harkway made no effort to call them back.

Cudyk, moving toward the exit with the rest, had much to think about. He had seen not only De Grasse's will, but

Rack's, part against the knife of human sympathy. And that was a thing he had never expected to see.

"At times like this," said Flynn, narrowing his gray snake's eyes in a smile, "I almost believe in God."

Father Exarkos smiled courteously and said nothing. He and Cudyk had been sitting in the back room of Chong Yin's since a half-hour after the meeting. Seu had been with them earlier, but had left. A little after twelve, Flynn had strolled in and joined them.

"I mean it," said Flynn, laughing a little. "There was Harkway, like a lamb for the slaughter, and there was little De Grasse standing in the way. And Rack backed down." He shook his head, still smiling. "Rack backed down. Now how would you explain that, gentlemen, except by the hand of God?"

It was necessary to put up with the man, who wielded more power in the Quarter than anyone else, even Seu; but sometimes it was not easy.

Flynn was particularly annoying tonight, because Cudyk was forced to agree with him. The riddle remained: why had Rack failed to finish what he had started?

It was conceivable for De Grasse to have acted as he did for reasons of sentiment; but to apply the same motive to Rack was simply not possible. The man had emotions, certainly, but they were all channeled into one direction: the destiny of the human race and of Lawrence Rack. De Grasse was at an age when the strongest emotions were volatile, when conversions were made, when a man could plan an assassination one day and enter a monastery the next. But Rack was fixed and aimed, like a cannon.

Flynn was saying, "He must be going soft. Going soft —old Rack. Unless it's the hand of God. What's your opinion, Father Exarkos?"

The priest said blandly, "Mr. Flynn, since I have come to live upon this planet, my opinions have changed about many things. I no longer believe that either God, or man, is quite so simple as I once thought. We were too small in our thoughts before—our understanding of temporal things was bounded by the frontiers of Earth, and of eternal things by the little sky we could see from our windows.

"Before, I think I would have tried to answer your question, yes or no. I would have said that I think Commander Rack was moved by a sudden access of human feeling, or I would have said that I think Commander Rack was touched by the finger of God. Perhaps I would have hesitated to say that, because even then I did not believe that God interferes with the small sins of men like Commander Rack.

"But now I would say that I do not think your question can be answered at all. I think that we do not understand enough, yet, to be able to answer it. In a few hundred or a thousand years, perhaps. The universe is so much bigger, Mr. Flynn, than we realized. We talked about eternity and about infinity as we talked about the time of drinking a cup of coffee, or the distance from our hotel to the nearest *estaminet;* for these were the touchstones of our culture, what Spengler calls the Faustian culture. And, in our appalling blindness and pride, we believed we understood the words. Now I comprehend that we knew nothing, and were not worthy to discuss the affairs of the Eternal. Nor, I truly believe, are we worthy yet."

Flynn smiled thinly. "Well, Father, that's the best excuse for an answer I've ever heard, anyway." He dragged on his cigar, narrowing his eyes and pursing his lips. "By the way, are those the orthodox sentiments these days? How does your Pope feel about it?"

"The Patriarch," murmured Father Exarkos. "To be exact, the Ecumenical Patriarch—there are three others."

"That's right, the Patriarch: I keep forgetting. How does he feel about eternity and infinity, Father? Agree with you, does he?"

Father Exarkos spread his hands; his leathery skin wrinkled in a smile. "Unfortunately he does not, nor do the other Patriarchs, nor the Pope of the Róman Church. It is a pity, I think, that so tiny a fraction of our world's population left Earth in all the emigrations taken together. It is certainly true that, in a sense, we who emigrated took the culture of Earth with us, but we are numerically unimportant in relation to those who are left behind. So that although new modes of understanding have opened to us here, we are like sterile mutants—we carry the seeds of a greater fulfillment within us, but they will die with our bodies. And, alas, the Church upon Earth can no longer hope to serve as the vehicle of enlightenment. She is conservative, now more than ever: that is her role, to conserve, and to wait."

"In other words," said Flynn, "you don't believe that the big blowup back home was a judgment on us for our sins. You think it was a good thing, only more people should have got out the way we did. That right?"

"Oh, no," said Father Exarkos. "I believe that, as you say, the Famines and the Collapse were a judgment of God. I have heard many theories about the causes of the Collapse, but I have not heard one which does not come back, in the end, to a condemnation of man's folly, cruelty, and blindness."

"Well," said Flynn, "excuse me, Father, but if you believe that way, what are you doing here? Back there"— he jerked his head, as if Earth were some little distance behind his right shoulder—"people are living like animals. Chicago, where I used to live, is just a stone jungle, with a few bare-assed scavengers prowling around in it. If the dirt and disease don't get you, some bandit will split your head open, or you'll run into a wolf or a grizzly. If none of those things happen, you can expect to live to the ripe old age of forty, and then you'll be glad to die."

He had stopped smiling. Flynn, Cudyk realized, was describing his own personal hell. He went on, "Now, if you want to call that a judgment, I won't argue with you. But if that's what you believe, why aren't you back there taking it with the rest of them?"

He really wanted to know, Cudyk thought. He had begun by trying to bait the priest, but now he was serious. It was odd to think of Flynn having trouble with his conscience, but Cudyk was not really surprised. The most moralistic men he had ever known had been gangsters of Flynn's type; whereas the few really good men he had known, Father Exarkos among them, had seemed as blithely unaware of their consciences as of their healthy livers.

The priest said, soberly, "Mr. Flynn, I believe that we also are being punished. Perhaps we more than others.

The Mexican peon, the Indian fellah, the peasant of China or Greece, lives very much as his father did before him; he scarcely has reason to know that judgment has fallen upon Earth. But I think that no inhabitant of the Quarter can forget it for so much as an hour."

Flynn stared at him, then grunted and squashed out his cigar. He stood up. "I'll be getting along home," he said. "Good night." He walked out.

Cudyk and Exarkos sat for a while longer, talking quietly, and then left together. The streets were empty. Behind them and to their left as they walked to the corner, the ghostly blue of the Niori beehives shone above the dark human buildings.

The priest lived in a small second-floor apartment near the corner of Brasil and Athenai, alone since his wife had died ten years before. Cudyk had only to go straight across Ceskoslovensko, but he walked down toward Brasil with his friend.

As they turned at the corner, Cudyk thought he heard a sound from behind them. He looked back, down the street of shuttered shops and blind entranceways. The spectral blue light from the Niori hives made the pavement shimmer like moonlit water; doors and windows were pools of blackness.

There came the sound again, faint but unmistakable: the sound of a blow, and then the groan of a man in pain.

"Astereos, wait," said Cudyk, and began to run across the street. Crime in the Quarter was rare, crime against the Niori nonexistent—Seu and the Council saw to that —but quarrels were continual; there were old enmities, even long-established vendettas, and at any time one of them might explode and destroy the Quarter.

As he ran, Cudyk fumbled for his pocket light—a tiny thing, Niori made, with a battery that had never had to be replaced since Cudyk had bought it nearly twenty years ago. Its blue-white beam lanced into a doorway— empty; another—empty; then down the stairs of a cellarway. Crouching at the bottom, one hand up to shield his eyes from the blue glare, was a boy Cudyk did not at first recognize.

"Who is that?" he demanded sharply. "Eleftheris? Gorciak? What are you doing down there?"

He shifted the light, and for the first time caught sight of another figure—dark, not moving—sprawled at the boy's feet.

In the dim wash of reflected light, the boy lowered his hand. Recognition came as Cudyk saw the square face, and heard the voice, raw with emotion: "Get out of here, Mr. Cudyk." It was Tom De Grasse.

Uneven footsteps came hurrying up the pavement. The priest's voice panted, "Laszlo, shall I go for help?"

But Cudyk was staring at the dark form huddled at De Grasse's feet. Even before the light picked out the bloody face, he knew who it must be: James Harkway.

He shifted the light again. In Tom's raised hand was something blunt and dark. "You, Tom?" said Cudyk, feeling sick and weary.

"What's it to you?" the boy yelled. "Get out of here, you two old crocks, before I give it to you too!"

"Never mind, Astereos," said Cudyk without turning. "This young hero only fights in dark doorways." He handed his light to the priest, then slipped off his jacket, wrapped it around one forearm, and started down into the cellarway.

"Be careful, Laszlo."

Cudyk did not answer. Advancing on De Grasse, with his padded forearm half-raised as a shield, he said firmly, "Your father was a good man. He had hopes for you. And what are you now, an assassin? A coward who strikes from behind?"

De Grasse, still shielding his eyes from the light, bent suddenly and raised his arm to strike at the motionless form on the pavement. Cudyk was barely quick enough to blunder into him, throwing him off balance so the blow fell, with a muffled, soggy sound, on the stone beside Harkway's head.

De Grasse staggered and recovered himself. His face was wild in the blue light, eyes glittering behind half closed lids, mouth savage. Cudyk said, "Today I was even proud of you, you did something that was actually human. Then what? Did Rack—"

"Shut up!" De Grasse shouted, clenching both fists.

"Shut up about Rack, just shut up! You ought to be glad to wipe his boots, you old crock!" He paused, caught his breath through pinched nostrils, then stared down wildly into the pool of darkness between their feet.

Cudyk stepped across Harkway's body and moved up to De Grasse, forearm high. The boy struck once; the blow was too short, without force, and Cudyk took it on his padded forearm, deflecting it, swinging the boy's arm wide. With his other hand, palm open, he slapped De Grasse stingingly across the mouth.

The boy's head rocked. He made a choked sound and came at Cudyk again. Cudyk blocked the blow once more, stepped in and pressed De Grasse against the back wall of the cellarway. He outweighed him by fifty pounds; leaning forward, he held the younger man pinned helplessly. He seized the wrist of the hand that held the blackjack; with his free hand again he slapped De Grasse across the face. He was coldly angry, and it was no light blow; the boy's head snapped around, and his knees bent.

Cudyk rapped the hand he held against the wall until it opened and the blackjack dropped, into the blue pool of light on the pavement. Then he swung De Grasse around, careful not to let him trample the body of Harkway, and propelled him up the steps.

"Laszlo, I was worried about you," said the old priest. The light in his hand was shaking with his excitement. "You should not have—"

Cudyk shoved the young man a few steps down the sidewalk and let him go. He stood reeling, dazed. Cudyk's anger was fading now, leaving weariness and a bitter foreknowledge. "Go and tell Rack," he said, "that an 'old crock' took your weapon away from you."

He turned to join Exarkos, who was halfway down the stairs anxiously holding the light for him, not daring yet to move it away from De Grasse. Glancing back, he saw the young man hesitate, then slouch away unsteadily down the street.

Exarkos knelt beside the still body, sucking breath between his teeth at the sight of the puffed, bloody face. His thin old fingers probed into Harkway's shirt. After a moment, he said, "He is alive."

"Any bones broken?"

"I don't think so . . . no. But he has been terribly beaten. We must get him to the hospital."

"No," said Cudyk. "Too dangerous." He thought a moment, breathing hard. The blue-lit street was empty. "Help me get him on my back, Astereos."

"You think they would attack him again in the hospital?"

"I am certain of it," Cudyk grunted, lifting the unconscious man upright. The old priest, propping himself against the wall, managed to take the weight and hold it while Cudyk turned. Taking Harkway's wrists, Cudyk pulled the body forward onto his own back. Half crouched, he began to toil his way up the stairs.

"What most appalls me," said the priest, following, "is that it should be De Grasse! When only a few hours ago—"

"I know," said Cudyk with difficulty. "But you see that was an anomaly, Astereos. The universe always smooths out anomailes, sooner or later." He shook his head irritably; blood, like a crawling insect, was trickling down the side of his neck.

They got Harkway into the back storeroom of Cudyk's shop, and laid him down on an improvised mattress of packing rolls. He was breathing stertorously, still unconscious.

"Concussion is what it looks like," said Moskowitz, half an hour later. "This isn't the place for him, but as long as he's here, leave him. Moving him again would be the worst thing you could do."

"You know better than that, Arnold," said Cudyk. "I have got to move him, and soon. Bringing him here was just a temporary expedient; it is the first place they will look."

"If you move him, he may die," said Moskowitz, closing his bag with an angry click.

"If I do not, he will die."

Moskowitz's broad, swarthy face was frustrated and angry. "It's ridiculous," he said. "We ought to have a decent police force, not a bunch of kids with pepper. Men, with guns."

He returned Cudyk's silent gaze for a moment, then

sighed and picked up the bag. "Do the best you can," he said. "I have to get back to the hospital."

Cudyk let him out, first making sure there were no watchers in the street. Moskowitz was a dedicated man, one of the few really selfless individuals Cudyk had ever met. He knew as well as anyone that the Quarter could not take the risk of open conflict; but it hurt him, deeply and shamefully, that he should have to turn an injured man away from the hospital for fear of Rack.

Exarkos, weary and shaken, had gone home to bed. Cudyk looked in on Harkway again, then went back to the door and waited. He had called Seu, on the Quarter's tiny Earth-style telephone system, just before calling Moskowitz; what was keeping him?

In a moment, two slender figures came drifting along the line of shop-fronts; they were carrying something long and thin between them. Cudyk recognized them through the glass, and let them in: Robert Wang and little Lee Far.

"Sorry it took us so long," said Wang, sliding through the doorway. "When we stopped at the hospital to get a stretcher, two of Rack's men were there. We finally went down to the morgue and got this."

"This" was a seven-foot roll of canvas and leather, with straps and buckles to hold it together. "But that is for corpses," said Cudyk, revolted.

"I know, but it's the best we could do. We'll leave the head end open. Where is he?"

"In the back." Cudyk gestured. "Where are you going to take him?"

"My uncle Lin has a spare bed. Don't worry." The two, carrying their burden, threaded their way carefully through the cluttered shop and disappeared.

Cudyk, abruptly depressed, stayed in the main room and stared gloomily at the ranked showcases glittering faintly in the light of a distant street lamp. He believed very much in symbols and omens, and he did not like Harkway's being taken out in a dead roll. Lately, it seemed to him, everything in the Quarter conspired to remind him of death; there was a stink of decay about it . . . But he was tired and depressed; probably that was part of the trouble. Once he had got Harkway safely into hiding, he would drink a glass of Calvados and go to bed.

His fingers, without being asked, had found the tobacco pouch and pipe in his jacket. He filled the pipe and lit it, taking some solace in the familiar actions.

The match's tall yellow flame blinded him for a moment. When he blew it out, the door was darkened with moving shapes.

The door-handle rattled suddenly, viciously.

Cudyk's heart hammered with shock. Trying to blink away the afterimage of the flame, he made out that there were two men in the doorway, now joined by a third.

Trying to think, Cudyk mimed bewilderment, gestured in a helpless way with the burnt match in one hand and the pipe in the other. Finally he put the pipe in his mouth and dropped the match into a pocket. One of the men outside was Biff—his apelike shoulders almost filled the doorway. Behind him was the skeletal silhouette of Rack's other lieutenant, the one called Spanner, and a third man, a nondescript ruffian whose name Cudyk didn't know. Cudyk fumbled with the lock, taking as much time as he dared.

He saw Biff pull a gun out of his windbreaker, saw him swing the butt. Glass exploded inward, showering Cudyk and leaving a stinging pain across his right hand.

Biff kicked at the broken pieces left in the frame; they clattered to the floor. He reached in, turned the key, and slammed the door open. The three men crowded in on Cudyk.

"Where's Harkway?" The big man's face was unpleasantly close, and his breath stank.

Cudyk said nothing, but let his eyes flicker upwards, as if involuntarily.

"What's upstairs?" Biff demanded.

"Nothing," Cudyk said. "My living quarters."

"Yeah? Spanner, watch him. C'mon, you." He shoved Cudyk ino the skeletal arms of Spanner and disappeared through the archway that led to the stairs, followed by the third man.

Spanner pushed Cudyk back against a display cabinet, hard enough to make the glass doors rattle, and smiled, showing pale gums. Cudyk held his breath, listening for some sound from the back room, but there was nothing.

Watching him, Spanner backed slowly away until he

reached the waist-high display case in the middle of the room. There were some fine gems inside, pink opals from Dromid in carved platinum settings. Spanner glanced down, took a wrench from the back pocket of his greasy overalls, and smashed the glass. He replaced the wrench, then reached down into the case and picked out the largest opals. He watched Cudyk as he dropped the gems one at a time into his breast pocket, and his pale smile grew broader.

Cudyk said nothing.

In a moment there was a clatter of feet coming pell-mell down the stairs, and Biff burst into the room again, followed by the other man. "Nothing up there," said the squat man. "Nobody been there all day, way it looks." He came close, gathered the front of Cudyk's shirt into his fists. "You joking with me?"

"It was you, not I, who said Harkway was here," Cudyk said impassively.

"What's that?" Biff demanded suddenly, looking at the broken display case. He glanced at Spanner, who grinned and patted the bulging pocket of his overall. Biff grunted.

" 'Taxes,' huh? Okay, Cudyk—"

The third man, who had been drifting around in the back of the shop, moved the screen aside and asked, "What's back here?"

Biff swore and followed him. After a moment's hesitation, Spanner went too, keeping a grip on Cudyk's arm.

They crowded into the doorway. The back room was dark at first, then glowed white as someone found the switch. Except for boxes and bales, the room was empty, but there was an unmistakable sense that it had not been empty long.

"Smart, huh?" said Biff, glaring at Cudyk.

Spanner scuffed a dark stain on the floor, smearing it. "Look at this here, Biff. Blood."

Biff swore again and made for the rear door, followed by the rest.

Outside, in the blue twilight, the blind courtyard was empty. The windows were dark, the spindling iron fire-escapes empty, the roofs empty. A mocking breeze lifted a curl of paper from the ground and dropped it again.

Biff turned to face Cudyk. "Where'd you send him to?"

Cudyk did not reply.

"Biff?" asked Spanner plaintively, showing the wrench in his hand.

"No," said the big man slowly. "All right, Cudyk, you were smart. You'll hear from the commander." He moved past Cudyk, with a certain dignity, and the others followed him.

When they were gone, Cudyk locked up again, feeling relief but no optimism. He looked glumly at the smashed and looted display case. There it was, and it was only the beginning, as he well knew. It was the price of being a fool. Harkway was a fool, and he himself was a fool for giving aid to fools.

He knew, with bitter certainty, that it had been a mistake to lift a finger for Harkway. But the circumstances had given him no choice; there were times when a man had to be a fool, or cease to call himself a man.

Harkway, in the back room of Wang Lin's apartment on Kwang-Chowfu, remained in a comatose state, cared for by Kathy Burgess and visited periodically by Dr. Moskowitz, who had to be smuggled in by a different route each time. Cudyk, when he looked in on the day following the attack, was struck by the rapt, almost hypnotized expression on Kathy's face as she sat by the bed. She sat with her eyes fixed on Harkway, hands in her lap, not moving, barely appearing to breathe. She was, Cudyk thought, less like a nurse at a patient's bedside than like a worshiper at a shrine; and the thought profoundly troubled him.

In the early morning of the second day, Cudyk was awakened by a crash from the shop below his garret. Hurrying down the stairs, he found the lower rooms choked by thick black smoke, so dense that the lights showed only as gray ghosts. He could see no flames, and there was no sensation of heat. Half strangled, he made his way through to the street door and found it broken again, the entrance-way full of glass. He opened the door, what was left of it, for more ventilation, and in twenty minutes the shop was clear enough for him to confirm what he already knew: in the middle of the floor lay the black cylinder of a smoke bomb.

Walls, ceiling, floor, display cases, hangings, papers,

everything was covered with a finely distributed coating of carbon. The place would have to be scrubbed from one end to the other; he would lose at least a day's business, more probably two.

Mounted gems displayed in open-back cases would have to be individually cleaned and polished; the cushions of purple velvet, the wall hangings, the clothing he had left in the shop would all have to be cleaned or thrown out.

Rack left the Quarter the next day, having stayed twice as long as usual. Cudyk, who had been up half the night, saw the ship take off from the spaceport north of the city, and watched the pale flame lance upward into the haze. Burgess, passing Cudyk's doorway at that moment, squinted up at the sky with his vague, watering eyes and said, "Ship leaving. Is that Rack's, by any chance?"

"Yes," said Cudyk.

"Good. A great relief to us all, I'm sure." He came nearer and blinked at Cudyk. "Now we won't have to worry about that young man any more."

Mistaking his meaning, Cudyk started to say, "I'm sorry I can't feel so callous about it as—" He checked himself. The expression on Burgess's face was bewildered and vague. "You don't know?" Cudyk said. "Kathy has not told you?"

"Told me what?" Burgess demanded. "I haven't seen Kathy since yesterday. Why, is something the matter?"

"Harkway died," said Cudyk wearily. "He died this morning."

III

One question of Harkway's kept coming back to Cudyk in the weeks that followed. "Would you live in a universe drenched with blood?"

Rack would, of course; for others there was a tragic dilemma. For them, the race had come to the end of a road that had its beginning in prehistory. Every step of progress on that way had been accomplished by bloodshed, and yet the goal had always been a world at peace. The paradox had been tolerable when the road still seemed endless; before the first Earth starships had discovered that humanity was not alone in the universe.

Human civilization was like a fragile crystalline structure, enduring until the first touch of air; or like a cyst that withers when it is cut open. The winds of the universe blew around them now, and there was no way to escape from the contradictions of their own nature.

The way forward was the way back; the way back was the way forward.

There was no peace except the peace of surrender and death. There was no victory except the victory of chaos.

As Father Exarkos had remarked, there were many theories about the Collapse. It was said that the economy of Earth had been wrecked by interstellar imports; that the rusts and blights which had devastated Earth's fields were of alien origin; the disbanding of the Space Navy, after the Altair Incident, had broken Earth's spirit. It was said that the emigrations, both before and after the Famines, had bled away too much of the trained manpower that was Earth's life-blood.

The fact was that the human race was finished: dying like the Neanderthal when the Cro-Magnon came; dying like the hairy Ainu and the Australian bushman. It was true that hundreds of millions of people lived on Earth much as they had done before, tilling their fields, digging stones from the ground, laboring over the handicrafts which sustained the men of the Quarter in their exile.

Humanity had passed through such dark ages before. But now there was no way to go except downward.

If the exiles in their ghettos, on a hundred planets of the galaxy, were the lopped-off head of the race, then the ferment of theories, plans, and policies that swirled through them symbolized the last fitful fantasies in the brain of a guillotined man.

And on Earth, the prelates, the robber barons, the petty princes were ganglia: performing their mechanical functions in a counterfeit of intelligence: slowing, degenerating imperceptibly until the last dim spark should go out.

Cudyk fingered the manuscript which lay on the desk before him. It was the last thing he had written, and it would never be finished. He had hunted it up this morning, out of nostalgia, or perhaps through some obscure working of that impulse that made him look out at the stars each night.

There were twenty pages, the first chapter of a book that was to have been his major work. It ended with the words, *The only avenue of escape for humanity is*

He had stopped there, because he had realized suddenly that he had been deliberately deceiving himself; that there was no such avenue. The scheme he had meant to propose and develop in the rest of the book had one thing in common with those he had demolished in the first twenty pages. It would not work.

Cudyk thought of those phantom chapters now, and was grateful that he had not written them. He had meant to propose that the exiles should gather on some uninhabited planet, and rear a new generation which would be given all the knowledge of the old, save for two things: military science, and astronomy. They would never be told, never guess that the bright lights of their sky were suns, that the suns had planets and the planets people. They would grow up free of that numbing pressure, they would have a fresh start.

It had been the grossest self-deception. You cannot put the human mind in chains. Every culture had tried it, and every culture had failed. In ten generations, or twenty, they would have reached the stars again. It would have been only cruelty to breed them for that.

He pulled open a drawer of his desk and put the manuscript into it. A folded note dropped to the floor as he did so. Cudyk picked it up and read it again:

You are requested to attend a meeting which will be held at 8 Washington Avenue at 10 hours today. Matters of public policy will be discussed.

It was not signed; no signature was needed. Everyone knew that Rack was in the Quarter again, after an absence of more than a month.

Cudyk glanced at his wrist watch, made on Oladi by spidery, many-limbed creatures to whom an ordinary watch movement was a gross mechanism. The dial showed the galactic standard numerals which corresponded to ten o'clock.

Cudyk stood up wearily and walked out past the carved screen. He told Nick, "I'll be back in an hour."

Eight Washington Avenue was The Little Bear, half a block from the corner where he had first met Harkway, a block and a half from the spot where Harkway had been attacked in a cellarway. Two more associations, Cudyk thought. After twenty years, there were so many that he could not move a foot in the Quarter, glance at a window or a wall, without encountering one of them. And this, he thought, was another thing to remember about a ghetto: you were crowded not only in space but in time. The living were the most transient inhabitants of the Quarter.

Cudyk stepped through the open door of The Little Bear, saw the tables empty and the floor bare. The bartender, Piljurovich, jerked his thumb toward the stairs. "You're late," he said in Russian. "Better hurry."

Cudyk climbed the stairs to the huge second-floor dining hall, where the Russians and Poles held their periodic revels. The room was packed tight with a silent mass of men. At the far end, Rack sat on a chair placed on a table. He stopped in mid-sentence, stared coldly at Cudyk, and then went on:

". . . or against me. From now on, there won't be any more neutrals. I want you to understand this clearly. For one thing, your lives may depend on it."

He paused, glancing around the room. "You all know that James Harkway was executed last month. His crime was treason against the human race. There are some of you here who have been, or will be, guilty of the same crime. To them I have nothing more to say. To the others, those who have considered themselves neutral, I say this: First, New Earth needs all of you and has earned your allegiance. Second, those of you who remain on an enemy planet in spite of this warning, will not live to regret it if that planet is selected for attack.

"You have two months to make up your minds and close your affairs. At the end of that time, a New Earth transport will call here to take off those who decide to go. It will be the last New Earth ship; and I warn you that you had better not count on galactic transportation after that date."

He stood up. "That's all."

The audience was over. Rack waited, standing on the table, thumbs hooked into his belt, jacket over his shoulders, like a statue of himself, while the crowd moved slowly out of the room. It was ludicrous, but you could not laugh.

Two months. For almost twenty years Rack had been a minor disturbance in the Quarter, no more important or dangerous or mad than a dozen others: appearing suddenly, at night, staying for a few days, disappearing again for a month, or two, or six. He brought stolen goods to Flynn—furs from Drux Uta, perhaps, or jewels from Thon—and Flynn paid him in galactic currency, reselling the merchandise later, some on Palu, some on a dozen other worlds, for twenty times the price he paid.

Rack had a following among the younger men of the Quarter; two or three a year joined him. Occasionally there were rumors in the Quarter of skirmishes Rack had fought with the Galactic Guard. It had never been a secret that he was building military installations on some backwater planet. But now, for the first time, Cudyk realized that Rack was actually going to make war on the universe.

Whatever the result, it meant the end of the Quarter.

The stairs were choked. Cudyk worked his way down, to find the barroom filled with little knots of men talking in low voices. Only a few were drinking.

Someone called his name, and then a hand grasped his sleeve. It was Speros Moulios, the gray little tobacco dealer, whose two sons drank too much. "Mr. Cudyk, please, what do you think? Should we go, like he says?"

The others of the group followed him: in a moment Cudyk was surrounded. He felt helpless. "I can't advise you, Mr. Moulios. To be truthful, I don't know what I am going to do myself."

Nobilio Villaneuva, the druggist, said, "I've worked fifteen years, saved all my money. What am I going to do with it if I go to this New Earth? And what about my daughter?"

Someone came elbowing his way through the crowd. He signaled to Cudyk. "Laszlo!" It was Moskowitz. "Some of the fellows want to form a delegation, to go back and ask Rack some questions. They asked me to serve, but I've got to get back to the hospital. Same thing with Seu—he's got six things on his hands already. Father Exarkos isn't here. Will you take over? . . . Good. I'll see you later."

Cudyk sighed. The men around him were watching him expectantly. He stepped over to the bar, picked up an empty glass and rapped with it on the counter until the room quieted.

"It's been suggested that a delegation be formed to ask Commander Rack for more information. Do you all want that?"

There was an affirmative murmur.

"All right," said Cudyk. "Nominations?"

They ended up with a committee of five: Cudyk as spokesman, Moulios, Chong Yin, the painter Prokop Vekshin, and the town clerk, Martín Paz. Cudyk had slips of paper passed out, and collected a hundred-odd questions, most of them duplicates and some of them incoherent. Paz made a neat list of those that remained, and the delegation moved toward the stairs.

At the foot of the stairway Cudyk saw Burgess standing, blinking uncertainly around him. He dropped back and put his hand on the man's arm. "Hello, Louis. I'm glad to see you. How is Kathy?"

Burgess straightened a trifle. "Oh—Laszlo. She's all right, thank you. Feeling a little low, just now, of course . . ." His voice trailed off.

"Of course. I wish there were something I could do."

"No—no, there's nothing. Time will cure her, I suppose. Where are you going now?"

Cudyk explained. "Were you at the meeting earlier?" he asked.

"No. I was not invited. I only heard—ten minutes ago. Perhaps it would be all right if I came upstairs with you? In that way—But if I would be a nuisance—" His features worked.

Cudyk felt obscurely uneasy. He recalled suddenly that it was a long time since he had seen Burgess looking perfectly normal. He said, "I think it will be all right. Why not? Come along."

Rack was sitting at the end of the long table on the far side of the room, talking to Flynn. Flynn's hatchet-man, Vic Smalley, was leaning watchfully against the far wall. Biff and Spanner were at Rack's left. De Grasse, pale and red-eyed, sat halfway down the table, away from the others. He stared at the table in front of him, paying no attention to the rest.

Rack looked up expressionlessly as the five men approached. "Yes?"

Cudyk said, "We have been chosen to ask you some questions about your previous statement."

"Ask away," said Rack, leaning back in his chair. Before him was a glass of the dark, smoky liquor Flynn imported for his special use. He was smoking a tremendously long, black Russian cigarette.

Cudyk took the list from Paz and read the first question. "What is the status of New Earth as to housing, utilities and so on?"

"Housing and utilities are adequate for the present population," said Rack indifferently. "More units will be built as needed."

Paz scribbled in his notebook. Cudyk read, "Will every

new colonist be expected to serve as a member of New Earth's fighting forces?"

Rack said, "Every man will work where he's needed. Common sense ought to tell you that middle-aged men with pot bellies and no military training won't be asked to man battleships."

"What is the size of New Earth's navy?"

"Next question."

"Will new colonists be allowed to retain their personal fortunes?"

Rack stared at him coldly. "The man who asked that," he said, "had better stay in the Quarter. If by his personal fortune he means galactic currency, he can use it to stuff rat-holes. Any personal property of value to the community, and in excess of the owner's minimum needs, will be commandeered and dispensed for the good of the community."

"Will new colonists be under military dis—"

"Look out!" said De Grasse suddenly. He lurched to his feet, upsetting his chair.

Someone stumbled against Paz, who fell heavily across Cudyk's legs, bringing him down. Someone else shouted. From the floor, Cudyk saw Burgess standing quietly with a tiny nickeled revolver in his hand.

"Please don't move, Mr. Flynn," said Burgess. "I don't trust you. All of you, stand still, please."

Cudyk carefully got his legs under him and slowly stood up. The men on the other side of the table were still sitting or standing where they had been a moment before. De Grasse stood in an attitude of frozen protest, one big hand flat against his trousers pocket. He looked comically like a man who has left the house without his keys.

They must have taken his gun away, Cudyk thought, after that affair last month.

Biff and the aged Spanner were sitting tensely, trying to watch Rack and Burgess at the same time. Rack, as always, was inhumanly calm. Flynn looked frightened. The gunman, Vic Smalley, had straightened away from the wall; he looked alert and unworried.

"Commander Rack," said Burgess, "you killed that man Harkway."

292

Rack said nothing.

"I did it," De Grasse said hoarsely. "If you have to shoot somebody, shoot me."

Burgess turned slightly. Rack, without seeming to hurry, picked up the glass in front of him and flung the black liquor in Burgess' face.

The gun went off. Burgess stumbled back a step and then toppled over, with a knife-handle sprouting magically between neck and shoulder. De Grasse came hurtling across the tabletop, dived onto Burgess' prostrate body and came up with the gun. Not more than two seconds had gone by since Rack lifted the glass.

The delegates were moving away, leaving a clear space around De Grasse and Burgess. Cudyk heard some of them clattering down the stairs.

Time had slowed down again, after that one moment. Cudyk saw De Grasse kneeling at Burgess' side, looking up across the table at Rack.

Rack was leaning over the table, supporting himself with one hand, while the other rested at his waist. His attitude, together with his frozen expression, suggested that he was merely bending to examine Burgess' body. But in the next moment he turned slightly, lifted the hand that was pressed to his side, and looked at the dark stain that was spreading over his shirt.

De Grasse stood up. Cudyk went to Burgess and knelt beside him. The man was conscious and moving feebly. "Lie still," said Cudyk. Someone pushed his shoulder roughly, and he looked up to see De Grasse transferring the revolver from his left hand to his right. The youngster's lips were compressed. "Get out of the way," he said harshly.

"No," said Rack. "Leave him alone." He sat down slowly. After a moment De Grasse went around the table and joined him.

Cudyk lifted Burgess' jacket carefully. There was not much bleeding, and he did not think the wound was dangerous. Burgess said weakly, "Did I kill him, Laszlo?"

"No," said Cudyk. "No one was killed."

Burgess turned his head away.

There were footsteps on the stairs, and Moskowitz came into the room, followed by Lee Far and two men with a stretcher. Moskowitz glanced at Burgess and at Rack, then knelt beside Burgess without a word. He pulled out the knife expertly, pressing a wad of bandage around the wound.

"I'll take that," said Spanner, bending over with his hand outstretched.

Moskowitz dropped the knife on the floor and went on bandaging Burgess. Spanner picked it up, glared at the doctor and went back around the table.

Cudyk waited until Moskowitz had finished with Burgess and started probing for the bullet in Rack's side. Following the stretcher-bearers down the stairs, he went out into the blue-white morning sunlight.

There was never any end to it. The Quarter was like a tight gravitational system, with many small bodies swinging around each other in eccentric orbits, and the whole shrinking in upon itself as time went on, so that it grew more and more certain that one collision would engender half a dozen more.

And in the mind, too, each event went on forever. Cudyk remembered Burgess, in the stretcher as he was being carried home, weeping silently because he had failed to kill the man who had murdered his daughter's lover. And he remembered Rack, sitting silent and weary as he waited for Moskowitz to attend to him: sitting without anger for the man who had shot him, sitting with patience, filled with his own inner strength.

And De Grasse, tortured soul, who had once more shown himself willing to sacrifice himself to any loyalty he felt.

Even Biff, even Spanner, lived not for himself but for Rack.

There were all the traditional virtues, dripping their traditional gore: nobility, self-sacrifice, patience, even generosity. By any test except the test of results, Rack was a great man and Burgess another.

And the test of results was a two-edged razor: for by that test, Cudyk himself was a total failure, a nonentity.

He thought, *We are the hollow men, we are the stuffed men . . .*

When every action led to disaster, those who did nothing were damned equally with those who acted.

IV

Someone touched Cudyk's arm as he left Chong Yin's. He turned, and saw it was Flynn.

"I've got something to say to you, Cudyk. I saw you were busy talking to Father Exarkos in there, so I didn't bother you. Besides, it's private. Come on down to my place."

The man was doing him an honor, Cudyk realized, in approaching him personally instead of sending an underling. And now, as Flynn stood waiting for him to reply, Cudyk saw that there was something curiously like appeal in his eyes.

"All right, if you wish," he said. "But I will have to go back to the shop within an hour—Nick has not had his lunch."

"I won't keep you that long," Flynn said.

They turned at the corner and walked down Washington, past Town Hall to The Little Bear. Beyond this point, everything was Flynn's: the dance hall, the casino, the bawdy house, the two cafés and three bars, and the two huge warehouses at the end of the avenue. But it was the casino that Flynn meant when he said "my place."

A white-aproned boy got up hurriedly and opened the heavy doors when they approached. Flynn strode past without looking at him, and Cudyk followed across the long, empty room. Dust covers shrouded the roulette table, the chuck-a-luck layout, faro, *chemin de fer*, dice and poker tables. The bar was deserted, bottle and glasses neatly stacked.

Flynn led the way up a short flight of stairs to the overhanging balcony at the end of the room. He opened the door with a key—a rarity in the Quarter, since ward locks were available only by scavenging on Earth, and had to be imported, whereas a mechanism used by the Niori as a mathematical toy could be readily adapted into an efficient lock.

The low-ceilinged room was furnished with a blond-wood desk and swivel chair, a long, pale-green couch and two chairs upholstered in the same fabric: all Earth imports, scavenged from stocks manufactured before the Collapse. The carpet was a deeper green. There were three framed pictures on the wall: a blue-period Picasso, a muted oyster-white and gray Utrillo, and a small Rouault clown.

Flynn was watching him. "Just like my place in Chicago," he said. "You never saw it before, did you?"

"No," Cudyk said. "I have never been in the casino until now."

"Sit down," said Flynn, pointing to one of the upholstered chairs. He pulled out the swivel chair and leaned back in it. He nodded toward the glass which formed the entire front wall of the room. "Sittin' up here, I can see everything that goes on downstairs. I got a phone"—he laid his hand on it—"that communicates with the cashier's booth in every room. I can handle the whole place from here, and I don't have to be bothered by the goofs if I don't want to. Also, that glass is bullet proof. It's Niori stuff, ten times better than anything we had back home. They tell me you couldn't get through it with a bazooka."

Cudyk said nothing.

"What I wanted to talk to you about—" Flynn leaned forward with his elbows on his knees. "You understand, Cudyk, this is confidential. Strictly between us."

"I don't want any confidence that will be difficult to keep," said Cudyk.

"What do you mean?"

"If it is something that touches the safety of the Quarter—"

Flynn waved his hand impatiently. "No, it's nothing like that. I just don't want it to get around too early. All right, use your own judgment. Here it is.

"Rack's coming back in about three weeks with his cruiser, to pick up anybody that wants to go to New Earth. I'm not going, and neither are any of my boys. On the other hand, I'm not going to stay here either. It isn't healthy any more.

"I don't know what Rack has got, but I've got a pretty good idea he's got enough to raise a lot of hell. Now you can figure the angles for yourself. Maybe he won't bomb this planet, because he thinks he can still make some use of the Quarter—but that's a big maybe. Even if he doesn't, it's a dead cinch there's going to be trouble. The Niori know he comes here, even if they can't prove it, and when the war starts they're going to be sore."

"Tell me something," said Cudyk after a moment. "If you knew all this long ago—and you must have, since you have been so closely associated with Rack—why did you help Rack, and so force yourself to leave Palu?"

Flynn smiled and shrugged. "I'm not complaining," he said. "Rack never fooled me. I got mine, and he got his— it was a business arrangement. When you figure everything in, I can clear out now and I'm still ahead. Don't you see, you've got to figure that nothing lasts forever. If I hadn't played along with Rack, he would have taken his business somewhere else. Maybe I could have stayed here a little longer, but then again, maybe I would have stayed too long. This way, I've got my advance information, and I've got my take from Rack.

"As a matter of fact, he thinks I and all my outfit are going to be on that cruiser when it goes back to his base. He knows I wouldn't take a chance on staying here when the shooting starts. What he doesn't know is that I've got someplace else to go, and a way to get there."

He sat back in his chair again. "I've got a Niori-built freighter hidden back in the hills. Had it for eight years now. It'll carry five hundred people, and fuel and provisions for a year, on top of the cargo. And I've got a planet picked out where nobody will bother me—not Rack, and not the Galactics."

He took a cigar box from the desk and offered it to Cudyk. Cudyk shook his head, showing his pipe.

Flynn took a cigar, twirled it between his lips slowly, and lit it. "You know," he said, bending forward, "there are plenty of planets in the galaxy that aren't inhabited. Some have never even been explored. They're off the shipping routes, no intelligent race on them, nothing special in the way of ores, so nobody wants them. Rack's got one—I've got another."

He gestured with the cigar. "But I'm not using mine to build up any war base. What for?" His long face contorted with violent disgust. "That Rack is crazy. You know it and I know it. If it wasn't for him, I could have stayed here, who knows how long? Or I could have moved to one of the other colonies if I saw a good chance. I like it here. This is civilization—all that's left of it.

"But"—he leaned back again—"you've got to take what you can get. If the odds are against you, cash in and walk out. That's what I'm doing. I'm retiring. On this planet I told you about, there's a big island. A tropical island. Fruit—all you can eat. Little animals something like wild pigs. Fish in the ocean. Gravity just a little under Earth normal, atmosphere perfect. And I'm taking along everything else we'll need. Generators, all kinds of electrical equipment, stoves, everything. It'll last your lifetime and mine."

He looked at Cudyk. "What more would you want?"

Cudyk said slowly, "You're asking me to go with you?"

Flynn nodded. "Sure. I'll treat you right, Cudyk. My boys will go on working for me, you understand, and so will most of the others I'm going to take. I'm going to be the boss. But you, and three, four others, you won't be asked to do any work. Just lie in that sand, or go fishing, or whatever you feel like. How does it sound?"

"I don't think I quite understand," said Cudyk. "Why do you choose me?"

Flynn put down his cigar. He looked uncomfortable. He said irritably, "Because I've got to have somebody to talk to." He stared at Cudyk. "Look at me. Here I am, I'm fifty years old, and I've been fighting the world ever since I was a kid. You think I can just cut loose from everything now and lie under a tree? I'd go nuts in a month. I'm not kidding myself, I know what I am. It takes practice to learn how to relax and enjoy yourself. I never learned, never had the time.

"When I get on that island, and I get all the houses built and the wires strung up, and everything's organized and I've got nothing else to do, I can see myself lying there thinking about this place, and all the other places

I ever owned, and thinking to myself, 'What for?' And there's no answer, I know that. But just the same, I'm going to be wanting to start in again, making a deal, opening a joint, figuring the angles, handling people.

"So there I'll be, with all these mugs around me. What do they know to talk about? The same things I do. Things that happened to them in the rackets, here or back on Earth. You've got to talk to somebody, or you go crazy. But if I've got nobody but them to talk to, how am I ever going to get my mind off that kind of stuff?"

He gestured toward the Rouault, on the wall to Cudyk's left. "Look at that," he said. "I bought that thing in 1961. I've been looking at it for, let's see, twenty-three years. For the first five or so I couldn't figure out whether the guy was kidding or not. Then, gradually, I got to like it. But I still don't know *why* the hell I like it. It's the same thing with everything. I got a Corot that I'm nuts about—I look at it every night before I go to sleep. It's just a landscape, like you used to see on calendars in the old days, except that the calendars were junk and this is art. I know that, I can feel it. But what's the difference between the two? Don't ask me.

"You see what I mean? That's the kind of stuff I've got to learn about. Art. Literature. Music. Philosophy. I always wanted to, before, but I never had the patience for it. Now I've *got* to do it. My kind of life is finished. I've got to learn a new kind."

He frowned at his cigar. "It isn't going to be easy. Maybe there'll be times when you'll wish you had anybody else in the world around but me. But I won't take it out on you, Cudyk. I'll give you every break I can."

He meant it, Cudyk knew. For a moment he wondered, *Why don't I accept?* He could see Flynn's island paradise clearly enough: the tropical trees, the log hut—with electric light, induction stoves for cooking, and hot and cold water—the sand, the sunshine, the long, lazy afternoons spent in talking quietly on the beach. There would be no strain and no tension, if everything went as Flynn planned —only a long, slow twilight, with nothing left to fear or to hope for: forgetfulness, lethargy; lotos and Lethe; a pleasant exile, a scented prison.

"You won't need to worry about the others, the guys

that work for me," Flynn said. "After they get through building the settlement, they can do what they want as long as they don't make any trouble. There'll be enough women to go around; they can settle down and raise kids. There won't be any liquor, and I'm going to keep the weapons locked up. About the ship—I'll disable that as soon as we land. Once we're there, we're there."

If it were not for Flynn himself, Cudyk thought, I believe I might do it. But Flynn, inside a year, is going to be a pitiable man. This is his own punishment, his lesser evil—he chooses it himself. But he is not going to like it. Even if nothing else happens, it will not be pleasant to watch Flynn suffer, day after day.

"I think I understand," he said. "Believe me, Mr. Flynn, I'm deeply grateful for this offer, and I am tempted to accept. But—I think I will stay and take my chances with the Quarter."

Flynn stared at him, then shrugged. "Don't make up your mind in too much of a hurry," he said. "Think it over. I'm not leaving for a couple of weeks. And listen, Cudyk, do me a favor. Don't spread this around."

"Very well," said Cudyk.

Flynn did not get up to see him to the door.

Seu was waiting at the doorway of Cudyk's shop. He said, "Let's go inside, Laszlo, where we can talk privately."

Behind the carved screen, pitching his voice too low for Nick Pappageorge to hear, he said, "One of my assistants saw you going into Flynn's casino. Did he offer you a place on his ship?"

"Yes," said Cudyk, raising an eyebrow. "What is your source of information this time? Did he make the same offer to you?"

"No." Seu blinked at him solemnly. "I don't think I am on his list. Flynn dislikes me, as you know. But he did offer to take Louis and Kathy Burgess—and Louis accepted."

"Are you certain? How do you know?"

"One of Flynn's employees—in or out of confessional, I don't know and didn't ask—told Astereos and Astereos sent for me immediately. I came from there only half an hour ago; then I heard about you, and came here to wait."

The two looked at each other.

"He can't go," said Cudyk finally. "He isn't responsible. We'll have to stop him."

"Yes. It would be very bad. Not just a little bad, *very* bad."

"Did Astereos try to change his mind?"

"Yes, of course. But you know Astereos; he's too good a listener to batter anyone down."

Cudyk nodded and stood up. "Can you wait a little longer for your lunch, Nick?" he called.

Nick looked around. "Sure, Mr. Cudyk. About how long will you be?"

"Not more than half an hour, I hope. If it's longer, I'll send someone to relieve you."

The front of Burgess' shop was plastered with signs in English, Chinese and Niori announcing a gigantic sale— *All Merchandise at Half Price.*

"He might as well have told everyone in the Quarter," Seu commented.

The tables in the long, low outer room were heaped with bolts of hand-woven cloth: woolens from Scotland and England, silks from the Orient, cottons from North and South America. The aisles were nearly filled with customers, most of them human; Burgess' two clerks were both sealing parcels.

They found Burgess sitting behind the half-open door of his office. He rose nervously when he saw them. "This is a pleasure, Laszlo. Min. I haven't seen as much as I'd like of you lately, either one of you. Here, sit down, do."

"May we have this door closed?" asked Seu.

"Yes, yes, of course. May I ask—"

"It's about Flynn's ship," Cudyk said. "We've learned that you have agreed to go on it. We want to dissuade you if we can, Louis. We think it would be a great mistake."

Burgess frowned. "I thought it was meant to be a secret," he said. "Unless you two are going. But then, in that case, why shouldn't I? I mean, I don't understand."

The mayor said smoothly, "Flynn approached Laszlo, who refused. The rest was not hard to gather from your

301

signs, outside. We were sure you weren't planning to leave on Rack's ship. Therefore . . ."

"Oh," said Burgess. "Yes, I suppose it was obvious. Well, why shouldn't I go?" He looked at them with hang-dog defiance. "I'm as good as the next one, I suppose?"

Cudyk felt a faint stirring of nausea. Pity lives in the stomach, he thought abstractedly. We were always too polite to say so—we said "heartstrings" instead. But pity is a cold, heavy writhing in the gut, and so is despair, and so is terror when it becomes so constant that it is a thing to be lived with, and the heart ceases to take any notice of it.

Burgess had been a good man: intelligent, strong, considerate, humorous. Even when the shell of his prejudices had begun to close around him, he had never for a moment turned toward the relief that cruelty offered. Now the shell had closed entirely, but it was not thick enough, and never would be. Like Flynn, Burgess had built a world of his own; and like Flynn, he was not happy in it.

Cudyk said gently, "Of course you're fit to go, Louis. It's the others that are not fit. Can you imagine your living out the rest of your life with Flynn and his gangsters for company? Also, have you considered what life would be like for Kathy in that environment?"

Burgess' strong fingers were moving nervously, gripping and shifting to grip again. He scowled at them and said, "We'll be safe, anyhow. Safe from that madman Rack, and safe from the natives. You can't overlook that . . . Anyhow, Kathy isn't afraid to go. I've talked the whole thing over with her. Thoroughly. Our minds are made up. We want to go."

"Have you considered that Flynn's party won't even have a doctor—unless he can persuade Moskowitz or Pereira to leave the Quarter, which I very much doubt?" Cudyk turned to the mayor. "You don't suppose Flynn would go so far as to take one of them forcibly, do you?"

"It's something to think about," Seu said. "We may as well take precautions."

Burgess was shaking his head. "It's no good trying to frighten me," he said. "I know you mean well, but my mind's made up."

"Louis," Cudyk said after a moment, "do you know that Flynn intends to scuttle his ship after landing? If you go, you will be marooned there. You will never see any of us again."

Burgess stared at his hands. "We've been friends a long time," he said, almost inaudibly. "I haven't forgotten all you've done for me, Laszlo. And you, Min, of course. Almost twenty years . . . But you don't understand what it's meant to me to stay here, either of you. Among these Niori . . . beetles, really. They're nothing but talking beetles.

"You two don't mind as much as I do. I don't know why. I mind dreadfully. Living here, knowing that we humans are superior to them in every way, and yet— there are so many of them! Billions, to our pitiful two thousand. They could rise up against us, you know, any time. This hour, if they felt like it. What chance would we have?

"And what future have we got here? What's there for Kathy to look forward to? There are fewer of us every year. When she is as old as I am, she might be the last human being on the planet.

"No. I've thought it all out, and Kathy agrees with me. We're going to get clean away, out of the whole mess. I can't say I like Flynn much, but he's human. He's human! That means a lot—it means everything."

He looked up. "You two must do what you think best, but I wish you would come along too. I don't know, perhaps it would be difficult for you to go to Flynn. But I'd be glad to speak to him; I'm sure he would consent." He blinked at them painfully. "You must do what you think best."

"I'm sorry, Louis," Cudyk said, and stood up. "We'll see you before you leave?"

"Of course, of course," Burgess muttered. "Good-by, Laszlo . . . Min."

"That island of Flynn's will be a hell-hole within two years," said Seu gloomily. They had been sitting for half an hour over coffee cups in the rear of Cudyk's shop.

"I believe it," Cudyk answered. "If Kathy goes, I would say not two years but six months."

303

"If it comes to the worst, I can kidnap them and hold them until Flynn leaves."

"No," said Cudyk. "You tried that once, with Harkway."

Seu blinked at him. "I would make certain this time."

"Don't misunderstand me. I was going to say that this case is altogether different. For one thing, I believe that even if we anticipate the sailing correctly, Flynn is capable of holding it up and searching until he finds the Burgesses. Or he might be more direct. He might take hostages. You have seen Flynn crossed."

"Yes."

"Even if that did not happen, I think you would lose your office afterwards."

"I admit the possibility. However, you are unnecessarily pessimistic. The thing could be handled more smoothly than that, Laszlo. For example, if we sent Flynn a letter of refusal, imitating Louis' handwriting, at the last moment . . ."

Cudyk was not listening. He said abruptly, "Kathy wants to go. It comes down to that, doesn't it? If she changed her mind for any reason, she would persuade Louis to stay also."

"Yes. What are you thinking, Laszlo?"

"I have a wild idea. Let's go and find Arnold Moskowitz."

Moskowitz was in the surgery; it was two hours before they could see him. When he finally entered the tiny, cluttered office where they were waiting, Cudyk said, "Arnold, we have a problem. Can you simulate a new and unheard-of disease of great virulence, well enough to deceive a person with some knowledge of illnesses?"

Moskowitz cocked a weary eyebrow at him. "Depends. Who's the person?"

"Kathy Burgess," Cudyk told him. He explained what he wanted done, and at the end Moskowitz nodded.

"Sure, I can do it," he said. "I can fake a fever for you —that's child's play—and I can inject some colored wax for pustules, and stain the skin a few gaudy colors. Is that what you want, something spectacular?"

"Yes. And unpleasant in the extreme," said Cudyk. "Perhaps you could also use an emetic?"

"It's all right with me, but it's going to be rough on the patients. You got anybody in mind?"

"I will undertake to provide the patients," said Seu. "But, Laszlo, it still seems to me that this is a very uncertain plan."

"I don't get it at all," said Moskowitz. "I'm supposed to make Kathy believe this phony disease is going to spread into a terrible epidemic that will probably wipe out the Quarter—and you think she'll persuade her father to stay here *because* of that?"

"I wish I did not think so," Cudyk replied. "But if I understand Kathy, that is what she will do. She will not tell herself that she must stay here, because here her sufferings will be greater. She will invent other reasons, I think, without any consciousness that they are only excuses. Probably, she will offer to come back to work in the hospital when she is needed. But I believe that she can no more stay away from death than a moth from a flame."

"And that's why she wants to go with Flynn now, is that it?"

"Yes. She herself does not know it, but I am convinced that that is her reason."

"You could be right," Moskowitz said slowly. "I never got to know her very well, but there's something unhealthy about her. A little too eager, every time we had a serious case. From what I've seen, I could put it down to either an honest desire to help people—a dedication—or a death wish. Except there's one thing, an observation, for what it's worth. She's the best nurse I ever had. She has a natural talent for it, she knows her business, and she works like a beaver. And she's got a lot of natural charm. But the patients never liked her."

Cudyk nodded. "No, they wouldn't." He stood up. "Then it's agreed, Arnold? You'll do it?"

"Yes, I'll do it. I'll tell you the truth, though, Laszlo: I don't enjoy this kind of thing. It strikes me that a fellow could work up a hell of a guilt complex, tinkering around with other people's wackiness."

Cudyk said, "I am willing to give the idea up, if you feel strongly against it."

Moskowitz smiled. "You'd have to. No, I'll go along with you. I was just putting an anchor out for the sake of my conscience, or what's left of it. If I really thought I knew all the answers, I'd probably turn this place into a butcher shop and get it over with."

Cudyk said to Seu as they left, "He is right about the feeling of guilt. If the charge of presumption were to be raised against us, we would have no defense. We do not know that either Louis or Kathy will suffer less here than on Flynn's planet. Have we any right to play God, Min?"

The mayor said soberly, "I've asked myself that question a thousand times since I was twenty. If I ever stop asking it, I'll know that I'm no longer fit to meddle with other people's affairs."

V

The *Armageddon* had the stink of an old ship, too long out of planetary. She was rusty and corroded, and one of her four McMichaels propulsion units was badly out of phase. Spanner did what he could, with profanity and barked knuckles, but it was not enough. When the ship came out of overdrive in the Törkas system, ten days from New Earth, she lurched underfoot and rang like a brazen gong.

De Grasse, who had a hangover, caught himself by the edge of the chart table and swore. Emergency bells were ringing down the companionway in the control blister: the strain had parted seams again, and they were leaking air. De Grasse ignored the bells, and the whisper of running feet going past the chart room, to ready the displays on his own board.

They had emerged into normal space well within the orbit of Törkas, some twenty billion miles from the G-type sun, and about ten degrees above the ecliptic. De Grasse took his readings and fed them into the scarred old computer, which whirred, chattered, and spat out a tape.

"All stations report," said Rack's cold voice on the intercom.

"Damage control, patching leaks," said May Wong promptly. "Five minutes, Larry."

"Engine room, building potential. Two minutes," Spanner's voice growled.

De Grasse palmed his plate. "Astrogator, it's on the tape."

"Fire control, we are arming. Ten minutes."

"Ultraphone, signal coming through from Törkas Orbital I, Commander."

Rack said nothing. Out of curiosity, De Grasse tuned

his own ultraphone to the frequency Sparks was receiving. On the screen a squat, blue-black amphiboid shape came into view. The inhuman features were working, and speech came out of the speaker—Galactic Standard—with such a blubbery accent that De Grasse could barely make out a word. Presumably the thing was asking them to identify themselves. The voice stopped, then the screen flashed red for a second and a bell rang, and the voice began again.

"Belay that ultraphone!" Rack's voice snapped.

De Grasse turned the receiver off. The ship's own emergency bells were falling silent, one by one; as they died, he could begin to hear the creaking in the ribs as the old ship balanced her strains. The chronometer clicked off a minute, then another.

"Engine room, on the green."

"Acknowledged."

The chronometer moved steadily on. De Grasse had nothing to do but sit and hold himself in readiness. Under his feet and a hundred yards to the stern, Barnes and the gunner's mate would be in the improvised bomb blister, sweating over the long, delicate task of arming the bomb. De Grasse was tinglingly aware of them down there, invisible and unaudible, but he could feel them with his skin. And all over the ship, he knew, crew members would be sitting at their stations, listening and waiting. They had crippled themselves, torn out the old fire-control center and made the *Armageddon*'s cannon useless, just to make room for that one tremendous weapon.

To take his mind off it, he read his instruments again and animated the visual-analog display. Krell, the Törkas sun, had seven major planets, four inhabited. Törkas, the dominant planet, was now near perihelion; the other three, all colonial worlds, swung farther out. Total population seventy-eight billion, including a human colony of some twenty thousand souls on the sixth planet, Trig. De Grasse glanced at the motionless red dot that stood for Trig, and looked away again. Near the red dot of Törkas, an intermittent white light indicated that the orbital station was still signaling them. After a moment a second white light began to blink, not near any planet, and simultaneously De Grasse's detectors showed a subplanetary mass at extreme range, in motion toward them.

"Ultraphone reporting, signal coming in from galactic ship at two point three parsecs."

Rack did not reply.

"Damage control, all leaks patched."

"Acknowledged."

De Grasse took readings, fed them to the computer. The galactic ship was closing on them at sublight speed, ETA too far in the future to bother about.

"Fire control reporting bomb armed and ready."

"Okay," said Rack crisply. The lethargy in his voice was gone; his voice was vibrant, eager, almost joyful. "All personnel *strap in!* Count down! Five! Four! Three! Two! One! Go!"

The ship lurched again under De Grasse's body: in the analog screen, the red dots that were planets suddenly took on depth as they began to float outward toward the viewer, while the golden star in the center slowly expanded. De Grasse involuntarily gripped his arm-rests, tensed his body. The seconds sped away, the last red dot drifted past and was gone. The golden star continued to expand, while the instruments showed they were closing on it at frightful, unbelievable speed: ten billion miles . . . seven billion . . . five billion . . .

"Bomb away!" grated Barnes' voice in the intercom.

"Acknowledged!" Rack shot back. "Reversing course!" In the screen, De Grasse saw the blue arrow that represented the *Armageddon* joined by a blue dot. That was the bomb: the instruments gave its distance as a horrifyingly close five meters. Abruptly the dial swung, the arrow reversed its direction, the blue dot drifted away from the arrow; the golden star hung steady a moment, then began to shrink, and one by one the red dots floated back toward it again. The blue dot went with them, then faster than they, and winked out at the limit of detection.

"Astrogator, report!" Rack snapped.

De Grasse ripped the tape out of the computer with shaky fingers. "Collision course, Captain!" he said.

In the screen, the Törkas system collapsed, shrank into itself and became one more star in a field of stars. De Grasse briefly tried to imagine it as a real sun, surrounded by planets with sentient beings living and working on them, traveling between them, but the effort was too much, he couldn't. He let the analog expand in a normal visual display, but kept an ultrabeam feeding in data on the Törkas sun. Two minutes passed, three, four; then the dot that was the Törkas sun blazed white.

"Well done, one and all," said Rack.

Once in overdrive and out of the Törkas system, there was nothing to do. De Grasse got out a bottle and sat with it discreetly in the chart room, looking at the wall.

Rack came by and leaned in the doorway. "Glum?" he asked.

De Grasse looked up. "I'm all right, Captain."

"Putting yourself in their place?"

"Who?"

Rack nodded sternward, without bothering to reply.

De Grasse turned to face the chart table, looked at it blindly and put one hand on it, palm down; his fingers worked at the smooth, scarred metal.

"Damn it," he said thickly, "there was a human colony on one of those planets, Captain. Not bugs. People."

"Don't you think I know that?" Rack asked quietly. He came into the room, closed the door. "We gave them warning, Tom. They had their chance to get out of the Minority Peoples' League, forswear treason, come to us."

De Grasse's fingers found a pack of cigarette papers. He peeled one off, creased it, rolled it, and began twisting it into a thread. "I know," he muttered.

"Tom, this is war we're talking about," said Rack, leaning over to punch the analog display. The screen lighted up with a chart of the central sector of the galaxy. "Here's Törkas." His finger stabbed. "Rud-Uri. Gerzion. Àlfhal. Shergo. The five biggest shipbuilding centers in the central galaxy. It isn't just killing bugs, Tom, it's immobilizing them—*that's* our job. We're men, and men have got to win. But don't forget the sheer monstrous size of what we've got to fight. Pin them down, isolate them—then we can mop up, even if it takes a century." He paused, turned off the display. "And make no mistake, it will—it's that long a job. But when we're done, the galaxy will be human, Tom."

"I know it," said De Grasse, turning toward him. "I'm sorry, Captain. I just . . ."

"I *understand*," said Rack, putting a hand on his shoulder. Then he opened the door and was gone.

Afterward, lying in his cubby, De Grasse heard Rack's and May Wong's voices murmuring through the thin bulkhead; and such a wave of loneliness took him that he turned and bit the pillow to keep from crying out.

Six days out of Törkas, they made planetfall on a world known to its natives as Yerez, but to the *Armageddon*'s crew as Hub's Rest. Hub's was a largely agricultural world where a few hundred humans had been allowed to homestead. Their leader was a shaggy, unwashed giant named Hub McAllister, who had three wives nearly as big and dirty as himself, and uncounted hordes of jeering children.

There were fields of native biologicals around Hub's settlement, but they were neglected and scraggly; "pig-nuts and grunt-weed," Hub called them. Hub did a thriving business in opium and marijuana, and in home-made white lightning; he also accommodated visiting humans with poker, blackjack, cockfights and girls. Hub did a little fencing of stolen merchandise, through the nearby transfer point of U1-Rouha; he could get nearly anything, fix anything, dispose of anything, at a price.

Hub himself met them on the veranda of the sprawling, ramshackle saloon and general store. Lean, wild-eyed children clustered curiously behind him for a few moments as Rack and his crew approached. The hide of a green-furred predator was pegged out on the wall. The air hung stifling hot. A slatternly woman leaned from an upstairs window, to be greeted with bawdy shouts from Biff and the black gang.

"Commander, God damn it, it's good to lay eyes on you again." Hub stuck out his hand, which Rack did not appear to see; fists on his hips, the commander was staring around at the huddle of neglected buildings, the dusty street, the rows of weedy plants.

"Place hasn't changed much!" roared Hub, choking with laughter. "Nor you, neither, Commander—same old high hat, God love you. Come in, come in!" He led the way into the dim barroom adjoining the general store. De Grasse and the rest of the crew made for the back bar, where Hub's unshaven bartender was setting them up unasked. Hub and the captain sat at a table.

311

"Now remember, all you space-apes," Biff was saying, "two shots or a quart of beer, that's all. We're lifting ship no later than eighteen hours, and any sonofabitch that gets drunk'll stay behind." He lifted the shot glass in front of him and poured the contents directly down his throat, as if into a jug.

Nursing his own drink, De Grasse could hear the rumble of Hub's voice behind him, followed by the captain's clear, cold tones. They were exchanging news and rumors, comparing notes on mutual acquaintances—the beginning of the elaborate ritual of doing business with Hub. De Grasse half turned to watch, and to hear better. There was a bottle of Rack's own special smoky liquor on the table beside him; Hub, opposite, was drinking beer from a tremendous stein. Rack was saying, ". . . a few opals from Dron. I don't know if that interests you."

"Not much market for gems now," Hub rumbled. "Have to transship halfway across the damn galaxy—cost more than they'll bring, probably. I might take 'em as a favor, though, if that's all you got. Couldn't pay much."

"It would have to be for barter, anyhow," Rack said. "I'm not interested in galactic currency."

"Yeah, I heard that," said Hub, wiping his nose with one sausage-like finger. His little eyes were shrewd. "Something about you taking anybody that'll go back to your New Earth. Put a new blister on your hull too, since last time, didn't you, Commander?"

"Want to come along?" Rack asked, swirling his drink idly. "I could send a transport for you in about a month."

"I'll think it over," Hub told him. "Well, dammit, in the meantime a fellow's got to live. I got some damaged slugs of galactic fuel I could let you have cheap . . ."

At the bar, Biff had his arm around a fat woman in a red print dress and was hailing her with loud cries of recognition. "Rosie, you old hooker!" Two or three of the other men had already drifted off to upstairs rooms.

In a few minutes, Hub had brought up the subject of spare machine parts, and Rack had delicately hinted that he could always use a few spares. In ten minutes more, they had established that Hub had the parts Spanner needed for the ailing propulsion unit, and settled on a price in opals, spilled out on the table from the pouch Rack wore around his neck.

Three hours later, when they were just clearing atmosphere, a pip appeared on the *Armageddon*'s screens: it was one of the rare galactic police boats, coming into line of sight in a parking orbit.

"Ultraphone signal from a galactic ship, captáin," said Sparks. "They're asking us to cut power and stand by for boarding."

There was silence for a moment. De Grasse palmed his plate, said bitterly, "Captain, this is Hub's doing. It's a sell-out!"

"He wouldn't dare," growled Biff's voice. "I'd stuff his tripes down his throat, and well he knows it."

Ignoring them, Rack said crisply, "Astrogator, how fast are they closing?"

De Grasse read his instruments, said, "A little over three G's combined, Captain. But they're loafing now. Those little speedsters will do anything the crew can stand."

Rack said, "What kind of bugs are they, Sparks?"

"Nimmoke, Captain—those things that look like ginger-colored apes. They can take up to fifty G's, I heard."

The intercom was silent again. The pip was closing rapidly.

"Spanner! Can we go into overdrive this close to a planetary mass?"

"Tear the guts out of her, Captain."

Biff's voice roared again: "You, Spanner! Did you tell any of Hub's gang about the cannon?"

"I did not! You probably spilled it to that broad you was with!"

"Belay that!" said Rack.

"Ram her!" shouted Biff's voice. "Only thing to do, ram her, split her open!"

"Negative," said Rack's cold voice. There was a pause. "Airlock detail, stand by to admit boarders."

The silence on the intercom was eloquent of disbelief. Not a sound came even from Biff. The pip was closing rapidly, decelerating now, matching course and velocity with the *Armageddon*. Now it was within visual range—a sleek, bullet-shaped vessel perhaps half the size of the Earth cruiser.

The galactic pilot nursed his boat closer, jockeying it with superb skill until the airlocks of the two vessels were in alignment. A clang echoed through the whole ship as the magnetic gasket of a boarding tube struck the hull.

The *Armageddon* was taken, without firing a shot.

Rack went down to the arsenal with Biff, and came back empty-handed. To questioning looks as they came back up the companionway, Biff only shook his head glumly.

After some delay, pressure was equalized in the boarding tube and the *Armageddon* airlock opened. The crew looked on in hostile silence as three squat beings entered. They were suited and helmeted; through the faceplates it could be seen that they had ape-like heads, thickly covered with Pekinese-colored fur.

One of the spacesuited figures looked around and spoke briefly in Galactic.

"He wants to know who's in charge, Captain."

Rack nodded indifferently. Sparks pointed him out to the Nimmoke, who spoke again.

"He wants to know if we're the human ship that was seen in the Törkas system just before the accident to their sun."

Somebody snickered nervously.

"Tell them no," said Rack, gazing bleakly past the three aliens.

Sparks and the Nimmoke exchanged a few more words. "He wants to see our galactic registry papers, Captain, and then he wants to take us to the galactic yards on Shergo."

Spanner, standing at De Grasse's elbow, whistled softly. "That means they'll impound the ship," he said.

"Tell him we'll co-operate," said Rack, "but we must go back to Hub's Rest first. There are witnesses and evidence there that will prove our case."

Sparks and the Nimmoke spoke at some length. "He says he'd like to extend you this courtesy, Captain, but it isn't practical for our two ships to land together."

"Tell him to release us, and we'll meet him after landing."

There was a stir of attention among the crew.

"He says he's sorry, but experience shows humans sometimes don't speak the truth. He says it will be necessary to take a hostage aboard his ship. Then he'll grant your request."

Silence fell; the crew members looked at each other. No one had to tell them what that meant: the ship would get away, but the hostage would be lost.

"I'll go myself," said Rack, pulling on his gloves.

There was a babble of protest. "Silence," said Rack sharply. "That's an order! Biff, you know what to do." He stepped over to the Nimmoke and stood waiting.

The Nimmoke spoke to Sparks.

"Captain, he says you can't breathe his atmosphere. You'll have to wear a spacesuit all the time you're aboard."

"Very well. Biff, break out a suit."

May Wong, tears streaming down her face, stepped toward Rack and said, "Captain, send me, for God's sake! What good is anything if—"

"I promise you I'll come back," the tall man told her. "Do you understand? I give you my word. *I'll come back.*" He was stepping into the legs of the spacesuit Biff held out, then zipping it up. The suit looked bulkier than usual; there was some nonregulation equipment strapped to it at the belt. Biff helped him on with the helmet, checked out the oxygen supply, radio and other devices. Stunned, the crew saw Rack raise his hand in token that he was ready. The three Nimmoke took him through the airlock, and the valve closed behind them.

"Stations!" said Biff, diving toward the control room. The crew dispersed.

After a few minutes came the clang as the boarding tube was released. In De Grasse's screen, the bullet-shaped vessel drifted slowly away.

"Gimme a landing tape," said Biff's hoarse voice on the intercom.

De Grasse punched the keys of his calculator. He could not guess what Rack's plan was, or how landing on Hub's Rest again would help the *Armageddon* to escape; but he fed Biff the tape he asked for. In a moment the ship's tubes fired. The distant globe of Yerez, turning far below them, steadied, grew insensibly larger, and seemed to revolve in the opposite direction. In the screen, the galactic ship was paralleling their course.

Suddenly a shout came over the intercom. Simultaneously, De Grasse saw a puff of vapor at the flank of the galactic ship; it looked as if it came from the region of the airlock.

"He did it!" Biff's voice bellowed happily. "Christ, was that sweet, or was it sweet?"

Confused and half deafened, De Grasse said, "Biff, I don't get it. What happened? What did he do?"

"Why, you chump, he took a delayed fuse demolition bomb with him—left it in the airlock. As soon as they had time to get out of their suits, blammo—it blew out both valves."

Under power again, they were drifting gently nearer to the galactic ship. De Grasse, bent over his screen, saw a tiny figure appear in the lock and leap free. It was Rack. A spacesuited crewman, standing in their own airlock, cast him a line and pulled him safely in while they were still in the outermost fringes of Yerez' atmosphere.

And the galactic ship, falling uncontrolled, struck and burst in the middle of the single street of Hub's Rest.

The *Armageddon* stayed in parking orbit, along with the eleven other ships of Rack's embryo fleet; the crew went down in the lighter, leaving a caretaker aboard: thus, there was no structure in the New Earth settlement bigger than the one-story sheds that housed the colonists. Little camouflage was needed. The sheds, of corrugated steel, were painted to blend with the dusty brown of the landscape, and were dispersed in random patterns. As for the ships, they might be natural satellites.

Should any galactic ship approach the planet—an unlikely event in itself—nothing would be visible from space to show that the arid world was not as deserted as it had always been. The planet was near enough to its G-type primary to be livable for men, but it was lifeless, bone-dry; there was nothing here that the galactics wanted.

It was past three in the morning, local time, when the

lighter touched down, but the colony was awake and active—a racket of riveting where new sheds were going up to ease the overcrowding; lights burning in the bomb shed, where the huge, deadly spindles of the T.C. bombs were assembled. Rack was working his scientists in three shifts, stockpiling weapons.

De Grasse got himself a steak in the mess hall, but found that he could not eat it. As he emerged, a guard detail passed him, half dragging a slight, brown-skinned man who had a dazed expression. In the spill of light from the mess-hall door, De Grasse recognized him: it was Villanueva. A few children followed, whistling and jeering. They must have been holding him until Rack returned; that meant the charge was treason. "Treason" meant anything from sabotage to slacking on the job. There was no room on New Earth for those who couldn't, or wouldn't, pull their own weight.

De Grasse walked on, past the poisonous yellow lights of the bomb shed. Behind him, he heard a scattered volley. So much for Villanueva . . . He came to the canteen and paused, wanting a drink, but the clamor of drunken voices, Biff's the loudest among them, drove him away and he went on. At the corner of the training shed he heard running feet and saw a few teen-agers sprinting past him in the darkness. A voice floated back: "Come on! They're showing films of the mission down at the rec hall!"

De Grasse went on, past the living quarters with their darkened windows, past the last building of the colony, out into the desert night. It was as black as your hat but, looking up, he could see the frosty glory of the stars. He never could quite believe that he had been up there himself, only a few days ago. It was a miracle that you never got used to. His trained eye picked out Palu's primary, involuntarily, and he found himself thinking of Kathy.

Standing in the darkness, he felt angry tears leaking from his eyes. It was unfair—things that life had promised him had never been delivered. His youth was up there, as distant and unreal as the stars; all that happiness, the anticipation of joy that had somehow been stolen from him when he wasn't looking.

He heard his name called softly, and whirled to see a dark

317

figure pass before the lights of the settlement. "Who's that?" he demanded.

The figure came closer. It was a woman, and now he recognized her by her whiskey-coarsened voice. "Tommy," she said plaintively, "what you doin' out here all by your lonesome?"

It was Edie Bannon, once a good-looking woman, now a hopeless drunk who hung around the camp, doing odd chores, shacking up now and again. She had been Biff's woman for a while, till he kicked her out for a younger girl.

"How did you know I was here?" he demanded.

"I followed you, honey." She sniffed. "You shouldn't be out here in the dark, all by your lonesome," Her form shifted against the lights of the camp, frizzy-haloed, and he saw her come nearer. "You want a drink, honey?"

The raw smell of whiskey.

After a moment, he took the bottle, put the sharp-tasting rim to his lips and drank. The liquor went hot down his throat, started a warm glow in his belly. He took another, bigger slug.

"Hey, don' drink it all," her voice said gently. He turned, lowering the bottle, offering it back. "You're a good old girl, Edie," he said, feeling as he spoke that it really was so, that she wasn't so bad after all, coming out here to comfort him.

"No, that's all right, you drink it," she said, pushing the bottle back. "I got more in my room. You drink it up. Go ahead, kill it."

He held the bottle up against the distant lights, a phosphorescent ghost-bottle, with a half-inch of amber at the bottom: one more jolt. He drank it down, tilting his head back. Off balance, he reached for her to keep from falling in the darkness; she was bare and mountainous under the thin dress.

"That's right, honey," she said. "Come on with Edie, we go get some more."

He put his arm around her, not giving a damn. "Why not?" he said, and went.

VI

There was a curious feeling of suspension in the Quarter. Trade was slow; only a few Niori and still fewer members of other galactic races strolled down the narrow streets, and for more than a week Cudyk had sold nothing.

Human faces were missing too. Almost two hundred of the ghetto's inhabitants had left quietly, during the night, when word had gone around that the New Earth transport was waiting. Villanueva had gone, with his family; so had Martín Paz; and Flynn had gone earlier with all his crew. The Burgesses had not gone with him.

Today, two weeks later, Cudyk had a consignment coming in on the weekly shuttle from Rud-Uri, and he went to the spaceport to see it through customs. It was shortly after sunset when he started out; the nocturnal city was just coming to life, the broad, curved avenues brilliant under the stream-lights and in the blue glare of the moon, Hut-Shera, which had just risen in the east. Cudyk walked north out of the Quarter, past the office and factory hives of downtown Lur, and at the Niu traffic center allowed himself to be sucked down into the blue hell of the transport tube, along with the crowd of Niori on their way to work.

The tube let him off at Oray Central, the huge elevated plaza around which were clustered the city's merchandise hives. Cudyk spent twenty minutes shopping here, lost his way, asked directions of a Courtesy Leader, finally found the hive he wanted and purchased some Oladi silks.

From Oray he walked northward again past the Niori legislative hives, attracting curious stares from pedestrians. He was beginning to be sorry he had come, as he always was when he ventured out of the Quarter; seeing himself through the Niori's eyes, he could not help feeling

319

soft and squashy, grotesquely shaped, disgustingly hairy. At a substation near the dream hives, he boarded an aircar, an extravagance, merely to have a little privacy. He arrived at the spaceport in good time, claimed his parcel, and took another aircar back to the Quarter.

At the foot of Kwang-Chowfu Avenue, he met Zydh Oran coming out of his office. The Niori said formally, "Greeting, Mr. Cudyk. I have recently seen the priest, Father Exarkos. He was endeavoring to find you."

Cudyk said, "Greeting. Do you know where he has gone now?"

"I believe he is at his home. Contentment to you, Mr. Cudyk."

"Contentment," said Cudyk wryly, and went on. The Out-group Commissioner had used the form of address which, in his language, was normally reserved for strangers. It was the nearest thing to insult that was possible to a Niori. Even these people, Cudyk thought, can learn to recognize the existence of evil in time. It has taken them more than twenty years, but I think they are learning now.

He remembered the three monkeys which had sat on the mantelpiece of his father's home: See-no-evil, Hear-no-evil, Speak-no-evil. The Niori were like that. *To the pure, all things are pure. Set a thief to catch a thief.* But even a saint's patience can be tried, Cudyk thought; and the deaf and dumb can be taught to speak.

Depressed, he walked down to Brasil and crossed over to the building in which Exarkos lived. He pressed the combination that opened the street door and went up. The priest answered his knock.

"You were looking for me, Astereos?"

The little man smiled, then looked concerned as he saw Cudyk's expression. "Yes, my friend," he said, "but it is nothing. Nothing has happened. I am sorry you were worried."

He pointed to the chessboard by the window, set between two comfortable chairs. "I only thought that perhaps you would like a game."

"I would," said Cudyk, and smiled. "Lately, whenever I see anyone, I think that he is going to give me bad news."

They sat down, and Exarkos held out two pawns in his closed fists. Cudyk chose the black. "As with all of us," said the priest. "Seu is badly worried, more than I have ever seen him. I think that he knows something he has not yet told."

"We'll find out soon enough," said Cudyk, and countered Exarkos' gambit. In five moves he lost a pawn, and in seven the priest had driven him out of the center.

"Your mind is not on it," said Exarkos.

"No. I concede, Astereos. If you don't mind, let's play another day."

The priest got up and brought two goblets and a bottle of white wine. "We will talk then," he said, filling the glasses. He held up the bottle. "This wine is from the vineyards of Agrinion, where I lived when I was a boy."

"Will you go back there, Astereos, if we have to go?"

The priest shrugged, smiling. "I will go where I am sent," he said. "It does not matter. I was a city man, Laszlo, like yourself. All wildernesses will be the same to me."

They looked at each other. At length the priest sighed. "Well," he said, "let us say what we are thinking. How much damage do you think the activists will be able to do before they are stopped?"

"I only wish I knew," said Cudyk slowly. "They can't have much armament—only a few ships from the Earth Navy, rebuilt to take galactic fuels, probably. Perhaps they have stolen some galactic ships, but those would not be armed. And I don't know how much ammunition they could have for the cannon in the military ships; I think not much. I give them credit for knowing where to use it where it will do the most harm—to disrupt communications, for example, or to destroy manufacturing centers on which many planets depend. But the galaxy is too big for them. They're ridiculous, in a way. They would not last a week against a fighting force of any size."

"You think that they have developed some defense against the stasis field?"

"They've had twenty years," said Cudyk grimly. "And that is the only weapon—if you can call it a weapon— that the galaxy has. What I am most afraid of is that they

321

have developed more weapons of their own—a workable total-conversion bomb, for example."

"Well"—the priest spread his hands—"perhaps nothing will happen. At any rate, we can do nothing but wait." He smiled. "Do you know, I have often had the heretical thought that if only the other races of the galaxy had been as warlike as ourselves, all would have been well. They conquered space long before we did. By the time we entered upon the scene, the worst of the wars between planets would have been over. Doubtless they would have achieved an order of some kind, even if it were only an armed truce. And they would have looked at us pityingly, and said, 'Mind your manners, little Earthmen, if you do not want to have your breeches warmed.' And we would have minded our manners."

Cudyk smiled and shook his head. "Can you imagine twentieth-century Europe, expanded to the size of the galaxy?"

"Oh," said the priest, gesturing widely, "It would have been very dreadful, of course. One would hear daily of some planet that had been blown up as the result of losing a quarrel. But it would have been no worse, for us, than the world we were accustomed to. And above all, we would not have had to bear *all* the guilt."

His eyes were narrowed with enjoyment. "But," he said, "it is a heretical thought. I make many penances for it."

Cudyk laughed.

"Ah, good," said Exarkos. "You have forgotten to be gloomy. When you are gloomy, you know that talking accomplishes nothing, but this knowledge only makes you gloomier. When you are able to laugh, you realize that the futility of discussion is the reason why it can be enjoyed. If it were otherwise, there would be no pleasure in it."

Cudyk laughed again, relaxing in his chair. "All right, Father Christmas," he said, "I will stop croaking of disaster. But let me hear you make light conversation on the subject of Rack."

"Rack," said Exarkos promptly, "is an amateur. The amateur, my friend, has been the curse of our people from the beginning of time. I do not mean simply the apprentice, who has not yet learned his trade. Unfortunately there are people who are amateurs by nature, and these people never become professionals even if they have seventy years of experience. I will give you an example."

He pointed a forefinger at Cudyk. "In writing," he said impressively, "you begin as a small boy. You read some author's works, you are struck with admiration, you are overwhelmed; you say to yourself, this is what I will do with my life. You write. It is bad, but you do not realize this. You continue writing, you learn a little—but still it is bad. Now you begin to doubt, but still you write. Then comes the turning point.

"Suddenly you discover that you have learned enough to see *behind* the things which so fascinated you in the works of others. With this knowledge, you write again— and now, perhaps, the work is not great, but it is not hopeless. At the same time, your attitudes have changed. You have become the least bit cynical. You work consciously for effects; you criticize yourself as you write. And you read the works which first inspired you, and think to yourself, 'Well, but after all, I was very young then!' This means, my friend, that you have become a professional.

"This has happened to you; but there are others to whom it will never happen. There are writers who never will recover from the awe they felt for their first idols. There are revolutionaries who never will cease to feel the pure, uncritical emotions of their first conversion to the Cause. There are priests who never will progress a step beyond their first investiture. These are bad writers, bad revolutionaries, and bad priests. I believe, truly, that nine tenths of the evil of the world can be traced to them and those like them; for professionals are rare. Amateur statesmen, amateur generals, amateur psychologists, amateur economists—can you picture the confusion they have spread?"

"Bravo," said Cudyk.

"You like it?" the priest asked, pouring more wine. "I have been saving it for someone who would come and tell me that Rack is dangerous because he is a professional soldier; but no one has felt the need to tell me this, so I give you the theory free of charge."

Cudyk rose to go a few minutes later, when one of Exarkos' congregation knocked on the door. He nodded and spoke to the man as he left: it was Speros Moulios, hat in hand, eyes frightened and humble in the little gray face. Both his sons had elected to go to Rack's New Earth when the cruiser had called, but Moulios himself had been too timid to leave; and now, without doubt, he was afraid to stay where he was.

Exarkos would soothe him, quiet his nerves, perhaps make him laugh—just as he had done for Cudyk. It was little enough to do, perhaps—soothing-syrup for the dead-alive—but Cudyk was profoundly grateful that there was someone in the Quarter who was able to do it.

We have very little left, he thought, except one or two minor virtues that have no bloodstains on them. Kindliness, humor, a sense of brotherhood—perhaps if we had stuck to those, and never learned the martial virtues, never aspired to be noble or glorious, we would have come out all right. Was there ever a turning point? When Carthage was sown with salt, or when Paul founded the Church—or when the first caveman sharpened the end of a stick and used it for murder? If so, it was a long way back, dead and buried, dust and ashes.

We took all that was best in three thousand years of yearning and striving for the right, he thought, and we made it into the Inquisition and the Star Chamber and the NKVD. We fattened our own children for each generation's slaughter. And yet we are not all evil. Astereos is right: if the other races had been like ourselves, it would have been bearable. Or if we ourselves had been creatures of pure darkness, conscienceless, glorying in cruelty —then we could have made war on the galaxy joyfully, and if we failed at least there would have been an element of grandeur in our failure.

Olaf Stapledon had said this once, he remembered— that there was an artistry in pure, uncontaminated evil, that it was in its own way as real an expression of worship as pure good.

The tragedy of human beings was that they were not wholly tragic. Jumbled, piebald parcels of contradictions, angels with asses' ears . . . What was that quotation from Bierce? *The best thing is not to be born. . . .*

Someone brushed by him, and Cudyk looked up. He was at the intersection of Kwang-Chowfu and Washington, three blocks from Exarkos' apartment.

Chong Yin's was only a few doors to his left; perhaps he had been heading there automatically. But the doors were closed, he saw. Seven or eight Chinese were standing in the street outside, and as Cudyk watched, Seu Min came down the stairs from the living quarters over the tea room. The other Chinese clustered around him for a moment, and then Seu appeared again. The others slowly began to disperse.

Cudyk went to meet him. The mayor's face looked strained; there were new, deep folds of skin around his eyes. "What is it, Min?" said Cudyk.

Seu fell in beside him and they walked back up the street. "Chong killed himself about an hour ago," said the Chinese.

How many does that make? Cudyk thought, frozen. *Six, I think, in the last two months.*

He had not known Chong well; the old man had been a north-country Chinese, not at all Westernized, who spoke only his own language. Now that he thought of it, Cudyk realized that he did not know who Chong's close friends had been, if he had had any. He had always been the same spare, stooped figure in skullcap and robe, courteous, unobtrusive, self-contained. He had a family: a wife, rarely seen, and six children.

"Have you some whisky?" asked Seu abruptly.

"Yes, of course."

"Let us go and drink it," Seu said. "I'm very tired."

It occurred to Cudyk that he had never heard Seu say that before. They turned the corner at Athenai and climbed the stairs to his apartment. Seu sighed, and dropped heavily into a chair while Cudyk went to get the bottle and glasses.

"Straight or with water?" he asked.

"Straight, please." Seu tilted his glass, swallowed and shuddered. Cudyk watched him in silence.

For the first time in more than an hour, Cudyk remembered his meeting with Zydh Oran, and the commissioner's coldness. Now, looking at Seu's tired face, he knew that he was going to hear something unpleasant.

Seu was the only one in the Quarter who owned a Niori communicator: an elaborate mechanism which reproduced sound, vision in three dimensions, odors, modulated temperature changes, and several other things perceptible only to Niori. There was no restriction on their sale, and they were cheap enough, but the Niori broadcasts were as dull or as incomprehensible to men as a Terrestrial breakfast program would have been to the Niori. Seu used his as a source of galactic news. Today, Cudyk guessed, the news had been very bad.

"It's Rack, isn't it?" he said finally.

Seu glanced at him and nodded. "Yes, it's Rack. I haven't told anyone else about it yet. The Quarter's in a half-hysterical state as it is. But if you don't mind my talking it out to you—"

"Go ahead," said Cudyk.

"It's worse than anything we expected." Seu took another swallow of the whisky, and made a face. He said, "They've got a total-conversion bomb."

"I was afraid of that."

Seu went on as if he had not heard. "But they're not using it on planets. They're bombing suns, Laszlo."

For a moment, Cudyk did not understand; then he felt his abdominal muscles contract like a fist. "They couldn't," he said hoarsely. "It would explode before it got past the outer layers."

"Under faster-than-light drive?" Seu asked. "I did some figuring. At one thousand C, it would take the bomb about two point six thousandths of a second to travel from the surface to the center of an average G-class star. I think that is a short enough interval, but maybe it isn't. Maybe they have also found some way to increase the efficiency of the standard galactic drive for short periods. Anyway, does it matter?" He looked at Cudyk again. "I have seen the pictures. I *saw* it happen."

Cudyk's throat was dry. "Which stars?" he said.

"Törkas. Rud-Uri. That's the Oladi sun. And Gerzion. Those three, so far."

Cudyk's fingers were nervously caressing the smooth metal of his wristwatch. He looked down at it suddenly, remembering that the Oladsa had made it. And now they were gone, all but their colonies and travelers on other worlds, and those who had been in space at the time. All those spidery, meticulous people, with their million-year-old culture and their cities of carved opal: wiped out as a man would swat a fly.

Seu took another drink. His face flushed, and drops of sweat stood out on his forehead and cheeks.

He said, "They'll have to learn to kill now. There isn't any alternative. They intercepted one of the New Earth ships and sprayed it with the stasis field. It didn't work; the ship got away. They'll have to learn to kill—do you know what that means?"

"Yes."

Seu drank again. His face was fiery red now, and he was gasping for breath. "I can't get drunk," he said bitterly. "Toxic reaction. I thought I'd try once more, but it's no good. Laszlo, look out, I'm going to be sick."

Cudyk led him to the lavatory. When he came out, the Chinese was weak and waxen-pale. Cudyk tried to persuade him to rest on the bed, but he refused. "I've got to get back to my office," he said. "Been gone too long already. Help me down the stairs, will you, Laszlo?"

Cudyk walked him as far as Brasil and Washington, where two of Seu's young men took over with voluble expressions of gratitude. Cudyk watched the group until it disappeared into Town Hall, and then turned back.

He could feel nothing but an arid depression. Even the horror at Rack's mass-murders, even his pity for Seu was blunted, sealed off at the back of his mind. The lives of saints, Cudyk remembered, spoke of "boundless compassion" and "infinite pity": but an ordinary man had a limited supply. When it was used up, you were empty and impotent, a canceled sign in the human equation.

Half instinctively, half by choice, Cudyk had chosen his friends among the strongest and most patient, the wise and cynical: the survivors. But he had leaned too much on their strength, he realized now. He had seen Seu crumble; and he felt as if a crutch had broken under his weight.

Someone called his name. He turned to see Kathy Burgess walking toward him. She looked incongruously fresh and happy, and it took Cudyk a long moment to recall that she did not know about the exploded suns; that no one in the Quarter knew except himself and Seu.

"You are in good spirits today," he said, trying not to sound lugubrious.

She smiled. "Yes. I have a wonderful new job, Mr. Cudyk. I'm helping a Niori—his name is Sef Eshon."

"Helping a Niori," Cudyk repeated. "What does he do?"

"Well . . ." Her smile became a trifle uncertain. "He's a psychologist. I'm really only a guinea pig, I guess, but he says I'm an excellent subject. He asks me questions, and I answer them as well as I can, you know, and then he puts me into a kind of a reverie state and asks more questions. He uses the same thing they have at the hospital—it's a Niori drug like sodium pentothal, but better. He's a *wonderful* person, Mr. Cudyk."

Cudyk asked, "How does your father feel about this?"

She frowned. "I haven't told him yet. I only got the job last night. I had a notice put up in their medical hive, and last evening a note came from Eshon. I didn't tell Father about it then, because of course I wasn't sure I'd get the job." She hesitated. "He won't like it, I know. But you can't imagine what it means to me to have this job, Mr. Cudyk. It gives me such a wonderful feeling to be useful, and at the same time to be free—to have some place to go outside the Quarter."

"Yes," said Cudyk. "That is something I think all of us would like to have."

He left her at her door and walked home, wondering why he was so sure that Kathy would not, this time, submit to her father. She had given up De Grasse at his order; why should she refuse to give up a job? Perhaps because marriage might have brought her happiness?

That evening he opened his shutters and looked out at the sky. The familiar constellations were there, unchanged: the light of the nearest star took more than three years to reach Palu. But in his mind's eye one glittering pinpoint exploded suddenly into a dreadful blossom of radiance; then another; then a third. And he saw the blackened corpses of planets swinging around each, murdered by that single flash of incredible heat.

During the night he dreamed of a black wasteland,

and of Rack standing motionless in the center of it, brooding, with his cold gray face turned to the stars.

It was Cudyk's birthday. He had never told anyone in the Quarter the date, and had all but forgotten it himself. This morning, feeling an idle desire to know what the season was on Earth, he had hunted up a calendar he had last used fifteen years ago; it translated the Niori system into Gregorian years, months and days. The result, when he had worked it out with some little trouble, was February 18th. He was fifty-six.

Now he was constrained to wonder whether the action had been as random as it seemed. Was it possible that subconsciously he had no need of the calendar? That he had kept track, all these years, and had known when his birthday came? If so, why had he felt it necessary to remind himself in this oblique way?

A return to the womb? A hunger for the comforts of the family circle, the birthday cake, candles, the solace of yearly repetition? Perhaps that was it. Cudyk, smiling a little, thought of the cycle of seasons, the long slow rhythm that was soothing at first, before the fact that you were going to die became in the least credible. Later, to most men, it was frightening, like the measured sweep of Poe's scimitar-bladed pendulum: each stroke shearing away a little of life. Still, even when you cursed the sweating silent heat of one season and the bitter chill of another, the rhythm was a part of you.

Cudyk was fifty-six. When he had been fifty-five, he had thought of himself as a man in his middle years, still strong, still able. Now he was old.

The same thing had happened to Seu: he had recovered from his first shock when the news had come about Rack, and for more than three weeks now he had moved about the Quarter, as quiet and as competent as before; but there was a difference. His swift furtive humor was gone except for rare flashes; his voice and his step were heavy.

It was the same with all of them, all the old settlers. Cudyk had met Burgess on the street the day before, for the first time in several weeks, and had been genuinely shocked. The man's hair was white, his skin papery, his gait stumbling.

Even Exarkos showed the change. More and more of his gray, woolly hair was vanishing. The umber crescents under his eyes were a deeper shade, almost black.

Watching him now, as he sat listening to Seu, Cudyk told himself that the priest was the strongest of them all, and the hardest to fathom. Strain was written in his face, but his eyes gazed through that wrinkled, clever mask as serenely as ever. There was a deep inner quietness in Exarkos that was the antithesis of Kathy Burgess': it was the pregnancy of life, not death.

Cudyk remembered what the priest had said on that evening, long ago, when Flynn had asked him about his beliefs. *We are like sterile mutants—we carry the seeds of greater fulfillment within us, but they will die with our bodies.* For himself, at least, Exarkos had spoken the simple truth.

In other times, Cudyk thought, this man might have flowered into greatness. As it is, he was born too late; the seed he carries will never grow; he will go down into darkness like the rest of us. And I believe he knows this, all of it. But there is no self-pity in him. Here is a man with every excuse to make himself a tragic figure; and yet he is a man at one with himself.

Seu was saying, "These problems have to be considered, but it would be simply asking for more trouble if I took them to a full Council meeting at this point. There would be five hours of argument, probably finishing with a free-for-all, and in the end nothing would be done." He raised his hand slightly and set it down again, flat on the table-top. "Perhaps that would be the best thing. I admit that I am unable to decide. I want you to help me."

The three of them were sitting in the assembly room at Town Hall. In one corner the speaker's stand was leaning against the wall, its base splintered; the last full meeting, two weeks ago, had ended in a brawl, and the damage had not yet been repaired. When the news about the war in the galaxy had leaked, as it was bound to do, the first reaction had been a stunned apathy; later it had turned to something dangerously close to hysteria. Tempers were short in the Quarter, moods unpredictable. There had been several stabbings in the Russian section, and half a dozen more suicides. And the bombings had continued: by now more than thirty suns had blazed into terrible brightness.

The mayor said wearily, "I don't think there is any doubt that if we do nothing to stop it, there is going to be a change in the Niori policy towards us. It was bad enough when our only offenses were crimes committed inside the Quarter, and in similar ghettos on other planets. Now it isn't just a few people like Zydh Oran, who are directly concerned with us and *have* to notice how disgusting we are, that we have to reckon with: every Niori on the planet is thinking about us now, and changing his ideas, if he had any.

"As I see it, there's only one thing we can do—reverse our own policy completely. Confess that there have been murders here in the Quarter, that we've harbored activists, and that we've lied about it—and explain our reasons as well as we can. After that, throw ourselves on their mercy; volunteer to fight against Rack—anything. The question is, simply, will that do us more good than harm?"

He looked at them in turn. "I don't think any of us would claim to understand the Niori completely, but perhaps one of you has some insight that has been denied to me. What do you think?"

"Very risky," said Exarkos after a moment. "We are dealing here with a people who do not understand what it is to sin. Now we are forcing them to understand it. I am afraid I do not believe that they would regard this confession as an evidence of repentance—because, you see, repentance cannot exist without sin. I do not think that they understand what repentance is. I think that, being forced by our statement to believe that we lie, they would most probably conclude that the statement itself is also a lie. What they would then do, I cannot guess. This is for them a completely new situation, without precedent. But what do you say, Laszlo?"

Cudyk said slowly, "I agree with you, but I think Seu's plan might be worth trying nevertheless. I myself believe that we are going to be expelled, no matter what we do.

I have no hope for the Quarter. But I think it would be as well to try whatever we can."

As he finished speaking, someone shouted, outside in the street. A door slammed in the hall, and they heard running footsteps on the stairs.

Seu stood up and started toward the windows. Before he got there, the door opened and Lee Far thrust his head inside. "Is Miss Burgess!" he said. "She walk down street with no clothes!"

Seu paused in mid-stride, half-turned, then went on and opened the nearest window. Cudyk and the priest followed him.

Two stories below, ivory in the warm sunlight, the slender figure walked down the middle of the street. She had already passed Town Hall, heading toward Rossiya Street and the Russian sector. She was walking slowly, arms swinging freely, looking to neither side.

A small crowd had collected behind her, and two half-grown boys were capering at her side, talking to her, reaching out to touch her. Three of Seu's young men were spaced along the sidewalk below, looking up at the windows, waiting for orders.

Seu called, "Miss Burgess!"

She did not turn or pause.

The mayor said, "Laszlo, you'd better get her." As Cudyk headed for the doorway, he heard Seu calling down to the waiting men, "Get one of the doctors, quickly!"

Cudyk hurtled down the stairs and out into the bright sunlight. Kathy had nearly reached the end of the block. The crowd was growing. As Cudyk came up to her, he saw that her lips were compressed and her face flushed with anger, although she was still staring straight ahead.

Her body was immature: slender, almost boyish hips and thighs, breasts no larger than a man's fists. Her skin was clear and silkily soft, like a child's. Virginal, Cudyk thought, remembering that the word had once been a synonym for "seductive." He stepped in front of her and took her arm. "Please come with me, Kathy," he said.

She stepped back with a swift, lithe motion, slipping her arm free. "But why won't you leave me *alone?*" she said.

She was staring at him, he saw, but her eyes did not quite seem to focus on him. They were glassy, the pupils so large that he could not see her irises.

Cudyk stepped toward her again, but one of the two boys moved into his way. He saw now that it was Red Gorciak, the wine merchant's son: not more than sixteen, but as tall as Cudyk and nearly as broad. The youngster's face was flushed, lips swollen, ears bright pink. He said breathily, "Sure, leave her alone, Mr. Cudyk. She don't want you to bother her."

Cudyk said, "Don't interfere, Red," and moved forward. Gorciak danced away from him, keeping between Cudyk and the girl, and said over his shoulder, "Get her, Stan!"

The other one, then, was Stanley Eleftheris. Naturally. Cudyk put his weight on the balls of his feet, brushed aside Gorciak's warding arm, and swung his fist to the youngster's jaw. Gorciak went sprawling down. He did not get up.

Eleftheris was standing just beyond Gorciak, two steps from Kathy: a loose-limbed boy with oversized nose and ears, and a pale adolescent beard on his pimpled cheeks. He looked from Gorciak to Cudyk, his mouth hanging open. When Cudyk stepped toward him he moved hurriedly away. "I didn't do nothing! What you want to hit me for?"

The crowd had gathered in a semicircle around them now: a few Russians and Poles, several Greeks, one or two Chinese. The situation had the making of a full-scale riot, Cudyk knew, but he had had no choice but to knock Gorciak down; otherwise the amorous pair would have been on his back as soon as he tried to lead Kathy away. Even now, there might be trouble. He said carefully, "This girl is sick. One or two of you help me to get her upstairs, but be careful not to hurt her."

Kathy said violently, "I'm not sick! I'm *all right*. Why don't you all let me alone?"

Cudyk stepped cautiously forward, seized her right arm and elbow. There was a furious strength in her slender body; Cudyk had all he could do to keep his grip without injuring her, and meanwhile she was raining a flurry of blows on his face and chest, kicking at his legs, kneeing him, doing her best to bite. This lasted perhaps six seconds, and then the blows stopped. One of the Greeks, a strongly-built, middle-aged man, had stepped forward and gripped her other arm.

Kathy stood trembling between them, tears running down her cheeks. She called piteously, "Won't somebody *help* me? *Oh!* Why are you doing this?" She screamed piercingly and began to struggle again, back arched and head thrown back, writhing as if in agony.

The crowd parted and Moskowitz came through, breathing heavily. He set his bag down on the pavement, opened it and took out the squat tube of a pressure hypodermic. He put the tube's blunt end against Kathy's left shoulder and pressed the trigger. In a few moments her taut body relaxed; she would have fallen if Cudyk and the other man had not held her up.

The two hospital attendants came forward with a stretcher and they put her into it. She lay breathing quietly, lips half-parted, arms crossed limply over her body. Damp strands of hair lay across her closed eyes.

The hospital was a narrow three-story building on Brasil Street, almost exactly in the center of the Quarter: morgue in the basement, then receiving rooms, clinic and surgery, and wards on the top floor. The place had a smell that was not like the smell of any hospital Cudyk had known on Earth. There were a few familiar elements in it, but they were smothered by the alien odors; the galactic drugs and antiseptics which filled the gaps in the human pharmacopoeia.

Moskowitz sat behind a tiny desk cluttered with unfiled forms and charts, and more than half covered by a rack of labeled bottles. He was obviously weary. His eyes were alert and steady, but the dry skin of the lids was taut and discolored around them.

He said, "As I get it, then, she just came home from work, took off all her clothes as soon as she crossed the line, and walked straight down Washington."

"That's right," Seu said. "We found her clothing at the foot of Washington Avenue. She didn't talk to anyone, as far as I can discover—just walked straight ahead, taking her time. According to Laszlo, she seemed outraged when he stopped her."

"Yes," said Moskowitz. He picked up one end of a pencil and let it drop. "It would help if we could find out what set her off. How did you make out when you tried to locate this Niori she was working for?"

"No one remembers his name, unfortunately."

"Sef something," Cudyk put in. "She told me last month, when she first got the job, but that is all I can remember."

"I sent word to Zydh Oran, however," said Seu. "I think he will find the Niori."

Moskowtiz raised one eyebrow. "That's against policy, isn't it?"

Seu shrugged. "I don't think we need to worry about the Niori finding out that one of us is insane. I only wish we could have found some way of concealing the fact that we're *all* mad."

Moskowitz grinned wryly and nodded. "True for you, Mr. Seu. I don't know how seriously you meant that, but I'll tell you one thing: the reason we never got any farther than we did with the treatment of psychoses back home, is that we never had a single mind we could point to and say, 'That's sanity. That's what we want to produce.' We were like a bunch of fellows tinkering with a garageful of beat-up Fords, trying to turn out a brand-new Cadillac. It can't be done. The best we can get is something that runs, and that's about all you can say for it. And we don't always get that."

Cudyk asked curiously, "Have you learned anything from Niori psychiatry, Arnold?"

Moskowitz shook his head sadly. "Not a thing. It doesn't exist. The galactic races just don't ever jump their trolleys. Well, I'm exaggerating; it happens once in a long while. Once or twice in a century, maybe. When it does happen, it knocks them over. They don't know what it is or what to do about it."

"So we have too many madmen, and they have too few," Cudyk commented.

"Sure. It makes sense. There are human diseases that have never been licked because there aren't enough cases on the books. To find a cure for galloping consumption of the toenails, you'd want to have a few consumptive toe-nails to study. If you can't get 'em, you're out of luck. But if everybody's got the same disease, and you don't even know what the disease is, just that something's fishy some-where—you're *really* licked then. All you can do is keep pushing buttons to see what happens—pure empiricism. That's what we do. Sometimes it works, after a fashion."

"I gather then," said Seu, "that you can't make any forecasts about Miss Burgess' recovery."

Moskowitz shook his head. "Not unless I get a dream about it tonight, or cast a horoscope or something. I'll push as many buttons as I know how, but it's really up to her. She may snap out of it in a month, or it might take five years, or she may never come out of it."

He added, "I won't tell Burgess that, of course. He's in bad shape, himself. Has he got someone to look after him, by the way?"

"I left one of my assistants with him," said Seu. "He is very disturbed. He wants to be with his daughter, and I am very much afraid he'll get his wish."

Cudyk stood up. "I'll look in on him before I go home," he said. "If you're through with us, Arnold?"

Before Moskowitz could reply, the door opened. Cudyk, turning, saw two Niori enter the room. One he recognized by the distinctive markings on the flat armor of the head; it was Zydh Oran. The other was a stranger to him.

Oran greeted them formally in his own language, and said, "This person is Sef Eshon, the scientist. Sef Eshon, I introduce to you Mr. Cudyk, Dr. Moskowitz, and Mayor Seu."

After greetings had been exchanged, Moskowitz said in Niori, "You are the person who employed Kathy Bur-gess?"

"I am that one. I was told that she has been taken ill. I have come to give what help I can. I hope that the illness is not virulent."

"The illness is of the mind," Moskowitz told him.

The Niori emitted the harsh grating noise that signified astonishment. "In this case I can give no help. She was not deranged, to my perception, when she left me."

He passed a many-jointed "hand" over the gleaming

translucency of his crest—a motion so like that of a bald man nervously caressing his pate that Cudyk was taken by a curious mingling of amusement and despair. If it were only true that they were that nearly human—if they could be laughed at!

Moskowitz asked, "Scientist Eshon, did she undergo any unusual emotional strain during her last session with you?" The question was hard to put into Niori; he stumbled over it several times.

Sef Eshon did not seem to understand. Moskowitz tried again, with a different phrasing. Finally the Niori scientist said, "I am not sure I have your meaning, Dr. Moskowitz. She felt emotion toward me, but surely this is not harmful to your race?"

The lines of Moskowitz's face tightened. He said haltingly, "Sometimes when one emotion conflicts with another —or when the emotion is one which by its nature cannot achieve its object—emotions can be a factor in precipitating mental illness."

Sef Eshon hesitated, turned and exchanged a few words of rapid Niori with Zydh Oran. Cudyk understood them to say, "Do you understand this?" and "Little, if any, more than yourself."

The scientist turned back to Moskowitz. "The emotions Kathy Burgess felt for me were respect, admiration, and love. In my understanding, these emotions do not have what you call an object, they are self-sufficient."

Moskowitz asked, "Did she express these emotions in words, at your last meeting?"

"She did."

"Can you recall the words she used?"

The Niori thought for a moment: then, mimicking Kathy's high, clear voice almost perfectly, he said in English, " 'You are so wonderful. I never knew anyone like you. I think I love you, Sef Eshon.' " In his own voice he added, "She said these words in her language, and then translated." He repeated the sentences in Niori.

Moskowitz glanced sidelong at Seu and Cudyk. He said cautiously, "Thank you. You have been very helpful, Sef Eshon."

The scientist said, "She then stroked my upper left hand with her fingers. I am trying to recall any detail which may be helpful, although I still do not understand what you say about the 'object' of an emotion."

"It is difficult to explain—" began Moskowitz, glancing again at the other two.

Seu said to the Niori, "Perhaps I can make it clear. I will try. With us, the word 'love' applies not only to the objectless affection any person may feel for another, but especially to the strong emotion felt by one person toward another with whom he wishes to mate. It is evident, from the words and the tone in which Kathy spoke to you, that this was the 'love' she meant. She has twice been disappointed in her choice of mates among us; apparently she turned to you in despair at achieving a normal relationship. But at the same time she knew perfectly well that union with one of another race was impossible, and the conflict of emotion with reality, as Dr. Moskowitz said, made her insane."

The two Niori stood perfectly still, not speaking, for what seemed to Cudyk almost a full minute. Then Sef Eshon said formally, "I am glad to have been of help. Contentment to you all." He turned to go.

Zydh Oran lingered to say to Seu, "It would please me to speak with you later, in private."

"I will come to your office in half an hour," said Seu.

"You are kind. Contentment to you." He followed the other Niori out.

"You shocked them," said Moskowitz after a moment. "You should have let me cover up."

"We've been covering up for more than twenty years," Seu said wearily. "I don't think we can do any more harm now by telling the truth."

VII

The Quarter's graveyard was an acre of ground, surrounded by trees, on the outskirts of the City; there the dead reclined in a more ample space than the living enjoyed. The Niori had allotted the ground, though the outline of the City was thereby disfigured, and had contributed slabs of a synthetic stone which carved easily when it was fresh, later hardening until it would resist any edged tool. The plot was ill tended, but the standing stones, translucent pearl or rose, had a certain beauty. To the Niori, the purpose of the graveyard was only that; they were not equipped to understand mankind's morbid attachment to its own carrion.

Cudyk had gone to Burgess' funeral, presided over by Kellin, the falsely hearty Protestant pastor; and the image of those ranked headstones, neatly separated into the Orthodox, the Protestants, the Buddhists, the Taoists and the unbelievers, had returned to him many times since. It was another sign of the change that was taking place in him: the images which formerly had dominated his mind had been pictographs of abstractions—the great globe of infinity, the tiny spark that was creative intellect; now they were the pale headstone and the dark curtain of death.

He had felt nothing, standing over Burgess' grave and watching the sod fall. What is there to say about a man when he is dead? The pastor's words were false, as all such words are false; they had no relevance; the man was dead. Nothing was left of him now but the dissolving molecules of his flesh, and the fragmentary, ego-distorted memories he had planted in the minds of others. He was a name written in water.

It was not Burgess who obsessed Cudyk, nor the many other half-remembered men and women whose names were clumsily carved on those stones. It was the cemetery as a symbol: the fascination of the yawning void.

When he looked at the stars now, they sparkled with the cold brilliance of death, and he could feel the icy stillness of the waste between them.

Always a man turned his face toward some dimly-felt goal, whether it were the sun-image, the suspected, yearned-for warmth of childhood and adolescence, or the bright, steely purity with the resounding name that replaced it in early manhood—the Socialist World State, the Rule of Reason, the Kingdom of God—or the immense nothingness, the sheer overpowering weight of transcience and unreason, that bowed a man's head and drew him into darkness when he was old.

Cudyk thought of all the words, the billions of words that had seemed so important at the time they were spoken. It was possible to live by words, to live so blinded that nothing existed beyond words; and to weave them tirelessly into bright, intricate structures that always collapsed and always were replaced by others. Only at the end, when you were close to that dark curtain, did their hypnotic hum fade from your ears—and then the stillness!

The majesty of that silence struck you dumb; you saw the universe as it had been before your first groping speech, in the forgotten time before words; and you felt that never once, in all the years between, had you seen the truth. But the truth was not to be borne, and the squeaking little phrasemaker, the cricket of the skull, once more began to spin its vulgar thread into the silence.

Cudyk had one other preoccupation: he thought often of Earth, seeing it as a dark globe turning, black continents dim against the gray ocean, pricked by a few faint gleams that were cities. Or, if he thought of the cities, he saw them drowned in shadow: the shapes of tower and arch melting into night-patterns; moonlight falling faintly, dissolving what it touched, so that shadows became as solid stone, stone as insubstantial mist.

For Earth, also, was a symbol of death.

There had been no more suicides since Burgess had poisoned himself, no riots. It seemed to Cudyk that the whole Quarter moved, like himself, through a fluid heavier than air. All motion had slowed, and sounds came muted and without resonance. People spoke to him, and he answered, but without attention, as if they were not really there.

Even the news about Rack's defeat had stirred him only momentarily, and he had seen in Seu's face that the Chinese felt himself somehow inadequate to the tale even as he told it. The galactic fleet, vastly expanded, had met the activist forces with a new weapon—one, indeed, which did not kill, but which was shameful enough to a citizen of the galaxy. The weapon projected a field which scrambled the synapse patterns in the brain, leaving its victim incapable of adding two figures, of lighting a cigarette, or of aiming a torpedo. Eleven New Earth ships had been captured, and it was thought that these were all the activists' armed vessels; there had been no further attacks since then.

He did not believe that anything which could now possibly happen could rouse him from his apathy. But he had forgotten one possibility. Seu came to him in Chong Yin's, where Yin's eldest son Fu now moved in his father's place, and said, "Rack wasn't taken. He's here."

Cudyk sat with his teacup raised halfway between the table and his lips. After a long moment, he saw that his hand was trembling violently. He set the cup down. He said, "Where?"

"The Little Bear. Half the town has gone there already. Do you want to go?"

Cudyk stood up slowly. "Yes," he said, "I suppose so." But he felt the tension that pulled his body together, the tautened muscles in back and shoulders and arms.

As they reached the corner of Ceskoslovensko and Washington, they saw scattered groups of men moving ahead of them, all hurrying, some frankly running. The crowd was thick around the doorway of The Little Bear when they reached it, and they had difficulty forcing a passage. Men moved aside for Seu willingly enough, but there was little space to move.

Inside, it was worse. The stairway was solidly packed; it was obviously impossible to get through.

"There is a back staircase," Seu said. He worked his way toward the rear of the room, Cudyk following, until he caught sight of the bartender. The press was not so thick here, and he was able to reach the man and lead him into a corner away from the others. "Can you get us up the back way?"

The Russian nodded, scowled, and put his finger to his lips. Following him, they went through the swinging doors at the back of the room, through the dark kitchen and up the narrow service stairs at the rear. The bartender unlocked the door at the top and helped them force it open against the pressure of the packed bodies inside.

The long room was heavy with the odors of sweat, tobacco smoke and stale air. Faces shone greasily under the yellow glare of the ceiling lights. The only clear space was the table top against the wall to Cudyk's right, where Rack stood.

Cudyk could see him clearly over the heads of those in front of him. He stood with legs planted firmly, hands at his sides. As always, the leather jacket was draped over his shoulders like a cloak.

He was alone. Spanner was not there, nor Biff, nor Tom De Grasse.

Rack was talking in a low, clear voice. Cudyk listened to the end of a sentence which conveyed nothing to him, and then heard: "After that, we got it. They gave it to us." Rack's hands clenched once, and then opened again.

"They intercepted us three minutes after we came out of overdrive in the orbit of New Earth. Twelve fighting ships, the whole fleet. We were in a line, just closing in after we broke C on the way down—the *Thermopylae*, the *Tours*, the *Waterloo*, the *Chateau Thierry*, the *Dunkirk*, the *Leningrad*, the *Acre*, the *Valley Forge*, the *Hiroshima*, the *San Francisco*, the *Seoul*, and the flagship last, the *Armageddon*.

"We didn't know they were there; they were out of our detector range. They had us like sitting ducks. The first thing we knew about it was when a teletype report from the leading ship, the *Thermopylae*, broke off in the middle of a word. Five seconds later the same thing happened to a report coming in from the next ship. Three seconds more, and the *Waterloo* was gone.

"I gave the order to reverse acceleration and scatter. But the field—whatever it was—came after us. It would have taken us at least two minutes to build up the overdrive potential again, and we all knew we wouldn't make it. They were getting us one ship every six or eight seconds.

"The men were looking to me for orders. I didn't have any to give them. Suddenly De Grasse turned around and looked at Biff and Spanner, and they all nodded. They jumped me. I don't know what happened. I struck my head against the deck when I went down, or one of them hit me with a gunbutt."

His fists clenched and opened once more. "When I came to, I was strapped into a one-man lifeboat, on overdrive, doing ten C's. They must have emptied the ship's accumulators into that lifeboat, charged it up to C potential and got me off just before the field hit them.

"I took my bearings, reversed, and went back. Eventually I found the fleet again. The galactics had matched courses and velocity with them and they were just beginning to tow them off, in the general direction of Altair.

"They hadn't got into overdrive yet. I slipped in—there were a hundred of their little scouts nosing around, about the same mass as my lifeboat—and berthed in the same port I'd come out of. I got out and walked into the control room.

"The crew was still there, still alive. But not men. They were lying on the deck, looking at nothing. Their mouths were open, and they were drooling."

Rack's head moved stiffly, and his sharp profile turned from one side of the crowd to the other. "Mindless idiots," he said. "They couldn't feed themselves, or stand up, or sit. But they had saved me.

"I built up the charge and took my time about it. When the galactics went into overdrive, I took off in another direction. I was a good seventy light-years away before they knew I was gone.

"I had a ship, an undamaged ship. But I had no crew to man her. I can astrogate and, when I have to, I can man the engines on top of that. But I can't fight her as well.

"I came here, put the *Armageddon* into a one-day orbit and came down in the lighter. I want to go back and find out what those slime-eaters did to us, and give them a taste of the same. *I want twenty men.*"

There was a silence.

Rack said, in the same even, low voice, "Will you fight for the human race?"

Someone called, "What did you do with your other crew?"

Rack said, "I gave them military burial, in space."

For the first time, the crowd as a whole broke its silence. A low murmur rose. Rack said sharply, "I would have given my life for those men, as they did for me, gladly. But they were already dead. If there's a way to restore a man's mind after that has been done to it, only the vermin know how. I would rather be buried in space, and so would they."

A deep voice called, "Are you God, Rack?"

"I'm not God," he said promptly. "Are you a man?"

There was another murmur, dying as a pulsing movement began near the back of the room: someone was forcing his way toward Rack. In the stillness, another voice said thinly, "My Demetrios . . . my Alexander . . ." It was Moulios, wailing for his two lost sons.

Red-faced, with a lock of black hair hanging over his forehead, the painter Vekshin squeezed through to the edge of the table on which Rack stood. He shouted, "I'm a man, all right. What do you call yourself, you assassin? You come here with blood dripping from your jaws like a weasel fresh from a poultry yard, and we're supposed to feel sorry for you because they wouldn't let you go on killing! The great god Rack! *Ptui!*"

Rack did not move. He said quietly, "I killed your enemies, while you sat at home and drank tea."

"Enemies!" Vekshin roared. "You're the enemy, Rack." He put his big hands on the tabletop and heaved himself up.

Rack let him come. He waited until the Russian was standing on the table; then he stepped forward with a motion so smooth it seemed casual. There was a flurry of blows, none of which landed except two: one in Vekshin's midriff, the other on the point of his jaw. Five men went down as Vekshin's body hurtled into them.

Rack stepped back. "I have very little patience left," he said, "but if there is anyone else here with a personal grudge, let him step up."

Two men at the table's edge moved as if to climb up. Rack put his hand to the gun at his belt. The two men stayed where they were.

Rack stared out over the crowd. He looked suddenly very weary; it occurred to Cudyk that he must have gone without sleep for a long time.

Rack said, "This is the last call. I am not trying to deceive you. I promise you nothing, not glory, not your lives, not even that you will be able to spend your lives usefully. But if there is any man here who will serve aboard the *Armageddon*, in the last fight for mankind—raise your hand!"

There was a long moment's silence. Rack turned abruptly, with his hand still on his gun, and said to the men in front of Cudyk, "Stand back!"

The silence held for an instant, while the men at the table's end moved uncertainly away; then sound broke like an avalanche. As Rack jumped down, the crowd surged toward him, no longer an audience but a mob. Cudyk felt the pressure at his back, caught a glimpse of Rack's face, then heard the deafening report of the gun as he went hurtling forward.

The gun did not fire again. Cudyk was squeezed tightly in the center of the struggling mass. He saw Seu, a few feet away. The mayor's mouth was open; he was shouting something, but the words were lost.

Suddenly Rack came into view again, charging straight toward Cudyk, hurling bodies to either side. The lower half of his face was a smear of blood, his cap and jacket were gone, his shirt torn half away.

Cudyk was half-aware of the constriction in his throat, the pounding of blood at his temples. He wrenched one arm free and, as Rack came near, struck him full in the face.

He had one more glimpse of Rack's white features, the pale eyes staring at him with a curiously detached expression: the eyes of a Caesar or a Christ, reproachful and sad. Then the crowd surged once more, the door to the back stairway slammed open, and Rack was gone.

Cudyk found himself running through the doorway with half a dozen others. He caught sight of Rack leaping down the stairs, just short of the landing where the narrow stairway doubled back on itself.

With a catch in his breath, feeling no surprise at what he was about to do, Cudyk put both hands on the railing and swung himself over into vacancy. Then there was an instant of wild, soaring flight, Rack's foreshortened body drifting beneath him, and the shock.

Dazed and numb, Cudyk felt the universe moving under him like a gigantic pendulum. He saw faces appear and vanish, felt someone push him aside, heard voices faintly.

After a long time his head cleared, and there was silence. He was lying at the foot of the stairs, one arm flung over the first step. Rack was not there; no one was there but himself.

He moved cautiously and was rewarded by an astonishing number and variety of pains. But apparently he had broken no bones. He felt weak and hollow: he was afraid he might vomit. He hoisted his torso up slowly, sat on the lowest step and then put his head between his trembling knees.

He heard a foot scuff on the concrete floor, and looked up. It was Seu.

The Chinese looked at him anxiously. "You're all right?"

"Yes. I think so. I have felt better in my life."

"Do you want to get up? Did you jump or fall?"

Cudyk leaned forward, trying the strength of his thighs to raise him, and Seu put a hand under his arm to help. "I jumped," Cudyk said. "What happened afterward?"

"The mob came down, me in the middle, and I couldn't stop to see if you were all right. They took Rack with them. He was unconscious then; he may have been dead."

"And?"

"They tore him apart," said Seu. "I have seen some bad ones in twenty years here, but nothing to match that. For half an hour, I think we were all insane."

They moved toward the exit from the kitchen, Seu holding Cudyk's arm firmly.

"I don't know if you felt this," the mayor said stiffly, "but the way it seemed to me was that Rack suddenly represented all of it—not only the bombings, but the Quarter, the galaxy, Earth—everything we hated. It was a feeling of release, a kind of ecstasy. Watch out for the sill."

"Scapegoat," Cudyk said, indistinctly.

"Yes . . . Zydh Oran saw it, you know. He was there when the mob came out. He saw it all. This finishes the Quarter, Laszlo. After this there won't be any more reprieves."

Cudyk glanced down at Seu's plump fingers. There was a thin film of blood on the skin, and a dark line of it around each fingernail.

Cudyk stood at the top of the gentle rise opposite the foot of Washington Avenue, and looked down at the Quarter. It was just after sunset, and the ranked street lights cast a lonesome gleam. The streets were empty. There was no one left in the Quarter except one man in the powerhouse. When the time was up, he would pull the switches on the master board and come out; then the Quarter would be dead.

The Niori edict had come on the Wednesday morning after Rack's death. They had been given four days to pack their belongings, arrange for assignment of cargo space, and wind up their several affairs. Cudyk's stock was small and his personal belongings few; he had been ready two days ago.

The evening breeze, fresh'ening, pressed Cudyk's trousers against his calves and stirred the hair at the back of his head. Looking into the east, he saw a few pallid stars in the sky.

Several hundred people had already been collected by the aircars which served the spaceport. Cudyk, Seu, Exarkos and a few others, by unspoken assent, had taken places at the rear of the crowd, to be the last to go.

He glanced at Seu. The little man was standing with his hands in his pockets,, shoulders slumped, staring dully at the Quarter. He looked up after a moment, smiled unhappily, and shrugged.

"It's absurd to feel homesick for it, isn't it?" he said. "It was a ghetto; we had no roots there. It was cramped, and it stank, and we fought among ourselves more viciously than we ever fought on Earth. But twenty years . . ."

"We could pretend that we had roots, at least," Cudyk answered. "We don't belong anywhere. Perhaps we'll be happier, in the long run, once we face that and accept it."

"I doubt it."

"So do I."

To Cudyk's right, Father Exarkos was sitting on his suitcase, hands relaxed on his thighs. Cudyk said, "If I were a believer, Astereos, I think it would do me a great deal of good to confess to you and be absolved."

The priest's dry, friendly voice said, "Why, have you sinned so terribly, Laszlo?"

"I killed a man," said Cudyk, "but that's not what I mean. I jumped over a stairway railing and stopped Rack. If it hadn't been for me, he might have got away. There would have been nothing wrong with that. He couldn't have done any more harm, one man by himself. The Guards would have captured him sooner or later, anyhow. And if he had gotten away, we wouldn't have given the Niori the one more straw they needed. In that sense, it is my fault that we were expelled."

"No, Laszlo," said Seu.

Exarkos said, "You have nothing for which to reproach yourself, on that score. You were only the instrument of history, my friend, and a minor instrument at that. And, speaking for myself, not for the Church, Rack deserved to die."

Cudyk thought, *At least it was quite suitably ironic. Cudyk, the man of inaction, hurls himself through the air to kill a murderer. And the citizens of the Quarter are deported, not because one of their race murdered a billion billion galactics, but because that same man was killed by them.*

That was one thin mark on the credit side. There was one more: the tension was gone, for some of them at least. Now the worst thing that could happen had happened; the Damocletian thread had snapped. The problems which had caused the tension no longer existed, and as yet there were no new ones.

Earth was two months away. Cudyk expected nothing and hoped for nothing. But the Niori had agreed to set each passenger down wherever on the globe he chose to go: each man, at least, could choose his own purgatory. The crews of the captured battleships, and the captured staff of the base on New Earth, were also being sent back. The weapon that had been used on them had done no permanent damage; they would simply have to be retrained, to learn all over again, as if they were born again. Seu was going to North America, where he hoped survival for a fat cosmopolite woud be a little less difficult than in Europe or Asia. Moskowitz had been born in New York, and was going back there. Kathy Burgess was going to England, where Cudyk supposed she had relatives. Exarkos was going to Istanbul first, for orders; he had no idea where he might be sent after that. Cudyk had not yet made up his mind. He thought that perhaps he would go with the priest; if he should change his mind after landing it would be no great loss. One wilderness, as Exarkos had once said, was as good as another.

It will all be anticlimax, he thought, *and perhaps that is the definition of hell; unending anticlimax. We are dying now, at this moment; what happens afterward does not matter very much.*

He wondered how it would feel to be Earthbound again. The repatriation ship was to be the last galactic vessel which would ever call at Earth. And there would be a constant guard. The Niori had learned, belatedly but well. If humanity ever climbed high enough again to reach the stars with its bloody fingers, the citizens of the galaxy would be ready.

Seu glanced behind him and said, "Nearly all the others have gone. The next aircar should be ours."

Cudyk looked at his watch. The man in the powerhouse must be a sentimentalist: he was waiting until the last possible moment.

He heard the soft hum of the aircar behind him, turned and saw it settling lightly to the clipped lawn. The remaining passengers were moving toward it; Exarkos stood up and lifted his suitcase. Cudyk turned back for one last look at the Quarter. It was full dark now, and all he could see of it was the blocky, ambiguous outline of its darkness against the glowing buildings beyond, and the cross-hatched pattern of yellow street lights.

The lights went out.

The Dying Man

I

It is noon. Overhead the sky like a great silver bowl shimmers with heat; the yellow sand hurls it back; the distant ocean is dancing with white fire. Emerging from underground, Dio the Planner stands blinking a moment in the strong salt light; he feels the heat like a cap on his head, and his beard curls crisply, iridescent in the sun.

A few yards away are five men and women, their limbs glinting pink against the sand. The rest of the seascape is utterly bare; the sand seems to stretch empty and hot for miles. There is not even a gull in the air. Three of the figures are men; they are running and throwing a beach ball at one another, with faroff shouts. The two women are half reclining, watching the men. All five are superbly muscled, with great arched chests, ponderous as Percherons. Their skins are smooth; their eyes sparkle. Dio looks at his own forearm: is there a trace of darkness? is the skin coarsening?

He drops his single garment and walks toward the group. The sand's caress is briefly painful to his feet; then his skin adapts, and he no longer feels it. The five incuriously turn to watch him approach. They are all players, not students, and there are two he does not even know. He feels uncomfortable, and wishes he had not come. It isn't good for students and players to meet informally; each side is too much aware of the other's goodnatured contempt. Dio tries to imagine himself a player, exerting himself to be polite to a student, and as always, he fails. The gulf is too wide. It takes both kinds to make a world, students to remember and make, players to consume and enjoy; but the classes should not mix.

Even without their clothing, these are players: the wide, innocent eyes that flash with enthusiasm, or flicker

353

with easy boredom; the soft mouths that can be gay or sulky by turns. Now he deliberately looks at the blonde woman, Claire, and in her face he sees the same unmistakable signs. But, against all reason and usage, the soft curve of her lips is beauty; the poise of her dark-blonde head on the strong neck wrings his heart. It is illogical, almost unheard of, perhaps abnormal; but he loves her.

Her gray eyes are glowing up at him like sea-agates; the quick pleasure of her smile warms and soothes him. "I'm so glad to *see* you." She takes his hand. "You know Katha of course, and Piet. And this is Tanno, and that's Mark. Sit here and talk to me, I can't move, it's so hot."

The ball throwers go cheerfully back to their game. The brunette, Katha, begins talking immediately about the choirs at Bethany: has Dio heard them? No? But he must; the voices are stupendous, the choir-master is brilliant; nothing like it has been heard for centuries.

The word "centuries" falls carelessly. How old is Katha —eight hundred, a thousand? Recently, in a three-hundred-year-old journal, Dio has been surprised to find a reference to Katha. Evidently he had known her briefly, forgotten her completely. There are so many people; it's impossible to remember. That's why the students keep journals; and why the players don't. He might even have met Claire before, and forgotten . . . "No," he says, smiling politely, "I've been busy with a project."

"Dio is an Architectural Planner," says Claire, mocking him with the exaggerated syllables; and yet there's a curious, inverted pride in her voice. "I told you, Kat, he's a student among students. He rebuilds this whole sector, every year."

"Oh," says Katha, wide-eyed, "I think that's absolutely fascinating." A moment later, without pausing, she has changed the subject to the new sky circus in Littlam— perfectly vulgar, but hilarious. The sky clowns! The tumblers! The delicious mock animals!

Claire's smooth face is close to his, haloed by the sun, gilded from below by the reflection of the hot sand. Her half-closed eyelids are delicate and soft, bruised by heat; her pupils are contracted, and the wide gray irises are intricately patterned. A fragment floats to the top of his mind, something he has read about the structure of the iris: ray-like dilating muscles interlaced with a circular contractile set, pigmented with a little melanin. For some reason, the thought is distasteful, and he pushes it aside. He feels a little light-headed; he has been working too hard.

"Tired?" she asks gently.

He relaxes a little. The brunette, Katha, is still talking; she is one of those who talk and never care if anyone listens. He answers, "This is our busiest time. All the designs are coming back for a final check before they go into the master integrator. It's our last chance to find any mistakes."

"Dio, I'm sorry," she says. "I know I shouldn't have asked you." Her brows go up; she looks at him anxiously under her lashes. "You should rest, though."

"Yes," says Dio.

She lays her soft palm on the nape of his neck. "Rest, then. Rest."

"Ah," says Dio wearily, letting his head drop into the crook of his arm. Under the sand where he lies are seventeen inhabited levels, of which three are his immediate concern, over a sector that reaches from Alban to Detroy. He has been working almost without sleep for two weeks. Next season there is talk of beginning an eighteenth level; it will mean raising the surface again, and all the force-planes will have to be shifted. The details swim past, thousands of them; behind his closed eyes, he sees architectural tracings, blueprints, code sheets, specifications.

"Darling," says her caressing voice in his ear, "you know I'm happy you came, anyhow, even if you didn't want to. *Because* you didn't want to. Do you understand that?"

He peers at her with one half-open eye. "A feeling of power?" he suggest ironically.

"No. Reassurance is more like it. Did you know I was jealous of your work? . . . I am, very much. I told myself, if he'll leave it, now, today——"

He rolls over, smiling crookedly up at her. "And yet you don't know one day from the next."

Her answering smile is quick and shy. "I know, isn't it awful of me: but *you* do."

As they look at each other in silence, he is aware again

of the gulf between them. *They need us,* he thinks, *to make their world over every year—keep it bright and fresh, cover up the past—but they dislike us because they know that whatever they forget, we keep and remember.*

His hand finds hers. A deep, unreasoning sadness wells up in him; he asks silently, *Why should I love you?*

He has not spoken, but he sees her face contract into a rueful, pained smile; and her fingers grip hard.

Above them, the shouts of the ball throwers have changed to noisy protests. Dio looks up. Piet, the cotton-headed man, laughing, is afloat over the heads of the other two. He comes down slowly and throws the ball; the game goes on. But a moment later Piet is in the air again: the others shout angrily, and Tanno leaps up to wrestle with him. The ball drops, bounds away: the two striving figures turn and roll in midair. At length the cotton-headed man forces the other down to the sand. They both leap up and run over, laughing.

"Someone's got to tame this wild man," says the loser, panting. "I can't do it, he's too slippery. How about you, Dio?"

"He's resting," Claire protests, but the others chorus, "Oh, yes!" "Just a fall or two," says Piet, with a wide grin, rubbing his hands together. "There's lots of time before the tide comes in—unless you'd rather not?"

Dio gets reluctantly to his feet. Grinning, Piet floats up off the sand. Dio follows, feeling the taut surge of back and chest muscles, and the curious sensation of pressure on the spine. The two men circle, rising slowly. Piet whips his body over, head downward, arms slashing for Dio's legs. Dio overleaps him, and, turning, tries for a leg-and-arm; but Piet squirms away like an eel and catches him in a waist lock. Dio strains against the taut chest, all his muscles knotting; the two men hang unbalanced for a moment. Then, suddenly, something gives way in the force that buoys Dio up. They go over together, hard and awkwardly into the sand. There is a surprised babble of voices.

Dio picks himself up. Piet is kneeling nearby, white-faced, holding his forearm. "Bent?" asks Mark, bending to touch it gently.

"Came down with my weight," says Piet. "Wasn't expecting—" He nods at Dio. "That's a new one."

"Well, let's hurry and fix it," says the other, "or you'll miss the spout." Piet lays the damaged forearm across his own thighs. "Ready?" Mark plants his bare foot on the arm, leans forward and presses sharply down. Piet winces, then smiles; the arm is straight.

"Sit down and let it knit," says the other. He turns to Dio. "What's this?"

Dio is just becoming aware of a sharp pain in one finger, and dark blood welling. "Just turned back the nail a little," says Mark. "Press it down, it'll close in a second."

Katha suggests a word game, and in a moment they are all sitting in a circle, shouting letters at each other. Dio does poorly; he cannot forget the dark blood falling from his fingertip. The silver sky seems oppressively distant; he is tired of the heat that pours down on his head, of the breathless air and the sand like hot metal under his body. He has a sense of helpless fear, as if something terrible had already happened; as if it were too late.

Someone says, "It's time," and they all stand up, whisking sand from their bodies. "Come on," says Claire over her shoulder. "Have you ever been up the spout? It's fun."

"No, I must get back, I'll call you later," says Dio. Her fingers lie softly on his chest as he kisses her briefly, then he steps away. "Goodbye," he calls to the others, "Goodbye," and turning, trudges away over the sand.

The rest, relieved to be free of him, are halfway to the rocks above the water's edge. A white feather of spray dances from a fissure as the sea rushes into the cavern below. The water slides back, leaving mirror-wet sand that dries in a breath. It gathers itself; far out a comber lifts its green head, and rushes onward. "Not this one, but the next," calls Tanno.

"Claire," says Katha, approaching her, "it was so peculiar about your friend. Did you notice? When he left, his finger was still bleeding."

The white plume leaps, higher, provoking a gust of nervous laughter. Piet dances up after it, waving his legs in a burlesque entrechat. "What?" says Claire. "You must be wrong. It couldn't have been."

"Now, come on, everybody. Hang close!"

"All the same," says Katha, "it was bleeding." No one hears her; she is used to that.

Far out, the comber lifts its head menacingly high; it comes onward, white-crowned, hard as bottle glass below, rising, faster, and as it roars with a shuddering of earth into the cavern, the Immortals are dashed high on the white torrent, screaming their joy.

Dio is in his empty rooms alone, pacing the resilient floor, smothered in silence. He pauses, sweeps a mirror into being on the bare wall; leans forward as if to peer at his own gray face, then wipes the mirror out again. All around him the universe presses down, enormous, inexorable.

The time stripe on the wall has turned almost black: the day is over. He has been here alone all afternoon. His door and phone circuits are set to reject callers, even Claire—his only instinct has been to hide.

A scrap of yellow cloth is tied around the hurt finger. Blood has saturated the cloth and dried, and now it is stuck tight. The blood has stopped, but the hurt nail has still not reattached itself. There is something wrong with him; how could there be anything wrong with him?

He has felt it coming for days, drawing closer, invisibly. Now it is here.

It has been eight hours . . . his finger has not healed itself.

He remembers that moment in the air, when the support dropped away under him. Could that happen again? He plants his feet firmly now, thinks, *Up*, and feels the familiar straining of his back and chest. But nothing happens. Incredulously, he tries again. Nothing!

His heart is thundering in his chest; he feels dizzy and cold. He sways, almost falls. It isn't possible that this should be happening to him. . . . Help; he must have help. Under his trembling fingers the phone index lights; he finds Claire's name, presses the selector. She may have gone out by now, but sector registry will find her. The screen pulses grayly. He waits. The darkness is a little farther away. Claire will help him, will think of something.

The screen lights, but it is only the neutral gray face of an autosec. "One moment please."

The screen flickers; at last, Claire's face!

"—is a recording, Dio. When you didn't call, and I couldn't reach you, I was very hurt. I know you're busy, but— Well, Piet has asked me to go over to Toria to play skeet polo, and I'm going. I may stay a few weeks for the flower festival, or go on to Rome. I'm sorry, Dio, we started out so nicely. Maybe the classes really don't mix. Goodbye."

The screen darkens. Dio is down on his knees before it. "Don't go," he says breathlessly. "Don't go." His last courage is broken; the hot, salt, shameful tears drop from his eyes.

The room is bright and bare, but in the corners the darkness is gathering, curling high, black as obsidian, waiting to rush.

II

The crowds on the lower level are a river of color, deep electric blue, scarlet, opaque yellow, all clean, crisp and bright. Flower scents puff from the folds of loose garments; the air is filled with good-natured voices and laughter. Back from five months' wandering in Africa, Pacifica and Europe, Claire is delightfully lost among the moving ways of Sector Twenty. Where the main concourse used to be, there is a maze of narrow adventure streets, full of gay banners and musky with perfume. The excursion cars are elegant little baskets of silver filigree, hung with airy grace. She gets into one and soars up the canyon of windows on a long, sweeping curve, past terraces and balconies, glimpse after intimate glimpse of people she need never see again: here a woman feeding a big blue macaw, there a couple of children staring at her from a garden, solemn-eyed, both with ragged yellow hair like dandelions. How long it has been since she last saw a child! . . . She tries to imagine what it must be like, to be a child now in this huge strange world full of grown people, but she can't. Her memories of her own childhood are so far away, quaint and small, like figures in the wrong side of an opera glass. Now here is a man with a bushy black beard, balancing a bottle on his nose for a group of laughing people . . . off it goes! Here are two couples obliviously kissing . . . Her heart beats a little faster; she feels the color coming into her cheeks. Piet was so tiresome, after a while; she wants to forget him now. She has already forgotten him; she hums in her sweet, clear contralto, "Dio, Dio, Dio . . ."

On the next level she dismounts and takes a robocab. She punches Dio's name; the little green-eyed driver "hunts" for a moment, flickering; then the cab swings around purposefully and gathers speed.

The building is unrecognizable; the whole street has

been done over in baroque façades of vermilion and frost green. The shape of the lobby is familiar, though, and here is Dio's name on the directory.

She hesitates, looking up the uninformative blank shaft of the elevator well. Is he there, behind that silent bulk of marble? After a moment she turns with a shrug and takes the nearest of a row of fragile silver chairs. She presses "3"; the chair whisks her up, decants her.

She is in the vestibule of Dio's apartment. The walls are faced with cool blue-veined marble. On one side, the spacious oval of the shaft opening; on the other, the wide, arched doorway, closed. A mobile turns slowly under the lofty ceiling. She steps on the annunciator plate.

"Yes?" A pleasant male voice, but not a familiar one. The screen does not light.

She gives her name. "I want to see Dio—is he in?"

A curious pause. "Yes, he's *in*. . . . Who sent you?"

"No one *sent* me." She has the frustrating sense that they are at cross purposes, talking about different things. "Who are you?"

"That doesn't matter. Well, you can come in, though I don't know when you'll get time today." The doors slide open.

Bewildered and more than half angry, Claire crosses the threshold. The first room is a cool gray cavern: overhead are fixed-circuit screens showing views of the sector streets. They make a bright frieze around the walls, but shed little light. The room is empty; she crosses it to the next.

The next room is a huge disorderly space full of machinery carelessly set down; Claire wrinkles her nose in distaste. Down at the far end, a few men are bending over one of the machines, their backs turned. She moves on.

The third room is a cool green space, terrazzo-floored, with a fountain playing in the middle. Her sandals click pleasantly on the hard surface. Fifteen or twenty people are sitting on the low curving benches around the walls, using the service machines, readers and so on: it's for all the world like the waiting room of a fashionable healer. Has Dio taken up mind-fixing?

Suddenly unsure of herself, she takes an isolated seat

361

and looks around her. No, her first impression was wrong, these are not clients waiting to see a healer, because, in the first place, they are all students—every one.

She looks them over more carefully. Two are playing chess in an alcove; two more are strolling up and down separately; five or six are grouped around a little table on which some papers are spread; one of these is talking rapidly while the rest listen. The distance is too great; Claire cannot catch any words.

Farther down on the other side of the room, two men and a woman are sitting at a hooded screen, watching it intently, although at this distance it appears dark.

Water tinkles steadily in the fountain. After a long time the inner doors open and a man emerges; he leans over and speaks to another man sitting nearby. The second man gets up and goes through the inner doors; the first moves out of sight in the opposite direction. Neither reappears. Claire waits, but nothing more happens.

No one has taken her name, or put her on a list; no one seems to be paying her any attention. She rises and walks slowly down the room, past the group at the table. Two of the men are talking vehemently, interrupting each other. She listens as she passes, but it is all student gibberish: "the delta curve clearly shows . . . a stochastic assumption . . ." She moves on to the three who sit at the hooded screeen.

The screen still seems dark to Claire, but faint glints of color move on its glossy surface, and there is a whisper of sound.

There are two vacant seats. She hesitates, then takes one of them and leans forward under the hood.

Now the screen is alight, and there is a murmur of talk in her ears. She is looking into a room dominated by a huge oblong slab of gray marble, three times the height of a man. Though solid, it appears to be descending with a steady and hypnotic motion, like a waterfall.

Under this falling curtain of stone sit two men. One of them is a stranger. The other—

She leans forward, peering. The other is in shadow; she cannot see his features. Still, there is something familiar about the outlines of his head and body. . . .

She is almost sure it is Dio, but when he speaks she

hesitates again. It is a strange, low, hoarse voice, unlike anything she has ever heard before: the sound is so strange that she forgets to listen for the words.

Now the other man is speaking: ". . . these notions. It's just an ordinary procedure—one more injection."

"No," says the dark man with repressed fury, and abruptly stands up. The lights in that pictured room flicker as he moves and the shadow swerves to follow him.

"Pardon me," says an unexpected voice at her ear. The man next to her is leaning over, looking inquisitive. "I don't think you're authorized to watch this session, are you?"

Claire makes an impatient gesture at him, turning back fascinated to the screen. In the pictured room, both men are standing now; the dark man is saying something hoarsely while the other moves as if to take his arm.

"Please," says the voice at her ear, *"are* you authorized to watch this session?"

The dark man's voice has risen to a hysterical shout—hoarse and thin, like no human voice in the world. In the screen, he whirls and makes as if to run back into the room.

"Catch him!" says the other, lunging after.

The dark man doubles back suddenly, past the other who reaches for him. Then two other men run past the screen; then the room is vacant; only the moving slab drops steadily, smoothly, into the floor.

The three beside Claire are standing. Across the room, heads turn. "What is it?" someone calls.

One of the men calls back, "He's having some kind of fit!" In a lower voice, to the woman, he adds, "It's the discomfort, I suppose . . ."

Claire is watching, uncomprehendingly, when a sudden yell from the far side of the room makes her turn.

The doors have swung back, and in the opening a shouting man is wrestling helplessly with two others. They have his arms pinned and he cannot move any farther, but that horrible, hoarse voice goes on shouting, and shouting . . .

There are no more shadows: she can see his face.

"Dio!" she calls, getting to her feet .

Through his own din, he hears her and his head turns.

363

His face gapes blindly at her, swollen and red, the eyes glaring. Then with a violent motion he turns away. One arm comes free, and jerks up to shield his head. He is hurrying away; the others follow. The doors close. The room is full of standing figures, and a murmur of voices.

Claire stands where she is, stunned, until a slender figure separates itself from the crowd. That other face seems to hang in the air, obscuring his—red and distorted, mouth agape.

The man takes her by the elbow, urges her toward the outer door. "What are you to Dio? Did you know him before?"

"Before what?" she asks faintly. They are crossing the room of machines, empty and echoing.

"Hm. I remember you now—I let you in, didn't I? Sorry you came?" His tone is light and negligent; she has the feeling that his attention is not really on what he is saying. A faint irritation at this is the first thing she feels through her numbness. She stirs as they walk, disengaging her arm from his grasp. She says, "What was wrong with him?"

"A very rare complaint," answers the other, without pausing. They are in the outer room now, in the gloom under the bright frieze, moving toward the doors. "Didn't you know?" he asks in the same careless tone.

"I've been away." She stops, turns to face him. "Can't you tell me? What *is* wrong with Dio?"

She sees now that he has a thin face, nose and lips keen, eyes bright and narrow. "Nothing you want to know about," he says curtly. He waves at the door control, and the doors slide noiselessly apart. "Goodbye."

She does not move, and after a moment the doors close again. "What's *wrong* with him?" she says.

He sighs, looking down at her modish robe with its delicate clasps of gold. "How can I tell you? Does the verb 'to die' mean anything to you?"

She is puzzled and apprehensive. "I don't know . . . isn't it something that happens to the lower animals?"

He gives her a quick mock bow. "Very good."

"But I don't know what it is. Is it—a kind of fit, like—" She nods toward the inner rooms.

He is staring at her with an expression half compassion-

364

ate, half wildly exasperated. "Do you really want to know?" He turns abruptly and runs his finger down a suddenly glowing index stripe on the wall. "Let's see . . . don't know what there is in this damned reservoir. Hm. Animals, terminus." At his finger's touch, a cabinet opens and tips out a shallow oblong box into his palm. He offers it.

In her hands, the box lights up; she is looking into a cage in which a small animal crouches—a white rat. Its fur is dull and rough-looking; something is caked around its muzzle. It moves unsteadily, noses a cup of water, then turns away. Its legs seem to fail; it drops and lies motionless except for the slow rise and fall of its tiny chest.

Watching, Claire tries to control her nausea. Students' cabinets are full of nastinesses like this; they expect you not to show any distaste. "Something's the matter with it," is all she can find to say.

"Yes. It's dying. That means to cease living: to stop. Not to be any more. Understand?"

"No," she breathes. In the box, the small body has stopped moving. The mouth is stiffly open, the lip drawn back from the yellow teeth. The eye does not move, but glares up sightless.

"That's all," says her companion, taking the box back. "No more rat. Finished. After a while it begins to decompose and make a bad smell, and a while after that, there's nothing left but bones. And that has happened to every rat that was ever born."

"I don't *believe* you," she says. "It isn't like that; I never heard of such a thing."

"Didn't you ever have a pet?" he demands. "A parakeet, a cat, a tank of fish?"

"Yes," she says defensively, "I've had cats, and birds. What of it?"

"What happened to them?"

"Well—*I* don't know, I suppose I lost them. You know how you lose things."

"One day they're there, the next, not," says the thin man. "Correct?"

"Yes, that's right. But why?"

"We have such a tidy world," he says wearily. "Dead bodies would clutter it up; that's why the house circuits are programmed to remove them when nobody is in the room. Every one: it's part of the basic design. Of course, if you stayed in the room, and didn't turn your back, the machine would have to embarrass you by cleaning up the corpse in front of your eyes. But that never happens. Whenever you saw there was something wrong with any pet of yours, you turned around and went away, isn't that right?"

"Well, I really can't remember—"

"And when you came back, how odd, the beast was gone. It wasn't 'lost,' it was dead. They die. They all die."

She looks at him, shivering. "But that doesn't happen to *people*."

"No?" His lips are tight. After a moment he adds, "Why do you think he looked that way? You see he knows; he's known for five months."

She catches her breath suddenly. "That day at the beach!"

"Oh, were you there?" He nods several times, and opens the door again. "Very interesting for you. You can tell people you saw it happen." He pushes her gently out into the vestibule.

"But I want—" she says desperately.

"What? To love him again, as if he were normal? Or do you want to help him? Is that what you mean?" His thin face is drawn tight, arrow-shaped between the brows. "Do you think you could stand it? If so—" He stands aside, as if to let her enter again.

"Remember the rat," he says sharply.

She hesitates.

"It's up to you. Do you really want to help him? He could use some help, if it wouldn't make you sick. Or else —Where were you all this time?"

"Various places," she says stiffly. "Littlam, Paris, New Hol."

He nods. "Or you can go back and see them all again. Which?"

She does not move. Behind her eyes, now, the two images are intermingled: she sees Dio's gorged face staring through the stiff jaw of the rat.

The thin man nods briskly. He steps back, holding her gaze. There is a long suspended moment; then the doors close.

III

The years fall away like pages from an old notebook. Claire is in Stambul, Winthur, Kumoto, BahiBlanc . . . other places, too many to remember. There are the intercontinental games, held every century on the baroque wheel-shaped ground in Campan: Claire is one of the spectators who hover in clouds, following their favorites. There is a love affair, brief but intense; it lasts four or five years; the man's name is Nord, he has gone off now with another woman to Deya, and for nearly a month Claire has been inconsolable. But now comes the opera season in Milan, and in Tusca, afterwards, she meets some charming people who are going to spend a year in Papeete. . . .

Life is good. Each morning she awakes refreshed; her lungs fill with the clean air; the blood tingles in her finger-tips.

On a spring morning, she is basking in a bubble of green glass, three-quarters submerged in an emerald-green ocean. The water sways and breaks, frothily, around the bright disk of sunlight at the top. Down below where she lies, the cool green depths are like mint to the fire-white bite of the sun. Tiny flat golden fishes swarm up to the bubble, turn, glinting like tarnished coins, and flow away again. The memory unit near the floor of the bubble is muttering out a muted tempest of Wagner: half listening, she hears the familiar music mixed with a gabble of foreign syllables. Her companion, with his massive bronze head almost touching the speakers, is listening attentively. Claire feels a little annoyed; she prods him with a bare foot: "Ross, turn that horrible thing off, won't you please?"

He looks up, his blunt face aggrieved. "It's *The Rhine-gold.*"

"Yes, I know, but I can't understand a word. It sounds as if they're clearing their throats. . . . Thank you."

He has waved a dismissing hand at the speakers, and the guttural chorus subsides. "Billions of people spoke that language once," he says portentously. Ross is an artist, which makes him almost a player, really, but he has the student's compulsive habit of bringing out these little kernels of information to lay in your lap.

"And I can't even stand four of them," she says lazily. "I only listen to opera for the music, anyhow, the stories are always so foolish; why is that, I wonder?"

She can almost see the learned reply rising to his lips; but he represses it politely—he knows she doesn't really want an answer—and busies himself with the visor. It lights under his fingers to show a green chasm, slowly flickering with the last dim ripples of the sunlight.

"Going down now?" she asks.

"Yes, I want to get those corals." Ross is a sculptor, not a very good one, fortunately, nor a very devoted one, or he would be impossible company. He has a studio on the bottom of the Mediterranean, in ten fathoms, and spends part of his time concocting gigantic menacing tangles of stylized undersea creatures. Finished with the visor, he touches the controls and the bubble drifts downward. The waters meet overhead with a white splash of spray; then the circle of light dims to yellow, to lime color, to deep green.

Beneath them now is the coral reef—acre upon acre of bare skeletal fingers. A few small fish move brilliantly among the pale branches. Ross touches the controls again; the bubble drifts to a stop. He stares down through the glass for a moment, then gets up to open the inner lock door. Breathing deeply, with a distant expression, he steps in and closes the transparent door behind him. Claire sees the water spurt around his ankles. It surges up quickly to fill the airlock; when it is chest high, Ross opens the outer door and plunges out in a cloud of air bubbles.

He is a yellow kicking shape in the green water; after a few moments he is half obscured by clouds of sediment. Claire watches, vaguely troubled; the largest corals are like bleached bone.

She fingers the memory unit for the Sea Pieces from *Peter Grimes,* without knowing why; it's cold, northern ocean music, not appropriate. The cold, far calling of the gulls makes her shiver with sadness, but she goes on listening.

Ross grows dimmer and more distant in the clouding water. At length he is only a flash, a flicker of movement down in the dusky green valley. After a long time she sees him coming back, with two or three pink corals in his hand.

Absorbed in the music, she has allowed the bubble to drift until the entrance is almost blocked by corals. Ross forces himself between them, levering himself against a tall outcropping of stone, but in a moment he seems to be in difficulty. Claire turns to the controls and backs the bubble off a few feet. The way is clear now, but Ross does not follow.

Through the glass she sees him bend over, dropping his specimens. He places both hands firmly and strains, all the great muscles of his limbs and back bulging. After a moment he straightens again, shaking his head. He is caught, she realizes; one foot is jammed into a crevice of the stone. He grins at her painfully and puts one hand to his throat. He has been out a long time.

Perhaps she can help, in the few seconds that are left. She darts into the airlock, closes and floods it. But just before the water rises over her head, she sees the man's body stiffen.

Now, with her eyes open under water, in that curious blurred light, she sees his gorged face break into lines of pain. Instantly, his face becomes another's—Dio's—vividly seen through the ghost of a dead rat's grin. The vision comes without warning, and passes.

Outside the bubble, Ross's stiff jaw wrenches open, then hangs slack. She sees the pale jelly come bulging slowly up out of his mouth; now he floats easily, eyes turned up, limbs relaxed.

Shaken, she empties the lock again, goes back inside and calls Antibe Control for a rescue cutter. She sits down and waits, careful not to look at the still body outside.

She is astonished and appalled at her own emotion. It has nothing to do with Ross, she knows: he is perfectly safe. When he breathed water, his body reacted automatically: his lungs exuded the protective jelly, consciousness ended, his heartbeat stopped. Antibe Control will be here in twenty minutes or less, but Ross could stay like that for years, if he had to. As soon as he gets out of the water, his lungs will begin to resorb the jelly; when they are clear, heartbeat and breathing will start again.

It's as if Ross were only acting out a part, every movement stylized and meaningful. In the moment of his pain, a barrier in her mind has gone down, and now a doorway stands open.

She makes an impatient gesture, she is not used to being tyrannized in this way. But her arm drops in defeat; the perverse attraction of that doorway is too strong. *Dio*, her mind silently calls. *Dio*.

The designer of Sector Twenty, in the time she has been away, has changed the plan of the streets "to bring the surface down." The roof of every level is a screen faithfully repeating the view from the surface, and with lighting and other ingenious tricks the weather up there is parodied down below. Just now it is a gray cold November day, a day of slanting gray rain: looking up, one sees it endlessly falling out of the leaden sky: and down here, although the air is as always pleasantly warm, the great bare slabs of the building fronts have turned bluish gray to match, and silvery insubstantial streamers are twisting endlessly down, to melt and disappear before they strike the pavement.

Claire does not like it; it does not feel like Dio's work. The crowds have a nervous air, curious, half-protesting; they look up and laugh, but uneasily, and the refreshment bays are full of people crammed together under bright yellow light. Claire pulls her metallic cloak closer around her throat; she is thinking with melancholy of the turn of the year, the earth growing cold and hard as iron, the trees brittle and black against the unfriendly sky. This is a time for blue skies underground, for flushed skins and honest laughter, not for this echoed grayness.

In her rooms, at least, there is cheerful warmth. She is tired and perspiring from the trip; she does not want to see anyone just yet. Some American gowns have been ordered; while she waits for them, she turns on the fire-bath in the bedroom alcove. The yellow spiky flames jet up with a black-capped *whoom,* then settle to a high murmuring

curtain of yellow-white. Claire binds her head in an in-
sulating scarf, and without bothering to undress, steps into
the fire.

The flame blooms up around her body, cool and caressing; the fragile gown flares and is gone in a whisper of
sparks. She turns, arms outspread against the flow. Depil-
ated, refreshed, she steps out again. Her body tingles, in-
vigorated by the flame. Delicately, she brushes away some
clinging wisps of burnt skin; the new flesh is glossy pink,
slowly paling to rose-and-ivory.

In the wall mirror, her eyes sparkle; her lips are liq-
uidly red, as tender and dark as the red wax that spills
from the edge of a candle.

She feels a somber recklessness; she is running with the
the tide. Responsive to her mood, the silvered ceiling begins to run with swift bloody streaks, swirling and leaping,
striking flares of light from the bronze dado and the
carved crystal lacework of the furniture. With a sudden
exultant laugh, Claire tumbles into the great yellow bed:
she rolls there, half smothered, the luxuriant silky fibers
cool as cream to her skin; then the mood is gone, the ceiling dims to grayness; and she sits up with an impatient
murmur.

What can be wrong with her? Sobered, already regretting the summery warmth of the Mediterranean, she walks
to the table where Dio's card lies. It is his reply to the formal message she sent en route: it says simply:

THE PLANNER DIO WILL BE AT HOME

There is a discreet chime from the delivery chute, and
fabrics tumble in in billows of canary yellow, crimson,
midnight blue. Claire chooses the blue, anything else
would be out of key with the day; it is gauzy but long-
sleeved. With it she wears no rings or necklaces, only a ti-
ara of dark aquamarines twined in her hair.

She scarcely notices the new exterior of the building;
the ascensor shaft is dark and padded now, with an endless chain of cushioned seats that slowly rise, occupied or
not, like a disjointed flight of stairs. The vestibule above

slowly comes into view, and she feels a curious shock of recognition.

It is the same: the same blue-veined marble, the same mobile idly turning, the same arched doorway.

Claire hesitates, alarmed and displeased. She tries to believe that she is mistaken: no scheme of decoration is ever left unchanged for as much as a year. But here it is, untouched, as if time had queerly stopped here in this room when she left it: as if she had returned, not only to the same choice, but to the same instant.

She crosses the floor reluctantly. The dark door screen looks back at her like a baited trap.

Suppose she had never gone away—what then? Whatever Dio's secret is, it has had ten years to grow, here behind this unchanged door. There it is, a darkness, waiting for her.

With a shudder of almost physical repulsion, she steps onto the annunciator plate.

The screen lights. After a moment a face comes into view. She sees without surprise that it is the thin man, the one who showed her the rat. . . .

He is watching her keenly. She cannot rid herself of the vision of the rat, and of the dark struggling figure in the doorway. She says, "Is Dio—" She stops, not knowing what she meant to say.

"At home?" the thin man finishes. "Yes, of course. Come in."

The doors slide open. About to step forward, she hesitates again, once more shocked to realize that the first room is also unchanged. The frieze of screens now displays a row of gray-lit streets; that is the only difference; it is as if she were looking into some far-distant world where time still had meaning, from this still, secret place where it has none.

The thin man appears in the doorway, black-robed. "My name is Benarra," he says, smiling. "Please come in; don't mind all this, you'll get used to it."

"Where is Dio?"

"Not far . . . But we make a rule," the thin man says, "that only students are admitted to see Dio. Would you mind?"

She looks at him with indignation. "Is this a joke? Dio

sent me a note . . ." She hesitates; the note was noncommittal enough, to be sure.

"You can become a student quite easily," Benarra says. "At least you can begin, and that would be enough for today." He stands waiting, with a pleasant expression; he seems perfectly serious.

She is balanced between bewilderment and surrender. "I don't—what do you want me to do?"

"Come and see." He crosses the room, opens a narrow door. After a moment she follows.

He leads her down an inclined passage, narrow and dark. "I'm living on the floor below now," he remarks over his shoulder, "to keep out of Dio's way." The passage ends in a bright central hall from which he leads her through a doorway into dimness.

"Here your education begins," he says. On both sides, islands of light glow up slowly: in the nearest, and brightest, stands a curious group of beings, not ape, not man: black skins with a bluish sheen, tiny eyes peering upward under shelving brows, hair a dusty black. The limbs are knob-jointed like twigs; the ribs show; the bellies are soft and big. The head of the tallest comes to Claire's waist. Behind them is a brilliant glimpse of tropical sunshine, a conical mass of what looks like dried vegetable matter, trees and horned animals in the background.

"Human beings," says Benarra.

She turns a disbelieving, almost offended gaze on him. "Oh, no!"

"Yes, certainly. Extinct several thousand years. Here, another kind."

In the next island the figures are also black-skinned, but taller—shoulder high. The woman's breasts are limp leathery bags that hang to her waist. Claire grimaces. "Is something wrong with her?"

"A different standard of beauty. They did that to themselves, deliberately. Woman creating herself. See what you think of the next."

She loses count. There are coppery-skinned ones, white ones, yellowish ones, some half naked, others elaborately trussed in metal and fabric. Moving among them, Claire feels herself suddenly grown titanic, like a mother animal among her brood: she has a flash of absurd, degrading

373

tenderness. Yet, as she looks at those wrinkled gnomish faces, they seem to hold an ancient and stubborn wisdom that glares out at her, silently saying, *Upstart!*

"What happened to them all?"

"They died," says Benarra. "Every one."

Ignoring her troubled look, he leads her out of the hall. Behind them, the lights fall and dim.

The next room is small and cool, unobtrusively lit, unfurnished except for a desk and chair, and a visitor's seat to which Benarra waves her. The domed ceiling is pierced just above their heads with round transparencies, each glowing in a different pattern of simple blue and red shapes against a colorless ground.

"They are hard to take in, I know," says Benarra. "Possibly you think they're fakes."

"No." No one could have imagined those fierce, wizened faces; somewhere, sometime, they must have existed.

A new thought strikes her. "What about *our* ancestors —what were they like?"

Benarra's gaze is cool and thoughtful. "Claire, you'll find this hard to believe. Those were our ancestors."

She is incredulous again. "Those—absurdities in there?"

"Yes. All of them."

She is stubbornly silent a moment. "But you said, they *died.*"

"They did; they died. Claire—did you think our race was always immortal?"

"Why—" She falls silent, confused and angry.

"No, impossible. Because if we were, where are all the old ones? No one in the world is older than, perhaps, two thousand years. That's not very long. . . . What are you thinking?"

She looks up, frowning with concentration. "You're saying it happened. But how?"

"It didn't happen. We did it, we created ourselves." Leaning back, he gestures at the glowing transparencies overhead. "Do you know what those are?"

"No. I've never seen any designs quite like them. They'd make lovely fabric patterns."

He smiles. "Yes, they are pretty, I suppose, but that's not what they're for. These are enlarged photographs of very small living things—too small to see. They used to get into people's bloodstreams and make them die. That's bubonic plague"—blue and purple dots alternating with larger pink disks—"that's tetanus"—blue rods and red dots—"that's leprosy"—dark-spotted blue lozenges with a crosshatching of red behind them. "That thing that looks something like a peacock's tail is a parasitic fungus called *streptothrix actinomyces.* That one"—a particularly dainty design of pale blue with darker accents—"is from a malignant oedema with gas gangrene."

The words are meaningless to her, but they call up vague images that are all the more horrible for having no definite outlines. She thinks again of the rat, and of a human face somehow assuming that stillness, that stiffness . . . frozen into a bright pattern, like the colored dots on the wall. . . .

She is resolved not to show her disgust and revulsion. "What happened to them?" she asks in a voice that does not quite tremble.

"Nothing. The planners left them alone, but changed us. Most of the records have been lost in two thousand years, and of course we have no real science of biology as they knew it. I'm no biologist, only a historian and collector." He rises. "But one thing we know they did was to make our bodies chemically immune to infection. Those things"—he nods to the transparencies above—"are simply irrelevant now, they can't harm us. They still exist—I've seen cultures taken from living animals. But they're only a curiosity. Various other things were done, to make the body's chemistry, to put it crudely, more stable. Things that would have killed our ancestors by toxic reactions— poisoned them—don't harm us. Then there are the protective mechanisms, and the paraphysical powers that *homo sapiens* had only in potential. Levitation, regeneration of lost organs. Finally, in general we might say that the body was very much more homeostatized than formerly, that is, there's a cycle of functions which always tends to return to the norm. The cumulative processes that used to impair function don't happen—the 'matrix' doesn't thicken, progressive dehydration never gets started, and so on. But you see all these are just delaying actions, things to prevent you and me from dying prematurely.

The main thing—" he fingers an index stripe, and a linear design springs out on the wall—"was this. Have you ever read a chart, Claire?"

She shakes her head dumbly. The chart is merely an unaesthetic curve drawn on a reticulated background: it means nothing to her. "This is a schematic way of representing the growth of an organism," says Benarra. "You see here, this up-and-down scale is numbered in one hundredths of mature weight—from zero here at the bottom, to one hundred per cent here at the top. Understand?"

"Yes," she says doubtfully. "But what good is that?"

"You'll see. Now this other scale, along the bottom, is numbered according to the age of the organism. Now: this sharply rising curve here represents all other highly developed species except man. You see, the organism is born, grows very rapidly until it reaches almost its full size, then the curve rounds itself off, becomes almost level. Here it declines. And here it stops: the animal dies."

He pauses to look at her. The word hangs in the air; she says nothing, but meets his gaze.

"Now this," says Benarra, "this long shallow curve represents man as he was. You notice it starts far to the left of the animal curve. The planners had this much to work with: man was already unique, in that he had this very long juvenile period before sexual maturity. Here: see what they did."

"It looks almost the same," says Claire.

"Yes. Almost. What they did was quite a simple thing, in principle. They lengthened that juvenile period still further, they made the curve rise still more slowly . . . and never quite reach the top. The curve now becomes asymptotic, that is, it approaches sexual maturity by smaller and smaller amounts, and never gets there, no matter how long it goes on."

Gravely, he returns her stare.

"Are you saying," she asks, "that we're *not* sexually mature? Not anybody?"

"Correct," he says. "Maturity in every complex organism is the first stage of death. We never mature,

Claire, and that's why we don't die. We're the eternal adolescents of the universe. That's the price we paid."

"The price . . ." she echoes. "But I still don't see." She laughs. "Not *mature*—" Unconsciously she holds herself straighter, shoulders back, chin up.

Benarra leans casually against the desk, looking down at her. "Have you ever thought to wonder why there are so few children? In the old days, loving without any precautions, a grown woman would have a child a year. Now it happens perhaps once in a hundred billion meetings. It's an anomaly, a freak of nature, and even then the woman can't carry the child to term herself. Oh, we *look* mature; that's the joke—they gave us the shape of their own dreams of adult power." He fingers his glossy beard, thumps his chest. "It isn't real. We're all pretending to be grown-up, but not one of us knows what it's really like."

A silence falls.

"Except Dio?" says Claire, looking down at her hands.

"He's on the way to find out. Yes."

"And you can't stop it . . . you don't know why."

Benarra shrugs. "He was under strain, physical and mental. Some link of the chain broke, we may never know which one. He's already gone a long way up that slope—I think he's near the crest now. There isn't a hope that we can pull him back again."

Her fists clench impotently. "Then what good is it all?"

Benarra's eyes are hooded; he is playing with a memo-cube on the desk. "We learn," he says. "We can do something now and then, to alleviate, to make things easier. We don't give up."

She hesitates. "How long?"

"Actually, we don't know. We can guess what the maximum is; we know that from analogy with other mammals. But with Dio, too many other things might happen." He glances up at the transparencies.

"Surely you don't mean—" The bright ugly shapes glow down at her, motionless, inscrutable.

"Yes. Yes. He had one of them already, the last time you saw him—a virus infection. We were able to control it; it was what our ancestors used to call 'the common cold'; they thought it was mild. But it nearly destroyed Dio—I mean, not the disease itself, but the moral effect.

The symptoms were unpleasant. He wasn't prepared for it."

She is trembling. "Please."

"You have to know all this," says Benarra mercilessly, "or it's no use your seeing Dio at all. If you're going to be shocked, do it now. If you can't stand it, then go away now, not later." He pauses, and speaks more gently. "You can see him today, of course; I promised that. Don't try to make up your mind now, if it's hard. Talk to him, be with him this afternoon; see what it's like."

Claire does not understand herself. She has never been so foolish about a man before: love is all very well; love never lasts very long and you don't expect that it should, but while it lasts, it's pleasantness. Love is joy, not this wrenching pain.

Time flows like a strong, clean torrent, if only you let things go. She could give Dio up now and be unhappy, perhaps, a year or five years, or fifty, but then it would be over, and life would go on just the same.

She sees Dio's face, vivid in memory—not the stranger, the dark shouting man, but Dio himself, framed against the silver sky: sunlight curved on the strong brow, the eyes gleaming in shadow.

"We've got him full of antibiotics," says Benarra compassionately. "We don't think he'll get any of the bad ones. . . . But aging itself is the worst of them all. . . . What do you say?"

IV

Under the curtain of falling stone, Dio sits at his work-bench. The room is the same as before; the only visible change is the statue which now looms overhead, in the corner above the stone curtain: it is the figure of a man reclining, weight on one elbow, calf crossed over thigh, head turned pensively down toward the shoulder. The figure is powerful, but there is a subtle feeling of decay about it: the bulging muscles seem about to sag; the face, even in shadow, has a deformed, damaged look. Forty feet long, sprawling immensely across the corner of the room, the statue has a raw, compulsive power: it is supremely ugly, but she can hardly look away.

A motion attracts her eye. Dio is standing beside the bench, waiting for her. She advances hesitantly: the statue's face is in shadow, but Dio's is not, and already she is afraid of what she may see there.

He takes her hand between his two palms; his touch is warm and dry, but something like an electric shock seems to pass between them, making her start.

"Claire—it's good to see you. Here, sit down, let me look." His voice is resonant, confident, even a trifle assertive; his eyes are alert and preternaturally bright. He talks, moves, holds himself with an air of supressed excitement. She is relieved and yet paradoxically alarmed: there is nothing really different in his face; the skin glows clear and healthy, his lips are firm. And yet every line, every feature, seems to be hiding some unpleasant surprise; it is like looking at a mask which will suddenly be whipped aside.

In her excitement, she laughs, murmurs a few words without in the least knowing what she is saying. He sits facing her across the corner of the desk, commandingly intent; his eyes are hypnotic.

"I've just been sketching some plans for next year. I have some ideas . . . it won't be like anything people expect." He laughs, glancing down; the bench is covered with little gauzy boxes full of shadowy line and color. His tools lie in disorderly array, solidopens, squirts, calipers. "What do you think of this, by the way?" He points up, behind him, at the heroic statue.

"It's very unusual . . . yours?"

"A copy, from stereographs—the original was by Michelangelo, something called 'Evening.' But I did the copy myself."

She raises her eyebrows, not understanding.

"I mean I didn't do it by machine. I carved the stone myself—with mallet and chisel, in these hands, Claire." He holds them out, strong, calloused. It was those flat pads of thickened skin, she realizes, that felt so warm and strange against her hand.

He laughs again. "It was an experience. I found out about texture, for one thing. You know, when a machine melts or molds a statue, there's no texture, because to a machine granite is just like cheese. But when you carve, the stone fights back. Stone has character, Claire, it can be stubborn or evasive—it can throw chips in your face, or make your chisel slip aside. Stone fights." His hand clenches, and again he laughs that strange, exultant laugh.

In her apartment late that evening, Claire feels herself confused and overwhelmed by conflicting emotions. Her day with Dio has been like nothing she ever expected. Not once has he aroused her pity: he is like a man in whom a flame burns. Walking with her in the streets, he has made her see the Sector as he imagines it: an archaic vision of buildings made for permanence rather than for change; of masonry set by hand, woods hand-carved and hand-polished. It is a terrifying vision, and yet she does not know why. People endure; things should pass away. . . .

In the wide cool rooms an air whispers softly. The border lights burn low around the bed, inviting sleep. Claire moves aimlessly in the outer rooms, letting her robe fall, pondering a languourous stiffness in her limbs. Her mouth is bruised with kisses. Her flesh remembers the touch of his strange hands. She is full of a delicious weariness; she is at the floating, bodiless zenith of love, neither demanding nor regretting.

Yet she wanders restively through the rooms, once idly evoking a gust of color and music from the wall; it fades into an echoing silence. She pauses at the door of the playroom, and looks down into the deep darkness of the diving well. To fall is a luxury like bathing in water or flame. There is a sweetness of danger in it, although the danger is unreal. Smiling, she breathes deep, stands poised, and steps out into emptiness. The gray walls hurtle upward around her: with an effort of will she withholds the pulse of strength that would support her in midair. The floor rushes nearer, the effort mounts intolerably. At the last minute she releases it; the surge buoys her up in a brief paroxysmal joy. She comes to rest, inches away from the hard stone. With her eyes dreamily closed, she rises slowly again to the top. She stretches: now she will sleep.

V

First come the good days. Dio is a man transformed, a demon of energy. He overflows with ideas and projects; he works unremittingly, accomplishes prodigies. Sector Twenty is the talk of the continent, of the world. Dio builds for permanence, but, dissatisfied, he tears down what he has built and builds again. For a season all his streets are soaring, incredibly beautiful lace-works of stone. Claire waits for the cycle to turn again, but Dio's work becomes ever more massive and crude; his stone darkens. Now the streets are narrow and full of shadows; the walls frown down with heavy magnificence. He builds no more ascensor shafts; to climb in Dio's buildings, you walk up ramps or even stairs, or ride in closed elevator cars. The people murmur, but he is still a novelty; they come from all over the planet to protest, to marvel, to complain; but they still come.

Dio's figure grows heavier, more commanding: his cheeks and chin, all his features thicken; his voice becomes hearty and resonant. When he enters a public room, all heads turn: he dominates any company; where his laugh booms out, the table is in a roar.

Women hang on him by droves; drunken and triumphant, he sometimes staggers off with one while Claire watches. But only she knows the defeat, the broken words and the tears, in the sleepless watches of the night.

There is a timeless interval when they seem to drift, without anxiety and without purpose, as if they had reached the crest of the wave. Then Dio begins to change again, swiftly and more swiftly. They are like passengers on two moving ways that have run side by side for a little distance, but now begin to diverge.

She clings to him with desperation, with a sense of

vertigo. She is terrified by the massive, inexorable movement that is carrying her off: like him, she feels drawn
to an unknown destination.

Suddenly the bad days are upon them. Dio is changing
under her eyes. His skin grows slack and dull; his nose
arches more strongly. He trains vigorously, under Benarra's instruction; when streaks of gray appear in his hair,
he conceals them with pigments. But the lines are cutting
themselves deeper around his mouth and at the corners
of the eyes. All his bones grow knobby and thick. She
cannot bear to look at his hands, they are thick-fingered,
clumsy; they hold what they touch, and yet they seem to
fumble.

Claire sometimes surprises herself by fits of passionate
weeping. She is thin; she sleeps badly and her appetite
is poor. She spends most of her time in the library, pur-
suing the alien thoughts that alone make it possible for
her to stay in touch with Dio. One day, taking the air,
she passes Katha on the street, and Katha does not recognize her.

She halts as if struck, standing by the balustrade of the
little stone bridge. The building fronts are shut faces,
weeping with the leaden light that falls from the ceiling.
Below her, down the long straight perspective of the stair,
Katha's little dark head bobs among the crowd and is
lost.

The crowds are thinning; not half as many people are
here this season as before. Those who come are silent
and unhappy; they do not stay long. Only a few miles
away, in Sector Nineteen, the air is full of streamers and
pulsing with music: the light glitters, people are hurrying
and laughing. Here, all colors are gray. Every surface is
amorphously rounded, as if mumbled by the sea; here a
baluster is missing, here a brick has fallen; here, from a
ragged alcove in the wall, a deformed statue leans out to
peer at her with its malevolent terra cotta face. She shud-
ders, averting her eyes, and moves on.

A melancholy sound surges into the street, filling it
brim-full. The silence throbs; then the sound comes
again. It is the tolling of the great bell in Dio's latest
folly, the building he calls a "cathedral." It is a vast enclosure, without beauty and without a function. No one

uses it, not even Dio himself. It is an emptiness waiting to
be filled. At one end, on a platform, a few candles burn.
The tiled floor is always gleaming, as if freshly damp;
shadows are piled high along the walls. Visitors hear their
footsteps echo sharply as they enter; they turn uneasily
and leave again. At intervals, for no good reason, the
great bell tolls.

Suddenly Claire is thinking of the Bay of Napol, and
the white gulls wheeling in the sky: the freshness, the
tang of ozone, and the burning clear light.

As she turns away, on the landing below she sees two
slender figures, hand in hand: a boy and a girl, both with
shocks of yellow hair. They stand isolated; the slowly
moving crowd surrounds them with a changing ring of
faces. A memory stirs: Claire recalls the other afternoon,
the street, so different then, and the two small yellow-
haired children. Now they are almost grown; in a few
more years they will look like anyone else.

A pang strikes at Claire's heart. She thinks, *If we could
have a child* . . .

She looks upward in a kind of incredulous wonder that
there should be so much sorrow in the world. Where has
it all come from? How could she have lived for so many
decades without knowing of it?

The leaden light flickers slowly and ceaselessly along
the blank stone ceiling overhead.

Dio is in his studio, tiny as an ant in the distance,
where he swings beside the shoulder of the gigantic, half-
carved figure. The echo of his hammer drifts down to
Claire and Benarra at the doorway.

The figure is female, seated; that is all they can dis-
tinguish as yet. The blind head broods, turned downward;
there is something malign in the shapeless hunch of the
back and the thick, half-defined arms. A cloud of stone
dust drifts free around the tiny shape of Dio; the bitter
smell of it is in the air; the white dust coats everything.

"Dio," says Claire into the annunciator. The chatter of
the distant hammer goes on. "Dio."

After a moment the hammer stops. The screen flicks
on and Dio's white-masked face looks out at them. Only
the dark eyes have life; they are hot and impatient. Hair,

brows and beard are whitened; even the skin glitters white, as if the sculptor had turned to stone.

"Yes, what is it?"

"Dio—let's go away for a few weeks. I have such a longing to see Napol again. You know, it's been years."

"You go," says the face. In the distance, they see the small black figure hanging with its back turned to them, unmoving beside the gigantic shoulder. "I have too much to do."

"The rest would be good for you," Bernarra puts in. "I advise it, Dio."

"I have too much to do," the face repeats curtly. The image blinks out; the chatter of the distant hammer begins again. The black figure blurs in a new cloud of dust.

Bernarra shakes his head. "No use." They turn and walk out across the balcony, overlooking the dark reception hall. Benarra says, "I didn't want to tell you this just yet. The Planners are going to ask Dio to resign his post this year."

"I've been afraid of it," says Claire after a moment. "Have you told them how it will make him feel?"

"They say the Sector will become an Avoided Place. They're right; people already are beginning to have a feeling about it. In another few seasons they would stop coming at all."

Her hands are clasping each other restlessly. "Couldn't they give it to him, for a Project, or a museum, perhaps—?" She stops; Benarra is shaking his head.

"He's got this to go through," he says. "I've seen it coming."

"I know." Her voice is flat, defeated. "I'll help him . . . all I can."

"That's just what I don't want you to do," Benarra says.

She turns, startled; he is standing erect and somber against the balcony rail, with the gloomy gulf of the hall below. He says, "Claire, you're holding him back. He dyes his hair for you, but he has only to look at himself when he has been working in the studio, to realize what he actually looks like. He despises himself . . . he'll end hating you. You've got to go away now, and let him do what he has to."

For a moment she cannot speak; her throat aches. "What does he have to do?" she whispers.

"He has to grow old, very fast. He's put it off as long as he can." Benarra turns, looking out over the deserted hall. In a corner, the old cloth drapes trail on the floor. "Go to Napol, or to Timbuk. Don't call, don't write. You can't help him now. He has to do this all by himself."

In Djuba she acquires a little ring made of iron, very old, shaped like a serpent that bites its own tail. It is a curiosity, a student's thing; no one would wear it, and besides it is too small. But the cold touch of the little thing in her palm makes her shiver, to think how old it must be. Never before has she been so aware of the funnel-shaped maw of the past. It feels precarious, to be standing over such gulfs of time.

In Winthur she takes the waters, makes a few friends. There is a lodge on the crest of Mont Blanc, new since she was last here, from which one looks across the valley of the Doire. In the clear Alpine air, the tops of the mountains are like ships, afloat in a sea of cloud. The sunlight is pure and thin, with an aching sweetness; the cries of the skiers echo up remotely.

In Cair she meets a collector who has a curious library, full of scraps and oddments that are not to be found in the common supply. He has a baroque fancy for antiquities; some of his books are actually made of paper and bound in synthetic leather, exact copies of the originals.

" 'Again, the Alfurs of Poso, in Central Celebes,' " she reads aloud, " 'tell how the first men were supplied with their requirements direct from heaven, the Creator passing down his gifts to them by means of a rope. He first tied a stone to the rope and let it down from the sky. But the men would have none of it, and asked somewhat peevishly of what use to them was a stone. The Good God then let down a banana, which, of course, they gladly accepted and ate with relish. This was their undoing. "Because you have chosen the banana," said the deity, "you shall propagate and perish like the banana, and your offspring shall step into your place. . . ." ' " She closes the book slowly. "What was a banana, Alf?"

386

"A phallic symbol, my dear," he says, stroking his beard, with a pleasant smile.

In Prah, she is caught up briefly in a laughing horde of athletes, playing follow-my-leader: they have volplaned from Omsk to the Baltic, tobagganed down the Rose Club chute from Danz to Warsz, cycled from there to Bucur, ballooned, rocketed, leaped from precipices, run afoot all night. She accompanies them to the mountains; they stay the night in a hostel, singing, and in the morning they are away again, like a flock of swallows. Claire stands grave and still; the horde rushes past her, shining faces, arrows of color, laughs, shouts. "Claire, aren't you coming?" . . . "Claire, what's the matter?" . . . "Claire, come with us, we're swimming to Linz!" But she does not answer; the bright throng passes into silence.

Over the roof of the world, the long cloud-packs are moving swiftly, white against the deep blue. They come from the north; the sharp wind blows among the pines, breathing of icy fiords.

Claire steps back into the empty forum of the hostel. Her movements are slow; she is weary of escaping. For half a decade she has never been in the same spot more than a few weeks. Never once has she looked into a news unit, or tried to call anyone she knows in Sector Twenty. She has even deliberately failed to register her whereabouts: to be registered is to expect a call, and expecting one is halfway to making one.

But what is the use? Wherever she goes, she carries the same darkness with her.

The phone index glows at her touch. Slowly, with unaccustomed fingers, she selects the sector, the group, and the name: Dio.

The screen pulses; there is a long wait. Then the gray face of an autosec says politely, "The registrant has removed, and left no forwarding information."

Claire's throat is dry. "How long ago did his registry stop?"

"One moment please." The blank face falls silent. "He was last registered three years ago, in the index of November thirty."

"Try central registry," says Claire.

"No forwarding information has been registered."

."I know. Try central, anyway. Try everywhere."

"There will be a delay for checking." The blank face is silent a long time. Claire turns away, staring without interest at the living frieze of color which flows along the borders of the room. "Your attention please."

She turns. "Yes?"

"The registrant does not appear in any sector registry."

For a moment she is numb and speechless. Then, with a gesture, she abolishes the autosec, fingers the index again: the same sector, same group; the name: Benarra.

The screen lights: his remembered face looks out at her. "Claire! Where are you?"

"In Cheky. Ben, I tried to call Dio, and it said there was no registry. Is he—?"

"No. He's still alive, Claire; he's retreated. I want you to come here as soon as you can. Get a special; my club will take care of the overs, if you're short."

"No, I have a surplus. All right, I'll come."

"This was made the season after you left," says Benarra. The wall screen glows: it is a stereo view of the main plaza in Level Three, the Hub section: dark, unornamented buildings, like a cliff-dwellers' canyon. The streets are deserted; no face shows at the windows.

"Changing Day," says Benarra. "Dio had formally resigned, but he still had a day to go. Watch."

In the screen, one of the tall building fronts suddenly swells and crumbles at the top. Dingy smoke spurts. Like a stack of counters, the building leans down into the street, separating as it goes into individual bricks and stones. The roar comes dimly to them as the next building erupts, and then the next.

"He did it himself," says Benarra. "He laid all the explosive charges, didn't tell anybody. The council was horrified. The integrators weren't designed to handle all that rubble—it had to be amorphized and piped away in the end. They begged Dio to stop, and finally he did. He made a bargain with them, for Level One."

"The whole level?"

"Yes. They gave it to him; he pointed out that it would not be for long. All the game areas and so on up there were due to be changed, anyhow; Dio's successor merely canceled them out of the integrator."

She still does not understand. "Leaving nothing but the bare earth?"

"He wanted it bare. He got some seeds from collectors, and planted them. I've been up frequently. He actually grows cereal grain up there, and grinds it into bread."

In the screen, the canyon of the street has become a lake of dust. Benarra touches the controls; the screen blinks to another scene.

The sky is a deep luminous blue; the level land is bare. A single small building stands up blocky and stiff; behind it there are a few trees, and the evening light glimmers on fields scored in parallel rows. A dark figure is standing motionless beside the house; at first Claire does not recognize it as human. Then it moves, turns its head. She whispers, "Is that Dio?"

"Yes."

She cannot repress a moan of sorrow. The figure is too small for any details of face or body to be seen, but something in the proportions of it makes her think of one of Dio's grotesque statues, all stony bone, hunched, shrunken. The figure turns, moving stiffly, and walks to the hut. It enters and disappears.

She says to Benarra, "Why didn't you tell me?"

"You didn't leave any word; I couldn't reach you."

"I know, but you should have told me. I didn't know . . ."

"Claire, what do you feel for him now? Love?"

"I don't know. A great pity, I think. But maybe there is love mixed up in it too. I pity him because I once loved him. But I think that much pity is love, isn't it, Ben?"

"Not the kind of love you and I used to know anything about," says Benarra, with his eyes on the screen.

He was waiting for her when she emerged from the kiosk.

He had a face like nothing human. It was like a turtle's face, or a lizard's: horny and earth-colored, with bright eyes peering under the shelf of brow. His cheeks sank in; his nose jutted, and the bony shape of his teeth bulged behind the lips. His hair was white and fine, like thistledown in the sun.

They were like strangers together, or like visitors from different planets. He showed her his grain fields, his kitchen garden, his stand of young fruit trees. In the branches, birds were fluttering and chirping. Dio was dressed in a robe of coarse weave that hung awkwardly from his bony shoulders. He had made it himself, he told her; he had also made the pottery jug from which he poured her a clear tart wine, pressed from his own grapes. The interior of the hut was clean and bare. "Of course, I get food supplements from Ben, and a few things like needles, thread. Can't do everything, but on the whole, I haven't done too badly." His voice was abstracted; he seemed only half aware of her presence.

They sat side by side on the wooden bench outside the hut. The afternoon sunlight lay pleasantly on the flagstones; a little animation came to his withered face, and for the first time she was able to see the shape of Dio's features there.

"I don't say I'm not bitter. You remember what I was, and you see what I am now." His eyes stared broodingly; his lips worked. "I sometimes think, why did it have to be me? The rest of you are going on, like children at a party, and I'll be gone. But, Claire, I've discovered something. I don't quite know if I can tell you about it."

He paused, looking out across the fields. "There's an attraction in it, a beauty. That sounds impossible, but it's true. Beauty in the ugliness. It's symmetrical, it has its rhythm. The sun rises, the sun sets. Living up here, you feel that a little more. Perhaps that's why we went below."

He turned to look at her. "No, I can't make you understand. I don't want you to think, either, that I've surrendered to it. I feel it coming sometimes, Claire, in the middle of the night. Something coming up over the horizon. Something—" He gestured. "A feeling. Something very huge, and cold. Very cold. And I sit up in my bed, shouting, 'I'm not ready yet!' No. I don't want to go. Perhaps if I had grown up getting used to the idea, it would be easier now. It's a big change to make in your thinking. I tried—all this—and the sculpture, you remember—but I can't quite do it. And yet—now, this is the curious thing. I wouldn't go back, if I could. That sounds funny. Here I am, going to die, and I wouldn't go back. You see, I want to be myself; yes, I want to go on being myself. Those other men were not me, only someone on the way to be me."

They walked back together to the kiosk. At the doorway, she turned for a last glimpse. He was standing, bent and sturdy, white-haired in his rags, against a long sweep of violet sky. The late light glistened grayly on the fields; far behind, in the grove of trees the bird's voices were stilled. There was a single star in the east.

To leave him, she realized suddenly, would be intolerable. She stepped out, embraced him: his body was shockingly thin and fragile in her arms. "Dio, we mustn't be apart now. Let me come and stay in your hut; let's be together."

Gently he disengaged her arms and stepped away. His eyes gleamed in the twilight. "No, no," he said. "It wouldn't do, Claire. Dear, I love you for it, but you see . . . you see, you're a goddess. An immortal goddess—and I'm a man."

She saw his lips work, as if he were about to speak again, and she waited, but he only turned, without a word or gesture, and began walking away across the empty earth: a dark spindling figure, garments flapping gently in the breeze that spilled across the earth. The last light glowed dimly in his white hair. Now he was only a dot in the middle distance. Claire stepped back into the kiosk, and the door closed.

VI

For a long time she cannot persuade herself that he is gone. She has seen the body, stretched in a box like someone turned to painted wax: it is not Dio, Dio is somewhere else.

She catches herself thinking, *When Dio comes back . . .* as if he had only gone away, around to the other side of the world. But she knows there is a mound of earth over Sector Twenty, with a tall polished stone over the spot where Dio's body lies in the ground. She can repeat by rote the words carved there:

> Weak and narrow are the powers implanted in the limbs of man; many the woes that fall on them and blunt the edges of thought; short is the measure of the life in death through which they toil. Then are they borne away; like smoke they vanish into air; and what they dream they know is but the little that each hath stumbled upon in wandering about the world. Yet boast they all that they have learned the whole. Vain fools! For what that is, no eye hath seen, no ear hath heard, nor can it be conceived by the mind of man.
>
> *—Empedocles (5th cent. B. C.)*

One day she closes up the apartment; let the Planner, Dio's successor, make of it whatever he likes. She leaves behind all her notes, her student's equipment, useless now. She goes to a public inn and that afternoon the new fashions are brought to her: robes in flame silk and in cold

392

metallic mesh; new perfumes, new jewelry. There is new music in the memory units, and she dances to it tentatively, head cocked to listen, living into the rhythm. Already it is like a long-delayed spring; dark withered things are drifting away into the past, and the present is fresh and lovely.

She tries to call a few old friends. Katha is in Centram, Ebert in the South; Piet and Tanno are not registered at all. It doesn't matter; in the plaza of the inn, before the day is out, she makes a dozen new friends. The group, pleased with itself, grows by accretion; the resulting party wanders from the plaza to the Vermilion Club gardens, to one member's rooms and then another's, and finally back to Claire's own apartment.

Leaving the circle toward midnight, she roams the apartment alone, eased by comradeship, content to hear the singing blur and fade behind her. In the playroom, she stands idly looking down into the deep darkness of the diving well. How luxurious, she thinks, to fall and fall, and never reach the bottom . . .

But the bottom is always there, of course, or it would not be a diving well. A paradox: the well must be a shaft without an exit at the bottom; it's the sense of danger, the imagined smashing impact, that gives it its thrill. And yet there is no danger of injury: levitation and the survival instinct will always prevent it.

"We have such a tidy world. . . ."

Things pass away; people endure.

Then where is Piet, the cottony haired man, with his laughter and his wild jokes? Hiding, somewhere around the other side of the world, perhaps; forgetting to register. It often happens; no one thinks about it. But then, her own mind asks coldly, where is the woman named Marla, who used to hold you on her knee when you were small? Where is Hendry, your own father, whom you last saw . . . when? Five hundred, six hundred years ago, that time in Rio. Where do people go when they disappear . . . the people no one talks about?

The singing drifts up to her along the dark hallway. Claire is staring transfixed down into the shadows of the well. She thinks of Dio, looking out at the gathering darkness: "I feel it coming sometimes, up over the horizon. Something very huge, and cold."

The darkness shapes itself in her imagination into a gray face, beautiful and terrible. The smiling lips whisper, for her ears alone, *Some day.*